AF228998

R E T

Dan Miwa

RET

Dan Miwa

Copyright © Dan Miwa 2023

All Rights Reserved

No portion of this book may be reproduced in any form or by any means (which includes mechanically, electronically, or by any other means, including photocopying), without written permission from the author.

Disclaimer

This book contains the ideas and opinions of its author. The intention of this book is to provide information, entertainment, helpful content, and motivation to readers about the subjects addressed. It is published and sold with the understanding that the author is not engaged to render any type of psychological, medical, legal, or any other kind of personal or professional advice. No warranties or guarantees are expressed or implied by the author's choice to include any of the content in this volume. The author shall not be liable for any physical, psychological, emotional, financial, or commercial damages, including, but not limited to, special, incidental, consequential, or other damages. The reader is responsible for their own choices, actions, and results.

1st Edition. 1st printing 2023

Cover Illustration: George Gausden

Cover and Interior Design: Steve Walters, Oxygen Publishing Inc.

Editor: Richard Tardif

Independently Published by
Oxygen Publishing Inc. Montreal, QC, Canada
www.oxygenpublishing.com

ISBN: 978-1-990093-83-8

Imprint: Independently published

Dedication

For my son,
Riley.

Introduction

Look into the sky on a clear summer night. Amid the infinite gathering of space, two dim stars are located just to the right of the Little Dipper, Sirra and Arris. From the surface of Earth, it's difficult to pinpoint these two specks of light. However, do not mistake their timid presence because it is here, far into the outer reaches of our galaxy, thousands of light years away, and inside a small binary system, that we find the first signs of intelligent extraterrestrial life.

As we embark on our long journey toward our two stars, we find ourselves outside our cosmic address. Hurled far beyond our solar system, we speed past ferocious black holes and gaze upon these fierce wonders as they consume the rich matter of our universe. Tracking back on our course, we encounter colossal and beautifully crafted nebulas. These immense clouds decorate the black surroundings with colorful plumes of ionized gasses.

We continue to peer out toward the Milky Way's galactic halo, witnessing vast gatherings of globular clusters. Spread over great distances, these collections of millions of stars shine brilliantly against the dark canvas. We extend ourselves toward the furthest reaches of our galaxy, leaving the boundaries of time and entering another existence of the cosmos.

We cannot comprehend the abyss known as space. Our passage through this barren cavity appears meaningless. However, we must believe in our yearning for hope; chance is the only equation. Every journey, even through time and space, eventually connects with something.

Here, another world is found.

Our two stars emerge. Home to a lone yellow planet ringed with billions of small iron rocks, it spins in perfect symmetry. The solitary planet orbits the two stars in a figure-eight pattern, working through its solar system, determined to complete its quest.

This planet has one giant, Pangea-like landmass surrounded by a liquid nitrogen ocean. As the planet moves closer to one of its governing stars, the ocean evaporates due to the sudden temperature change. A thick mass of nitrogen cloud engulfs the planet's simple atmosphere. As the cloud mass thickens, the temperature on the surface becomes hotter. The planet is now subject to an extreme greenhouse effect until it moves away from the star and to a more stable environment.

The nitrogen cloud will eventually, through precipitation, return the liquid matter to the depleted oceans. The nitrogen ocean is clear and would appear blue if the planet's atmosphere were rich in other compounds. On Earth, light particles, which amplify a prism's most abundant colour, affect water particles in the sky. On this planet, the atmosphere is meager and displays the ocean in a deep yellow hue. There is no current or tide. The ocean is still. Gravity from moons and satellites influences the oceans back on Earth. As for this world—it has no moon.

The brownish-red land formation has many elevation changes. Large mountain ranges decorate the landscape with nitrogen ice-covered tips, and large dark green pillars shoot up from the ground along the bottom edge of these rocky giants. These alien trees are dense and grow wild throughout the rough terrain. This species of tree is essential to the planet's ecosystem. They grow strong, so extreme temperatures do not affect their lives—they easily survive the stresses of violent summers.

At the onset of the intense summer heat, strong metallic liquids will seep from the top of each tree and gradually solidify as it extends to the surface floor. A ring of iron at the base of each tree will attract the coating through magnetism, eventually connecting this natural protective layer around the tree.

These trees also depend on outside nutrients. And this time, the temperature change from the extreme summer has a nurturing effect on this remarkable species. They need a continuous supply of exterior nutrients to keep the tree community healthy.

This is the duty of a snug.

Throughout the planet's history, organisms have struggled with the intense heat during summer. This threatening season has always impeded the advancement of life. However, at this moment, after thousands of years of trial and error, these clever prehistoric snugs were the first to discover trees as a suitable life source.

Below the surface, a young snug is sleeping through his first hibernation. He has two arms, two legs, an elongated torso, and a smooth rounded head with two large glossy eyes protected by thick, ruggedized eyelids. He is dark blue, almost black, and curled up in a ball, submerged inside a large reserve of liquid nitrogen.

These harsh two months are demanding for every snug, let alone an infant. While the little one seems dormant, his body performs an essential task; delivering viable nutrients to the tree.

A Snug's skin is very porous; it becomes saturated with microscopic minerals and metals throughout the year. These components complete the mineral composition of the tree species, perpetuating the life cycle for another season.

Hopefully, the tree will not consume too much of the infant's valuable resources. It is still very young and has not yet been exposed to the world long enough to attain large quantities of matter.

Symbiotic systems like this are alike all over this environmentally stable world. Over millions of years, evolution helped create a secure existence, especially for the snug species. They have now developed into an advanced civilization.

We focus on a northeastern part of the continent in a mountainous region called Terin, home to a large seaside megacity enclosed by a massive stone wall. One side of a large mountain is encased inside the structure. The stone wall snakes its way down into the valley regions of the land and stretches far into the yellow ocean, where both ends meet to form an oval-shaped perimeter.

Prominent buildings and infrastructure prove the snug species' intelligence. The city is fast-paced. They uphold and abide by forms of government and use contemporary modes of transportation. They perform modern skills and practices to their highest potential.

Large buildings and complex systems are less prevalent outside the stone border. Thousands of gray and white two-story homes surround the wall. As we look closer, we can see a long, winding path leading to an old square house. Wide windows and a long flat black roof help decorate this dated home. Directly above the dark brown front door is a large open window. Let's look inside.

<u>Act</u>

———

Homework

Ret tried to hang on to his father's nattering voice. He sat slumped over with his head tilted to one side, and his eyes glazed over. From where he sat, on the end of the long bench, the sounds of his father's boisterous delivery weren't enough to keep him from tuning out. His body may have been present inside the classroom, but his mind was racing away.

In his dreams, he stood atop a large stage, waving to a cheering crowd. Holding up a decorative red medallion above his little blue body, Ret rejoiced as beams of light shined directly on him. Savouring the moment, he wrapped the thick red ribbon around his head and secured the medallion on his chest where it belonged. With the crowd chanting all around, Ret looked down and inspected the medal. All red and trimmed in gold, the piece glimmered in the light as edged contours and well-cut rubies sparkled from within the setting. He adored his fantasy, and as he gazed into his prize Ret couldn't wait for this fantasy to become a reality.

"Ret! Hey, Ret! Welcome back."

Jerked out of his imaginings, Ret shook his head, blinked a few times and turned his attention towards a large whiteboard centered in the classroom's front, and then to his father standing just beside it.

Still caught in a daze, Ret stretched his arms and glanced over to his sister sitting at the other end of the long green bench, also paying little attention to her father.

"Alright, let me start over now that you are with me. Once a year, when our planet moves closer to one of our two suns, the nitrogen ocean evaporates because of the sudden temperature change; the surface will heat and you both need to find a suitable tree to hibernate inside so you can survive the hot summer season. Now, how do you know what makes a suitable tree? Can either of you tell me?"

"Dad, you're acting as if we've never hibernated before. We know this already. You don't need to keep telling us the same thing over and over again."

Caught in a playful stare down with his father, Ret cocked his brow and smirked out the corner of his mouth. And, to his surprise, he received the same sarcastic expression in return.

"That's not the answer I'm looking for; a suitable tree is at least twice your height."

"Dad, can we talk about more interesting things, like me winning the champions medallion tomorrow?" interrupted Ret.

"But what could be more interesting than hibernation?" asked Sert.

"Umm, I'd rather you tell me that I'm going to win the competition and that everyone will praise me for my victory."

"Oh, little guy, you're that sure, eh?" said Sert.

"Come on, Dad. I'm the smartest snug my age. You should know that by now. I'm going to outsmart everyone tomorrow."

Sert gawked at his son and rolled his eyes before sauntering over to his desk in the front left corner of the room.

"Ok, I'm done with my lesson. Unless you want me to keep talking about hibernation?"

Looking back at his children, Sert watched Ret and his sister Terri vigorously shake their heads "No."

"Yep, that's what I thought! Alright, now it's your mother's turn. Hella, they're all yours!"

Ret shot up from his slouched position, eager for Hella to finish scribbling down the last few thoughts on a sizable ten-month calendar. She finalized her notes and pulled her head up to face her audience. Her vibrant blue eyes met with her children's.

"When I was young, just like the two of you, a few of my friends and I snuck out at night during one of our banquets. They warned us—just like I'm warning you now—to stay inside the banquet hall and never leave the building without consent. But, if you ever want to see a geyser erupt high into the sky, trust me, it's best to see one during the night season."

"Uh, Hella…" said Sert

Hella continued. "As you know, our banquet hall is in the shrubs. Here, let me show you."

Ret tapped his toes as he watched Hella shake her fist. Before she could write on the white frostboard, she had to wait for the slender black object in her hand to heat.

Because of the planet's cold climate nitrogen frost occurred naturally, and the snugs used it to their fullest potential. Behind the layer of white frost, a solid black lining made up the undercoating of this panel. A special heated pen melted the frosted over face, leaving a visible line in its place; the board refreezes over time, slowly erasing its contents.

Hella addressed the frost board and began her demonstration by drawing a general vicinity map. And, after detailing a few last sketches, she turned back to her children sitting impatiently in their seats.

"Now, our plan when we got outside was to try to find a giant geyser," Hella explained. "We had to walk through here very carefully. Not only is the area scattered with thick vegetation, but small lakes can't be seen in the pitch black during our night season."

"I don't think you should be telling them this," said Sert, interjecting from his chair in the corner.

"There were six of us—three sets of children—and we were all carefully stepping with one burnlight between us. Getting there was pretty tough. The shrubs are not what you think. They're thick and dense and will tighten themselves around you if you stop moving. And they will steal the frost off your back."

Ret asked, "No, really? They'll take the frost right off our backs?"

Hella began. "Everyone took turns being the leader. I remember my friend Gin was leading for a while when he almost stepped into an unsuspecting pond. His sister pulled him out just before he fell in."

Hella re-enacted a series of dodging and pulling motions to help illustrate her story. Everyone in the room paid close attention—their eyes wide open and focused directly on her.

"Eventually, after a long time of exploring, we finally found ourselves at the edge of the flat rock plains."

Hella walked back over to her cluttered desk; took a big sip of liquid methane from a half-filled container, swished it inside her mouth, swallowed it and turned back to Ret and his sister.

"We walked all around on the flat rock but had to watch for big geyser holes. It was so dark we couldn't see them if they were right in front of us!"

"What did the geyser look like?" asked Ret. "The one that you saw?"

"We didn't see a geyser, unfortunately. We were waiting the entire night and didn't see a thing."

"Oh, that's too bad. I hope I get to see a geyser one day," said Ret, turning to Terri. "When do we get to see one?"

"Right after you learn to hibernate." interrupted Sert before bursting out in laughter.

Sert couldn't stop his smooth, elongated head from flinging right back as he howled a deep reverberating hum. Sounds of glee poured out of his wide-open mouth. The two eyes in the middle of his head were bright green as he cried in enjoyment. His eye colour reflected his emotion; green was a sure sign of delight.

Sert crossed his arms across the front of his body and addressed his children. "In all seriousness, we shouldn't be encouraging your children. If the chancellors found us instructing you to break the rules and go out into the flat rock, especially during a banquet, your Mom and I would get into a lot of trouble. So please, don't leave the banquet hall searching for a geyser."

Ret mounted the desk and started jumping up and down, acting out the actions of the geyser.

"Well, I hope I see one up close one day. I've heard of some being all sorts of colours. And they cast far into the sky!" shouted Ret.

"Ok, settle down, Ret. And don't get your hopes up," said Sert. "Besides, you have more important things to focus on; I want you to be ready for your final competition tomorrow."

Ret nodded in confidence. "I'm ready, Dad! Stop worrying. You know I'm the smartest."

Sert was ready to temper his son's ego but was interrupted by a loud knock at the front door. He hopped to his feet, graciously made his way through the open doorway, and trotted through a long corridor to a tall flight of stairs at the end of the hall.

Ret's competitive nature deflated—he lost his ambition to argue and climbed off his desk. He showed minimal interest toward his sister Terri, piping up from her side of the bench.

"Mom, why are you and Dad trying to force us to do well tomorrow? I mean, Ret and I both made it into the final competition. And all of us children are going to get into Pagan, right? So why do you make us compete against one another? I don't know why this is so important."

Hella used her thumb to pull up on a thick red strap attached to a shiny red medallion hanging around her neck. She illustrated it to her daughter; however, this one in particular, was not trimmed in gold or impressed with rubies.

"Come on, Terri. You know why. You want one of these, right?" said Hella.

"Of course I do."

"If you want to be a red society member, Terri, you have to be smart," Hella said. "Our community and everyone at tomorrow's red society banquet are counting on you children to represent our society inside Pagan. If, and only if you perform well in the competition, you will have every advantage and opportunity inside Pagan: better living quarters, more resources, and most importantly, a reputation. Members from the green, blue, and yellow societies will want you to join their idea groups. That is what Pagan is all about; it's a chance for you to progress this civilization forward—a chance to develop a great invention that will make you famous. Every opportunity is inside Pagan, and I'll tell you this, Terri: if you do well in the competition tomorrow, your chances of being a success in Pagan are that much greater."

"I'm not going to settle for a standard red society medallion, Mom," declared Ret. "I'm going to win the champions medallion and become a huge success when I get to Pagan!"

Hella tried to hide her saddening emotions. "Well, I hope you do, Ret. But it still doesn't change the fact that after you two enter Pagan, your father and I are never going to see you again. That's the worst part. I'm still having trouble with that."

"Mom," said Ret.

"I want to see the both of you do well before you get sent off into Pagan, and out of my life forever."

Ret looked over at Hella, holding in her emotions, and gave her exactly what she wanted to hear. He knew the gravity of her situation and graciously smiled before answering.

"Alright, we'll do well tomorrow, Mom, just for you."

"And for your father."

"Dad, too."

*

Sert marched down the long hallway that led to the front door. After trotting around a white stone hourglass-shaped feature that accented the middle of the foyer, he opened the door to the much expected visitors.

Two small children, both three years of age, were standing at attention, each holding a checklist in one hand and an orange bag filled with folded-up pamphlets in the other. Their upright bodies and smiling faces hid a wonderful view of the sharp peak of Mount Nite. The entire mountain, most noticeably the tall pointed peak, was splashed in a light violet hue, showcasing the atmosphere's abundant ultraviolet rays.

Sert's attention moved down the smooth granite face to the bottom of the mountain, where he focused on a massive enclosed stone wall encapsulating one side of the expansive base. The wall extended a great distance and conquered much of the view from his doorstep. As it snaked its way throughout the land, the towering stone wall stretched far down the valley and out into the yellow ocean, encompassing a large part of the sea within its oval-shaped boundaries.

He returned his attention to the two snugs standing in his doorway.

"Hey, Sert. Have you taken time to read any of the pamphlets we've left here?" asked the little male snug.

Sert crossed his arms and leaned up against the brown door frame. "You know, I truly admire your dedication," he said mockingly. "You walk the neighbourhood every day trying to impose this absurd lifestyle on others. I have to ask you both, is anyone interested?"

"Of course, Sert. We want to build a new banquet hall, and we're trying to get enough supporters to do it. You wouldn't be our first," answered Bri. "Here, take a look at our new pamphlet. Look at our new banquet hall."

Sert spoiled any impression they could have made on him and cut into their lecture.

"Why would anyone want to be a part of this made-up society? Why are you trying to change things around here? It's perfect the way it is. If I were the chancellor, I would banish you—permanently!"

Standing in the middle of his doorway, Sert raised his brow and pointed to the massive stone structure.

"Inside that wall are some of the world's most sophisticated and intelligent snugs; snugs working on ground-breaking ideas that will help advance the entire planet. Out of all the civilizations in the world, our Pagan—Terin's Pagan— is the brightest and most promising Pagan. We are ranked number one for productivity and ingenuity. So tell me, you two, why would any of us Terinians want to join you?"

Bri started his response. "Well…"

"Here's the real question. Why don't you want to be a part of our Pagan? Other civilizations can't even compare to the size, technology, and opportunity we have inside that wall. Your futures are secured, and you are promised a good life inside our Pagan. And you two want to throw that all away." Sert looked at Bri, expecting him to answer.

"I'm not saying that the Terin Pagan is bad…"

"I mean, who even has the audacity to come to my door and try to tell my family how we should live our lives? I'll tell you what, come to the red society's banquet hall tomorrow and explain how ridiculous your idea is to everyone there. Better yet, participate in the red society's competition tomorrow. Both of you wouldn't even make it past the first stage," screamed Sert as he bent down and pointed a skinny finger at their shocked faces.

"Alright, enough! Just read the pamphlet."

Bri shoved the folded-up piece of paper in Sert's hand, spun around and stormed down the steep pathway in front of Sert's white stone house.

"I can't wait to say 'NO' next time you come by!"

With a cocky smile, Sert walked back into the house and slammed the door.

"You know what? It's time Sert gets what he deserves!" shouted Bri. "I've got an idea. Gimmie some of the frost off your bump."

"Hey, I need that. Why don't you use your own?" exclaimed his sister.

Nevertheless she turned around and did nothing but cater to her brother's hands. He scraped a good portion of the frost off his sister's frost bump on the upper part of her back, and began smoothing out the edges of the snowball into a perfect sphere. He gathered the last bit of snow from her frost bump, leaving his sister gasping for energy, and after crafting this trusty weapon, Bri advanced with his vengeful plan.

Quickly, he ran back up the hill, stopped when he felt he was in striking distance, planted his skinny blue legs, and stretched his arm far behind his body.

"This is for you, Sert."

Bri hurled the snowball through his range of motion. The high-velocity ball of revenge was perfectly in line and heading straight for the center of the doorway; he savoured the sight.

Ret's face was buried in a book upstairs in the classroom, stuck on a tricky question. He closed his eyes, sat back in his chair, and dove deep into his memory, trying to find the answer to a math problem. He was almost there. The thoughts were making a familiar shape in his mind, and then to his surprise, a loud bang came from downstairs.

"What was that?" he screamed before racing toward the window.

He spotted the mischievous youngsters running down the steep hill in front of their house, and watched as Bri pushed his sister's bare back, trying to make her run faster. As they picked up speed, Bri's sister stumbled down the heavy incline and nearly fell to the ground; however, a quick tug from her brother helped her regain balance before the two made out with their escape.

Ret, admiring the children, chuckled to himself.

Let's Go

"**C**ome on, Ret. We have to go," yelled Sert from the bottom of the staircase.

Ret finished packing the rest of his belongings into a brown bag. "Be right down!" He slung both straps over his shoulders and tightened the bag around the front of his chest, avoiding the frost bump on his back. He darted out of his room, ran down the hallway and leaped onto the silver hand railing, sliding down and holding out his arms to help steady the shaky ride. After striking the floor, he anticipated a galvanized reaction. However, his family paid little mind and rushed the crowd-pleaser outside.

"Ok, ok, let's go. We have to get a move on. You and Terri still need time to prepare before the competition," said Sert while closing the front door.

"Do you have everything?" asked Hella.

"Yes," Ret responded in a monotone voice, his back turned, walking down the flat stone pathway.

"Are you sure?"

"Yes, Mom. I have everything."

"How about a burnlight?"

Ret continued to stroll, smirking out the side of his mouth, knowing that Hella was smiling behind him.

Sert followed close behind and hurried his family toward an ice-filled parking lane connecting their house to the street. There, glimmering in the sunlight, sat their trusty glider vehicle.

Ret gawked at his father as he approached the glider. He slowed his stride, placed his finger on the edge of the rounded bumper bordering the vehicle, and slipped it along the surface. He walked toward the small extendable step in the middle of the chassis and stared at the glider with a crafty grin as if it were a well-earned prize. He hopped in, plopped down on the driver's side, settled his hands on the steering wheel and checked over the dashboard to ensure all the gauges were set and indicator lights were operational. He waved the rest of his family in, directing Hella to sit up front and Ret and Terri to sit in the back.

Ret chuckled as he waited for his family to climb on and took a moment to gaze around the glider mimicking his father's prideful persona.

The open-top vessel sat on four long reinforced blades cutting deep into the ice: two in front and two in the back. The steel blades ran along both sides of the glider, fastened to the bottom of the chassis. A series of thick copper cables attached to each blade snaked under the vehicle and into a panel behind the back seats.

Every street interacts with the sled using a series of large copper plates installed below the ice. Magnetism is the source of energy here; as the front blades come in contact with the copper plate they attract due to the magnetic pull of opposing poles. As the glider passes over the middle of the plate, the polarity of the vehicle quickly changes, forcing the glider to be pushed away and, in turn, propelling it forward to the next copper plate.

"Can I drive, Dad? Come on, please?" asked Ret sarcastically as he climbed in.

"After you win the competition, I'll let you!" replied Sert, chuckling.

Without a second thought, Sert pressed the ignition, and instantly bursts of electricity sounded off as the mechanical system ignited. The initial rough sounding racket was replaced by a gentle sixty-cycle hum, capturing the authentic sound of the vehicle.

"Ok, here we go. Put your seat straps on," said Sert.

The glider shot out of its parked position and raced down the steep, icy hill. A bright green light signalled from the dash indicated the road was clear. Gradually taking his foot off the brake pedal, Sert made a smooth left turn from his parking lane and accelerated onto the open ice road.

"Ok, you two. Time for a quiz. I want to sharpen your wits."

Terri cried out from the back seat. "Come on, Dad. I don't want to."

"I don't want to either," answered Ret, winking and nodding to his sister.

Sert shook his head. "You two are not going to win with an attitude like that.

It's a long ride there, and there is plenty of time to quiz you both before the banquet."

"Alright, fine. Start with an easy one," suggested Ret, with a subtle hint of regret for encouraging his father.

"Hmm," said Sert as he tapped the steering wheel with his finger. "I'll begin with a math question. What is the mathematical value we use to find the diameter or radius of a circle?"

"Three point one four one five nine two six five."

"That's good, Ret, but three point one four was all I needed to hear. Ok, on to geography. What area is home to the giant slug?"

"The great plains located in the middle of the continent."

" Now, let Terri answer the next one."

Looking back at Terri in the back right-hand seat, Sert flashed an encouraging smile. "Terri, can you tell me what forces this glider to move?"

"Big magnets?"

"Yup. And what powers the lights on the glider?"

"Electric… charges?" responded Terri, unsure.

"That's right. One last question—do you know the source of the electricity?"

"From the copper plate, right? The blades cut deep enough into the ice to connect to the plate when it glides over."

A look of pride blossomed on Sert's face. "Yeah, that's it. Well done. You're right!"

Ret moved his vision to the sky and focused on the planet's massive planetary ring. Iron and copper rocks of all different sizes organized themselves into a perfect symmetrical arch that cut a vertical line through the middle of the sky, and in turn, around the entire planet. Two suns perched on either side of this natural display radiated a rich, deep yellow atmosphere.

"I've got a question for you, Dad."

"What's that, Ret?"

"Why isn't our planet hot?"

"What do you mean?"

"Both of the suns are superhot, right?"

"Ya."

"Then why is our planet cold?"

"Well, it's because of the… it just is, alright."

Ret sat in disbelief, entertained by his mom, rolling her eyes and gawking at their father. Sert lowered his brow and tightened his lips.

"What?" Sert asked her defensively.

"Our atmospheric layer is too weak. Our planet is mostly ocean, and the rest is hard rock. As a result, the ocean reflects most of the sun's heat away." Hella answered.

Hit with inspiration, Hella unbuckled her seat strap and flung around to face her children.

"Hey, you need to put that back on," said Sert.

Hella shrugged her shoulders and faced back to her children.

"Our skin can actually take a lot of heat. In Pagan, I worked with an idea group that tested the resiliency of our bodies in extreme conditions. We learned a lot. Did you know that your body can withstand the heat of hibernation? Do you want to know how?"

"Wait, if we can take a lot of heat, then why can't we live through hibernation? Hibernation is superhot, right?" asked Ret, sitting puzzled in his seat.

"Well, hypothetically speaking, if you were to get stuck outside during hibernation, you would only have a short time to live. All the frost on your bump would melt, and you would have no energy to survive. But, nothing would happen to your body."

Ret glanced over to Terri, who was looking out the side of the glider, paying little mind to Hella's lecture and then to his father; he was distracted and deep in thought. Hella leaned in closer to Ret, her eyes half open, conveying a sarcastic little expression, and whispered the next part of her explanation.

"I know your father was trying to explain hibernation to you, but do you know why we hibernate?"

"Not really, no," he whispered back.

"Our planet moves around both of our suns in a figure-eight pattern like this," she said, acting out the motion with her hands. "And for most of the year, the days are full of light, all day long. However, we get the night season three months out of the year. See, as we circle Sirra, the smaller of the two suns, the face of our planet spins away from the star and into darkness; this is our night season. Are you with me so far?"

"Ya, Mom. I'm with you."

"Once we move away from Sirra and continue our orbit, we head towards the other sun, Ariss. As our planet moves around Ariss, it becomes hot. And I mean, really hot! So hot that the ocean evaporates into the sky."

"Eva…po…rate?" said Ret.

"Yes, evaporate. It means the liquid ocean turns to a mist and forms huge clumps of vapour in the sky, called clouds."

"Wow, that really happens?"

"Well, to be honest, no one knows, but that's what the specialists say."

"That's amazing. I would love to be outside during hibernation."

"Me too, Ret, me too. To this day, no snug has ever been outside to witness what really happens. I guess it's something we'll never see. Anyways, where was I? Oh ya, because snugs cannot live in these conditions, we need to find protection; a tree. Every tree root has a large cold liquid sac beneath the ground. Before hibernation, we must find a suitable tree, bury ourselves below ground and make our way into the liquid sac until hibernation passes. That's what we've been doing for thousands of years."

"Huh, I get it now. Thanks, Mom," answered Ret, smiling back at Hella.

"You're welcome, Ret. Do you want to hear another fascinating discovery my idea group was working on? Our bodies are actually warm on the inside."

"Really?"

"Yes, our suns deliver something called radiant heat and our skin, and…"

"Ahh, there's the sharpening station," interrupted Sert. "I might as well do it now. Come on, who wants a refreshing bottle of Jax? I know Terri wants one. Don't you, Terri?"

"I sure do!" responded Terri, speaking over Ret and Hella's conversation.

"I'll tell you later on," winked Hella as she turned around in her chair and felt the glider begin to slow.

The long road split in two, and before merging into the right lane, Sert watched for the green light to appear on the dash. He carefully piloted the glider and kept his eyes focused on the road, gradually applying the break as he approached a small hut on the shoulder.

Slowing the vehicle, Sert lined up his glider onto two bright orange lines printed on the ice lane beside the building, indicating where to park. Sert stopped at the checkpoint, faced the serving attendant behind an open window, turned off the ignition and showed his red medallion dangling from his neck.

"Full sharpen, front and back," said Sert.

The attendant stood up from behind a small counter inside the tight corners of his shed and inspected the identity piece hanging around Sert's skinny neck. "Let me see your red medallion. Good. You are a true red society member. I have to always check, you know. At the odd time, a green, blue, or even a yellow will drive from their society's borders and try to sneak in a free sharpening. Don't they have their own sharpening stations in their societies?"

"Maybe they all secretly want to be reds?" suggested Sert.

The elderly attendant chuckled over Sert's comments as he routinely hovered his finger over a flashing control panel and pressed firmly on a yellow button. The glider started to shake as the orange lane retracted, and a large grinder beveled an edge in the middle of the glider's blades.

"Anything else today?" asked the attendant.

"Ya. Four bottles of Jax and that will be all," said Sert.

"Thank you, and enjoy yourself at the banquet hall," said the attendant.

"Thank you very much," answered Sert while passing around the bottles. "Don't drink it too fast, you two. There's water in it."

Ret snatched the long clear glass bottle from his father's hands and popped the cap. He tilted his head back and chugged the fizzy concoction. "Ahh, this is why I love our trips to the banquet hall! Jax makes the long ride worth it!"

After handing a bottle to Hella, Sert rested his Jax in one of two holders in the middle of the dash and pressed the blue ignition button next to the steering wheel. A red light on the dash turned green after another glider passed. He turned the steering wheel and took his foot off the brake pedal, accelerating away from the sharpening station and back on route.

2
Community

A dark green, leathery protective layer covered every tree trunk in the overgrown forest. Shoots of sturdy trunks yearned their way to the canopy, aspiring upward in an effort to expose their sharp gray metallic tips in the open sky. The canopy, brimming within the sea of trees covering the valley of Mount Nite, sparkled a sheen of glitter across the rolling land, reflecting the rich sunlight back into the sky.

The glider weaved down the ice road through dense forest. It tried to stay in its lane by turning on sharp switchbacks and coasting down steep hills. It performed the odd speed check and puttered along emitting a moderate hum from the vehicle, echoing through the forest and piquing the interest of a nearby haze.

The large female haze was galloping on four muscular legs through the maze of trees, trying to catch up with the glider. The brown wide backed animal dodged every trunk, picking up speed and trying to reach the vehicle's tail end. Her elongated head and sharp jawline stayed still as her four legs pounded, carving a preplanned path through the forest floor. These evolving creatures have eyesight five times as superior as a snug. Her eyes worked with her brain to judge the time and distance between the two objects so accurately, she was able to do this while running through the forest.

"Go away!" screamed Terri.

Ret turned his head to his side of the glider. "Wow, look at that!"

Hella, in shock at the speed of the haze, could not believe her eyes. "Sert, take a look at this."

"That's amazing. I've never seen one up close like this before," said Sert, hinting with some sarcasm in his voice.

With his body rigid in his seat, Ret noticed that the thick layer of frost that covered the haze's frost bump was melting, causing her head to bob and her strides to shorten.

"Go away!" Terri shouted.

Terri unbuckled her seat strap, stood up, and held tight to Sert's backrest.

"It's ok, Terri." said Sert. "She is starting to slow down, see."

The glider shot ahead of the haze. But before the creature gave up, she stopped, sat on its hind legs, opened her mammoth mouth and projected a loud, thunderous roar. Terri cringed and grabbed her father's seat again as the glider sped down the road and away from the howling animal.

Sert shouted. "It's over, Terri. Put your strap back on. We're approaching the shrubs!"

Terri sat back in her seat, placed her heels on the edge of her chair and wrapped her arms around her legs. She drove her head down between her knees and closed her eyes.

The flickering sunlight and shadows streaming from the forest toyed with her imagination. She pictured the haze's piercing red eyes locked onto her as a cold chill petrified her frozen body. Even the sight of the animal's ravenous wide open-mouth couldn't shake her paralyzed state. It came closer, closer.

Terri vigorously shook her head between her legs, trying to force the image out of her mind, but it was useless. She couldn't take it anymore; her thoughts were overwhelming, and right before she burst out in a horrified shriek, the flickering of light that encouraged her self-torment stopped.

Terri pulled her head up, rubbed her eyes and noticed the sun's uninterrupted bright light again shining on them. Dumbfounded, she stared out and realized the glider had passed the border of the forest line and had made its way into shrub territory.

The sky may have looked the same in the mountain valley, but the landscape was very different inside the shrub territory. The entire rock surface was swarmed with a thick bountiful blue weed. Expanding in all directions and conquering the land, the smooth light blue vine covered the sprawling plains. The living tangle overtook small rolling hills, while dark blue areas of wet, twisted vegetation charted the location of randomly placed lakes of liquid nitrogen.

The curving ice-filled road stretched again into another impressive world.

"Are you alright, Terri?" Sert asked calmly.

Terri wiped her brow with her forearm. "Yeah, I'm alright,"

"Why don't you sit back and enjoy a sip of your Jax, Terri? We're just about there," said Hella.

The glider carved around the edge of a small vine-covered lake before pushing up the last rolling hill on their trip—everyone was waiting in anticipation as they reached the top. After crossing the summit, the glider descended into a valley. Ret and Terri leaned forward and tilted their heads toward the middle of the glider, trying to get a clear view of the banquet hall.

At the bottom of the ice road stood the red society's beautifully crafted second home. An enormous coliseum stood out as a vibrant centrepiece within the lush valley of dense blue. The rough granite foundation of this gigantic half sphere would be noticeable if it weren't for a thick layer of shrubs decorating the bottom half. As for the top, a deep smooth red crowned the upper half, standing prominently against the yellow sky. Ret and his family were not the only ones approaching; thousands of gliders filled with red society members flooded in on roads leading from all directions.

"Yes! We're here!" exclaimed Ret.

Ret and his family found themselves on a busy three-lane road curling around to the back of the banquet hall and stopping just before the parking lot entrance. Sert sat impatiently in the driver's seat and started tapping his thumb on the steering wheel, waiting for a break in the oncoming traffic. He watched for the red light on the dashboard to turn green.

"Finally," he said, turning down a long lane filled with gliders.

He parked in one of the last available spots, locked the pedal down to the floor and pressed the blue button on the steering wheel. The sixty-cycle hum gently decreased until the sound disappeared.

"Ok, everybody. Let's go," said Sert.

Ret jumped from his seat, slung his bag over his skinny blue arms, and sprinted down the glider's extendable staircase, only waiting for the rest of his slow-moving family. He stood avidly, staring at his webbed toes, tapping vigorously on the ground. In the midst of gawking at his family, he heard a familiar voice from behind him.

"Hey, Ret. You're going down!"

"Please, Rony, I'll be shocked if you make it past the first round." said Ret lightheartedly as he turned to face his approaching friend.

"I couldn't wait to see you, Ret. I have so much to tell you. My family just got back from the other side. The other side! We saw a giant sand mound and went to the north rimmed mountains."

Jealous, Ret flagrantly turned around and followed his family toward the banquet hall. He tried to drown out the enthusiastic details of Rony's family adventure, however Ret couldn't calm his envy. His family never had the opportunity to visit the other side of their planet; his father never believed in travelling outside of Terin. As Ret paced behind his family, he stared unkindly at Sert's backside, silently criticizing him for having never partaken in an adventure.

"Hey, Sert. Hella," said Marc, Rony's father.

Rony's parents interrupted at the perfect time. With Rony still chattering on, Ret glanced up ahead to see Rony's parents standing at the edge of a parking lot with their daughter Bes at their side.

He watched his father hurry over to Marc, and when Sert reached his friend, he turned to show off his half "egg" shaped bump coated in a healthy layer of frost. The pure white overlay covering Sert's bump speckled in the light. Even the top side (the bigger portion of the egg) was solid from edge to edge, indicating he was full of energy; small cracks and liquid runoff would form in this location at the first sign of fatigue.

With Marc returning the gesture, both snugs turned and took a big step inward until their frost bumps came into contact. Being a little shorter than Marc, it was tough for Sert to extend a proper greeting. Marc couldn't help but crack a lighthearted chuckle before returning to face his friend.

"So, did Rony tell you? We just got back from the other side," said Marc.

Ret rolled his eyes.

"We met the north rimmed, green skinned snugs," exclaimed Marc. "The snugs in that civilization are out of their mind. They would climb to the top of the tall mountains and jump off, just looking for a thrill. They were wearing what they called flysuits that helped them soar through the sky—for scientific research, apparently." added Marc. "And way over on the far east is Tarni. And believe me; it's as broken down and dilapidated as you can imagine. It's so sad. Their Pagan is broke, they have no homes, and everyone just sits around doing nothing to help their society. It's an utter disgrace."

"Tell them about the frost," said Sandy, piping into the conversation.

"Oh right, the frost on your back turns bright yellow on that side of the world," said Marc.

"Really? Your frost bump turns yellow?" inquired Hella. "Oh, tell me more!"

Ret shrugged his shoulders and marched on, knowing this would be a long walk to the entrance.

*

Hella and Sandy sauntered along a curving white flagstone pathway beside the clutter of blue shrubs that swathed the entire base of the banquet hall. They headed the pack and walked to the front of the group, trying to keep a quick pace. Terri and Bes were at the back and were responsible to keep the pack moving to their mothers' satisfaction; however, at the moment, they were distracted.

Terri and Bes were taking turns trying to balance their bodies on the tips of their toes. After a few frustrated attempts, Terri was shocked to realize her toes were holding her up. "I've never been able to do this Bes! Look over here!"

Before Bes could see, a careless pedestrian walked right into Terri. She hit the ground hard and instantly her eyes turned pale black. Terri glared around the busy walkway, identified her assailant and demanded an apology. However, all she received was a careless shrug from the snug before he walked off further into the crowd.

Terri, hunched over on her hands and knees, burst out a high-pitched shriek.

"Why is it always my family?" asked Hella sarcastically, picking up the sound of Terri's scream.

Hella turned and approached her daughter, bent down on one knee and placed her hand on her shoulder, smiling.

"What's the matter, Terri? Was a haze chasing you?"

"You can be so..." snarled Terri.

"I know," chuckled Hella, finishing the thought for her daughter. "Listen, we're almost at the entrance, and I want you to look great."

Hella pulled Terri to her feet, wiped the dust off the front of her brown bag and then turned her around towards the rest of her family awaiting their inspection. The entrance to the hall was around the corner, and Hella's professional standards needed upholding, as this was their opportunity to make a meaningful impression with the head chancellors.

Built out from the base of the red dome, hundreds of granite blocks, stacked atop one another, culminated in an arching summit. It served a profound impression on those entering the building. Detailed hieroglyphics describing the history of the snugs' primordial life were carved on the surface of these giant rock faces. The stories that retell these images were so valued within the community, it was considered sacrilegious not to pay homage as one walked beneath. Every member of the community felt a sense of unity as each snug entered the banquet hall, reflecting on their significant history.

"Is everyone ready? Let's go!" commanded an eager Hella.

Inside the banquet hall, another visually pleasing space encompassed a long slab of polished black quartz with two red walls and a tall white ceiling. Framed images of former head chancellors were hung evenly spaced along both red walls.

The lineup of snugs approached the red society's two head chancellors standing atop a tall cylindrical red coloured podium at the end of the hallway, waving to each passing snug.

"Remember, everyone. We have to make this great. Are you ready?" Hella asked in an excited tone.

Both chancellors displayed their nobility and addressed the public with a gracious smile and a strong upright posture. Each wore a long red sash decorated with hundreds of jewels that sparkled flawlessly in the sunlight pouring in from an overhead skylight. Hella was the first to address the chancellors. She marched towards the podium, turned to the noble figures, and delivered an endearing smile and well-practiced wave; Ret chuckled as he watched Hella beg for their acceptance. As he glanced away, he noticed something about his father. Sert was always personable and usually excited to see the chancellors, yet Sert was not himself; he smiled dreadfully and gave a pitiful wave. Ret glanced back at the chancellors and noticed their smiling faces instantly frown at the sight of Sert, at which point his father scurried past and made his way into the great hall.

Ret approached the podium, and after showing a sign of respect, he received the same scowl his father received from both chancellors. He dropped his hand and walked into the hall, confused.

"What was that all about?" Ret asked Sert.

"What are you talking about?" responded Sert, turning to Hella, who was reuniting with a few of her friends.

Ret stared at the back of his father's head while tugging on his leg.

"Dad, they both looked pretty angry when you passed by."

Ret cocked his head, spun around, looked to the entranceway and noticed Dek fiercely staring back at Sert from the podium.

"What did you do?" whispered Ret.

Sert pulled away from Ret's tight grasp, turned his body and began walking away. Ret followed closely behind.

The family made their way over to a short granite wall bordering the perimeter of a circular, glossy white stone floor in the middle of the banquet hall. Ret glanced at the floor and noticed a few snugs dressed in red uniforms polishing the surface. He then turned his head upwards and looked to the top of the dome ceiling.

Thousands of large open windows were cut out from the rough gray sandpaper-like surface that encircled around the dome, all casting a bird's eye view down to the stage. Ret peered around the ceiling, trying to locate the window that belonged to his family.

"Shall we?" asked Ret, indicating his eagerness to visit their living quarters. "I want to study a bit more before the competition!"

"Let's wait until the crowd dies down and for the chancellors to close the doors to the Great Hall," said Hella.

Ret glanced towards the entrance to the foyer.

Dek was securing the iron doors with its hefty latch. He tugged it a few times to ensure it was in place and turned around, perusing the busy foyer. After catching Ret's trenchant gaze, Dek glared in his direction and then at his father standing beside him.

"Or we can go right now!" exclaimed Sert after peering back at the chancellor.

Ret grabbed hold of Sert's hand. He rushed his family through the busy foyer to the room's far end. Eager to step foot on the escalation machines, Sert wasted no time hustling his family onto the ascending platform used to transport snugs up to the top levels of the hall.

Behind the expansive granite wall were two large conveyor belts lined by two gradually inclined curving ramps. They stretched upwards to the highest level of the building, giving access to every floor. Ret quickly stepped to the edge of the large moving belt and stood beside his father, ready with a list of questions.

"Did you teach us something you shouldn't have?"

"What? No. What are you talking about?" said Sert, startled, turning his head away.

"I know. You were covering for one of Mom's outlandish stories, weren't you?"

"For the last time, no. Now stop it and get ready for tonight."

Ret sneered at his father and pulled his bag off his shoulders. He reached into the front pocket, pulled out his green notebook, and flipped it to the first page.

A large entryway appeared as the escalator reached the fourth and final floor. Sert was the first to step off the conveyor belt and lead his family down a long hallway. Etched on both walls were intricate designs of concentric red circles, ellipses and cardioid shapes all intertwined together.

"Why are you in such a hurry?" asked Hella

Ret felt the frost on his bump start to melt as he scampered down the hall, trying to keep up with Sert. He reached the door to their family quarters and bent to one knee as his father frantically turned a silver knob and swung it open.

Flaunting a luxurious living residence and showing off their social value as red society members, a series of recessed lights illuminated the inside of their quarters. Centred within a lavish sitting area was a square brown table, and around it were three long red couches fabricated from threads of carbon fibre. Four red hoses snaked out from small compartments on the table's polished edge, outfitted to deliver fresh liquid nitrogen to anyone nearby.

Beyond the living room set, stretching from floor to ceiling was a large angled window facing down toward the white stage. Four swivelling padded chairs provided a perfect vantage point to the stage below.

Terri ran underneath Sert's extended arm as he held the door open.

"I get the good room; said it first!" screamed Terri, scurrying past the couches and down a long hall to the left of the foyer.

Ret moseyed to the living room, sat down next to Sert and pulled a nitrogen tube out from the table's hidden compartments. He sized up his father sitting uneasily on the other end of the couch while sipping fresh cold liquid nitrogen from a tank underneath the table.

Sert chuckled, knowing his interrogation was imminent.

"What's so funny, Dad?"

After taking a big chug from the nitrogen reserve, Sert slammed the hose down on the surface of the table and rose to his feet, looking into Ret's bright orange stunned eyes.

"I've got to go talk to the chancellors!"

*

Sert hurried down the descending side of the escalator belt and reached the empty foyer. He walked to the centre of the communal area and inspected a few distant snugs for a red-jewelled sash hanging across their chests.

He stood alone in the middle of the foyer, and while examining the room for anything that could help him with his search, he heard the sound of the two iron doors leading into the great hallway squeak behind him. He unlocked the latch, swung the solid gray door open and walked inside.

The red podium illuminated by natural light was starting to dim through the skylight, the only light source inside the now-darkening hallway. Sert walked towards the podium and, acting before thinking, looked up through the ceiling window and right into the beam of light. He pulled his head back and rubbed his eyes.

"You're a foreigner?"

Sert recognized the voice behind him and stumbled forward, trying to gain his balance. He squinted open a thin sliver in his vision and glanced toward a scowling Dek.

"You know, you could have saved yourself a lot of trouble if you had just come to me years ago," said Dek. "Did you think I wasn't going to find out?"

Sert grew defensive and wanted to explain his actions, but he kept quiet.

"Do you realize that no one in the history of Terin has ever done what you have done?"

"I didn't have a choice, Dek. I had to protect Ret and Terri."

"Protect them? You just hurt them."

Sert extended his open hands in front of his chest and pushed his palms down to de-escalate Dek's emotions.

"I'm a foreigner, Dek; I'll be the first to admit. But when I came here years ago, you weren't in power. I had to lie to your predecessors because I knew they would've expelled my whole family if they ever learned about my past."

"Do you think that puts me in any easier of a situation? I've never faced something like this before, Sert. You're from Tarni, the other side."

Sert studied the chancellor's emotions to gauge a feel of his temperament. Sert was on a slippery slope and needed to sway Dek's opinion. After all, this conversation could change his children's future so he trod carefully.

"How did you manage to keep this a secret for this long?"

"I had a friend that did administrative work for the chancellors when I forged my parental information, and she made sure no one saw them. Then, when you took over as chancellor, I thought you would find out, but you didn't. I noticed that after a while, nothing had happened. No one was wiser about my situation, so I raised my kids and lived my life. It wasn't until six years later, eight months ago, that I had to submit the children's Pagan application forms. I knew right then and there that someone would discover my past, but what could I do? I wasn't going to run. Where would I go? Then, I passed you today and I knew you had found out."

Dek stood with his hand covering his eyes, struggling to process the information.

"Well, I don't know what to tell you, Sert. You broke the rules. And a big rule at that. For the sake of everyone else, especially the young ones inside Pagan, I have no choice but to expel you and your family. What else can I do?" asked the chancellor, pulling his hand away from his face and shrugging his shoulders. "The last thing anyone wants around here is a foreigner, especially one from Tarni—where you are from."

"Come on, Dek. You can't be serious!"

"Why should I keep you? You're from a civilization that destroyed your own Pagan. I don't know what is, if that's not a reason to expel your kind. My father told me over a generation ago what really happened in those days in Tarni. Your civilization annihilated your own Pagan!"

"Listen, Dek, that's not how it all happened; you weren't there, I was."

"Well, I know that the elders in your civilization were so selfish and felt so entitled that they destroyed their own Pagan. You must have known that was going to obliterate your way of life. Tarni was a very successful civilization before all of that. You were leading the world in innovation. You were developing groundbreaking inventions and in an instant, destroyed them. It's more than sad. And with all this being said, the last thing I want in our Pagan is to have Tarni half-breeds trying to influence the lives and minds of our snugs. How can you even question my verdict, Sert?"

"I'm not my parents, Dek; I never believed in what they did, and I have never instilled that idea in either Ret or Terri."

"That's another thing. I can't trust that you have been a good parent up to this point. I have to protect Terin. How do you expect me to trust your kids?"

"I resent that, Dek! Hella and I are great parents. We attend every banquet, participate in activities, and teach our kids from your curriculum. And trust me, the last thing I want is anyone else intruding on our ways…"

"On our ways?"

"Yes, Dek. Our ways. Just ask those two little snugs Bri and his sister. They come to my door every week," argued Sert, trying to distill some understanding with the chancellor.

Faintly amused by his comment, Dek chuckled and continued listening.

"I know my kids are brilliant; I assure you of that. I can see them being amongst the greatest minds of their time."

"Oh really? As half-breeds? Please, I've seen your kind. Your cities don't even have roads or gliders. In fact, how did you learn how to drive anyway?"

"This is not about me. It's about my kids. Two months, that's all I need. Once they're behind that stone wall, you can do whatever you want with me."

"Does Hella know?"

Sert replied with silence.

"Hella doesn't even know?"

"No, she doesn't. I met her after her Pagan years. Listen, I understand your duty as chancellor, but I don't have to stand here and explain my relationships to you."

"And you listen. I cannot afford to have our Pagan tainted by your kind. We only accept bright young snugs into our society."

"How about this? Ret is going to win the competition tonight. I guarantee it."

"Well, I highly doubt that."

"And when he does, you will approve his Pagan application and Terri's."

"You are crazy, Sert, if you think I will allow that."

"Ret is going to win tonight, Dek. And when he does, you will let both of my children into Pagan and bury this secret of ours."

"How do you expect me to ignore years of tradition—not to mention our entire belief system—for your children? How many times do I have to tell you? They are half-breeds. That's the reason they won't be allowed in."

"Does it matter? They can be great! Ret is smart, Dek. Plain and simple. And you would be giving up a great opportunity if you disregard him. Pagan would be worse off if you didn't let him in."

"Well…" he faltered.

"Ret will be great. I know it. And it would be for the good of Terin to let him into Pagan. Not only is he smart, but he's creative. He will make Terin proud. Trust me."

"I don't know, Sert."

"Give me this, Dek. Give me this chance. Let Ret prove to you how smart he is, and then once he wins the competition and my children enter into Pagan, I'll leave."

Just like that, Sert?"

"Just like that, Dek."

"I don't know if I…"

"Listen, Dek," said Sert while pointing to his fingers. "I have fought and struggled my entire life up until this point. You think the stories from Tarni are bad? That's nothing compared to living through it. I've done it all. I've lived in ruin. I was exploited by a corrupt government. Why do you think I ran away from Tarni and came here? After all that time, there is no way I will let you throw away my kids' futures when in only two months, they will move into Pagan and we will never see them again. Please, chancellor. Give me two months."

"So, what if he is smart? You're asking a lot from me, Sert. How am I supposed to hide this secret from the chief director, not to mention every snug inside Pagan?"

"I'm sure if you were to recommend Ret after he wins the competition, the Pagan counsel wouldn't even look at his file. This will stay between just you and me."

"Well, I won't recommend someone who doesn't deserve it."

"Trust me. My children deserve it, and Ret will prove that to you tonight."

"You better ensure Ret is ready for the competition because I'll be watching him closely. Your children are your only saving grace, Sert. Remember, if he doesn't win, you are all out!" added Dek before turning his back and walking towards the two iron doors. "Don't forget to close the latch. We're about to begin."

Sert stood baffled as he gazed up at the dimmed skylight shining down onto the podium. He placed his hand on the side of the pillar and sighed in relief before trotting over toward the iron door. He stepped back inside the Grand Foyer, looked around cautiously for any witnesses, and slammed the door shut, locking the iron latch behind him.

Town Hall

Ret sat in his chair, his feet casually kicking over the front edge like two small pendulums swaying back and forth. His face was buried in a notebook, trying to cram the last bits of information into his memory, when he felt a familiar hand caress the back of his neck. He rolled his eyes, pushed Hella's comforting hand away, and even shot her a glare after his second attempt to swat her hand failed. To his surprise, he noticed her gazing out the viewing window at a single worker snug hanging from a rope and setting up a high-powered spotlight.

"Where did all these worker snugs come from?" Hella asked.

"I know. I think they're new. I hope I never get this duty after Pagan." answered Ret.

The door swung open and Sert trudged inside. He plopped down on the corner of the couch, pulled a nitrogen tube out of the table, and began chugging down the cold liquid.

"So, what did you say to the chancellor?" asked Ret, peering towards his troubled father.

"I just told him how well you would do tonight, that's all."

Sert followed his comment with a trusty smile, but Ret wasn't buying it. Before he could follow up with another question, Terri came trotting down the corridor and sauntered over to Sert, resting on the couch.

"Hey Dad, aren't you excited? Ret and I are going to do extra well for you tonight!"

"Ya, I hope you do," said Sert. "Let's go over to the viewing window with your brother."

The beginning of the red society banquet couldn't have started at a better time for Sert. Ret was still peering at his father and was ready to grill him when all the lights in the building turned off, leaving everyone in the darkness.

"Oh, it's about to begin! Everyone. Quiet." Hella said.

Thick beams of light from four spotlights cut through the darkness illuminating the white circular stage, as a low-pitched sound blasted through multiple sound accelerators hanging from iron brackets secured to the ceiling. Everyone in the grand hall stood on their feet with their eyes closed, savouring the comforting tone until it stopped.

"Welcome, everyone. "It's our pleasure to host you tonight."

Both chancellors spoke out from the center of the stage under the bright lights. Outfitted in their distinguished red jewelled sashes, Dek and Deea simultaneously raised their arms above their heads, gesturing a warm sign of greeting.

"It has been two and a half months since our last banquet, and there have been a lot of improvements to our Great Hall," announced Dek, turning his torso to face everyone. "I'm sure most of you have noticed the newest additions to our maintenance team. Let's first give them a round of appreciation! Let me introduce the 'Flyers'!"

Suddenly small compartments sprang open over the dome ceiling, and a long rope unravelled to the stage from each one. Snugs dressed in red jumpsuits flew out from the opened hatches and raced down the ropes, moving their bodies to the sound of a beat. The Flyers dazzled the audience with their routine—some were cartwheeling down the ropes while others slid face first, doing front flips in complete control.

The crowd cringed in fear as they performed their amazing act. A few flyers jumped from rope to rope; others swung out to the audience, anchoring themselves to the rope with one hand, and more were executing a series of flips as they descended to the ground. Sounds of "Oohs" and "Aahs" scattered over the audience.

The performers spun down to the white floor and let go of their ropes, all landing firmly on the ground. The performers formed a circular pattern around the stage as the long lines quickly retracted back to the ceiling. A colourful pyrotechnics display burst from the ceiling, finalizing the act and sending a loud "BOOM" across the hall.

"That was amazing," screamed Ret. "I wish every banquet was like this!"

"Please show your appreciation!" said the chancellors.

Whistles and claps rained down from the audience as the performers made their way off stage, raising their hands and nodding confidently to all their fans.

"Wow, they're not lying—they can fly!" Deea said to the audience. "I am very excited to speak in front of you because tonight marks a new chapter in our community. We have consistently reached our goals while maintaining our vision throughout the entire history of the red society. For that, we only have you to thank," continued Deea. "Our brilliant young minds are doing so well representing us inside Pagan. I'm informed of their progress and accomplishments daily, and I promise you this: today, our middle-aged citizens are amongst the smartest and most productive of all Paganers. Let's keep up the good work, parents!"

As she outlined the additions to the community's education program, a projection shined down from above, illuminating the stage and broadcasting clear written instructions beneath her feet.

"Our Pagan representative informed me that our children should be learning more about physics and other naturally occurring phenomena around the globe," said Deea pointing down to the enlarged image. "The Pagan counsel is trying to educate all children on the importance of technological progression. When you return home tomorrow, a detailed lesson plan will be in everyone's community box, so be sure to teach your children."

Deea discussed other changes to the curriculum and guided every parent in the audience, each one paying close attention. She summarized her presentation, gave a quick nod to the audience, and instantly the room went black.

A thin spotlight shined down on Dek, standing behind Deea. He cleared his vocal cords with a slight cough and raised his arms.

"Now, please give warm regards to our send-off snugs. I would like to present to you our eight parting souls."

Eight twenty-five-year-old snugs walked onto the stage, formed a straight line and looked up at the crowd. Their spirits were mixed. All of them had good posture, displaying a prideful demeanour as a reflection of a well-lived life. However, their eyes were jet black, indicating their uncertainty, sadness and fear.

Deea addressed the first elder snug in line. She revealed one of the eight silver charms attached to a chain and smiled before offering this unique piece of jewelry. Every charm was tailored specifically to each snug, signifying their life's accomplishments.

"To Jo, I present you a silver blade," said Dek before instructing Deea to place the chain around the first snug's neck.

After receiving their gift, the elder snug approached Dek, and turned his body, exposing his frost bump; Dek graciously responded.

"Jo, the progeny of Reg and Kym, was a big part of our society!" announced Dek facing back to the audience. "Throughout his Pagan years, he contributed to the field of transportation. Jo is the reason why all our glider blades work. He discovered how friction causes ice to melt and developed a method to deliver electricity to the glider's polarity switch. After he left Pagan he met Lyn, the mother of his children," said the chancellor as large pictures of Jo's life changed from one to another on the white stage below his feet.

"And your two young children are doing great! They are leading a project inside Pagan to redesign our gliders so they can move even faster. I think they call it aerodynamics or something," announced Dek. "Looks like they took after their father."

Jo longed to hear more as the chancellor spoke of his children inside Pagan. However, due to the timeline of Pagan, children were never present for their parents' death.

"All of us here appreciate what you have accomplished. You should feel proud, Jo. You've had a great life, and your children are doing so well." said Dek, putting a hand on his shoulder.

Jo took one final look at his personalized montage on the stage below him and turned his head up, facing the silent audience. Without any reaction or forewarning, his eyes instantly changed from a dark empty black to a bright glowing white.

"Goodbye, my friend! You will be missed," Dek said in a comforting tone.

Everyone whistled as he turned around and walked toward Deea, showing off the radiating white from his eyes. He stepped closer to Deea, who at that moment unlatched two large gray doors leading outside. The doors swung open, unveiling the first sign of darkness in a year. In front of the door, Jo bent his legs, shifting his body into a sprinter's position, and ran full speed into the night, never to be seen again.

"Where is he going, Mom?" asked Terri, looking concerned.

"Everyone has a different belief. The truth is, no one knows. We all run off into the night when we get to that age. Some say we vanish into the atmosphere. Some say we turn completely into frost," said Hella. "I can tell you this, though; one day you'll find out for yourself!"

Hella watched as Terri scrunched her brow, grimacing over the thought of dying.

"Ooh… don't worry, Terri. Please, don't worry!" soothed Hella.

The chancellor continued on, reciting warm farewells to the remaining send-off snugs, and performing the same ritual before each snug followed suit, running off into the night.

Deea shut both doors and locked the iron latch, finalizing that portion of the assembly. She strode toward the center of the stage and paused in a state of reflection; everyone in the audience followed suit.

After a long drawn-out moment, Deea raised her head, clapped her hands and continued with the presentation.

"Ok! All you young soon-to-be-Paganers, please start to make your way down here. We will begin the competition right after the news bulletin," announced Deea.

Ret and Terri jumped out of their seats and ran to the front door; Sert followed close behind. Excited and nervous, both children were reciting questions, trying to sharpen their minds at the last moment. To their surprise, Sert bent down on one knee and gave them a long affectionate hug. Ret looked over Sert's shoulders at his sister and received the same befuddled expression he was giving her.

"I hope you two do well!" whispered Sert.

Ret trode backward into the hallway and tugged on his sister's arm, pulling her away. They both shot their father an awkward glare and took off down the hallway.

"What was that about?" asked Terri.

"I don't know. He's been acting weird since we got here. Don't let this distract you. We're here to win this!"

The two hopped on the escalating machine. Still uneasy, Ret turned around and glanced back down the hall and witnessed his father holding his head and pacing back and forth. Ret stood transfixed looking on, and right before the angle of the escalator slid out of sight, Ret locked eyes with his father one last time and received a genuine look of desperation. He turned to his sister.

"Terri, we need to win!"

•

Healthy Competition

Ret and Terri ran down the escalator, reached the foyer and gathered with the other contestants. Ret could feel the stress in the room. He looked around the foyer and noticed a few children hopping on their feet, while others tried relieving some tension from their shoulders by stretching out their arms and shaking their heads from side to side.

The chancellors finished presenting the last portion of the news bulletin to the audience, warning the crowd of massive geyser predictions in the area. Dek took one last look over his sheet and gave Deea a nod.

"You're going to love this!" Dek exclaimed with excitement in his voice.

As he pointed up to the ceiling, several compartments swung open and out came the famous Flyers. With one hand, each flyer held firmly to the rope, and with the other they grasped a tall cylindrical shaped podium wedged between their curled- up arms, as if they were giving the bulky red object a tight headlock. The snugs, dressed in red, zoomed down from high above. Diving head first from the ceiling and reaching the ground, each flyer placed their cargo in a circular pattern on the floor, and then rappelled up the long rope performing their crowd-pleasing stunts on their way back up.

"I'll never get tired of that!" said Rony as he approached Ret. "So, let's see you flex that big brain of yours! Are you nervous? Are you scared? Cause I'm not. I will beat you and everyone else!"

Ret turned around, chuckling. He was unafraid of Rony's intimidation and knew better than to give in to his cheap scare tactics. With a sarcastic smirk and quick roll of his eyes, Ret ignored Rony's empty threat and faced back to the stage in front of him.

"Alright you young ones, show everyone what you know," said Deea.

All sixteen children walked out on stage in single file. Ret approached his podium. His legs shook. His hands trembled.

"What's wrong," Ret said, mouthing his words. "This never happens."

Ret was bent over. A shiver, one he had never felt before shot down from his neck underneath his frost bump to his webbed toes and the points of his fingertips. He couldn't shake it. Thankfully, he wasn't alone—all the other contestants were battling their own reactions.

Why wouldn't they be? All the effort and dedication led to this very moment. Every question, lesson, and test was all in preparation for this defining event in their lives; that was enough pressure.

Every parent cringed as they sat within their resident windows, staring at their petrified children. It seemed so cruel to put these children and parents through such an arduous validation test. However, this was Terin, and performing well in this competition would provide an advantage for their children inside Pagan and confirm their hard work as parents.

After looking around the room, Ret forced away his anxiety and slammed his hands flat on the smooth podium surface. He shook his head, focused his red eyes and leapt to the top of the podium.

He stared as all the other children struggled to climb up. He smiled as he panned the room, waving his hands upward, trying to encourage the other children to follow. His eyes managed to change to a faint greenish hue that sent a comforting message to each child as they made it up to the top of their podiums.

The chancellors welcomed the contestants, presenting each with their identity piece and a welcoming bow. Ret glanced over as Dek approached the snug next to him. The little snug's posture froze, and his black eyes made it clear he was terrified. The chancellor smiled and waited for his legs to stop shaking before placing the society identity piece around his neck.

"You will do great," encouraged Dek.

Ret tried to lock eyes with Dek, butDek did not return the gesture. After tilting his head over and peering directly into Dek's face, he received a simple nod as Dek tossed the medallion to him. He glared back at Dek as he placed the medallion around his neck.

"My children, this medallion marks the end of your primary life," said Dek, centering himself on the stage. "Seven years of preparation has made you all fit to proceed into your next life. Now is the time to prove yourselves! These years have equipped your minds with knowledge, and now you must use it. A life of competition, dedication, and great reward awaits you inside Pagan. Let these medallions remind you of who you are representing."

"We will now begin the competition. Is everybody ready?" asked Dek, looking at each firm, standing snug. "Let's begin the first round!"

Sixteen spotlights fixed to the ceiling illuminated every contender.

"First question: What is the main difference between green and red trees?"

The lights flashed rapidly. Ret and all the other contestants shut their eyes as pulsing strobes purposefully distracted them from finding the answer. The uncomfortable flashing only lasted a few moments until two solid beams randomly selected two snugs; Rony was one of them.

"Red trees cannot be used for hibernation because they take too many resources from our bodies," answered Rony.

"You are correct!" said Dek.

Another small beam of light projected the number "one" on the front of Rony's podium, indicating his correct response and awarding him the point.

Looking over to Ret, the confident Rony smiled and cocked his brow.

"Next question: What is the highest frequency our vocal cords can hit?"

Again, the spotlights began flashing; this time Ret was chosen to answer. He pinpointed in his mind the lessons his mother tried to teach him about frequency.

"One thousand ripples," said the other snug, beating Ret to the answer.

"I'm sorry. That is incorrect," answered the chancellor. "Ret, you can take the point."

Ret dove back into his memory attempting to recall. He vaguely pictured a few examples of waveforms on the frostboard; some were short and small, and others were big and long. What did that mean, he wondered. Panicked and running out of time, he tried thinking of anything to help jog his memory.

He remembered Hella delivering a lesson in the classroom a few years ago. She bragged about a team inside Pagan that discovered how sound travels using frequency. She talked about how ambitious they were, how the team worked together when faced with challenges, and even how she played a part in their discovery. It went on and on. Ret pictured Hella relishing her story, but in his mind he was trying to push Hella's boisterous body aside, and clarify the images of waveforms on the white frostboard next to her. Ret's eyes closed, and his head tilted ever so slightly.

"What was that number?" he whispered.

Right before the timer ran short he found the answer, opened his eyes and gave his response. "Ten thousand ripples!"

"Correct you are, Ret. Ten thousand ripples," Dek repeated.

Ret reached around to the small of his back, wiped away the drip off his bump and looked up at the family quarters. He tried to make out their faces but couldn't see much as their viewing window was dimly lit.

The competition continued as more and more children got eliminated from the first round, and Terri still needed to answer her question. Her turn came next.

"Why is the nitrogen snow yellow on the south side of the planet?"

The spotlight centred on Terri as she closed her eyes. Ret could see she was mouthing the events in her memory. With the timer counting down, Terri was starting to panic. Her arms began to flail.

"Large deposits of particulate metals have settled on the south side of the planet over time due to the planet's magnetic pull. Their yellow snow has more trace amounts of metal than ours," answered Terri's competitor, Kin, beating her to the answer.

"Yes, Kin. That is correct! And Kin, that was a great response!" said the chancellor before signalling the end of the first round. "I'm sorry Terri, you do not move on."

Everyone in the building watched Terri deflate. Her head pointed down and her shoulders drooped as she left the podium. She kicked the gate open and stomped into the foyer.

The chancellor positioned himself in the middle of the circle.

"You eight have made it through to the second round of the competition. In this round, you will be racing against each other," instructed the chancellor. "The first four to get more than three points over any other snug will move onto the third round."

The ceiling compartments opened again, but no flyers. Eight long ropes unwound from above, carrying small pen-like objects delivered to the corresponding contestant. Each device projected a small coloured beam of light unique to each contestant.

"Is everybody ready?"

Ret grabbed the green pen dangling before his eyes and pumped his fist.

"Let's begin!" announced the chancellor.

An enlarged picture of a giant slug alongside a large world map image projected on the floor. A question above the photographs read, "Where did this species originate from?"

The contestants raced against the timer, pointing their beams at a specific location on the map before locking in their answers. Once the clock ran short, a still snapshot captured all the coloured beams, as a light blue region slowly appeared on the map indicating the correct area. Any coloured dot inside the light blue vicinity would be deemed correct.

"Great! That is one point for orange, green, red, and purple!" explained the chancellor.

Ret felt confident after answering this question correctly, which increased his score to two points. He glanced over to Rony, who responding to the crowd's applause raised his arms above his head; a pompous smile written over his face. Ret chuckled and looked down at his podium. The number on his display changed from one to two.

The round continued.

All eight contenders were keeping pace with one another. Questions ranging from math equations to foreign affairs came one after another. Ret was tied with Kin for the lead nearing the end with five points on his board. Most contestants were sitting on four points, leaving two snugs on three. Any player outside three points of the leader would be eliminated.

Ret and Kin set a great pace and answered nearly every question correctly. As it stood, Kin secured first place, Ret a close second, and Rony third with one point less. The fourth-place snug received a sarcastic laugh from the audience after realizing he was one point away from losing the round.

Dek approached the remaining snugs. Applause filled the hall.

"Round three. Is everybody ready? Do I need to explain the rules for this round?" asked Dek.

He received a clear "no" from his contestants and raised his hand above his head. He waited until everyone was paying attention before dramatically chopping his arm down, leaving everyone in darkness.

"Let's begin!" said Dek.

Four squares appeared on the floor, representing each of the snugs through their corresponding colours, and inside every square were five pictures rotating in sequence. Staring down at the projection, Ret looked into his square (bordered in green) as the five different pictures flipped. Ret's mind was racing, trying to find any relationship between them. A still photo of a baby snug screaming his first words flipped first, followed by an exaggerated picture of large sound accelerators bursting with power. The third picture was split into two; a snug with a white frosted back standing next to another snug with a yellow frosted back.

The fourth was a collage of four Pagans that belonged to civilizations from other parts of the world. Ret took a moment to confirm his answer. He didn't wait for the last picture.

"A global communication system?"

Silence fell over the crowd as the chancellor approached the impatient Ret.

"Are you sure, Ret?" asked Dek.

"Yeah," answered Ret in an uncertain tone. "Is it correct?"

"Let's congratulate the first finalist! Ret! Maybe one day you will develop the world's first global communication system."

Swept by relief, the crowd burst into an enormous cheer. The front display on Ret's podium turned from six to seven. Excited, he glanced up at his family's viewing window but couldn't see anyone. He squinted his eyes, only to see a vague silhouette of Sert pumping his arm and cheering him on.

"Electrical power?" Rony answered, being the second in line to finish.

"Unfortunately, that is incorrect, Rony. I'm sorry, your answer was electromagnetic induction; close though," said Dek.

Rony was devastated. And as he dismounted from his podium, Ret shot a heavyhearted look and an apologetic shrug. Rony half smiled as he puttered off the stage.

"I know the answer to mine!" announced Kin. "Sustainable energy!" The chancellor took a moment to confirm the answer. Dek teased the audience and paused before delivering his pronouncement. He would leave everyone hanging on his word many times, holding them in suspense. Dek turned his body to face the sizeable adolescent snug standing with an uneasy look, and chuckled before delivering his response.

"Yes! That's correct. You, too, move on to the final round!"

Moment of Truth

The chancellors stood on opposite ends of the stage, pumping their arms above their heads, chanting to the audience, all looking down from their ceiling windows and cheering on the two finalists.

Ret felt confident standing behind his podium. He glared at Kin, sizing him up. Coming in first place in two out of the three rounds boosted Ret's ego. He ignored the sight of Kin's one point lead. Nothing would stop him from winning the champion's medallion.

Ret lifted his arms over his shoulders, encouraging a loud cheer throughout the hall. Every spectator replied with a surging roar. The sound shook the building and resonated across the ceiling, amplifying the chaos as loud echoes showered back down onto the two finalists. Ret lowered his arms and looked at his opponent with certainty in his eyes.

The natural high Ret felt was among the greatest a snug could ever feel; an audience cheering on your every movement with applause and acceptance. Ret raised his chin and pushed out his chest; however Kin held in his emotions. Instead of reacting in kind, he stood composed and emotionally steady.

"Is everybody ready?" asked Deea as the audience burst into another huge applause. "Welcome, Ret! Welcome, Kin! To the final round!"

Both chancellors raised their hands to their jewelled sashes and removed pear cut green emeralds from their collection of jewels. Both stepped towards a contestant on either side of the stage, held the crafted stone in their hands, and addressed each finalist. Ret followed Kin's lead and extended a graceful bow to the approaching chancellor, smiling back at Deea after she attached the stone to the middle of his red medallion.

"Let these stones signify your brilliance inside Pagan. Being a finalist is quite an accomplishment!" said Deea before leaving the stage.

The competitive stare down continued. Ret was cocking his head from side to side and displaying signs of disrespect. Kin stood calm, staring right back at him.

"Let me have your attention!" announced Dek. "The final round is straightforward. We will pose one question, and the first to answer correctly will receive two points," he said, looking at both scores. "Ret, you are behind by one, so you must answer correctly to win. Is everybody ready?"

"Yes!" shouted Ret.

"Yes," answered Kin.

Dek raised his arm and swung it back down, pointing his finger towards the stage. Immediately, all the lights in the building turned off, leaving the platform glowing white.

A timer set to ten appeared, and as Ret gazed into the projection, he found himself in a bit of a trance. He had a hard time believing that all the lessons he had endured, all the challenging examinations, and all the hard work he had put into his childhood came down to this very moment. Shaking his head, Ret tried to suppress his thoughts. It was time to focus.

"How do our bodies keep warm?"

Ret closed his eyes. "What was Mom saying in the glider?"

The timer started counting down, and loud shouts and chanting filled the room.

Kin fed into the crowd's rowdy excitement and took the first shot. "By heating the melted nitrogen inside our bodies?"

Dek's solemn face looked at Kin. "I'm sorry, but that is not correct. Alright Ret, it's down to you! I will set the timer back to ten. Good luck!"

"Our skin," whispered Ret. " What was Mom saying about our skin?"

He closed his eyes tightly, whispering to himself as he tapped his forehead with the palm of his hand.

The timer was passing five.

"There was one word mom was in the middle of saying," answered Ret's inner voice.

Sert was leaning far over the window's edge in their family quarters, staring down at his son with fiery red eyes.

"Answer, Ret!" shouted Sert, along with the thousands in attendance.

The timer was passing two and he needed to make a move. Hunched over atop his podium, Ret paid little attention to the clock. His ego was in the way of his rational thinking. Instead of watching the timer and taking a shot, he was too determined to find the answer.

Up above, Sert was hopping up and down with frustration. He was dancing in front of his chair, watching in horror as the clock turned from two to one. He shook his head in disbelief, knowing his son was lost in his mind.

"Answer!" Sert screamed.

And then, the timer ran short, sending a loud buzzing tone throughout the building, signifying the end of the competition. Rets eyes shot wide open. He dropped to his knees in disbelief.

Kin released his built-up emotions and screamed in delight. His accomplishments were accentuated by a massive, colourful display of pyrotechnics bursting from the ceiling. The Flyers swung from their trusty ropes, performing their exhilarating stunts as everyone in the crowd chanted his name.

Ret climbed off his podium, captive to his pride, as the chancellors rushed past him and presented Kin with the champion's medallion.

Disappointed, angry, and helpless, Ret left his podium and traipsed through the gate and into the foyer. He stopped before the ramp, hesitated, turned around, marched over to the iron doors leading to the grand hallway, and unhooked the latch. Before stepping inside, he glanced at the main stage and saw Kin hoisted up by the chancellors. His arms extended over his head, beaming a jubilant smile as sparkling confetti rained over him. Ret stomped his foot on the ground, turned around and trotted inside.

He paced back and forth in the dark hallway, his head down, searching for peace. He walked to the corner, slid to the floor and placed his head between his knees.

Ret just wanted to be alone.

Family Feud

Sert felt lifeless.

He stared out at the crowd, his eyes glazed over, blank. Not even the sights of the Flyers could shake the numb feeling of shock, petrifying his body.

Hella and Terri clapped along as Kin waved back to the cheering crowd, his glorious smile still brimming. As for Sert, he glared down at Kin, soaking in his moment. He shook his head, faced Hella and Terri, and edged closer.

"There's something I have to tell you both," said Sert

"What?" asked Hella.

He hesitated momentarily, "There's something important I have to say."

"What is it, Sert? Let me guess. You're upset because he didn't come in first? I think Ret did great, and I don't want to hear what you have to say."

Hella jumped out of her seat and marched towards the living area. Sert and Terri followed close behind. All three sat on different sides of the glossy brown table and sipped from nitrogen hoses.

Sert cleared his throat. "You're going to hate me. I am so sorry."

"Please, Sert. Get over yourself." Hella replied.

"No, you don't understand."

Then suddenly, a knock came from the front door.

"Oh, that must be Ret. I wonder why he's knocking?" said Hella.

Sert cringed as Hella walked towards the front door. He closed his eyes and lowered his head when she grabbed the handle and opened the door.

"Wow, Dek, Deea?" responded Hella. "Well, thank you for coming to our quarters. I'm sure this is about Ret. He performed so well, didn't he? Ret hasn't returned yet. I'm not sure where he is?"

Sert kept his head down. The clanging sounds of jewels from the chancellors were all he could hear as they advanced toward the living room table; Sert felt every step they took. He slowly opened his eyes and saw four blue feet pointing in his direction.

"Well, Sert, a deal is a deal," said Dek, standing over him.

"Wait, what's going on?" asked Hella.

"Do you want to tell her, or should I?" asked Dek.

Sert answered with silence.

"Sert is a foreigner!" shouted Dek.

"Ya, good joke Dek. No, really, why are you here?" asked Hella.

"Hella, listen to me," began Dek. "Sert is a foreigner. I have proof, and he admitted it to me just before the competition."

Hella chuckled. "Yes, I heard you say that the first time, but how can that be true? It can't be."

Hit by the total silence in the room, Hella turned to Sert, hunched over, still hiding his face with both hands.

"Is this true, Sert?" she asked. "Answer me!"

"Yes, I'm not from Terin. I'm actually from Tarni."

"Uh-huh, and I'm a green-skinned snug from the north. Come on, really? You're telling me that you have been living a lie for the last seven years?" Hella chuckled. "Really, though, that can't be? It's impossible. You were a blue society member in Pagan, weren't you? You told me you were."

Hella looked over to the chancellors. Her brow lowered, lips shrugged downward. "No, really? Are you serious?"

"Yes," said Sert.

Hella clenched her fists, her eyes turned red, fixed on Sert, cowering on the couch. He didn't need to look up; he could feel the anger emitting from Hella's body.

"You little puss bag! I should have known! It all makes sense now that I think about it," screamed Hella. "We never met in Pagan; we met after I left Pagan.

Wow! You slimy coward. I can't believe you lied to me all this time. Who would do that to someone? Get away from us, you deceiver! I can't even look at you!"

"Is everything going to be okay?" Terri asked softly.

"No, it's not! And you can thank your wonderful father for this! I'm so embarrassed. So what's going to happen now?"

Sert slid his hands over to the side of his face and glimpsed up at Dek, with one of his black eyes.

"You are all hereby expelled from Terin. This act of fraud committed by one Sert, the progeny of, well, I don't know, do I?" said Dek before pausing. "The act of fraud is punishable by these terms. Deea, do you concur?"

"I concur."

Hella's eyes filled with despair. "This cannot be your decision. You are going to expel all of us? Even my children? For one snug's actions? Please, no."

"Sert and I made a deal before the competition, Hella. If one of your children had won the competition, we wouldn't be here now."

Hella's frightened face turned into outright rage. She glared at Sert, still sitting helplessly on the couch; his hands back covering his face.

"You dirty slug! You gambled our future on our kids? You're going to pay for this!"

Hella marched to the couch, grabbed Sert by his arms and dragged his body to the floor. Sert didn't resist. She harnessed her rage and began stomping on his body. Sert pulled his arms over his head, trying to block Hella's swarm of kicks.

Hella eventually succumbed to the realization of their situation. Her eyes turned black as she screamed out. Sert watched as she fell to her knees, weeping in grief.

"Okay, Dek. I think I've got all their belongings," said Deea, holding four bags. "Where's Ret?"

"We'll find him on the way out. Let's go, everyone. Pick up your belongings and get out these quarters," instructed Dek.

Sert crawled over to his bag. He picked himself up and wandered into the hall. Hella, being hauled out by Dek, was still trying to negotiate with him.

"No, please, Chancellor, please don't do this to my family!" she pleaded, pushing back against Dek, twisting in an attempt to escape.

Dek forced her out the door by grabbing her neck, pushing her down, and leading her through the hall by her lowered head.

"You can throw me out, Dek, but not my kids! Please, not my kids!" begged Hella.

"Your kids are the reason we're expelling you!" stated Dek. "We don't want any foreign seeds in our Pagan. We would have overlooked it if Ret had won the competition, but he didn't."

On the main floor, a large group of snugs celebrating with Kin learned what was happening after Hella's screams sparked their interest. Everyone scurried over and formed a circle around Sert and his family, and without any sympathy, began throwing half-filled cups of liquid methane. Hella swung her hands, swatting at the cups coming in from all directions; Sert did nothing to protect himself and simply walked in shame as the debris rained down on him.

Dek reached the grand hall entrance, grabbed hold of the iron latch, swung open the door and led the family into the hallway, closing the door behind him. He shoved on Sert's back, forcing him to stumble to one side of the hall and instructed Hella and Terri to stand next to him. Dek staggered to the greeting podium with his arms held out and unlocked a latch from a hidden storage compartment underneath the platform. He pulled out a burnlight and cranked the device's base; a thick light illuminated the room.

"What's going on?" spoke a faint voice out of a darkened corner.

"Who is that?" asked the chancellor as he pointed the light toward the source of the sound.

Ret stepped out of the shadows. Growing concerned, Ret looked at his mother, who stared back with black eyes and an agonizing grimace. He turned to Dek for an explanation.

"We're all being expelled, Ret. I'm really a foreigner," announced Sert, beating Dek to the answer.

"Yeah, sure. And I actually won the competition." Ret responded sarcastically. "Really, what's going on here?"

A heavy silence filled the room as Ret weighed his comment.

"It's true, Ret," cried Hella. "We're all just finding this out now."

"This is a good joke, Dad, and I'm not going along with it."

"Ret, I swear this is no joke," Hella answered.

"But how? You're actually serious? And now we're getting expelled because of this? Wait, this is it, isn't it? This is what you were worried about today? You're a foreigner? And we're all getting expelled? Really?"

"We wouldn't be here if this weren't real, Ret," answered Dek.

"Alright, but you can't do this, Dek!"

"Yes, I can! And I am!"

"Dad, be honest. Is this really happening?"

"Yes, Ret. I'm so sorry. If you had won the competition,"

"Don't you tell him that! You've done enough, you stupid puss bag!" screamed Hella.

"Alright, enough stalling. It's time to go," interrupted an impatient Dek.

Pointing toward the entranceway, Dek signalled for Ret to join his family.

"Our skin." shouted Ret.

"What?" said the chancellor.

"Our skin."

"What about our skin?" asked the chancellor.

"Our bodies take in the sun's radiant heat, and our skin acts as an insulator to keep the heat inside our bodies. This is what keeps our bodies warm."

Dek flashed the beam of light in Ret's face. Ret squinted, raised his hands in front of his face and turned his head away.

"How did you know that?"

"I just figured it out. It's right, isn't it?"

"Okay, how did you figure it out, then?"

"Well, why don't you get that blinding light out of my face, and maybe I'll tell you."

After lowering the beam, Dek asked again. "Okay, Ret. Honestly, how did you know that?"

"On our glider ride over here, mom was teaching me about heat from our sun until my dad interrupted her," said Ret, rubbing his eyes. "I learned that our skin protects us from the sun's radiant heat."

"Keep going," said the chancellor.

"To be honest, I just figured this out right now. If our skin protects us against radiant heat from the outside, it must do the same inside. The heat from the sun is insulated inside our bodies. That's why we would suffocate during hibernation, but our body would be okay."

Kneeling beside Ret, Dek placed his hand on his shoulder and smiled. "That's impressive, Ret. I didn't expect you to know the answer to that question. I posed that question, figuring neither of you would get it right. To be honest, I wanted you to lose."

Ret sneered back at Dek and watched him rise to his feet. He kept his eyes locked on Dek's face, sporting a slight smirk and a raised brow. Ret could see Dek was weighing something heavily in his mind; his eyes were closed, and he was tilting his head side to side. He hummed and hawed before landing a decision. Finally, Dek opened his eyes and marched over to Ret's family in the corner.

"Well, Sert. It seems your son is your family's saviour, after all. Ret impresses me, Sert. I will pass him and Terri into Pagan to represent our society," Dek announced.

A wave of relief rushed through their bodies.

"Can we go now?" asked an exhausted Hella.

"Yes, Hella, you can go too," stated Dek.

"Thank you! This means so much to us!" exclaimed Sert.

"Sert, I didn't say your name."

Ret watched Sert's back straighten at attention. He turned to face Dek with a pair of glossy black eyes. He pushed up his bottom lip, outstretched his chin, and nodded his head before turning around to face Hella and Terri, both slouching and leaning on the wall.

"I'm so sorry, Hella. I didn't mean for this to happen. But if it gives our children a good future, then we must do this."

She didn't look at him.

Sert puttered over to Ret, smiled and hugged him, patting him hard on his back.

"Good luck Ret! I'm so proud of you!"

"Let's go, Sert, stop wasting time!" shouted Dek

Sert released his hug and slowly stepped over the stone floor, making his way to the entrance, trying to hide the dripping liquid from his hand as he clenched his fist inconspicuously, forming a hard-packed snowball. He reached the main doorway, forced open the latch, and spun around.

"Goodbye, Dek!" screamed Sert.

In a quick, purposeful movement, Sert released everything projecting the snowball in the direction of the chancellor.

Dek pinpointed the snowball heading straight at him. He slid his body out of the path, as the ball grazed his chest before exploding on the wall behind him. Dek regained his balance, glared toward the door, and saw that Sert was gone.

"What a puss bag. I better not be missing a jewel," muttered Dek fingering through his sash.

Ret noticed the burnlight loosely held in Dek's other hand. He glanced at the chancellor, realized he was distracted and snatched it whilst racing towards the doorway. The chancellor spun around, reaching out his free arm, trying to grasp Ret's little body, but it was too late. All he could make out was Ret's fading silhouette running through the door and into darkness.

Dek stood in disbelief. Tilting his head and half chuckling, he turned to Hella.

"See, Ret's very impressive!"

Outcast

s Ret ran, he didn't know how to feel; one moment, humiliation and anger, and the next, confusion and sadness. Strobes of colours radiated from his eyes, changing from green to red, then black to blue as he sprinted along the walkway outside the banquet hall. He ignored the large quantities of melted nitrogen spilling off his back. He tried to push himself, but his legs slowed.

Ret glanced over his right shoulder and noticed his bump was nearly out of frost. He slowed to a stop, knelt, and stretched his back toward the sky, waiting for his bump to replenish. He dropped his head and looked at his burnlight. It was flickering. Like him, it needed a recharge.

Magnesium and frozen water are the key components that power one of these beams. Inside the rectangular iron casing is a block of solid magnesium surrounded by a thick layer of frozen water used to induce a bright chemical reaction. A small crank attached to a lever on the back of the apparatus connects to a sharp grating device inside the front end.

Both components must be broken into small shavings before the metal catches a spark. By turning the crank, the shaved metal and the oxygen in the ice combust from sparks caused by a small piece of flint rock. Inside a durable layer of clear glass, the bright reaction will shoot out the front of the burnlight, piercing through a great distance into the night.

Ret stood and patted his back, feeling a thick layer of frost. He pointed the burnlight across the ice road and into the parking lot filled with hundreds of unoccupied gliders.

"The glider!"

He raced through the parking lot until he reached the family vehicle. Stepping up into the interior, he held the light steady inspecting every compartment, nook and cranny, searching for clues. Rustling through the front seats, he noticed only one bottle of Jax sitting in the front holder. He was confident there were two when they parked.

"Dad was here," he thought. "He must have gone into the shrubs."

Ret slowly turned around and shined his light into the living shrub field. Blue branches of different sizes were brimming over the land. All entwined, a sea of dense interlacing vines were slowly crisscrossing within the massive jumble of vegetation. Loud pops and cracking echoed over the ground as the shrubs gradually shifted throughout the massive swathe. Constantly turning, each limb rotating around, trying to coat itself with an even layer of frost.

Ret climbed down from the glider and stepped towards the shrubs. His legs were trembling.

The beam from his burnlight disturbed the living tangle issuing louder sounds of cracking within the locations where the light shone. Ret stood transfixed.

"Enough was enough," he thought. "Do you want to see your father again?"

Ret lifted his right knee, his leg hovering over the edge and held it there, second-guessing himself. Finally, after a big courageous sigh, he lowered his foot into the shrubs.

The slithering roots instantly climbed up his legs. Weeds approached him from every direction in search of his frost. He snapped into action and began pushing his way through, trying to locate his father's trail. The burnlight flashed from side to side as he plowed through each step, struggling to maintain his direction.

He tried to keep his balance, but constant jabs from the shrubs made it harder to penetrate deeper. He threw a flurry of kicks as each spear poked his legs, testing the little snug for weaknesses. One curly vine hooked onto his shin and pulled so hard that it flipped him right off his feet, his body crashing to the ground. Instantly, slick blue branches wrapped around his arms and shoulders, pinning him down.

"No! Get off me!"

He was face down, struggling to get up, but the swarm was relentless. Sharp tips from each vine clawed up his back, scraping the frost off his bump. Ret was suffocating. As he lay there, he closed his eyes, feeling the energy drain from his body. He flailed around on the hard-packed soil bed, helpless, like living prey defeated and at the mercy of its captors. He was no longer courageous, wasn't strong, and felt like a failure.

Ret relaxed his body and thought of his father one last time. It wasn't a pleasant recollection from his childhood that he fonded over. No, he pictured Sert running out into the flat rock, alone in the dark, misguided and screaming for help.

A surge of power coursed through Ret's body.

He opened his fiery red eyes in a rage, heaved his leg up, planted his knees on the hard-packed soil, and pressed his body up to his feet. Forcefully swinging his arms, he grabbed the sharp little vines on his back and flung them away. He looked down at his legs and clenched the vines that coiled around his shins, tearing them off.

"No, you're not going to get me!" he screamed.

He trudged, gained ground, and struggled with every step, throwing kicks and punches at the flock of attackers. He had no time to consider the risk, danger, or fear. The deeper he went, the more the vines became aggressive.

He pressed forward until he noticed a source of relief in the form of an enormous root sticking out of the ground.

A thick shrub trunk was lying sideways and sprawled out under the weight of the top growing shrubs. Unlike tree species, shrubs produce thousands of vines, and the structure of the trunk cannot support the weight of the growth. Right at the apex, where the trunk turns downward, sat an exposed and undisturbed area elevated just high enough that the vines could not reach. It was the only safe spot. Ret raced right toward it.

He ran with precision, stepping into small gaps and over the top of bulky sections of more mature slower moving shrubs until he reached the edge of the root. After hurling the burnlight up to the top of the root's hump, he dug his fingers into the thick layer of frost covering the trunk's surface. Pulling himself up, grasping hand over hand, Ret edged up to the top, kicking away branches that tried latching onto his feet. He fell on his belly at the summit, forcing a reassuring sigh.

"Where are you, Dad?" he thought.

Ret slowly pushed himself up into a kneeling position and retrieved the burnlight. He reached his other arm behind his back, catching the dripping nitrogen leaking off his bump. With a cupped hand, he recycled it back to the top, pouring it over his half-melted bump until he restored a healthy layer of frost.

He stood firm on his feet and shined the light from his burnlight far out to the horizon, but something was different. In the distance, at the end of the beam, there were no shrubs in sight, no vegetation—nothing but brown and flat land.

Ret howled in delight. Smiling, he raised his arms, jumping up and down, the beam of light flinging in every direction. He stopped and thought twice about celebrating so loudly, considering all the commotion would stimulate the shrubs beneath him; however, to Ret's surprise, his actions acted as a perfect beacon.

"Ret!"

"Dad?" he yelled.

Ret shined the light toward his father's voice and found him standing beyond the border of the flat rock, wildly waving his arms. Ret jumped down from the root and fought his way through the shrubs until he reached the border of the flat rock.

It looked just how Hella had described it. The brownish coloured ground extended to the edge of the darkened skyline, covered by a light dusting of sand swirling over the land from a gentle wind. Hundreds of geyser holes were punctured into the surface.

Ret wanted to explore the flat rock; he'd been waiting his whole life for this moment, but without hesitation he shook his head and took off, running along the flat rock border toward his father.

Sert knelt on one knee and smiled as Ret ran toward him, and to his credit, Sert was wearing his shoulder bag and holding the missing bottle of Jax.

"Dad!"

"You actually made it this far out here? Wow, Ret. You're so brave."

Ret lowered his head. "I don't want you to leave, Dad," he said, his eyes changing from green to black. "Where are you going?"

"Ret, I'm so sorry. You don't deserve any of this."

Ret stood baffled. It was the first time he could process what had happened.

Yes, it was unfair and irresponsible, and Sert's actions will affect everyone in the family, but what mattered more was he simply didn't want to see his father leave. Staring down at the ground, Ret cried.

"I, I don't want you to leave, Dad."

"I know; I don't want to leave either."

"But, if I had won tonight, you could have stayed."

"Hey, hey. I want you to know that none of this is your fault. It is not your fault Ret. I'm sorry I brought you into this mess."

Sert gently placed his hand under Ret's chin and pulled his son's head up to look into his eyes.

"Ret, I know you are strong. I raised you that way. You are going to do so well in Pagan. I know it. What will hold you back in life are your doubts and regrets. Don't be afraid, Ret. Don't ever be afraid. If there was anything in my life that I would take back, it's my fear."

Sert looked up at the dark sky before he readdressed Ret.

"Fear will always stop you from getting what you want. It will shape you and make you push away opportunities if you let it. Embrace the struggles life throws at you. Work through your obstacles and learn from your mistakes. Be strong like I know you are. To accomplish, you must first overcome."

Ret hung onto his father's words and nodded. He stared deep into Sert's eyes, hoping this moment would last.

Suddenly, a steady vibration shook the ground, and a low reverberating hum crescendoed into a loud rumble.

"Do you hear that? Ret, point the light over there, down the rock line."

"Is it the shrubs?" asked Ret,

"I don't think so," replied Sert.

"What's going on?" screamed Ret.

The ground shook harder; the rumbling grew louder. Ret couldn't hold the light steady. He dropped the burnlight and fell to the ground, curling into a ball and clenching his knees into his chest.

The sound was defining. The build-up increased as a harmony of commotion engulfed the space around his body. Then, like a spark before a surge, a powerful explosion erupted next to Ret, tossing his curled body toward the shrub line. He covered his ears with his forearms and gripped the back of his head as powerful tremors shook the ground. Scared and trembling, Ret opened a sliver of his vision and slowly stood up, swaying his legs to match the oscillation of the ground. He pulled his quivering hands to his face, rubbed his eyes, and noticed his shadow was cast onto the shrubs from a light source behind him. Flickering back and forth, up and down, like it was dancing to its own tune.

In one fast motion, Ret turned around and stood in absolute awe after witnessing a geyser exploding next to him. Stretching high into the night sky and raging out from a massive geyser hole, large quantities of oxygen and other gasses were bursting up from the deep cavern below. Tones of red poured out from the base of the geyser, changing to deep shades of green as it expelled off the top.

The only thing that pulled Ret's vision away was the urge to see his father's presence but he was gone. Ret frantically panned around the geyser and screamed out. He circled the massive eruption and desperately searched over the rock plain, using the light produced by the geyser to scan the surrounding area. But Sert was nowhere to be found. After panic coursed through his little body, Ret dropped to his knees, realizing this time his father was truly gone.

Guardians

Hella felt shocked, angry, upset, humiliated, worried, suspicious, frustrated, and tired. Her mind, body, and soul were enduring unimaginable torture. How was Sert able to fabricate such a lie? Why didn't she catch on sooner? Where does Sert plan on going? What would her life be like now, disgraced and painted with a dishonorable reputation, and how would that impact her children, especially inside Pagan?

Hella stared down at Terri, her head tilted and resting on her hip. Terri's black eyes were open and fixed on the doorway her father and brother had just run through, but to Hella's surprise, she didn't react in the way she expected. Terri didn't burst into a shrieking cry, stomp in a rage, no expression of maniacal retaliation. She stood in silence, petrified, as she stared into the darkness. Hella placed her hand on Terri's head and tried to soothe her daughter with a motherly stroke. But Hella could feel through Terri's cold, stiff skin, that her shattered spirit weighed heavily on her, and would carry through the rest of her life.

Hella glared at Dek and sneered as he sauntered over to the Grand Foyer iron door. He shouted to Deea, waiting on the other side of the door, to unlock the latch. The door swung open, filling the hallway with bright artificial light. Hella covered her eyes with one of her hands and clenched firmly onto Terri's arm with the other.

Everyone walked back inside the foyer. A mob of persecutors surrounded them. A large gathering of snugs had already learned of Sert's identity, but the sight of Hella and Terri stepping back through the entranceway drew fiery coloured eyes from the mob. The crowd poured on their disgust by shouting obscenities and pumping their fists.

She tried to shield her daughter by tucking Terri under her arm. She could feel that Terri's bump was beginning to drip as her body trembled in fear. Panicked and humiliated, they scurried toward the escalation machines, but the crowd was unceasing.

"Traitors!" they chanted.

"Ban them! Get them out of here! Never to return!" another shouted.

Hella couldn't run fast enough. She dipped and weaved her way to the escalators, but no matter which route she took, rows of snugs surrounded them, all glaring through their deep red eyes and shouting crude cutting insults. The two managed to edge their way to the ramp, and before Hella stepped onto the escalator, she turned around.

"You are all puss bags! I found out just moments before you all did! We're in just as much shock as you! Now, get out of my sight!"

Hella turned her back and stepped onto the rugged black belt, grabbed a tight hold of her daughter's shoulder and pulled her close.

"I'm so sorry, Terri."

Terri finally broke her silence. "They hate us, Mom; they all hate us."

As the escalation machine approached the third level, Hella and Terri stepped off and walked down the long corridor, stopping in front of a solid red door. Hella rapped a quick knock and stared down the hallway, scanning for trouble. The door abruptly opened.

"Hella?" questioned Marc.

Hella paused and stared into Marc's face. Looking back with a raised brow, he shot her a contentious glare. Hella tried to examine his nonverbal cues. She knew the weight of her situation but never thought Marc and Sandy would turn on them as quickly as the rest. They were all she had. Hella pursed her lips to one side of her mouth and shrugged her shoulders, communicating her helplessness.

"It's ok, Hella. Come in, come in," said Marc, waving them in.

"Oh, thank you, Marc," answered Hella.

Marc and Sandy's quarters had a viewing window overlooking the centre stage. She glanced around the room and observed two clashing bright orange couches arranged around a brown table, unfashionably characterized by an immense stress split down the middle of the surface. Hella weaved around the furniture and walked Terri over to Rony and Bes sitting near their viewing window. Finally, she released her grasp on her daughter's hand and walked back to Marc and Sandy.

"Who would have ever thought?" asked Sandy.

"I know."

Sandy raised her brows. "You never knew this whole time?"

"No, I never knew. It is a surprise to all of us. Still is," answered Hella, attempting to diffuse Sandy's leading question.

"Wow," Sandy said, lowering her brows.

"Hey, do you have a shot of water? I could use one," asked Hella before sitting on their couch and resting her head on the padded headrest.

"I'm already ahead of you," answered Marc, pouring a shot from a large insulated bottle. "Quick, before it freezes."

The shot went down hard. Hella clenched her fists and shut her eyes as a low rumbling sound resonated inside her midsection. The water reacted with the stored nitrogen inside her body, resulting in the by-product of the two chemicals mixing; a thick white mist. At first, the reaction is painful, but then a sense of euphoria takes over.

Tilting her head back, a thick white cloud of mist rolled out of her mouth, and a blissful feeling spread over her body, mind, and spirit.

Hella began blowing out the cloud of nitrogen vapour. She gazed into the dancing blanket of mist as the cloud contoured around her body, forming different shapes and patterns. Her limbs felt weightless, and her mind opened as the thick white fog filled most of the room.

She stared into the cloud, letting her subconscious take over; Hella started to have fun with her high.

The image of a calm yellow ocean stretching far in every direction formed within the moving white mist, and underneath the bright sun-filled sky Hella ran toward a never-ending horizon. Striding across the glossy calm ocean, every frolicking step left a trail of perfectly spaced ripples on the calm ocean surface.

Now, sprinting at her top speed, Hella looked upwards, jumped off the silken liquid surface and shot high into the sky. She pushed out her arms, reaching out both her hands in front of her rocketing body and climbed higher into the deep yellow atmosphere. She aimed for one of the bright suns and soared toward it.

She pushed her arms forward as much as she could and stretched her fingertips toward the star; however, suddenly she lost herself. Even in her wild imagination, no matter how much she tried to reach the dazzling star, it was too far away.

Hella gave one last effort and performed a giant loop in the sky before she stared down below her blue feet and noticed huge mountain ranges suddenly growing out of the calm sea. Before she could comprehend her vision, Hella found herself sliding down steep snow-covered peaks.

As she zipped down the mountainside, she tried to gain as much velocity as possible by bending her knees and tucking in her body. She cut perfect lines in the smooth powdery surface and raced across the vast slope that funneled deep into a valley below. Hella picked up speed as she navigated through her dream, and after gaining more momentum; she noticed a giant snowy jump at the end of her run. She focused her eyes on the edge of the snow-packed ramp, planted her feet and found her line. She barreled right for the incline, and her path transformed into a perfectly groomed lane that led up the massive kicker. Tucking her body, Hella took the pitch flawlessly and leaped off its edge.

She extended her arms in front of her body and fell carelessly through the sky, hands and legs fully extended, performing slow-moving cartwheels. Her soul felt at peace and her mind presented a pleasant blankness.

The serene feeling didn't last. Hella came back from the hallucination and stared soberly into the fading mist. Reality hit her harder than ever as she waved the remaining white fog away from her face.

"Thanks, you two. I needed that!"

"No worries," Marc answered.

"So, there is another reason I came here. It wasn't just for the shot of water."

"Oh, alright, Hella. What is it?" asked Sandy.

"I'm going after Sert."

Sandy squeezed her lips tight before saying, "You're what? You're going after Sert? Are you sure that's a good idea?"

"My kids are moving on in two months. I'll be alone, and everybody in this place hates me except for you two, which I appreciate," said Hella, looking into Sandy's eyes. "I can't stay here. I would much rather get lost out there than live another day here with these snugs."

"Well, what about somewhere local?" suggested Sandy. "Why can't you start over in another civilization, and one a lot better kept than Tarni? Trust me, Hella. I've been there. It's not where you want to be."

"I know what you two are trying to tell me, and again, I appreciate it, but honestly, I'm not looking for your opinions. Besides, I have a much bigger request to ask of you," explained Hella, looking over to Terri, conversing with Rony and Bes. "I need you to look after Ret and Terri for two months and send them off to Pagan."

The room went quiet. Sandy and Marc's eyes were wide open, awkwardly staring. The lines around Marc's eyes tightened. "That's a big request. Is it even possible?" His lips were pursed. When he spoke, he sounded confused. "Wait, you want us to be with your children when they go to sleep?"

"Yes."

"Seriously?" asked Sandy.

"I know how it sounds, But I don't have a choice. If I wait two months, it will be too close to hibernation, and I'll have to start my search after hibernation. I can track Sert now, not after hibernation."

Hella glanced at Terri and noticed her sitting slumped over with her hand curled into a fist, propping up her head. Terri fabricated a pitiful smile and played alongside Rony and Bes, but from the dark shade of her eyes, she felt mortified. Hella sprung from the couch and walked over to her daughter.

Sandy turned to Marc. "I know how this sounds, Marc. But look what just happened. Sert is a foreigner. Honestly, who saw that coming?"

"Yeah, I know."

"Well, what do you say, Marc? They're our friends. And if this—by some chance—ever happened to us, they would do the same," replied Sandy. "One thing's for sure, though. I wouldn't be chasing after you if this happened to us."

"Yes, you would. Don't even try to pretend. I make your life worth living." Marc responded with a charming smile.

"Anyways, let's do this for Hella; what do you say?" asked Sandy.

"Alright, let's help her out. Besides, it's not even that big of a responsibility. We have to give them a place to stay for a little while. That's it,"

They turned towards Hella, kneeling with her daughter, and shot a questionable glance back at one another.

"Hey, my little snowflake," said Hella.

Terri answered with silence.

She picked up her daughter's hands and caressed them gently.

"None of this is your fault, Terri, and for what it's worth, I'm sorry. You did nothing wrong. But I have to tell you something that will make things worse, and I'm sorry for this too."

Terri looked up into Hella's eyes with an expression so disheartening it made Hella question if things could even get worse for her.

"I'm going after your father. I have no other choice."

"What? What do you mean?" questioned Terri.

"I know you're scared, and I'm so sorry about all of this, Terri. But I have to go and find your father. Tonight."

"You're leaving us?" whimpered Terri as she shuddered and cried. 'How can you do this? Right now? Why?"

"I know," whispered Hella. "There's nothing left for me here. Once you and Ret move into Pagan, I will be left alone and surrounded by snugs that hate me. I have to find your father before it's too late. I know this is sudden."

"No, you can't go, Mom. You can't go. What am I going to do?"

Hella smiled deeply into Terri's eyes and cleared her throat.

"Hey, do you remember that one day in the classroom when your father and I were testing you both, and I asked who invented the sound accelerator, and you beat Ret to the answer?"

"Ya. That was only a few months ago."

"Do you remember what Ret said after your father and I rewarded you with a bottle of Jax instead of him?"

"He made fun of me. He said that was the first time I beat him to an answer, and it was an easy question, so he didn't even try."

"Do you remember how angry you got after he said that?"

"Yes. Look, I know I overreacted. I shouldn't have hit Ret. But he stole the bottle of Jax from me and drank the whole thing."

"Do you know why he did that?"

"Well, no."

"He was jealous of you, Terri. He stole it because you showed him that you were smart," said Hella as she moved her hand and caressed the top of Terri's head. "He couldn't accept that you were just as good as him, and he took out his anger on you by drinking your Jax."

"Why are you telling me this? What does this have to do with,"

"The truth is, I was really proud of you that day. Don't get me wrong, it's not right to hit anyone, but deep down I know Ret deserved what he got, and I was so happy that you stood up for yourself and what you believed in, and you were right."

"Well, he never tried that again," answered Terri.

Hella chuckled, "No, he didn't."

"Mom, why are you telling me this? What's your point?"

"You need to fight Terri, just like you did that day. You are about to enter Pagan, which will be hard for you. Snugs will try to put you down and bully you; they will avoid you. If you do land an idea, when they find out who you are, they will manipulate you and try to take things from you, even though you are smart."

"So what do I do?"

"You have to fight, Terri. You have to be the one to make a change in Pagan. You have to show everyone there that you don't stand for injustice; you need to show everyone that you are not afraid and willing to fight to make a difference." announced Hella.

"How do you expect me to do that, Mom? You saw for yourself they all hate me."

"Fight to make a change, Terri. If anyone can do it, I know you can."

Terri's face didn't change. She was still harbouring that same dispirited expression. However, the only confirmation Hella received was a slight glint of green that sparked within Terri's eyes.

"This will be very difficult, Terri. I can't imagine what Pagan will be like for you and Ret, but if anyone can make a statement, make a change and show others what is wrong with this world, it's you, my precious daughter."

Hella stroked Terri's head as they swayed side to side, holding each other and savouring their last moments. Hella gracefully picked up Terri's body, walked to one of the viewing chairs and placed her down gently. She pulled her arms out from under her daughter, curled Terri's knees into her little chest, and kissed her forehead.

Marc and Sandy looked on, and with a gentle nod, they conveyed their acceptance of being guardian parents. Willing and ready to tell her the good news, Marc and Sandy smiled at Hella before she came walking back into the room.

"We'll do it for you, Hella!" Sandy announced.

"Thank you, Sandy. Thank you, Marc," said Hella, relieved.

"This is probably the strangest thing we'll ever do, but it's for a good friend. And honestly, Hella, I know why you're doing this. I think it's the right thing to do."

"Thanks, Sandy. I've got a long journey in front of me. Don't I?"

"Yes, you sure do," said Sandy.

"Yeah. And tell Sert I'm taking his glider when you see him." Marc said jokingly.

"He's going to hate you. I think hearing that would make Sert come back here."

"When are you going?" asked Sandy.

"Right after Ret gets back. I have to say goodbye to him, and he's got the chancellor's burnlight. I'm going to need that."

Hella looked down at the large insulated bottle on the floor, smiled, and turned back to her friends.

"One more thing? Can I have another shot of water?"

••

Here we go

Ret glared over at Rony, lounging back in his padded blue chair. He couldn't make out Rony's bottom half as the edge of his curved desk extended an arm's length around the sides and front of his body. But he could see Rony sitting back with his fingers interlaced behind his head, staring at the ceiling. His eyes were wide open, glowing a healthy deep green, and his smile was impervious; nothing could break his joy, not even Ret's resentful scowl.

Ret sat on a warped, rickety chair that tilted from side to side. Unfortunately, this chair was all Marc and Sandy could provide without having to take one from their children. He leaned over and put his weight on one leg, stopping the chair from teetering back and forth. Another annoyance in this awkward surrogate arrangement.

"I can't wait! I wish I were there right now!" shouted Rony.

Ret glanced over to Marc and Sandy. Their glum faces were tilted down, staring blankly at the desk in front of them. Their slouched bodies sat motionless as each cheer from their children stifled their spirits, reminding them that today was the last day with them. Marc looked up and forced out a smile, but Ret could see it was only out of courtesy as his eyes were filled with the darkest shade of black he'd ever seen.

"Hey, do you remember that day the chancellors came to our house because they thought Dad was teaching us from his material and not their curriculum?" said Rony, trying to lighten the mood.

"Yeah, I remember. You two were young." chuckled Marc as he forced another smile. "What I remember the most was when you told the chancellors I was smarter than them."

"Ya! They lost it after you said that," said Bess sitting behind her desk on the other side of Ret. "And Rony, when the chancellors approached, you started yelling at them. At first, they thought you were adorable until you called them both puss bags."

Everyone laughed except for Ret, who sat hunched over with a crusty look on his face.

"And then you started to cry," said Marc. "You must have thought they were taking me away or something? Because the last thing you said before dropping to your knees was, 'No! Take me instead!'"

"We had to scrape you off the floor and calm you down," said Bes before erupting with laughter.

The family fell into hysterics. Even Sandy bubbled up with a genuine smile, but not for long. Everyone forced out a few last chuckles before an unsettled silence cloaked the room.

"I'll be right back. There's one more thing we need to do before we send you off," said Marc, standing up behind their long shared desk, leaving Sandy alone, suffering.

Ret cringed as he looked at Sandy. He couldn't help but empathize as he watched her crumble with emotion. Her eyes closed, her shoulders were lifeless, her arms dangled at her sides, and her brow pulled down her gloomy face. The most noticeable feature was her mouth; it lay deeply frowned.

"I wish I had one more day with you," said Sandy. "That's all I need—one more day. You two are my whole world. I can't say goodbye to you right now. Please don't make me say goodbye to you."

The children were silent. Ret could see they were trying to console her the best way they could, but their glowing smiles completely contrasted Sandy's feelings. She smacked her hand firmly against the face of the desk, gasped, and looked away.

Ret broke the tension in the room by sliding the worn-out chair out from under him and switching positions with Terri, who was standing behind him and waiting for her turn to sit.

"Here, sit down, Terri. It's your turn."

"Thanks, Ret," answered Terri.

Marc walked back into the room, holding a stack of old hardcover books and rushed to the desk, trying not to drop them. Finally, he planted the heavy books onto the tabletop before his grieving other.

Submitting a written account of their ancestry was a timeless custom every snug practiced. Right before the transition into Pagan, every child received their own personal ancestry book and the obligation to include their accomplishments throughout their Pagan life. All ancestry books are gender specific. After making an entry of their own, each parent must deliver this time-honoured tradition to their children—a mother passes her book down to her daughter, and a father passes his book down to his son. Every book is unique; not one is the same.

Marc proudly stood and addressed the young ones in the room. "You are probably wondering what these are. These are your ancestry books." He picked up the first thick, square book from the top of the pile and held it up high, presenting it to the group.

Ret examined the face of the worn-out book. In the middle of the cover was the faintest image of a well-known star constellation, best translated by the words "Worthy Expression."

As seen from the planet's surface, this constellation was densely populated. One hundred and fifty-seven stars made up this intense cluster, arranged within an area that appeared to be no bigger than Ret's thumb tip.

Without the constellation's pattern, this grouping of stars wouldn't be much to obsess over; however, one of Rony's ancestors first claimed that the stars' random configuration resembled a snug's face, hence the origin of the constellation's name.

"Every snug has a duty to uphold this tradition that dates back thousands of years. These books record the accomplishments of all its previous owners, our family's line to date," announced Marc, staring directly at Rony.

Lowering the book, Marc walked toward his son, sitting eagerly at his desk.

"Take this, Rony. This is our family line. You have a responsibility to add to this book until one day you give it to your son,"

Marc placed the large book in front of Rony and proudly patted him on the shoulder. Rony opened up the dark brown rustic dried-out cover and rifled through it.

"Take it easy, Rony. That's very old. Some of those etchings have already been restored, so please be careful with it," explained Marc.

Most of the entries were basic images coloured with natural minerals. For these more primitive images, solid carbon and talcum helped with shading and outlining. Rony's green eyes absorbed all the information and flipped through old pages until one caught his eye. He pulled out the page, pale yellow with chipped and ragged edges. It read: Pulo, the grand astronomer and greatest leader of his time.

Rony was hooked.

The biography exaggerated this ancient snug's early struggle through life. His dramatic story elaborated on how he overcame a troublesome childhood with torturous parents who would use him for his brilliant mind. In his early Pagan years, he wrote about how he felt too admired by his fellow snugs and could not cope with all the stresses of being famous. And with his discovery, Pulo bragged about how he was the first to name every star in the constellation. The drama continued.

Pulo was a professional at his craft. In his time, they considered him a master of storytelling. After claiming that he discovered a cluster of stars in the night sky in the shape of a face, he wrote in his memoirs that he was the greatest leader to have ever lived. It was, of course, quite an overstatement to anyone outside this family. However, to Rony and Marc, this was their family's best accomplishment and deemed fit for the honourary position of representing the cover of their ancestry book. The cover will remain affiliated with Pulo's life until someone else in his family succeeds with an achievement greater than Pulo's.

Rony felt proud, and his inner will strengthened. His ancestor's written words empowered him with a genuine sense of purpose, and he began crafting his life's philosophy. This was the essence behind these timeless resources—every story and accomplishment from Rony and Marc's family tree lived through these delicate pages.

Ret watched as Marc reached for another ancestry book from the desk and noticed only two books were on the table. Marc paused before he picked up Terri's ancestry book and approached her, sitting uneasily.

"Is there another book for Ret?" asked Terri.

"No," answered Marc.

"Where's Ret's book? Doesn't he have a book?" Terri asked.

"I'm sorry, Ret. You had a book, but the chancellors had it confiscated and destroyed. I tried to stop them, but Dek ruled the book fraudulent, and he grabbed it right from my grip." recalled Marc.

Ret sat unaffected and looked straight past Marc's worried expression. Entering Pagan without an ancestry book was the least of his worries. Ret glanced over as Marc slid Terri her ancestry book. It was light green, hard-covered, and bound with a long piece of yellow twine tied together horizontally from front to back. Terri sat uninspired when presented with her book; she didn't open it up.

"Don't you want to learn about your ancestry, Terri?"

"I will, later."

A sudden knock came on the door.

"No! They're not here already, are they?" screamed Sandy. "Marc, see who that is. I can't go."

"Ok, Sandy. Are you going to be alright?"

Marc received a slight nod from her before walking out of the room.

Sandy pulled her emotions together. She picked up the last ancestry book on the desk and brought it to Bes, who waited patiently. She carefully placed the book on Bes's desk and examined her daughter for the faintest signs of sympathy.

Over the years, Sandy listened to other parents discuss how they handled their Pagan send-off day. The chancellors offered parents coping strategies to prepare them for their children's departure. However, Sandy's insides were churning, her bump slowly dripping, and at that moment, she realized how underprepared she was.

"How can they not be just as upset as I am?" thought Sandy.

She silently yearned for her daughter to show her some emotional reassurance. But Bes was too busy exploring her new ancestry book and unknowingly ignored her mother's request. Sandy backed up in her tracks, petrified.

The sounds of fast-paced footsteps racing up the stairs were traumatic for Sandy. She began pacing back and forth, trembling with anxiety as she looked beyond Marc entering back into the room, her fear turned into reality. Four midsized teenage snugs wearing red medallions around their necks followed

Marc. They walked in single file, each carrying a small black metal box clenched in their right hand.

Each snug took a position in front of a child and addressed them with comforting smiles. Well, all but one. Marc slowly nodded, signalling to the snug that Ret was the half-breed.

Ret received a glaring eye squint from the snug. He looked him up and down and raised his brow. Ret responded by standing firm and staring right back into the larger snug's yellow eyes. The teenager chuckled over Ret's tough façade, disregarding his feelings and addressed the rest of the children.

"Hello, young ones. Do not be afraid."

"Why would we be afraid? We're going to Pagan!" screamed Rony.

"A new life awaits you inside Pagan. Your life's purpose awaits you," he shouted, becoming more enthralled with his speech. "We need young developing team members like you to push yourselves to your highest potential throughout your time in Pagan and represent our society. Can you do that for us?"

"Yes!" screamed Rony and Bes

Ret and Terri answered in silence.

All four simultaneously dropped their black iron cases to the floor and opened the latch. Each snug pulled out a small, clear container filled with red liquid from their case

"Alright, children, I need you to take the bottle with your right hand and open the cap with your left," announced the leader.

Rony and Bess went right for the bottles and immediately opened the caps. Ret and Terri both took their time.

"Say your last goodbyes and drink up. All of it," announced the snug.

Sandy stood hunched under Marc's long blue arm and forced out a terrible smile. Her children admired her effort and waved one last goodbye before downing all the contents in the bottle; Terri followed suit.

Ret looked around the room.

"For you, I can wait; really, there's no rush." snarked the snug standing before him.

Ret sneered back before popping the cap and chugging down the contents. The taste was good, like Jax. He dropped the bottle and watched it bounce off the floor. The empty container sent a sharp, high-pitched sound through the room, but Ret didn't hear the racket; the liquid started working immediately. Ret tried to keep control as his vision tunnelled and his speech slurred. Before falling to the ground, he mustered up three broken words:

"Here. We. Go."

Dan Miwa

Act

Search…

Hella grasped Ret's burnlight as she traipsed along the rock plain, tracking Sert's footprints. She'd been following his trail for almost half the night and was starting to tire.

The landscape was barren. Dust and granular stones covered the flat rock floor; the only movements were from random tremors reverberating within the ground, forcing the dust and particulate materials to shake throughout these minor quakes. This frequent seismic activity was a natural cycle for this planet and something Hella could've done without.

She stopped for a moment and shined the light around her. The burnlight was strong and could penetrate far into the darkness. Still, in terms of finding prominent landmarks and gathering a general idea of where she was geographically, the powerful beam of light was a disappointment.

Alone in the middle of the rocky plains, with only her burnlight and the stars as company, Hella took a brief moment to relish in the comforting darkness.

Hella found that being alone and lost in the middle of nowhere was relaxing. She felt liberated. Sert was the only thing on her mind. She wasn't worrying about chores in the house, being pulled in every direction by her family, and she didn't miss the social pressure of being a "good parent" one bit.

Coming out of her daze, Hella shook her head and looked up into the black sky and the blanket of stars. She glanced to confirm her location before pointing her light in front of her. Dragging foot over foot, she trudged on. The only thing Hella could do to help pass the time was to reflect on her past and replay old memories, some of which were on endless repeat. This time her mind drifted back to the first time she met Sert.

*

Hella was racing down a rugged pitched valley, hurling her body over large rocks and manoeuvring her footing around hundreds of small stress cracks pitted all over the course ground. Her wide-open eyes were bright red as she glanced at the sky, noting how much time remained before hibernation. The once calm yellow atmosphere changed into a troublesome orange, and the abnormal feeling of wind gusts pummeled her back. Large quantities of melted frost splashed off her bump as she frantically approached the forest for a good spot to enter.

She reached the treeline and slowed her pace to conserve her energy. She grasped a tight hold on a young brown trunk and secured herself before visualizing a path down in the forest. Her balance was tested after her shoulders took the odd blow from another frantic snug running into the forest, searching for one large and unused tree—exactly what Hella wanted.

She noted her path and scurried down the forest valley, slipping down the slick ground, clutching anything for support. Small rivers started forming from the melted nitrogen, expelling off the trunks, and small pools of liquid gathered around the base of each tree. She glanced at the canopy and saw that the trees were starting to expel a protective iron coating from the tip of their trunks. Hibernation was beginning.

At the onset of the summer, a strong metallic liquid will seep down from the top of each tree and solidify as it extends down to the surface floor. A large ring of iron at the base of each tree attracts the coating through magnetism, eventually connecting this natural protective layer around the tree. The trees form an inverted funnel throughout the hibernation season.

Although necessary, this natural shield is impenetrable and will stop any snug from entering once in place. Understanding the urgency, Hella anxiously searched for a vacant tree big enough to fit her body.

She hurried down the valley, leaping over established rivers with fast-moving currents. The liquid nitrogen levels were rising, and Hella knew these small rivers would grow into roaring rapids in moments. She looked around, noticed a perfectly sized tree further up the hill, and climbed toward it.

Hella edged her way up, fighting the current and exclaimed a joyful cheer when she reached her target; the tree was free for use, and the protective iron coating was nowhere near the base. However, her relief quickly turned to frustration when she bumped into someone else in just as much panic.

"I don't think so!" yelled Hella.

"What do you mean? I was here first," the little snug retorted.

"There's no time left. You have to find another tree. This one is mine."

"No, no, I was the first one here. You crawled up here after—I saw you! Besides, why don't we just share it?"

"Share it? What do you mean, share it?"

Liquid nitrogen was rushing down the valley floor, leaving only a few areas untouched, and the protective iron coverings from the top of every tree had seeped halfway down to the ground on all sides of the trunks. As the wind gusts picked up, the sky changed from orange to a violent red. The ground shook as the first sounds of thunder broke the sky's silence. Followed by an immense crackling, a sudden flash of white light lit up the valley of trees and concluded with a loud rumbling roar that rolled throughout the mountain vale.

"See that tree? It's not used! Jump in it—quick!" shouted Hella, pointing across the steep hill.

"I would still rather share this one with you," the snug responded, smiling insatiably at her.

"What do you mean, share it? I've never heard of such a thing. Just go before it's too late."

Hella grabbed the little snug's shoulders and turned his body around, pointing him toward the vacant tree. Before he walked over, the little snug turned his head and addressed her one last time.

"Nice to meet you. My name is Sert."

"Ya, I'm Hella. Now go!"

She was adamant this time and turned him around again, pushing on his dripping frost bump. The flushing rapids flowed against his ankles as Sert inched toward the tree, balancing his body with his arms stretched out. He leaned into the current as the flow grew stronger.

By the time he reached the other side, the nitrogen had reached his knees, and with one final push, Sert lept toward the tree and grabbed hold of the trunk. He signalled to Hella with a reassuring smile and gave her a modest wave with his open palm.

Hella was at a loss for words. Staring into each other's eyes, she instantly connected with Sert. Crouched against her tree, she smiled back and shared one last moment before the protective layer draped over her vision, sealing the iron shield to the magnetic iron ring.

She shook her head and began burying herself face-first into the ground beside the trunk. Digging into the softened soil, she went below the tree's base and into its cold dark nitrogen reserve. It was pitch black and half-filled with a pool of cold liquid nitrogen. She used her hands to feel around the space and locate the liquid's deepest part. Keeping her bump submerged throughout the entire hibernation season was essential for survival.

After rustling back and forth a few times, she tried to settle in and get comfortable but couldn't. It wasn't the need to acclimatize her body to the murky tree bottom that toyed with her; it was the odd little snug she had just met. For some reason, Hella couldn't take her mind off him.

Reflecting, Hella formed a little smirk on one side of her mouth.

The long traverse affected her physically and emotionally; at this point Hella was exhausted. She'd been staring into one beam of light focused on the pale ground, surrounded by blackness, for too long. Her vision had etched the same repeating image into her mind's eye, and it was now difficult to concentrate on her search. She needed a break. After running a long stretch into the open darkness, she finally sat on the hard rocky surface, rubbed her eyes, turned off the burnlight and rested her mind and body.

Tilting her head back, she delved into her mind and recalled another fond memory with her family; however, before she could even begin savouring her recollection, a loud rumble broke the silence. Hella's back straightened.

The noise grew louder, and screams of a high-pitched shriek vibrated her body.

She felt the ground shake as the noise gathered around her. She grabbed hold of the burnlight, slowly wound the bottom and shined the light in front of her.

Ironically, the instant her trembling hands turned on the light, all the commotion around her stopped. Standing perplexed, she noticed a giant wall of yellow frost in the light. She squinted her eyes and examined the image.

"What could this possibly be?"

It didn't take long for her to figure it out. She let out a silent yelp and pulled her hand to her mouth, her eyes pinned on the target as she backed away.

The frosted object began to rock back and forth as the ground rumbled below her feet. Hella slowly moved the light over the silky-smooth body and finally up to reveal the massive bulbous head of the mammoth frost-covered slug.

The giant beast began to shake harder and harder. On the verge of exploding through his thick frost shell, the creature pounded from inside his cocoon, and after one big heave, the giant slug exploded out of his frozen crust in one captivating scene.

It had shattered right through the protective layer. Shards of ice scattered everywhere as the animal shook its enormous body, casting large pieces high into the sky. The animal erupted with a monstrous scream as ice chunks rained down from above. The beast shook his huge bulging brown head and focused one of his red eyes on a terrified Hella.

In two words, she summed up her situation.

"Oh, No!"

We're here

Ret opened his heavy eyelids and cracked the faintest sliver in his vision. Blurry specs of white and red danced from side to side as he swayed his head shaking off the effects of the drug. After a few moments, Ret felt a little stronger, extended one of his arms to his face and rubbed his eyes. Prying them open and turning his head to the ceiling, he took his first glimpse inside Pagan.

Suspended in the centre of the ceiling was a complicated piece of art. Multiple red squares protruded down from the surface in four layers, forming an inverted pyramid that dropped from above. Being a wondrous first sight for any Pagan newcomer, Ret lay firmly on his back; his eyes wide open and fixed on the beautifully crafted pendant.

He snapped out of his daze, turned his head and spotted the top edge of a wide doorway. Ret swung his legs over the edge of the soft resting cushion and rubbed his smooth head. He shook his body, jumped off his cushion pad and took his first steps inside his new personal quarters.

Walking out of his room, Ret stopped in pure astonishment. The shimmering finish of polished black quartz grounded the open room as rich red, gray and white colour tones were splashed on every wall. In the middle of the room were two deep red, semi-circular couches curled around a dark brown oval-shaped table. He looked closer at his new furniture and realized every seat had a personalized nitrogen hose attachment. Ret nodded his head in approval,

He glanced down to the brown table top and raised his brow after noticing a small empty cabinet meant to display the current resident's ancestry book recessed within the centre of the table. A small spotlight attached to a stand illuminated the unfilled case underneath a clear glass surface.

Ret turned away.

The rest of the room exceeded his expectations. The sheer size and elegance compelled Ret to appreciate his state of privilege. Soaking it in, he noticed a series of red offset triangles, squares and oval shapes of intricate patterns stencilled on the wall behind his couch.

The most inspiring feature inside his quarters was a black-trimmed floor-to-ceiling window stretching across one residence wall. He sauntered toward the window and savoured the moment before looking out at the Pagan city.

He starred out to a metropolis standing thirty stories high and was astonished by the difference in scale. On the east side of Pagan, buildings upon buildings lined all around one end of the curved shaped stone wall. On the west side, the other end of the curved perimeter, the giant wall encased part of the ocean. Ret squinted his eyes and made out a little island far away and in the middle of the enclosed ocean.

Returning to land, he looked at an immense open courtyard in the middle of the city. Surrounding the courtyard was the long encircling chain of buildings divided into four sectors with four distinct colours: green, blue, yellow and red. Right away, he knew what each one of these colours represented.

For some reason, Hella disliked the green society and would always argue with the children whenever the topic of the four societies came up in class. Ret remembered Hella's long rants about the greens.

She could never understand how an entire society could be interested in labour-intensive work. "All just a bunch of worker snugs," she used to say, "instead of trying to research an idea that would further advance their civilization, they'd rather swing a hammer." Hella would constantly advise Ret and Terri to push themselves to their highest potential while they were in Pagan and to never settle for anything less. Ret disagreed, and even before meeting a green, he thought it was commendable for a society to be dedicated to the pursuit of construction and manufacturing. After all, their civilization required it.

Ret chuckled as he stood in front of his window. The green society was across from him, at the other end of the long stretch of buildings that curved around Pagan in the shape of a "U." One indication that the area belonged to this society was the evidence of deep green that outlined every building. However, the most prominent landmark was a vibrant green archway stretching high into the sky that extended to both sides of their borders. The tall structure was the main focal point for that part of the city.

Ret was impressed by the green society, and after following the archway from one side to the other, he arrived on the border to another coloured city division.

Blue was the distinguishing colour in this section of Pagan, but it didn't seem as prevalent compared to the greens. The brilliance behind this society was the elegant architecture that showcased the essence of the blue society's ideology; an entire society dedicated to craftsmanship, design and engineering.

Their buildings were fashioned in dark polished stone. Most were traditional shapes, but some were conceptual designs that stood out for their artistic individuality. Floodlights highlighted the deep stone texture on the surfaces of these stylish edifices, and rising to the tops were tall peaking roofs lit by a deep blue light cast evenly on all sides. The most inspiring feature was a large cavern that peered into the planet's crust, situated front and center within the blue society, surrounded by a stone encasement.

"They have their own geyser hole?" whispered Ret. "Why didn't Mom tell me that?"

Prying his focus away from the blues, Ret wanted to see the yellow society he and Terri had learned so much about. Unfortunately, the view from his quarters faced both the green and blue sectors. He could only make out one corner of the yellow society before the edge of the window blocked his angle.

The yellow society was, architecturally speaking, a work of art. Three distinct levels climbed up the incline of Mount Nite, giving this society an edge in terms of creativity. Giant buildings were erected atop massive stone platforms that shot straight out from the sharp slope of the mountain. Each platform was supported by stone pillars on the outside edge of the square foundation. The design was so sophisticated that the Pagan government inspected and maintained these platforms to ensure the safety of the yellows after every hibernation.

Ret pressed his face against the hard glass, trying to get a better look at the yellow society directly situated next to the blue's. He felt this was something he wanted to see— his mother spoke highly of these yellow society snugs.

Hella always commended the yellow society, encouraging Terri and him to share their ideas with the yellows. Hella seemed to think that the true brilliance of Pagan came from this organized society, but Ret didn't feel persuaded.

The yellows were well-versed in business conduct, developing and launching ideas, dealing with team politics, and managing projects. But, they weren't at the developing forefront of innovation and technology. That's where Ret felt his strengths lay, a true citizen of the red society.

Ret pushed his face hard into the window. He peered towards one of the stone pillars holding up one of the platforms, the only part of the yellow society he could see. He stood in disbelief.

"The gliders are driving up the sides of the pillar?" he said to himself.

"Yes, they are!"

Startled by the voice. Ret jumped from the glass window and turned to the front door.

"So you're the half-breed, huh. I'm Juke, your trainer. "

Juke stood tilted to one side, resting his shoulder on the doorframe, the corner of one lip tight, raised.

Ret nodded his head and peered back. Unimpressed with Juke's demeanour, Ret turned around and looked back out the window.

All around his residence were markers of his society's colours—bright red lined the corners of all the buildings outside. Down on ground level, he saw an intersecting street and a few snugs climbing onto a glider train stopped at the corner.

"You are lucky even to be here," Juke said sharply.

"Maybe luck will be the reason I become successful!" responded Ret, turning to look at Juke.

Juke rolled his eyes and pursed his lips. "Ya, you keep believing that."

Ret glared right back, but realizing his sharp attitude would not favour him, he cooled his emotions and shook away his feelings. It was not the impression he wanted to make, especially on his first day in Pagan. Ret lifted his brow and cracked a kind smile.

In Training

"Let's get this over with," said Juke.

Still slumped on the edge of the doorframe, Juke managed to summon enough effort to present Ret with a small black pocketbook at the end of his loosely extended arm.

"Pagan Laws and Guidelines," said Ret, peering at the cover.

"Did your parents tell you about our governance structure, or must I teach you everything?"

He tossed the book down in front of Ret's feet; the pages flailed and rustled before the book smacked the ground and lay open on its spine. Ret slowly lifted his head and glared at Juke, staring at the ceiling. Ret snatched up the book, flipping through the first few pages, skimming over the content, then slapped the book shut.

"I'll read all of this later! What's next?"

Juke pressed his lips and rolled his eyes. "You know, you really should look over all this before we meet with the board."

"The board?"

"Yes, the board. If you take some time to read the reference book, you will see how our chain of command works. Now just read it so that we can move on."

Ret stifled his desire to erupt in anger and stared back with fiery red eyes and a scornful scowl. He saw the same shade of red radiating from Juke's eyes.

"Alright, fine! What page?"

"Twenty-five."

Nine photographs showcased the Pagan board of directors, eight of which were evenly spaced in a circular pattern around the page. Each portrait had a small written column summarizing the personalities and characteristics of the directors (two directors per society) and, of course, their society colours that bordered the trim. The ninth picture was enlarged and printed directly in the centre, highlighting Terin's Chief Director.

"So, this is Sal," asked Ret, pointing to the centre of the page.

Sal's blue shoulders were horizontal and aligned with the picture's frame. His oversized oval head was tilted just to the left, and his blue eyes were wide open and engaging. Ret examined the image of Sal sitting proud, posing with a good posture and a charming smile.

"Ok, I'm all set with the board of directors. What's next?" Ret asked cockily.

"You know, Ret, you really should take some more time. Ah, it doesn't matter; you will fail miserably in this place. So, I am supposed to show you around your living quarters, one of our most accommodating suites. I'm shocked you came in second place. Still not as nice as Kin, though. If only you came in first… but you didn't."

"Well, I'm sure I will be pretty comfortable here. And where did you place in the competition? Did you get past the first round?"

"Maybe I did, maybe I didn't. But I'll tell you, Ret. I would rather come in last place than be labelled a half-breed like you."

Ret stormed down a long corridor to the left of the front entrance. He stopped before a reinforced dark grey door, smacked both hands on the smooth iron surface and heaved the heavy door open.

Inside the small square room, four spotlights shined down from each corner and exhibited a polished silver sphere vessel in the middle.

Juke walked over to the left side of the structure, sneering back at Ret before pressing a round blue button on a flashing panel next to the machine.

"It's your personal and modernized hibernation chamber."

Suddenly the sound of a sturdy mechanical latch unhinged from within, and the vessel split horizontally from one side to the other. The face slowly opened upward, detailing a comfortable space inside. A hydraulic hiss finalized the unveiling as the top half of the clamshell came to a rest.

Inside, the shell was lined with a soft cushion designed to contour a snug's body once enclosed. The dark green interior was well upholstered, with just enough room for Ret to extend his body in all directions.

Ret leaped into the soft padding and settled into position. His comforting smile infuriated Juke.

Juke's quarters were nowhere near as luxurious as Ret's. He didn't score as high as Ret when he competed in the red society competition. And to this day, he still hadn't developed an idea worth the board's approval. Forced to live in residence with little more than basic needs, Juke had to wait until he contributed a worthy idea before being awarded upgraded quarters. However, Ret's living space was second on Juke's list of reasons to dislike him.

Every snug was required to fulfil certain obligations within Pagan, and being a trainer for a newcomer was one of them. Teenagers must participate at least once in their Pagan life in guiding another young snug through their first months inside Pagan.

These teenagers were always quite busy and determined once they had an idea. You would think one would detest the thought of dropping everything instantly to tend to young inductees, but it was the contrary. Every red society snug made a tremendous effort to build their younger colleague's skills and confidence. It made it easier for the freshman snugs to feel welcomed and ensured all citizens were keeping with their society's traditions.

As a reward, if a trainee one day made the cover of their ancestry book, their trainer's name would also be engraved on the bottom right corner of the cover page. This was a reachable goal for every red society snug, except for Juke.

Ret was quite the anomaly. No foreign snug had ever entered into Pagan without possessing an ancestry book. In addition, being a descendant of Tarni would make Ret's life within Pagan more difficult. Ret's reputation was already tainted, and Juke's chances of getting his name on the cover were impossible. So, why even try?

"Alright, let's go and check in with the board. They'd like to meet with you young ones before you settle in."

"Ok, great! I want to discuss my idea with them!"

Juke stopped short of the doorway, squinted his eyes, and slowly turned around.

"You have an idea?"

"Yep!"

"Even if I believed you, do you know how to get it approved?"

"Well, I don't think it's going to be that hard!" Ret replied.

"You think you know everything, Ret? Well then, do everything yourself so I don't waste time on you."

Before Ret could answer, Juke walked to the front entrance, swung the door open and ran out into the hallway. Ret raised his brow, shook his head, and followed.

*

Ret was lost in a crowd of snugs. Meandering his way through the stampede, he was constantly nudged off balance as waves of bigger snugs marched past, shooting down an inconsiderate glare every time he got in their way. Frustrated, Ret squared his body and pushed himself through the busy hallway. Swinging his arms, he rifled through the oncoming horde until he caught up to Juke, standing smugly beside a set of silver double doors.

"What is your problem?" shouted Ret.

"I thought you already knew everything. Besides, if you think that was difficult, brace yourself for when we go outside," answered Juke before turning his back to Ret and pressing a button beside the silver lift doors.

Distracted by the mass of snugs walking past, Ret stepped aside and tried to hone in on a few passing conversations. Their articulation was advanced, and he could only make out a few short words.

Juke tapped Ret on the shoulder and pointed to the open lift doors. Ret stepped inside the small enclosure and noticed the space was lined with mirrors on all sides. On the wall next to the silver doors was another panel lined with flashing buttons corresponding to each of the building's floors. Juke pressed the button for the first floor.

"So, we're going straight down?" asked Ret, a puzzled look on his face.

"Yes."

"Does it work using magnetism just like the gliders?" posed an uneasy Ret.

"Yes."

"Huh…"

They reached the ground level, and the doors slid open. In an instant, a crowd of snugs barged in, pinning Ret's frost bump against the back wall. Ret braced himself. The horde engulfed the entire space, and a barrage of conversations went on at once. Ret was in awe; their arms were flailing, months were barking orders, and their eyes quickly cycled through colours. Such an emotional bunch, he thought.

Ret snapped himself forward as the lift doors closed. He slipped his body beside his peers and slid his way out. He glanced back into the lift and saw Juke trying to swim through the crowd. He snickered through the closing doors before they trapped Juke inside.

Ret sauntered onto an elevated platform beside the lift and looked out into a massive assembly of snugs. He tried to gather his bearings and get a good sense of the layout, but the sheer size and energy of the gathering amazed him.

The room was designed in a similar dome fashion to his banquet hall. A smooth polished white granite stone framework curved up to a high summit. A giant cube mounted on its side was suspended in the middle of the ceiling. One of the cube's corners was attached to a mount, slowly rotating around on its edge. This centrepiece was solid red, but Ret was not just amazed at the size of the fixture; he was astonished by the radiating red light that glowed from within. The glowing light gradually morphed from a dull to a rich, vibrant red.

After catching himself in a daze, Ret slowly pulled his head down and observed the busy floor.

The ground below was packed with snugs, all mingling and conversing in groups. The sound of all the rustles was almost ear-piercing. Ret instantly felt motivated. He started jumping on his feet as the energy emitting in the room began to course within him. He glanced at several groups and studied them. Some were five snugs large; others were twenty or thirty, but each group had a mixture of yellow, blue, green and red society members. He climbed down from the platform and approached one small group assembled close to him. He crept up beside them, trying to be nonchalant, and peered in.

First, he examined their physiques and straightened his back as everyone around him stood in perfect posture. Second, Ret started flailing his arms, re-enacting their ability to use dramatic arm gestures and body language to help position their argument.

He was jotting down as many mental notes as possible, cramming in as much information as he could until he was taken back by a female snug who took front stage in the conversation. Utterly captivated, he dropped his act of charades; he couldn't look away.

Her sharp green glossy pupils and attractive facial appearance first caught Ret's attention. And then her body's curvature and sensually inviting shape captured the rest. Ret walked ever so slowly towards her, focusing on her striking body. He examined every detail as he approached the group, especially her long, toned blue legs. They shot straight up from her perfectly shaped feet, gradually gaining in size as they passed her knees and conformed to her vivacious waistline. Ret's excitement grew.

Her tight blue skin wrapped around her well-defined abdomen and flat chest area, then curved to the small of her back, which ran up to the bottom of her bump. The brilliance of her blue society identity ring sparkled on her hand as the three shimmering sapphires waved in all directions. She emphasized her words using graceful arm gestures as her soft mouth moved in perfect sequence with her impressive voice.

Ret tried to hang on her every word, but it was difficult for a novice; not only was he caught in a trance, but the rate at which words were being spoken was too quick to comprehend; the only words he could make out were "research" and "hibernation."

For a moment, Ret took his eyes off her. He was so determined to decipher her words that he closed his eyes and leaned in, not realizing that he had drawn himself into the middle of the circle.

"Whose trainee is this?" shouted one of the group members pointing towards Ret.

Ret turned his head towards his accuser and noticed his yellow society identity piece wrapped around his skinny arm, a long yellow metallic bracelet reaching his elbow. Distracted for only a moment, Ret stared back at the snug who stood unimpressed with his social faux pas. He mustered up some courage and addressed the group.

"I… I'm Ret," he said in an apprehensive tone.

Being his first interaction with real Paganers, Ret found himself dazed. And as much as he wanted to say something, the anxiety he felt inside muted him.

"Hello, Ret. I'm Rox," answered Ret's admirer. "And who is your trainer?"

"Hi, well, his name is Juke, and he's a puss bag!" shouted Ret, finding some courage.

The crowd burst into a shouting laugh and began to applaud his response. Ret's tense shoulders relaxed when he heard waves of laughter roaring from everyone around him.

"I have to say, Rox. You are beautiful! I can't take my eyes off you."

The crowd giggled over his innocence, and Rox smiled before responding.

"Thank you, Ret. You're not bad yourself. You know, this is all kind of new to me, too. It's only my fourth month here."

"Four months? And you have an idea already? Wow, Rox. You are one smart blue!"

"I do have an idea. A great idea! And I hope it will get approved by the board," said Rox. "My idea group will meet with the board soon, and I hope they give me the materials I need to start building."

"I'm sure it's groundbreaking. I can tell you're the smart one leading this group," said Ret. "You know, I have an idea as well."

"You have an idea? This is only your first day inside Pagan." exclaimed a yellow citizen. "What is it? I'm really curious."

"Imagine communicating with every Pagan from all the other civilizations. We would no longer need to send messengers to all sides of the world to learn what other Pagans are inventing and how they are progressing. It will be a cutting edge invention."

Ret took over the conversation. Standing firm and presentable, Ret spoke clearly about his idea and held court throughout his pitch, a promising first impression. That was until Juke approached from behind and slapped him on the shoulder.

"So, what does everyone think of my new trainee?" Juke announced to the crowd of snugs. "Isn't he remarkable?"

Juke toyed with the group. He agreed with everyone's comments regarding Ret's skills and personality. He nodded and smiled back after they all commended Ret and wished Juke luck in his training.

Juke waited for a pause in the conversation and took the opportunity to break Ret's short-lived popularity.

"Ret does have some great potential, doesn't he?" Juke gawked. "Oh. Wait, I forgot to tell you. This is Sert's progeny."

Ret couldn't believe how long it took for his adoring crowd to turn against him. Everyone's smile turned into a cringeworthy scowl.

"You're the Tarni snug?" asked one of the snugs.

"Yes, my father is Sert. But I'm only half Tarnician." cried Ret. "It's not like I was born there. Plus, you don't even know my father. How can you feel this way toward someone you haven't even met?

"It doesn't matter, Ret. You are something that just doesn't belong here," he replied.

Hateful comments sparked heated debates within this circle of snugs. Without evidence or reasoning, they all chanted to one another, exercising their prejudiced views. Rox was the only one in disagreement and fought back in Ret's defence.

"You can't be serious, everyone. First off, none of you have ever been to the other side. And second, you don't even know him." she shouted, showing her emotions through arm gestures. "You're all judging him without even knowing him."

"Oh please, Rox. You've heard all the stories of what it's like over there. I can't imagine anyone from Tarni having any good or useful qualities. It's absolute chaos. And I, for one, don't want any part of him inside this society. Give him back to Tarni!" shouted an accuser, inciting a huge hooray from the rest of the group.

"That's wrong!" screamed Rox, trying to fight the intensifying bunch.

Ret realized that his argument was no match against the long-standing principles that set the rules in this Pagan. Their scrutiny and persecution were not just opinions that needed swaying but a deep-rooted idealistic tenet grounded in years, if not centuries of tradition. Stricken of all the goodwill within him and left empty and hollow, Ret turned away and ran into the crowd.

"He is quick; I'll give him that." chuckled Juke.

... and Rescue

11 Years Ago...

Sert clenched a handful of loose skin on the back of his haze and let out a powerful "hah" as he raced across the flat rock. The haze rode flawlessly and followed each of Sert's commands. Dashing over potholes and maneuvering around the edges of deep geysers, the two moved together in a well choreographed routine, perfectly in tune, riding in pure harmony.

The haze picked up speed when her target came into view. She cut across the land, sprinting as fast as possible; kicking up a long trailing plume of brown dust. In her final push, Sert guided the haze to an old, dilapidated building standing alone in the desert.

Both suns shone down on this lonely structure. The small, decrepit, worn-out building was situated in the most central location on the planet, making it a prime location to house an annual gathering between civilizations.

Once a year, members from all over the globe assemble to update the group on their progress. Their government appointed each snug present, given the honorary title of "messenger snug." Each messenger had a duty to exchange inventions, breakthroughs, or essential information with the other members; the benefits were shared by all. If a new idea were discovered, the entire world would be informed, keeping everyone on the same progressing page. For some civilizations, this meeting was an excellent opportunity to prove their worth; for others, it was an indication of concern, especially to those civilizations that have been struggling to keep up; Sert never looked forward to these meetings.

Sert posted on his haze as he approached and waved to his peers standing inside the glider parking lot waiting for him to arrive.

"I can't believe they still ride hazes over in Tarni. "Is it that hard to build roads?" inquired an amused green-skinned snug harbouring a spiteful expression.

"He'll never drive a glider, Tras. His society is in absolute shambles. It would be a miracle if Tarni ever became a productive society again. We all know what will happen today if Sert has nothing to share.

"Yeah, I remember," said Tras, the green-skinned snug.

Sert rode through the parking lot gate and steered his haze to his personalized spot equipped with a sturdy rope and iron anchor. He dismounted the animal, brushed her bulky brown head, and tied her down.

"Make sure that savage doesn't scratch my glider!" shouted one of the snugs.

Sert smiled back at the group, trying to laugh off the apprehension, but everyone responded with an awkward grimace. It was a typical welcome for Sert, for he was the Tarni messenger snug and endured this treatment every year.

"You just make sure your glider doesn't scratch my haze," responded Sert as he walked through the crowd, leading everyone through a weathered doorway.

The interior of the building comprised a single empty room with a crumbling framework and rustic architecture. Thick brown pillars that held up two old eroding balconies lined both sides of the building. Up above, hundreds of small stress cracks and holes were scattered over the ceiling letting in bright beams of natural light filling the room. As the group assembled at the center of the floor, Sert tried to point out his concerns regarding the unsafe roof; however, the group of snugs commenced their meeting.

"Good to see you all here!" said a moderately sized snug. "First off, does anyone have any breakthroughs to announce?"

"I do, Tal. My civilization will be flying soon!" said Tras as he stepped into the formed circle.

"Flying is impossible!" shouted another snug, "My civilization has spent years developing a machine that can fly, and we got nowhere."

"I promise you, I will have proof the next time we meet," answered Tras.

"I wish you luck, but I'm telling you, it's a waste of time and resources."

"Alright, everyone. Let's move on to other topics," announced Tal.

Tal discussed every new idea or invention his civilization discovered the previous year. Everyone stayed quiet, listened closely, and proffered their full respect to Tal, for he was from Terin, the most prosperous nation in the world for productivity and ingenuity. Everyone else's turn to share came after.

Sert was always uncomfortable when it was his turn to contribute to the group. He tried to hide that Tarni was the most unproductive society on the planet. He would always embellish the truth, try to seem convincing, and sometimes Sert even fabricated his ideas. But no one ever believed him.

Hesitant to speak, Sert tried to stay out of sight. He backed up slowly, not making any noise. However, to his surprise, Tal pointed right in Sert's direction and chose him to present first.

"How about you, Sert? What inventions or innovations has Tarni developed this past year?"

A cold shiver ran up Sert's back. He pushed back his anxiety by standing up straight and clearing his throat.

"I... I don't have anything."

Everyone burst out laughing.

"Well, as you all know, we are trying to rebuild our society. That takes up much of our time and effort," Sert argued. "It's going to be much better, I promise. We're starting to rebuild our Pagan and planning a huge development for ice roads. We're hoping it will be complete within five years. We just need some more funding."

"Enough, Sert!" shouted Tal. "We can't do this anymore. How is it that Tarni is so far behind? Why is it that you still have so much work to do? I thought that's why we all come here every year—to ensure we're all evolving at the same rate. I'm speaking for everyone here, Sert. Your civilization has taken advantage of our charity. We bail you out repeatedly, and you still come back here with nothing."

"Well, I wouldn't say nothing," answered Sert.

"Your civilization lacks motivation, and you're so far behind the rest of the world that it's almost impossible to catch up now! With all this being said, Sert, we have unanimously decided. We have decided to banish you and Tarni from the United Civilizations."

"What?"

Sert's eyes shot wide open. Tal's words hit him like a forceful chime from a hard struck bell. And the anguish, much like the resulting sound waves, reverberated inside Sert's body as the shock of the moment throbbed within. His jaw hung open, his head tilted forward, and his mind completely baffled. All he could feel was the weight of all the glowering stares and slick condescending quips from all the other snugs.

"I'm sorry, but there are consequences for those that take advantage and do not cooperate," warned Tal.

"You can't do that! I have just as much right to be here as you all do!" screamed Sert.

"No, you don't!" shouted another snug before he stepped into the circle and exposed his yellow-coloured frost bump.

"I'm also a yellow back, Sert, and my civilization had the same problems as yours. But we recognized our issues and worked hard to escape our societal situation. The problem is with your leader, Lip. He's corrupted and incompetent."

"You use your citizens!" screamed another troubled snug. "The majority of your snugs live in rundown buildings. The city is a complete mess. No one has any respect for themselves. And your younger generation? All they do is take shots of water every day. All day long! Everyone is either mistreated or simply just wasting time. And your leader does nothing. He doesn't even try to improve Tarni? That's unacceptable to us."

"I understand. We have some problems to work out. I promise the next time we meet, Tarni will be in a better state."

"Sert, you are banished from these proceedings," shouted Tal. "You will no longer be able to partake in this gathering, and Tarni will be removed from the Union of Civilizations. I'm sorry Sert, but those that do not contribute to the world go unrecognized as affiliates. I wish you all the best; please leave this gathering."

"What? What are you talking about? You can't do this, Tal. The decision isn't up to you only."

"All in favour?" asked Tal.

Sert stood helpless in the middle of the circle as he surveyed the room of all Tal's supporters holding up their arms. He slowly gathered his composure and fretted as he moped toward the entrance. Before exiting the building, he looked back at the group. Regrettably, no one was sympathetic to his situation, and instead of bidding a kind farewell; everyone ignored Sert and continued with their business.

*

Present Day

Coming back from his recollections, Sert struck two flint rocks together to create a spark that gave off just enough light to navigate through the flat rock. He found himself in a perpetual state of reflection as he recalled overworked memories, memories that played heavy on his mind. As anger set in, he struck the rocks harder and harder until tiny shards of flint broke off and scattered to the ground.

He paused for a moment and tried to compose his emotions. Deep down, he didn't feel angry with Dek, Deea or Union of Civilizations. Sert felt mad at himself and was just too stubborn to admit it.

He reached into his bag for his bottle of Jax; he took a sip and continued marching. After a couple of steps he stopped after hearing what he thought was the faint sound of a screaming female snug far in the distance. He reconsidered, shook his head and kept moving.

Sert approached a wide geyser hole cut deep into the ground. As he stood near the edge, trying to figure the best way around, he looked up after hearing another loud shriek coming from the opposite side of the cavern. Instantly, he sprung into action and scurried around the geyser hole, searching for the source of the sound.

*

Hella howled for help as she raced over the land in a tumultuous panic. The light beam scattered across the sky as her arms flailed above her body. Totally out of control, Hella sprinted in a zigzag pattern, racing away from the giant slug that was regrettably gaining ground on her.

She noticed a flashing spark in the distance and took off in its direction.

Completely disoriented, her instinct took over, and she now found herself heading toward the massive geyser hole, completely unaware of the danger.

She kept her eyes centred on the flashing spark. Unexpectedly, it shot high into the sky as if someone threw the flaming bottle in her direction. The lit bottle of Jax burst behind her, sparking a searing ball of flames right in the slug's path. The giant animal wailed in horror and tried to stop, but the momentum pulled its body into the blaze. Wholly engulfed, the slug rolled around over the flat rock, but it was too late; the fire penetrated the outer layer of its skin and spread into the methane rich layer of flesh beneath. Like the head of a dry match struck with force, the slug seared on all sides, and its agonizing wail echoed over the land as it slowly burned to death.

"Is anybody out there?" shouted Sert, cupping his hands over the sides of his mouth.

He looked all around, desperately searching for any sign of movement. His head was on a swivel, and his ears were wide open, trying to hear anything that would lead him to the voice he had heard earlier.

"Help!"

Sert turned around and approached the geyser hole. He slid his head over the edge and peered into the deep dark cavern.

"Is anybody down there?"

"Help me!"

"Here, grab onto my hand!"

Sert extended his arm into the darkness and felt another hand frantically grip his. Using all his might, he gave one big heave and pulled. Both snugs were flung backwards out of the hole and landed chest to chest, facing one another.

"What took you so long?" chuckled Hella.

"Hella?"

"I couldn't help myself; you Tarni's have a certain charm about you."

He looked into Hella's face to confirm the reality; her warm smile was all the validation he needed. He gracefully wrapped his arms around Hella's body and pulled her close. Sert closed his eyes and clenched her tight as the two rocked back and forth, lying on the ground. Still caught in disbelief, he placed his hands on the side of Hella's face and stared his bright green eyes into hers.

"I didn't think I was ever going to see you again," said Sert.

"You know I've always wanted to see the world."

"So, does this mean you aren't mad?"

"Let's not go that far, you Tarni snug, you," answered Hella, charmed. "Let's just say you owe me a pretty good adventure from here on out."

"Deal!"

Sert unlocked his eyes from Hella's, got up and brushed all the sand off his chest. He picked up his bag, grasped Hella's hands, and pulled her to her feet. He gracefully rubbed her head and smiled.

"Where are you going anyways? Do you have a plan?"

"Ya, I'm, well, I guess *we* are heading to the North Rimmed Mountains to meet up with an old friend of mine, Tras. Last I heard, they were working to be the first civilization to build a flying machine.

"I've heard about those snugs. Isn't their skin green?"

"Ya, it is."

"And what about Tarni? Are we heading over there?"

Sert paused, turned away, and started trotting back on his course.

"Well, are we?"

"Yes, we are… right after we meet with Tras."

Meet with the Board

Trillions of small iron rocks hovered above the planet's surface, forming the world's most magnificent natural feature: the planetary ring. It cut sharply across the sky and flaunted its presence against the deep yellow atmosphere. It was quite the view from the Pagan courtyard. Dividing the sky in two, this elegant feature stood prominently as both stars shined down from either side of the ring, flaunting an elegant setting for all the hardworking snugs to enjoy below.

The famous courtyard spreads over the middle land of Pagan. Hundreds of glass partitions built in a grid fashion were constructed within the city's centre, all clearly visible to the four societies that towered along the perimeter of the Pagan wall. Provided in each workspace was a small brown building equipped with supplies and room for storage, and each plot granted its members full glider access. Not one of the hundreds of working spaces was vacant—a great indication Terin's economy was booming.

From the middle of the courtyard, a tall white stone tower stood as the centrepiece of Pagan. White granite panels were stacked like bricks on all four squared off sides. Constructed on a broad and sturdy base, each panel stretched upwards and gradually slimmed as it reached its peak. The summit was not sharp, but blunt-nosed and expansive bay windows crowned all sides of the high rise, providing a vantage point to all corners of Pagan.

The Pagan Tower boasted its authority and stood proud of the city centre. It conveyed its power to the rest of Pagan, but not by sheer presence alone. The board of directors and Chief Director Sal resided within, holding counsel at the summit of the building, and Ret was on a public glider train heading directly for it.

Ret had no interest in observing the sights around him. The only thing in his vision was his trainer sitting across from him. He snarled at Juke, cursing his name over in his mind. His experience inside Pagan was disheartening, and Juke was a big reason for that. He sneered again at his ignorant trainer and turned his attention towards the approaching tower from the front of the open-top glider.

The tower cast a shadow on the train and blocked one of the shining stars as the glider entered the large glass trimmed entranceway. Ret studied the feature. Blocks of moulded glass lined the large circular entry; it sparkled flawlessly in the light.

The train stopped beside a gray platform, and a high-pitched sound signified that passengers were safe to exit.

"Governing Tower. Governing Tower," shouted the driver.

Ret stepped off the glider train and tried to dodge the swarms of snugs transferring between gliders. He weaved through the crowd, as his aggravation started to build. Ret was about to erupt in public until a familiar voice behind him prevented the spectacle.

"Hey, Ret! So how do you like this place? I love it! I bet you have pretty nice quarters. I gotta see it, I gotta see it!"

"It's good to see you too, Rony," replied Ret, smirking over Rony's overexcited announcement.

Before Ret could say anything else, Juke shouted from the top of the stairwell that led to the grand foyer.

"Come on, Ret. This way!"

Taking his time, Ret walked over to the stairs and began making his way up each granite step.

"Isn't this place amazing? My trainer said I have all the ability I need to make it as a cover snug," said Rony. "I can't believe we're here, you know?"

"Yeah, and I can't wait to present my idea to the board," said Ret. "I know I'm going to impress them right away."

"You have an idea? I never knew that." Rony said excitedly. "What is it?"

"I don't want to spoil it for you; you'll find out."

"Wow. I hope the board approves it right away. That would be something else." said Rony, full of enthusiasm. "Oh, Wow! Ret, look at that."

A clear lift shaft stretching to the peak of the building was located directly in the centre of the foyer. A clear cylinder pipe shot straight up the middle of the tower and transported passengers to the summit of the building. Ret and Rony looked at the moving vessel above them, mesmerized.

Ret shook his head and looked around the room for Juke. He paused to view an excited little girl smiling as she gripped her ancestry book.

One question popped into Ret's mind. "Hey, have you seen Terri? I've been looking for her but can't find her."

"No, sorry, Ret, I haven't seen her. I'm sure she's fine."

Ret was not so sure.

"My trainer is waving me over to him; I gotta go. See you up there!" said Rony.

"Alright, see you up there, Rony."

Ret trudged over to Juke and stared up the clear lift shaft. He noticed a circular silver platform speeding down from the top of the glass tunnel. It started to slow, eventually reaching a controlled stop at the bottom. A large glass door unlatched from one side of the cylinder, welcoming a group of snugs.

The platform was filling up. Everyone tried accommodating other snugs by packing tightly in until the last little snug entered.

The glass door closed behind her, and the silver platform took off without warning, racing up the shaft. Every trainee reacted by screaming "oohs" and "ahhs" as the platform sped upwards.

The lift reached the uppermost level and began to slow before coming to a comfortable stop. The door opened. Each trainee hesitated before stepping off, shaking off their angst and calming their nerves.

Ret rubbed his eyes and observed the chamber. Huge rectangular bay windows stretched from floor to ceiling, encircling this remarkable space. Rich sunlight cut through the room from all directions, heightening the open concept and free feeling design. From their vantage point, everything within the Pagan was visible; all four societies, the courtyard, the ocean and even Pagan island were located way out in the distance. Focusing his attention back inside the room, Ret looked up to his leaders appointed to this honourable space.

Nine powerful snugs held counsel in this chamber, all sitting attentively on tall white podiums assembled in a perfect circle. Everyone was sporting gracious smiles and ready to address their new arrivals.

"Hello, Pagan children!" announced one of the superior snugs sitting proudly on his podium. "I'm Sal, the chief of directors. It is good to meet all of you. Trainers, ensure you have all the appropriate paperwork and ancestry books for your trainees and line up in the order we requested."

The group of snugs formed a line in the middle of the room facing Sal, with the other eight circled around. Ret looked out from midway down the lineup and noted that he was the fourth trainee from the front. Juke pulled Ret back into position and shot a warning glare that clearly indicated for him to conform like the others. Ignoring his demands, Ret pushed Juke's hand away from his shoulder before stepping back in line.

"Alright, first we have Rony and his trainer Les," said Sal

"Yes, we are both present and accounted for," announced Rony's trainer waving up a few loose-leaf pages. "Here are his society papers, and I've also got his ancestry book."

Rony took a brown bag off his chest and handed his ancestry book to Les, who presented the artifact to Sal. Sal inspected the thick book cover and immediately recalled the origins of the young snug he presided over.

"Well, the old story of Pulo. And here is his descendant." acknowledged Sal. "How is your father? Marc, if I'm not mistaken."

Rony paused momentarily before answering the chief of directors; his nerves were being tested. Being the first snug put on the spot in front of this powerful circle of leaders gave any newcomer a good dose of insecurity. Terrified, Rony stuttered out an answer.

"G…G…Good, I guess."

Rony lowered his head, trying to escape this terror; his hands started shaking, and his bump dripped. He glanced around the room at the rest of the board of directors, looking for support.

Eight noble snugs made up the rest of the leaders. One female and one male from the four defined societies were perched on podiums trimmed in their society colours. Everyone was awkwardly staring down at Rony, hoping he could bounce back and respond to Sal with confidence.

"He was a good father. He taught me a lot. In fact, both my parents were gr…"

"No need to hear about Sandy. I'm only interested in your father. Bes will answer for your mother. Now, go on about your father."

Rony looked back to his trainer in shock, and Les indicated with a quick distinctive nod to hurry his answer. Rony turned around and continued but talked in vague detail about Marc, concealing any of his negative qualities.

"My father always taught us what the chancellors told him to teach us. And he always gave my sister and I a fair chance when answering questions. He was a very kind and knowledgeable snug."

"Ok. Thank you, Rony. Do you have anything else to say?" asked Sal, peering down at Rony with his wide framed body and large green eyes.

"No, that's everything."

"Good. Before we go on, I want to ensure everyone here knows the idea process. Your trainers should have educated you on this before coming here."

Ret faced Juke with an annoyed expression and shook his head.

"There are expectations of each of you inside Pagan," announced Sal, starting his formal lesson. "You must perform to your highest ability and represent your society with honour. Being successful will require sound knowledge and determination. Your societies are very much counting on you."

Standing with a commanding demeanor, Sal hoped to empower these young snugs. His booming voice and strong gestures showcased his authority; everyone was paying close attention.

"This is Pagan! How you spend your time here impacts the rest of your lives. We need all of you to strive as a team to achieve your society's goals and make Terin the most prosperous nation in the world."

Directing the crowd, Sal pointed to the blue society leaders and began his introductions.

"Each society has its own strength. Blues are the architects; they can formulate designs and construction plans to help you develop your idea and get it off the ground. Not only do they excel in planning, but they also have a keen eye for style and ingenuity," exclaimed Sal. "Our reds are still ranked first worldwide for mathematics, science research and technology. A few years ago, an idea created by a red society member greatly impacted the world; they claimed that we could convert our sun's rays into energy. After one year of development and some hard work inside our courtyard, solar generators are now available everywhere to power tools and equipment. Even the red society banquet hall, where some of you have spent your childhood, is powered by our suns. That good idea put Terin on the map as world leaders in technological advancements."

After a quick salute to the red society leaders, Sal turned to the yellow society directors sitting atop their podiums.

"Our yellows have made a mark in Pagan as the most important member of any idea group. When pitching your ideas to us, dealing with the politics of working with other group members, and keeping your idea group on track, there is no better snug to manage your projects. Every idea group will need a yellow to help keep you organized and motivated."

"And lastly, our greens. The most hardworking and task-oriented group members will persevere and accomplish any labour-intensive duty you give them. Their persistence and determination to see things through to the end make them invaluable to society and your idea group. Greens are the driving workforce your idea group will need to be successful."

Sal readdressed the trainees, stretching his arms and hailing the young group of snugs.

"You all have the opportunity to help advance our Pagan. When you discover an idea, you and your team must return to the governing tower and propose your plan. Only after our approval will you be granted access to work in a space down in the courtyard, where all your supplies can be stocked and machinery stored. However, you must be productive and always reach your quarterly goals, or your plot will be taken away and given to another idea group to use."

Sal paused and waited for any questions. When no one spoke, he finished his introduction and looked back toward Rony.

"In the meantime, each of you will be assigned a remedial job to fulfil. Until we approve an idea, you must continue to work on these daily obligations. So reds, where will Rony be going?"

Sal turned towards the two red society directors; Rony followed suit.

"I have good news, Rony. There is a perfect fit for you in the agriculture industry," announced the female leader. "We need help in the inventory sector. You are now part of the team responsible for ensuring we have enough trees for each of our citizens before hibernation. Well, that is, all the citizens that do not have a personal hibernation chamber."

"Is this good?" asked Rony, looking confused.

"It's what you deserve, young one," said Les

"Thank you, Rony. Work with pride, and we hope to see you soon," said the red society leader. "Les, see to it that he finds his way to his remedial, and introduce him to his new team."

Ret stood with confidence and waited for his turn to present. While Sal introduced the next few newcomers, Ret rehearsed what he would say. In his mind, he pictured everyone in the room praising him for his intelligence. He even wondered if another snug in history had an idea approved so early in their Pagan life. Marvelling over his intellect, Ret couldn't wait to be recognized as a famous Pagan snug; his time was almost here.

Rivalry

Ret swayed his body side to side and smiled at the ceiling, relishing the thought of being associated with fame and fortune. He pictured everyone praising him for his brilliance, and even imagined Juke's horrified look after being hoisted up and everyone chanting his name. Too busy in his own fantasy, he was gleefully ignorant and not paying attention to a hesitant trainee currently being addressed by Sal; it would have better prepared Ret for his shining moment.

"I'm sure your parents are great snugs. I remember reading about both of their lives. Of course, I was not inside Pagan at the time. If I'm not mistaken, they were both yellows, weren't they?" asked Sal.

Sal leaned back and pondered his delivery before beginning his lecture.

"They were dedicated snugs. I remember that about them. Didn't your mother make the cover of her ancestry book? And your father? He almost did? That's right. There was a long debate over his idea. Unfortunately, the former yellow directors did not grant him the cover."

The little snug focused on Sal, speaking in detail about her family's history. Standing captivated, she nodded her head, confirming every point he made.

"Yes, that's right," said the nervous little snug. "Wow. You know everything about my family."

"I have to, I'm the Chief Director, and soon I will learn all about you. All nine of us are here to guide you to build on your natural strengths. We are all mentors," he explained, as he stretched his arms out and proffered an inclusive gesture to all his fellow directors in the room. "We all know what's best for you. Trust our system, and I assure you little one, you will be just as, if not more successful than your parents, something every snug should strive to do."

"I really miss my parents, though. I don't know if I can live here without them," said the little trainee, as her voice began to weep.

"I understand you miss your parents, and I know they miss you too, but you must let go of the past and focus on your future."

"I know. I just wish I could see them again, that's all."

"Your parents lived a very successful life here. That is what we want from each one of you. Do you admire your parents' success?"

"Sure I do. I want to be just as successful."

"Use your time here productively. Every moment counts," said Sal. "This is something you will have to overcome. You are in Pagan, and your parents are now only fond memories; you are who they raised. Do not disappoint them by entertaining guilty feelings that will cloud your logical and organized mind. You are a true yellow citizen. I know that about you."

Showing his care for both aspects of her life, the Chief Director validated the little snug to honour her parents instead of dwelling on what cannot be undone. Refocused and reassured, the trainee looked back to Sal with pride.

"You are absolutely right. I feel…"

"Motivated!" announced Sal standing from his seat, pleased with her reaction. "I am certain I will see you soon. Stay with your trainer, he'll show you to your first remedial duty."

Ret missed every word of Sal's speech. Too busy rehearsing his introduction, Ret crammed in the last of his thoughts before strutting toward the Chief Director. He stopped and stood before Sal's podium, his body filled with courage as he looked up and introduced himself.

"My name is Ret. I'm part of the Red society."

Juke sauntered up behind him and indicated with an open hand that Ret did not have an ancestry book. Sal instantly caught on.

"Oh, so this is the progeny of the Tarni snug," said Sal in an ill-mannered tone.

"It is good to meet you, Sal. I can't wait to tell you my idea."

Sal squinted. "Have I permitted you to speak? It seems I have to inform you of your rights. Listen, foreigner; you are a miracle! Never in the history of this Pagan has any chief allowed the entry of a foreigner inside its walls. You make me feel tainted. You are a contamination. And if it weren't for Dek's approval, I would have never let you in. You and your sister will not take advantage of the purity inside our great city. Make it known directors; Ret and Terri will never be our primary focus. I order all resources and funding for pure Terin descendants. True Terins will come well before any half-breed!"

Ret stood with his mouth wide-open stunned at Sal's delivery.

He shook his head and crunched his brow. "You have no clue who I am and what I'm capable of, Sal!" said a wrathful Ret. "I can't wait to develop my idea. I will influence the whole world; you'll get no credit for it. Call yourself a leader. Go lead the slugs, you puss bag!"

"What? Do not offend me!" roared Sal from his podium. "I can make things very difficult for you."

"Yeah, well, I'll be waiting for your charity."

"You'll only wish I could help you, you Tarni snug! I only give help to snugs I know. Who are you? Your history is unknown to me. I don't even know which society you should belong to. How can I trust you?"

"My father was smart, and so am I, Sal," shouted Ret, holding out his arms. "If you just hear me out, I have a great idea."

Sal paused to suppress his anger, and Ret felt the moment starting to turn. In his mind, all he needed to do was present his idea, and everything would work out.

"I've never seen a trainee deliver an idea on their first day. It better be good."

Ret lowered his arms, turned around and snarled at Juke.

"Imagine you could communicate with someone else over great distances. Imagine you knew exactly what the rest of the globe was doing now?"

Intrigued by the idea, Sal's ears pricked as he listened on. Ret could see in his eyes he was impressed. However, as his pitch continued, it was clear Ret's beginner's luck was running short.

"And that's why having a global communication system would benefit the whole world! That's my idea."

Sal sat forward. "Is that all you have?"

"Yes..."

"Let this be a lesson to all of you, trainees. Ensure every question is answered before coming here. Presenting such a loose idea with no scientific background and no plan or design to execute is juvenile. Do not jeopardize your reputation by coming back here over and over again, trying to get the same idea approved. For this little half-breed, it doesn't matter. His name is tarnished. However, for the rest of you, ensure every aspect of your ideas are covered, how they work, how to construct them, who can use them, and why we need them. Does everyone understand? Never do what Ret did and propose only a simple idea, especially one that every snug in the world has pondered."

Sal waved his hand, directing Ret to return to the line.

"That means get out of the way," said Juke.

Ret turned around and trudged to the back of the room. Sitting on the glossy floor, he lowered his head. Rony plopped down beside him.

"I would have never thought of a global communication idea like that, Ret; that's amazing." cheered Rony. "I believe in you, Ret, and I want to work on this idea with you. I can be a great worker; you know I'm smart, so how about it?"

Ret lifted his head, rolled his eyes, and was about to respond; however, his attention peaked when Sal announced the final snug left to introduce.

"Kin: the winner and recipient of the champion's medallion. Welcome. We are so happy you are here with us."

Kin turned around and showed off his red champion's medallion sparkling in the sunlight.

"And how are your peak level quarters? I imagine you'll be comfortable in the red's most luxurious living space," asked Sal.

"Yes, I will be very comfortable, thank you." proudly answered Kin.

"That's great. I want you to be comfortable, Kin. But I need you to be successful."

Sal's voice turned serious. "To honour this position, you must take on a bigger share than everyone else. We have expectations for you, Kin. Make us proud."

"Sal, he will make you proud right now," responded Kin's trainer.

Ret pounded his fist on the floor, knowing Kin was about to live another one of Ret's dreams. He painstakingly watched on.

"Just like Ret back there, I also have an idea to propose to you. I have it here. Can I show it to you?"

"Yes, you can, Kin."

Kin and his trainer opened the large flap on his bag and pulled out a sheet of thick pliable material and two fabricated convex glass lenses. They rolled the flexible material into a long cylinder and fastened the lenses to either end. After making a few final adjustments, they presented the prototype.

"What is it?"

Kin directed Sal toward the Blue Pagan society in the distance. Sal swung his body around and awaited further instructions.

"Now, pick something to focus on and look at it through this."

Sal pulled the contraption to his eye and pointed it down to his target.

"Wow! I can see all the way down there!" said Sal. "It's clear as day. This is so impressive. What is this called?"

"A magnifying contraption," announced Kin, addressing the other directors in the room.

"Everyone in the world will want one of these, and it's so easy to make. I'm so proud of you, Kin; this is terrific!" answered Sal.

Sal passed the cylinder around to the other directors. Conversations started buzzing about the future of this idea and the social value it would bring to their Pagan.

Kin took in everyone's admiration. Modest and composed, he nodded around the room, relishing his accomplishment. Kin made his rounds, accepting the praise from everyone in the chamber. Smiling, he trotted to the back of the room, where he noticed Ret, the only one unimpressed with his achievement.

Adventure

A little green skinned snug looked down from one of the highest peaks in the great northern mountains. The young male prepared for the thrill of a lifetime as he stood at the summit, visualizing his route.

Deep within this mountain range, the entire landscape around him inhabited the sharp faced Alps spearing up from the planet's crust, towering over the land. A sedimentary mix of granite and limestone provided a rough light brown shade against these rocky giants, and a thick coating of nitrogen snow covered every peak. The mountain belt extended to the horizon in every direction, conquering the land, each standing firm and prominent.

Surrounding the base of each mountain was a dense green tinged forest that rolled throughout the valley. The forest would have stayed pristine if not for a small clear-cut area off in the distance, situated on a steep decline and filled in with orange sand; the young snug peered down from above and burned the landing spot into his memory.

He took a moment to gather his courage. He shook his head and hopped on the spot, psyching himself up. The time drew near. He inched towards the cliff's edge and stretched out his arms showing off his flysuit.

The durable black fabric was tailored around his body, and three distinct flaps gave the snug an odd shape when he extended his appendages. Two large triangular extensions stretched from his wrists to his waist, expanding from either side of his body, while another piece of material filled the space between his legs.

Without wasting another moment, the suited snug faced his target, bent his knees, and jumped.

Speeding down the face of the mountain, he flew parallel to the steep rocky edge and whipped past the rough shale surface. Diving straight down through the sky in a direct line with the mountain slope, he stylishly slalomed his body from side to side and managed a few maneuvers showing off his expertise. He controlled his body and accelerated through his descent, bombing down toward the canopy below.

His speed was increasing, as was his confidence. So much so that he began pumping his fist mid-flight, pulling his attention from his route for just a moment. In the midst of his boasting, a fast approaching cliff put his derring do in check. His eyes opened wide, and his body straightened out, reacting on pure adrenaline. He swerved his body to the side at the last moment and grazed his chest on the edge of the rough granite cornice protruding from the face. He shook his head and regained his composure. Lesson learned.

He powered on, showing no fear as he soared down the vertical slope. His eyes squinted, fighting the wind pressing on his face as his body reached terminal velocity. Then, after testing his limit, the little snug pulled up his suit, changed his trajectory, and started to fly horizontally and away from the mountain face until the planet's gravitational pull started to drag him back down. Spotting the clear-cut decline in the forest, he gauged his momentum and glided down towards his landing spot.

He harnessed all of his focus as he drew closer to his landing, and in one swift motion, he pulled his feet out from underneath his body into a sitting position. Marking his spot he used his bottom to touch down on the sandy incline and slid to a stop at the bottom of the hill. He hopped to his feet, brushed off his body and turned to the few spectators waiting at the edge of the landing ramp.

"That was incredible!" Hella said to Sert. "Wow. I've never seen anything like that before, except maybe the flyers," added Hella, remembering the banquet hall antics. "But this was way better!"

She glanced at the mountain's summit and replayed the impressive free fall in her mind. With a brimming smile, she turned towards Sert, who was playfully challenging his old friend Tras, and high-fiving his son Ty, at the bottom of the landing area.

"Yeah. That was okay, I guess," said Sert whimsically. "But you know, Tras, technically, that's still not flying.

Sert glanced over to his friend fast approaching and received quite a snarl. Sert was teasing the tall green skinned snug and knowing Tras's defensive nature, he readied himself for an argument. He snickered as he stared into Tras' red eyes and noted his slightly oversized forehead. He saved this piece of social arsenal for a future comeback.

"You haven't changed since our messenger days, eh Sert? You and Hella are only halfway to Tarni, so I would watch what you say. You don't want to get banished from here too," playfully warned Tras.

"We wouldn't fit in here, Tras." chuckled Sert. "Hella and I don't have the skin colour or the big foreheads to be part of the Torres civilization. Anyways, how long will you keep up this idea that you are going to fly one day? I don't see any real progress."

"Hella would fit in just fine; not too sure about you, though," Tras replied lightheartedly. "And we are getting somewhere. I have full faith in my son. Ty is already lined up to be one of the first snugs of his age group to be let into Pagan. It's snugs like him that will make a difference."

Hella's inquisitive mind was sparked by Tras's comments; she jumped right into the conversation.

"What do you mean being the first of his age group allowed into Pagan?"

"Really? Didn't you teach her anything, Sert?" exclaimed Tras. "Here in Torres, our children must undergo rigorous physical and intelligence examinations before entering our Pagan. Only after a child has met all standards will they be allowed in. The sooner our children can meet the standards, the sooner they go."

"They don't all leave together at the same age, do they? What happens if they never meet those standards?" asked Hella.

"Then they never go to Pagan. It's rare, but it happens."

Trying to comprehend the differences from Terin's social order, Hella stood perplexed. Sert watched from the corner of his eye as Hella reacted just like he anticipated.

Different cultures from all over this planet have always strived to be as knowledgeable and advanced as Terin. Terinians were consistently awarded respect from other civilizations for their global contributions, technological advancements, and revolutionary ideas. However, acknowledgements from others were never valued or appreciated. For as long as Terin was deemed the most productive civilization, not one citizen ever felt a reason to appreciate the outside world. As Terinians strived to become even more advanced, their awareness of the rest of the world diminished. Playing her role perfectly as a Terin citizen, Hella felt dumbfounded by the idea.

"Oh…" answered Hella.

Tras smiled as Hella soaked this in; she was curious to know more. While posing another intriguing question, she paused as Ty grabbed their attention.

"Hey! Watch this, everyone," shouted Ty from the base of his landing area.

Ty took off running toward the group. Pushing himself, he picked up speed moving closer to his spectators.

In mid-stride, he bent down and threw his arms to the ground. Rounding off his cartwheel, Ty set off on a series of back handsprings, loading his body for the finale. He soared through a double backflip, tucking his body and planting his feet firmly on the ground. Hesitating momentarily, Ty ensured his balanced landing was spot on before pumping his arms above his body.

"How was that, Dad?"

"Great, little guy! Keep it up," answered Tras. "But don't think I didn't see you almost hit that cliff in the middle of your flight. You got lucky."

"You saw that, eh? Yeah, that was close," said Ty as he walked over to his father. "I'm way too talented to let something bad happen, though."

"Oh, right. I forgot how skilled you are," Tras responded, rolling his eyes. "Just be glad your mother didn't see that. Keep your head up out there."

Tras turned back to his friends with his arm loosely over his son's shoulder, displaying him as his protégé. Beyond astonished by his abilities, Sert and Hella applauded Ty for his exhilarating performances.

"Alright, let's go home. You've shown us a lot today, little guy.

The group walked towards the public parking area, leaving the sharp mountain slopes and the deep tree-covered valleys illuminated by the bright suns.

Parked in the middle of the glider lot and presenting itself as an embarrassing display was Tras' outdated family glider. It ran smoothly, of course, but the bodywork and the unfashionable design were questionable.

The once glossy blue exterior was riddled with dents and large gouges. The interior was no better. The soft black upholstery in the front seats had worn down to its base materials underneath the cushions, and the back seats, torn open, exposed a good amount of padding. As for the extendable ladder, it was hanging off the side, fastened by a loose hinge.

"Can I sit in the front seat this time?" asked Sert.

"No. It's fine, Sert. We'll sit in the back again," Hella quickly answered. "It's not that far, anyways."

Sitting in the back, Sert glanced over and grinned at Hella before he tied both ends of his frayed seat strap together. Hella felt amused by the situation and tried to reign in her laughter. She pulled firmly on the knot to make sure it was tight. Then she patted the strap with the palm of her hand and smiled at Sert, confirming that he would be safe.

"Are we all ready?" asked Tras.

"Ready when you are." shouted Hella before laughing out loud.

"Step off the brake pedal, Tras. I'll be fine back here." laughed Sert.

Tras paid little attention to the scene behind him as he attempted to start the glider. The embarrassing clicking sound from the faulty starter transformed an amusing scene into an outright spectacle for Sert and Hella. Outbursts of laughter assaulted Tras from the backside of the beaten down glider.

"Stop laughing. I'm getting a new glider soon," growled Tras.

After a few failed attempts, the glider started up, prompting a sarcastic "hooray" from everyone inside. Tras took his foot off the brake pedal; the glider sped through the parking lot and cut a sharp right turn onto the open road.

"So, Ty, you must be one of the best students in your age group. What do you want to focus on when you go to Pagan?" Hella enquired.

"Flying. I'm going to study flying. Didn't you get that?" Ty answered rudely.

"Smarten up, Ty. Don't be so rude." shouted Tras.

"Well, she doesn't care, Dad. She's from Terin."

A series of sharp, heavy emotions struck Hella; feelings only a Terin outsider would feel, emotions that were now growing familiar to her.

"Ty, I've been a Terin citizen my whole life. I want you to know something. I never thought I would have to leave Terin. I never thought I would see other parts of the world. But I'm so glad I met snugs like you and your dad. You are really interesting, Ty, and so talented. I'm very grateful that Sert and I got to see so much on our way to Tarni. And honestly, I feel bad for every Terinian who doesn't get a chance to experience this."

Ty faced back with a kind expression. He thanked her with a simple smile, feeling moved by Hella's words.

"Yes, the rest of the world is something to experience," said Tras. "And Terin wouldn't be so bad if it wasn't for Sal. He's too controlling with his citizens, and doesn't give them a choice with anything. Everything Terin accomplishes is what he wants from his citizens. There's no freedom of choice in Terin."

"I've been trying not to think about him or anything that reminds me of Ret and Terri," whispered Hella. "It upsets me too much to wonder how they are doing. I know the chancellors told Sal about Sert, and well, that's what scares me."

As they drove through the final stretch of the mountain road, Hella battled her thoughts, unable to stop thinking about her children. She reached her hand towards Sert's and grasped it tight.

"They will be great. We have to believe that," whispered Sert.

With the highlands behind them, the road approached a small town shadowed by the mountain's jagged peaks. As they passed through a residential area of small gray granite houses, Hella tried to calm herself by filling her head with family memories. One recollection in particular came to her mind when Terri was young.

She recalled Sert erupting on Terri after pulling her out of the glider's driver's seat just before she ignited the electromagnets. A sound off ensued as Sert yelled at Terri, telling her she couldn't drive the glider because of her age. However, Terri jumped back into the driver's seat without regard for rules, and took off when Sert wasn't looking. Chuckling to herself, she pictured Terri laughing as she mocked his father, running after her down the road. Smiling, Hella sat back in her seat and relaxed as the glider slid over the last stretch of road before reaching Tras' home.

They pulled into the parking area, and Tras cut the engine. Everyone stretched out their bodies and took turns descending from the glider one at a time. Sert was eager to exit the vehicle, and as he jumped out his toe caught the edge of the siding. He fell hard to the ground and took the impact directly on his shoulder.

Rolling over the hard and rocky surface, he rubbed his arm to dampen the pain.

"Are you alright, Sert?" shouted Tras. "That's it! I'm getting a new glider!"

"And you're giving us this one." ventured Sert, rolling on the ground.

Laughing out loud, Tras looked down at Sert with a big smile.

"You can drive a glider? You sure you don't want a haze instead?"

Teamwork

Ret paced back and forth in his quarters, one hand balancing a black notebook in front of him, the other tracing his finger on the page. He was buried in the logs, thinking deeply. Whenever he looked up, he squeezed his eyes shut.

"Ok, the sound is a vibration," mumbled Ret. "Hmm, How will we find a suitable material that can resonate at the same frequency as our voices? And how will we power that over a long distance? That's what we need, right?"

He opened his eyes and turned towards the other eight members sitting unenthused, slouching over chairs, lazily sprawling over the couch, showing little interest in Ret's question.

"Anyone listening?" asked Ret, snapping the book closed.

One group member, in particular, finished sipping from her nitrogen hose, kicked her legs off the side of her chair, and stood up.

"Why am I putting my time into this outlandish idea?" She said, shrugging her shoulders and raising her arms, showing her intricately designed yellow bracelet. "I would much rather think of an idea and try to form my own group. I'm a yellow Ret. A lot of snugs would love to have me in their group. How much time will you spend trying to get this idea off the ground?

"It's not a loss, Gia; you know it."

"Yes, it is, Ret!"

"Hey! None of us would even be here if it weren't for Ret. Let's all remember that." shouted Rony, popping up from his chair.

Ret placed the book on a small table next to the couch. He extended his arm towards his old friend and gestured to Rony to sit back down.

"Alright, everyone. Let's stay together here," said Ret. "I don't know if you have realized, but we are progressing. We only need to figure out a few more things, and then we can go back to Sal and ask for a courtyard space to start building."

"See, that's another problem. How can we return to Sal with you as our red?" argued one of the blue society group members. "He hates you. I'm better off going myself with a lame idea."

Ret moved around his living room to face every snug, especially the blue member Gris, who was, at the moment, pointing his decorated hand towards him.

A series of three blue rings spread over the first three knuckles on Gris' right hand. The beautifully cut stones reflected the bright sunlight pouring in from the window beside him and caught Ret's eyes. Ret gazed into the deep blue sapphires sparkling in the light.

"Well, Gris," said Ret, regaining his attention. "It's not like I forced you to join. You made the decision knowing my history with Sal. Why are you putting this on me now?"

At first, Ret threw his arms over his head, unable to understand their attitude. However, wanting to act more like a leader, he calmed himself and tried his best to handle the situation, appreciating his team's concerns.

"Alright, listen. You do have a point, Gris. Sal will think whatever he wants about me; I have come to terms with that. But what can he say if this idea works? This idea has the potential to make him the most decorated chief of directors in history. A big head like Sal could never say no to that."

"You know what I think?" shouted Gia as she stood abruptly from the couch. "Some snugs spend their whole Pagan life trying to get an idea approved. There's no way I will be stuck watching all my friends move on while I'm here waiting for Sal to like you. I will not be one of those snugs."

"Gia, please don't start this again. Let's all just get back to work here." Ret stepped toward the small table and picked up the book, balancing it in his right hand and sliding his finger over the page. "This idea and this team cannot be smeared anymore by your attitude."

"Excuse me, Ret? My attitude? At least I'm being realistic. There is no way we're going to build this. I've wasted my first six months with you. That's it, go and find another yellow willing to work with you and your idea. I'm out!"

Ret took a moment to gather his thoughts. It wasn't the first time she lashed out. Gia was notorious for showing up with a poor demeanour, and leaving at pivotal moments in the group's progression. Still trying his hardest to see beyond her brashness, Ret bit his lip and endured her outburst. After all, the only thing she had going for herself was that she was a yellow.

"Listen, I know it's close to hibernation. Trust me; we're all a little edgy. I get it. But Gia, we need you. Look how much you have done for us already," Ret pleaded, holding up his notebook. "When I met you at the blue geyser hole a few months ago, you said this idea was worth the struggle. And that you were excited to start with us. Remember that?"

"That was before I actually understood what your idea entailed. And I didn't know how much Sal hated you. I mean, am I wrong here? Doesn't everyone else feel this way?"

Looking around the room, she tried to convince other group members to side with her. "Gris, how do you feel? Do you want to stay or leave?"

"Don't listen to her. Stop trying to take my team with you!" said Ret. "I've had just about enough of you, Gia. If you want to go, then get out of here. You and only you!"

Amid their bickering, some group members lowered their gaze to the floor, and others whispered, sharing their views.

"Why is Gia always starting arguments with Ret? She should know when to relax." whispered a blue group member.

"What? No way. Gia has a point. It's Ret with his wishful thinking. I agree with Gia. We are wasting our time with this idea and with Ret," another red group member stated. "What do you think?" He pointed his finger towards the only green member in Ret's crew.

Trying to ignore the dispute, the green busied himself by polishing the thick green belt around his waist.

"Well, what do you think?" repeated the red member.

"Honestly, I don't care. I'd rather just go home."

The two opposing snugs chuckled over his inane answer.

"See that empty showcase in the middle of your table?" said Gia, forcing the argument. "You don't have an ancestry book, Ret. How can you honestly say that you are a true red? You can't! You believe you're a part of the red society, but I don't see any family history proving it. And we're following you?"

"We are so close, Gia. And I can't spend any more time working on my remedial job! You're absolutely right, too. I can't imagine spending time in Pagan, never being part of an idea group. That would be terrible. I wouldn't wish that on my worst enemy," said Ret, facing back to Gia. "Go and find another group, Gia. I'm not stopping you. You have put a lot of time into this, and we're very close to getting our idea approved. I can feel it. Can you just do me one favour and make your decision after hibernation?"

Gia marched towards him and glared into his eyes.

"I'm going, Ret. I can't stay here and waste any more time. I don't have the same passion that you do. Your idea isn't even an idea yet. It's still just a thought. Sorry, Ret, but your team will need another yellow."

"You're going to force me to go to the yellow society, knowing I don't have a guide? Will I have to find a yellow and bring them up to speed? And now of all times!"

"You can always wait until after hibernation. Ah, that's up to you, Ret. I don't have to care anymore."

Gia looked around at her former teammates and silently said goodbye.

"Wait, Gia. I'm coming," announced Gris as he stood and quickly gathered his bags. "I'm sorry, Ret. But I think a fresh start after hibernation will be good for all of us. I have to go."

"Is that everybody? Who else wants to leave?" shouted Ret.

A few other snugs packed up and made their way over to Ret's doorway, exiting quickly. Awkwardness lingered inside the living room, and Ret's bump started to drip. He slowly turned his head around the room, facing everyone's uneasy grimace and raised brow. He reigned in his anger, and instead of reacting with an outburst, he tried to comfort everyone with a smile. With one final attempt to instill confidence in his teammates, Ret stepped up and addressed the group as a leader, something a red society member was not accustomed to.

"Uh, Well, first off, you are all making the right decision by staying with me. I will need some more time now to try and find a yellow, but hopefully, I will get things working soon. Let's just all stay focused on this, and, uh ya, everything will be fine."

The four remaining snugs considered Ret's gawky speech with grave concern. In a time like this, even Ret knew that his leadership skills were the only thing that could keep this battered team together.

"Really, everyone. It's not going to be bad at all. My idea is a hard concept. We all know that. It will be worth it. We are so close. We have discovered many properties and concepts of how sound works, and we can modulate it on a frequency band. Now, we just need to get it around the entire globe. That's it!"

Everybody who remained considered Ret's desperate plea with an un easy feeling.

Failing to reassure his team, Ret received another metaphorical blow from the group after a stern blue society member stood up from the corner seat and spoke out.

"We are taking a huge risk staying with you. I'm speaking for everyone here when I tell you that we will only stay after hibernation if you have a yellow member that won't encourage a walkout halfway through this project. I've spent too much time developing this idea with you and want to see this come together. But you must come through for us now and get a decent leader. Because if you think you can manage this group, I'm sorry, Ret, but think again. For one, you just really aren't that good at being the face of this project, and two, you have other more important work that needs to be done to get this idea off the ground. You can't be both red and yellow."

The outspoken blue nodded to each remaining member, confirming everyone was aligned with his message.

"Let me simplify it for you: no yellow, no us!"

Ret smirked, appraising the situation whilst staring at the vacant ancestry bookcase in the middle of his glass table. He gathered his paperwork, shoved it into his trusty brown bag, and ran towards the open doorway.

"Where are you going?" demanded Rony.

"I have to go find a yellow!"

"Right now? You won't have enough time before hibernation. How are you going to find one that quick? You can't expect him to find someone that fast," said Rony, turning to the blue member shrugging his shoulders.

"Are you coming or not?" asked Ret.

"We are a team, Ret. Of course, I'm coming."

*

The two raced out the door and headed toward the lift area. Ret reached the double doors and slammed his hand on the lift button, pounding it repeatedly with his tightly clenched fist.

"You sure you want to do this now?" asked Rony in a mild panic.

"You heard them. I have no other choice!" said Ret before stepping through the silver lift doorway. "Well, are you coming?"

"Alright, let's do this."

They scurried across the lobby floor, trying to make their way outside the building and onto the first glider train heading westbound. Ret glanced back as they dodged through the crowds and caught a glimpse of the large projector screen hanging from the ceiling. A timer was counting down to the hibernation lockdown.

"See, Ret. There's not much time before lockdown."

Too wrapped up in his plan, Ret ignored Rony, raced outside and took off up the street and over to the closest glider train platform.

Beside the road was a waiting area designed for public transit. Stretching more than a few glider lengths, this usually busy space was equipped with a wide stone platform trimmed in red. Rony stood uneasily on the platform's edge as he looked at the sky.

"The sky looks a little deeper in colour. It's turning orange. Are we going to have enough time to get back, Ret? We can't get stuck out there and not have a way back."

"Come on, Rony. Don't be a puss bag. We have plenty of time before the last glider train. Let's go. I see a train coming!"

Tilting his head, Ret stood in dread as the public glider reached the platform. Ret began waving his hands, trying to move the train quicker. A long, orange, open top, vessel pulled up to the frosty curb and extended a staircase next to Ret's tapping toes. A welcoming conductor greeted the two young snugs with a smile.

"Where to?" asked the green society member sitting in the conductor seat.

"Yellow society. Near the city centre would be perfect," said Ret, jumping on.

Staring back, the conductor looked puzzled before considering the young ones' request.

"I hope you're coming right back, you two. I wouldn't spend much time over there. You do realize hibernation is…"

"Yeah, we know," interrupted Ret.

"Well, there will only be three trains returning from the yellow society between now and then. Do you know anyone over there just in case something…"

"I appreciate it, but I think we'll be just fine," answered Ret.

Showing his medallion, Ret proved his citizenship and his admission. The conductor glanced at both of their medallions and gave a rueful smile before turning back around in his seat.

"Youth will always have a mind of its own," he murmured.

Ret and Rony stepped through the open aisles and made their way between the long bench seats and towards a few swivel chairs at the back of the locomotive. Closing his eyes, Ret did the best he could to block out any doubt creeping into his mind. He sat back in his seat, hoping for a miracle.

No Time to Waste

The sky was blanketed with a deep shade of orange, and large curling cumulative clouds swirled through the sky. The cloud formation was always a precursor to hibernation and provided a foreseeable warning for snugs to find cover.

As the glider approached the yellow society, not only did the sheer magnitude of the construction display an epic impression, but also the darkening sky added to the scene and conjured a looming feeling of disquiet to anyone approaching. The yellow society was always something to marvel at; however, as the two snugs drew near, a sense of panic set in. Ret could see that Rony was wrestling with his decision to come, but Ret suppressed his emotions and stayed focused as they advanced toward the first platform support leg.

This first level was the largest within the yellow sector. And above that, the other two platforms diminished in size as they rose along the granite slope reaching the city's highest point on the mountain.

The architecture was a work of art. One long building curled into itself, forming a distinct spiral shape and creating a distinct vacant eye shape directly in the middle of it. Each platform supported a structure identical to its counterpart; the only difference was the scale as the top two buildings decreased in size.

The highest building crowned the yellow society, and a slender copper tower stood at the top of Mount Nite that peaked into the sky just below the cloud layer; the tip aiming directly at the planetary ring.

Due to the style of the building, there was a complex system of tight corridors, bridges, and hard-to-find entrances used for getting around inside. Finding your destination within this multi-level city was always a challenge for any newcomer, which contributed to the list of concerns playing heavily on the two snugs minds.

"You know, it's getting dark really fast, Ret. Maybe we should just stay on this train and go back home."

"You can, Rony, but not me. I came here for a reason."

"Can we find a yellow for our group and return on time? I'm letting you know right now if we can't find someone and we get caught up scrambling around, I'm not going to argue or put up with your ego. If time is running short, I will leave you here!"

"Well, look at this; I didn't think you had it in you, Rony; good for you! I'm letting you know I can't leave without a yellow. That being said, if the world comes crashing down on us, then yeah, Rony, I'll understand if you want to leave," Ret said, cracking a faint smile.

"Return to your seats everyone and buckle your wrists. We are approaching the yellow welcome ramp. Repeat, return to your seats everyone. We are approaching the yellow welcome ramp."

Underneath every seat were two steel clasps fastened directly to the metal support of the chair. Once tightened around a snug's wrists, these simple devices secure any passenger from falling out of the open-topped vessel, especially during a vertical traverse. Rony's thick blue wrists had trouble fitting into the last notch on the self buckling latch.

"It won't lock! Seriously, why isn't it locking?"

Sitting comfortably, Ret ignored the situation behind him and stared toward the approaching support pillar. The massive yellow trimmed structure towered over the little glider train that was, at the moment, heading for the long curving ramp leading right up the stone support leg.

Rony frantically worked to wrench the clasps around his wrists, shouting out in panic until finally, he secured himself. Ret was already regretting bringing Rony along.

The conductor stepped off the brake pedal and accelerated towards the ramp. The train lined up and accelerated toward the incline as it shot up the enormous stone support.

Ret leaned back as far as his confined wrists would let him and glanced out in all directions looking out to the Pagan city.

"You still back there, Rony?" Ret said, half chuckling.

"Yes," said Rony in a monotone. "Why did I do this with you? We didn't have to come here until after hibernation."

"If I wait until after, our entire team will dissolve away and ruin my reputation with other snugs—even more so than it already is!"

Ret stared over his left shoulder and stared at his resident red society, marvelling at the design. Four identical high-rise buildings stood out with authority at the four corners of the red society borders. One expansive structure shaped like a half sphere was built in the middle, connecting the four buildings. Resembling their old banquet hall, the terraced construction acted as an atrium, a grand vestibule for large social gatherings, perfect for intermingling with idea groups.

Approaching the top of the stone platform, the glider train pushed up the last stretch of the vertical road and over a wide welcoming ramp. Quickly unlatching from the iron clasps, the two snugs got up from their chairs and ran for the extendable ladder.

The conductor looked back from his seat one more time before stopping.

"Ok, you young ones. I will return to this station with enough time to get you back home before Pagan lockdown. I'm the last glider ride back home. Do you understand? Go and do whatever you must, but please be here when I get back."

Rony urged Ret to listen to the green snug's warning, but he boorishly nodded in response and took off running down the steps.

As the two snugs approached the yellow society buildings, Ret looked to the top of a tall cresting entrance cut out from the structure. Inside, things were not in order. Chaotic sounds echoed around the open room as snugs hurried to get ready for hibernation. Yellows were running along the floor and racing down corridors and staircases throughout the hall. The scene impressed on the little inexperienced reds the need to move quickly.

Ret led the way. He scurried to the middle of the foyer and turned his head in every direction. The many doors and entryways lead to different areas, but only one would lead him to the city centre, where he and Rony needed to be.

He glanced around the busy room, trying to jog his memory, but it was fuzzy. He mustered up his courage and followed his intuition. Darting their way up a black stairwell under an arched doorway, the two snugs began their quest.

"We don't have that much time, Ret!"

"All we need to do, Rony, is get to the big concourse in the centre of the building. It won't take long."

The yellow society's community of socializing snugs sat in the middle of the city. Every society was required to provide adequate space for gatherings of snugs to converse and mingle with one another. Expressing ideas and sharing personal views was culturally vital for each Pagan. The large red sphere shaped building was the centre point of socialization for the red society. However, the yellow communal courtyard was not that easy to find. Deep within the complicated interior of the spiralling building was a large quad specifically built to accommodate all visitors searching for yellow group members.

Ret's problems were quickly intensifying. Running through a tight corridor decorated with the society's distinctive colour, Ret second-guessed his plan.

"Rony, do you remember the way? I have a hard time remembering where to go. It was a while ago when we came here to meet Gia. I don't remember going this way, but I could be mistaken."

Coming to the end of the tight yellow corridor, they stopped and looked at what seemed to be a common occurrence in this place, another moderately sized room full of multiple doorways and stone staircases. Ret gazed around the vacant room in search of anything that could help. To their misfortune, the space rendered them no clues.

"What do you think? Should we just go for one?" asked Ret.

"It's not worth the risk if we get lost here after everyone's left for hibernation. We might get lost inside and never get out!"

Rony's words were starting to play heavy on Ret's mind; he considered Rony's concern, and his own views were on the verge of swaying. But right then, the sounds of fast-paced steps echoed from down one of the hallways, and with that Ret surged back into high gear. He turned right around, keen on finding the source.

"Oh, come on!" screamed Rony.

Suddenly, a teenage snug wearing a yellow bracelet on his wrist darted out from one of the doorways.

"Excuse me, there," shouted Ret, trying to get his attention. "Are you part of a group at present?"

Stopping in his tracks, the older yellow turned and addressed the two desperate younger snugs. He squinted his eyes directly at the pair.

"A group? Are you joking?" answered the yellow citizen.

"Not at all. I have quite the idea to propose, and if you have a moment, I would love for you to…"

"What are you two doing here?" interrupted the yellow snug. "Are you really looking for a group member? Now?"

"It's quite an offer. I'm sure you will want to join our group after you hear it."

"I'm already part of a group, little one. Now go back home and find a cover. You two don't have much time."

Turning on the spot, the yellow snug ran up a staircase on the far side of the room. Desperate and knowing this could be his last opportunity, Ret addressed him again.

"Do you think you can help us find the city centre?"

"Little one, you sure are persistent, aren't you? Go home," answered the hurried snug.

Ret's humbled feelings turned sour, his body tensed, and his frost bump dripped down his back.

"Don't call me 'little one'!" screamed Ret. "I have an idea that will change the world, and honestly, the fact that we're here right now only shows our dedication. Do you know any yellows searching for a team, or can you lead us to the city centre? That's all I'm asking!"

The yellow society member stood stunned, his eyes on full alert.

"Alright, I'm going right by the city centre. So come along, little… young ones, and I'll show you the way. By the way, what is your idea?"

"It's about a…"

"You can explain it as we go. I'm in a hurry, and so should you be."

Ret followed the yellow citizen's lead. Rony stayed put. Ret glanced back and tried to wave his friend along, but inside he knew he was going forward alone.

He cocked his head to the side and shrugged his shoulders, hoping to sway Rony's decision, but it didn't work. Rony cracked a gangly smile that conveyed encouragement for Ret to go on.

"Just find your yellow and make it back in time, Ret. I'll be waiting."

"I will, I promise!"

The Harsh Reality

"We've learned so much about the science of sound. Did you know that sound moves in ripples? Yeah, it's true! We also discovered that the ripple's size determines the sound's pitch. The high-pitched ripples are smaller, and the low-pitched ripples are bigger. The bigger ripples are more powerful and tend to carry further over distance. You're probably thinking, 'Why don't we just make a giant sound accelerator and face it toward the edge of the flat rock? That's what I thought, too. But trust me; it wouldn't work. Even if a thousand snugs got together and yelled as loud as they could, the sound wouldn't make it around the globe. So, that's the question. What can we build to sustain the sound of our voices over long distances? We tried many methods using materials and metals to transfer the best results. We did the testing inside my quarters. I want to go in front of Sal with all our findings. We're on the verge of putting together a theory on long-distance communication. We're almost there! But my team fell apart. Some teammates, especially my yellow, lost all faith in me, and our idea, and betrayed us. To be honest, it's their loss. I will continue with this idea and reap all the success after I figure this out. The only thing is, I can't do it without a yellow, especially a yellow that won't fly out the door when things get tough. My new team will consist of snugs that take orders and listen for a change. I'm just sick of everyone else's negative views. Sick of everyone trying to change the group; anyways, as I said, it's their loss. My team breaks up before our big breakthrough, and here I am. Go figure that."

Ret summarized his idea to his yellow guide, who focused more on getting to their destination than praising Ret for his wisdom. Midway through the tour, the yellow rolled his eyes and snickered back to Ret, trying to temper his ego.

As the two snugs sped through the maze of corridors, foyers, and staircases,

Ret did his best to stay close to his guide. The yellow's fast feet were the only thing Ret focused on.

The yellow snug stopped beside a white marble staircase and cupped his right hand underneath his dripping frost bump.

"It could be worse, you know. You could be one of those snugs that never get an idea launched," the yellow said.

"Never launch an idea? And never make it to Pagan island for my last year?" said Ret. "Could you imagine? No, that's not going to happen. I need to get a yellow and get on with my idea."

"You youngsters. You all think you are a bunch of geniuses and will change the world with your brilliant ideas."

"Yeah, what's so wrong with that?"

"Listen to me. Cut it out. All the self-entitlement, all the ego, all the pride. This whole place, all of Pagan, is about communicating and connecting with others, wouldn't you agree?"

"Yeah."

"Well, little one, consider this advice a freebie. You can easily get ahead in this place if you simply understand others and their views. Listen before you delegate. Everybody should have a fair chance of being heard before they're judged."

Ret was purposely holding back from identifying himself throughout their entire discourse. The yellow's advice was in the right place, and Ret agreed as he discussed his views on equality and fair play. He wondered if this yellow would practice his own preaching once he learned about his origins. Ret concurred.

The yellow guide turned around and continued up a white stone staircase. Ret discreetly reached around to his bump and grasped a handful of frost. He formed it into a snowball and tossed it into the corner beside the staircase. He didn't want his guide to know, as it was merely a precaution, but deep down, Ret had to be responsible as the thought of being abandoned for his origins was a reality he was getting accustomed to.

Ret continued to recite his idea until they approached the final stretch. The small entranceway to the city center was normally shimmering with bright white sunlight. This time, however, the entrance was very ominous, glowing deep dark orange.

The two snugs ran down the hallway towards the stone quad. Ret kept his hopes high that others were still around.

This public space, usually busy and packed with thousands of conversing Pagan snugs, was shaped in a perfect circle and bordered by tall stone walls. The floor was made of polished yellow granite. The quad was enclosed except for two entranceways on either end of the room.

Standing in the middle of the quad was a yellow citizen staring at the darkened sky. Hard at work, he was observing the changing atmosphere. A touch of jealousy coursed through Ret when he noticed that the snug was holding Kin's magnifying contraption to his eye and staring up into the atmosphere.

"Wow. There is one snug still working. Now that's dedication," Ret's guide said.

The lone yellow snug lowered his magnifying cylinder and fixed on the approaching pair. The sight of Ret's red medallion stole his interest.

"Is that really a red rushing towards me? What do you think you're doing here? You should return to your hibernation chamber or find an open tree."

Ret made direct eye contact, cleared his throat, and offered a warm greeting.

"Hello yellow; I've come from the red society searching for you. I have a groundbreaking idea, and I promise it'll be worthwhile. I have a proposition for you, and the rewards will be massive. I will also promise that this accomplishment alone will get you on the cover of your ancestry book. If you haven't already obtained it, that is." answered Ret, charming his way through his story. "I'm here to tell you we have the answer to the age-old question of global communication. Is it possible? I'm here to tell you it is! The days of messenger snugs and delayed information are over. And with your help, I'm positive we can accomplish this. Ask your friend here. I've been explaining it to him for the last little while. He's even excited."

The yellow snug closed his notebook and stared into Ret's bright orange eyes. He shook his head and turned to the yellow guide, smiling sarcastically.

"First off, I don't know if you could tell, but I've got something else going on at the moment, and…"

"This is bigger and better," Ret interrupted.

"And two, I don't even know who you are. At first impression, you seem, well, insane. Really though, what are you doing here? And how old are you? You need to find a cover, young one."

"You think you're dedicated? I'm just as devoted to my team, maybe even more. I'm here because I was put in a hard spot and had to find a yellow immediately for the best interest of my team. I'm risking my safety being here, but I need a yellow. And I'm not going anywhere until I've got what I came for. Can you help?"

"I gotta say, little one, you are persistent, thorough, and dedicated; everything I look for in a red team member. You're tough; I'll give you that. But I'm already part of a group and couldn't leave them. It would be the worst time to leave," he answered regretfully.

Ret didn't want to listen. He slowly shook his head from side to side, kicking his foot against the floor before responding.

"I understand. It's all about timing, and this was just off. Thanks for listening to my pitch at such short notice." Ret said jokingly, addressing both yellows.

The yellow snug responded, "For as crazy as you seem, you must be twice as smart and talented. I'll tell you what. My sister completed her first idea, locking her down for a spot on Pagan Island. But she doesn't want to sit and do nothing until her retirement. So how about after hibernation, I'll ask her and see if she is interested in joining you?"

"That would be great. How much time does your sister have until retirement?"

"Another four years!" exclaimed the yellow snug.

"Wow, she must be brilliant. What was the idea that got her credited so early?"

"She was in a three-member group that developed a more productive way of evaluating group ideas, believe it or not."

"Huh? What do you mean?"

"Apparently, the chief can only approve ideas that meet a certain list of criteria. It's a set of laws passed down from generation to generation. These laws often prevent idea groups from performing meaningless or dangerous projects; over the years, there have been more than a few mishaps and worthless ideas. And so, because of those failures, the directors decided to create a list of ideas that could never be approved again."

"Oh," answered Ret, trying to follow along.

"For years, technology never really changed. However, times are much more different today, and things seem to evolve faster; something new is being created daily. Look at gliders, for example. No more having to ride big clumsy hazes. And even us Terin snugs aren't hibernating in trees anymore—well, most of us aren't. We have made a light source that can be held in our hands, and if you are successful, soon the world will have a global communication system!" said the yellow snug while playfully embellishing Ret's idea. "Our world is not the same today! And my sister and her idea group offered her services to rewrite a new set of guidelines. She proposed it, Sal liked it, and right away it was passed. She sparked a movement in him. And now, apparently, this new Pagan outlook of 'technical progression' that everyone is talking about indirectly results from her idea."

Gathering a sense of her idea, Ret thought more about how useful this information was to him. He prompted the conversation to continue as best he could, digging for more guidance.

"That's interesting. She's lucky to be working that closely with Sal. I didn't know civilians could do that. Good for her. I have to ask, what were some of the changes she made? Anything an ambitious snug like me can use?"

The yellow snug forced out a loud chuckle. "Well, I do know that environmental standards are being considered. In particular, all the waste created from our courtyard projects is beginning to accumulate faster than anticipated—and more than we can currently handle. Apparently, she says our way of living is exponentially growing, and we must act before it's too late."

"Wow, really? I would have never guessed that would have been such a problem," said Ret, still trying to keep the conversation going.

"She says it will become a serious issue soon if we don't fix it now. Also, ensure you can tie future innovations to your existing ideas. The directors are looking to invest in " expanding ideas." Actually, your idea, little one, would be perfect. It's versatile and can be marketed to the whole globe. Now that's expanding!" shouted the yellow, chuckling over his clever comment.

"Well, I hope it's not just a dream," said Ret, trying to be modest. "I'm not going to stop until I find a way to get this idea approved."

"Oh, to be a young wishful thinker again," chuckled the yellow, bringing his book back close to his chest.

"Ok, thank you. I've got a better idea of how to pitch my idea to Sal now. Good to know."

"No problem, and keep this quiet. I shouldn't be telling you this. I'll pass on your information, and she'll contact you after hibernation."

"That sounds great!" answered Ret, expelling his first sigh of relief.

His image and attitude secured Ret a better social standing with these two yellows. Ret's confidence radiated, and he felt he was starting to fit in; if only this could have lasted forever. Before he could make a clean break from the situation, that dreadful question arose.

"Hey! What's your name again?" asked the yellow with a laugh. "I gave all this information to a stranger."

Furrowing his brow and tilting his head, the yellow guide glanced over at Ret, appearing perturbed.

"Yeah, what is your name? I forgot to ask earlier."

Ret wanted to hold onto his newly acquired image and didn't want to spoil this moment. Stuck on the spot, Ret paused, which caused the two yellow snugs to cock their heads and ask again.

"Your name, little one?"

Ret braced himself and prepared for the worst.

"My name is Ret."

The guide instantly looked up. "Ret, Ret, Ret. I've heard that name before and quite recently."

Ret stepped back and glanced at the other yellow, staring at him. "The Tarni snug. Are you serious?"

"That's it. You're right. He's the Tarni snug," confirmed the guide.

The room went silent leaving Ret in a wretched position as he watched the yellow snug slam his notebook shut and shake his head.

"Why didn't you tell me earlier that you are the Tarni snug? Now you know something you shouldn't know, you foreigner. I'll be ruined if this gets out. Listen, you little liar, don't tell anyone about what I just told you. You understand?"

Ret dropped his shoulders as the two snugs ripped into him.

"I can't believe you would lie to me like that. I helped you get here. I took precious time from my hibernation prep to help a half-breed?"

"What did you expect? He's a liar and a phony. How can you trust a snug like this? Is that medallion even real?"

"What are you so scared of?" shouted Ret. "Am I someone to fear? Tell me!"

"You don't have a real identity. How can I trust you? That is the biggest and most threatening problem for you," said the yellow citizen.

"Yeah, and how can you believe you are as smart as the rest? We're all pure breeds," sneered the yellow guide.

"Besides that, when you leave Pagan, you'll raise your children in Terin. Then we're going to have to deal with that problem. You are not one of us! And I'm not going to help you in any way."

"Yeah, me either!"

Both snugs gave Ret a final withering glare and crude remarks before fleeing for the entrance.

"Good luck getting out of here on your own." said the yellow guide.

"They'll probably find his lifeless body curled up in a corridor after hibernation."

Ret hunched over, his eyes jet black. He knelt on one knee, lowered his head and counted to ten; however much he wanted to break down and pity himself, he needed to be responsible and think of a way to get out. Wiping away the drips off his back, he put his fears aside, dashed towards the doorway, and exited the stone quad.

Ret wasted no time. He made a few rushed decisions while trying to jog his memory, relying on instinct over judgment. As he made his way through the maze, he second-guessed himself as all the doorways, corridors, and staircases looked worryingly familiar.

He was frantic, but he wasn't hopeless.

"The snowball," he said, shaking his head, mordantly raising his brow.

Ret entered another open chamber at the top of a staircase with two other doorways evenly spaced beside him. As he moved down the stairs, he glanced to the bottom and saw another set of doors.

Ret pounded his head and clenched his eyes before scurrying down the stairs. He stood amongst six doors and inspected each one. He narrowed his decision to two but was still left with a dangerous gamble.

He tapped his toes, weighing his options and then before he could change his mind, he chose a door, opened it, and found himself running through one of the many yellow trimmed corridors again and again until he reached another room with six doors.

"Are you kidding me!" screamed Ret before stomping on the floor.

Out of the corner of his eye, he garnered some hope. This room had a white stone staircase built in the centre, and beside it he made out what he thought were snowflakes.

"Please! Please be the one!" shouted Ret.

He edged toward the staircase and peered over the side. He was stricken with doubt; part of him didn't want to look. To his dismay, there was no sign of a frost ball.

Ret turned his head to the ceiling in a rage and shouted as loud as he could. He released his pent-up emotions and pounded his fists against the wall. Furious, he held nothing back and let out a ferocious howl.

He knelt in his spot and put his hands to his face. His emotions were playing fast and loose as he sat in the corner coming to terms with his reality, his eyes changing from red to black and his face expressed anger and despair in perfect harmony; there was nothing he could do.

"Ret!"

He shot right up and joyously exclaimed, "Rony! I'm over here! Follow my voice!"

A wave of relief swept over Ret. He dropped his shoulders and closed his eyes. Right then and there, he saw his friend in a different light. Even though his behaviour towards Rony wasn't nearly as despicable as the two yellows, he had always treated Rony with a similar disregard. He realized that for all the guff, snide comments and shoddy character jabs he would throw at Rony, what he got back was a friend he could put all his trust into. A friend who would stand by him through thick and thin, and save him when needed. Most importantly, Rony was a friend who would never judge, abuse, or abandon him. Rony deserved more and Ret knew it.

After a moment, he got up and listened at each door, trying to pinpoint the source of Rony's bellowing. Ret shouted back until he saw Rony dart out one of the doorways, motioning to him with a frantic wave. Ret chuckled and smiled graciously before following his friend down the corridor, through the yellow society and out of the building.

Family Obligation

The glider train swerved down the road. Covered in a thin layer of glossy melt, the road reflected a clear image of the deep orange sky above. Windy gusts pushed against the long vessel, veering from shoulder to shoulder, taking the odd blow from the curb.

Ret shifted his legs, matching the sways of the glider and gripping one of the many vertical holding poles fastened to each seat. He glared at the yellow society towers and flicked the back of his hand in its direction. He slowly swung his hips around and his shoulders, but before turning his head Ret shot one last scowl up to the yellow towers by way of a final derisive goodbye.

"We can't thank you enough for waiting. We wouldn't have made it without you," said Rony to the conductor as Ret approached the front of the train.

The conductor nodded and tried to be receptive, but his eyes were fixed on the road. His mouth grimaced in stress; his hands glued to the wheel.

"This better not happen again. Next hibernation, tie up all your loose ends before it's time to find cover. Ok?"

Sensing the greens citizen's edgy undertone, Ret and Rony patted him on the shoulder, thanking the Pagan veteran for his service. The conductor accepted their gratitude with a grin.

"You know, this place needs courageous ones like you two. Keep up the good work, whatever you're trying to do. I have never seen such dedication from anyone in my seven years inside these walls."

"Well, honestly, I didn't get what I came for. I kind of failed today," answered Ret.

"Failing is all part of progressing, little red. It takes ten failures to get one success. The question is, can you get through all of your failures without giving up? Never give up. I wish I hadn't."

The conductor's eyes started to turn black as he reflected on his experience inside Pagan. Ret nodded his head in sympathy and smiled at the aged conductor.

"Well, I hope you remember us next year when you leave Pagan. You're going to invest in our idea group when you're outside, right?" said Ret, giving him a kind slap on his shoulder.

"Oh, don't worry. I'm going to keep a close watch on the quarterly results. And if I think your group's idea is worth it, I'll invest the day you receive a courtyard plot. That's a promise."

"Much appreciated," replied Ret.

"Hey, what was your name again?" asked the conductor.

Ret shrugged his shoulders and dropped his head in disappointment. Trapped in this ongoing social issue, he realized that his identity problem would never disappear.

"My name is Ret."

The conductor shot him a questionable glare. Ret braced himself. He didn't know what to expect. Was he going to bully him, attack him or kick him off the glider? Surprisingly, the conductor stared back at Ret, lifted his cheeks, and cracked a friendly smile.

"Beat them, Ret. Beat all of them. Beat them down at their own game until they have to respect you. Don't lose hope. You can do it, little one. I know you can," answered the conductor. "Don't worry about your past. Just make sure you win. Trust me; everyone will love you if you win."

Ret was shocked. He stood back and fixed his green eyes on the conductor as a warm, comforting sense of gratitude swelled inside him. Ret opened his mouth and was about to say thank you, but the glider suddenly stopped at the red society station.

"Ok, you two are home. Go on already, I have to get home too."

Ret locked eyes with the conductor and delivered his kindest smile. The conductor responded with a quick head nod and waved his hand, signalling to the two snugs to disembark quickly.

Ret and Rony stepped down the ladder and ran along the melting road. Weakened by the warming environment, both snugs neared their residence building.

They sighed in relief when they approached the entrance. Ret looked up as they ran over to the foyer, spotted the world clock and pointed it out to Rony.

"A little bit longer and we would have been locked outside," said Ret. "Good hibernation to you. And thank you, Rony, for saving me."

"Anytime Ret. You just make sure you get that yellow." chuckled Rony. "Good hibernation to you too."

*

Ret checked his essential belongings ensuring they were protected from the elements. He ran back and forth across his quarters and transferred all his study notes into a large square box, filling the space right to the top. Then he pulled a long length of heat-resistant wrapping off a spool and covered the box with a few layers.

"Alright, I'm all set."

He strolled down the hallway leading to his hibernation chamber and stopped when he heard the sound of a loud knock at his door. He turned around and raced to answer it.

Ret was stunned after opening the door. Terri was slumped over; her eyes were pitch black and her arms crossed her chest. Helpless, she stood stupefied as she glowered at Ret, looking for comfort.

"Terri? Where have you been? I've been looking for you. Get in, get in."

Terri didn't answer.

Grabbing one of her hands, Ret pulled her inside and hugged her. And as he wrapped his arms around her shoulders, he felt her body was cold, lifeless and vacant.

Terri pried herself away from his grip and plodded around his space, eying up his lavish surroundings. She gazed around the room and slowly turned to face Ret. Her eyes were now bright red.

"You've been living here? This whole time?" She demanded with an irritated tone. "I've been through torture, Ret! Torture! And you've been living a great life in this incredible place?"

Ret softly placed his hands back on her shoulder.

"Please. You don't want to know what I've been through," said Ret. "What's going on with you? I have worried about you since we left for Pagan."

"I've been treated like puss, and you're living the life you always wanted. How great is that for you? Why would you want to hear my side?"

"Where have you been, Terri? I've searched all over the red society for you and couldn't find you anywhere."

"I was in the blue society."

"The blue society? Doing what? And why didn't you contact me?"

"I didn't have time to write to you, Ret. I was with Cliff. Remember him?"

"Umm, no, I don't. Who is Cliff?"

"He was my transporter snug when we left Marc and Sandy's, remember?"

"Ok, I think I remember now. He was a blue?" asked Ret, trying to piece together her broken story.

"He was the best blue. At least, I thought he was. I stayed with Cliff in his place the entire time we've been here, and he showed me everything about the blue society."

"So, what happened?"

"Cliff said I had strong wits and could work through anything. He said everything was going to be alright and not to worry about my past," she explained. "We had the perfect setup. Our team was great, and our idea was within grasp. We all worked so hard. All of us! Then, after a few months, Pana, a yellow society member joined our group. That's when it all fell apart. I was part of something exceptional, Ret. I was even considering changing to a blue society. I was having a great start to Pagan until Pana showed up. That miserable snug ripped it all to pieces and destroyed my reputation. In front of my whole team; it was so embarrassing."

Ret rolled his eyes. He knew her dramatic tendencies and temperamental attitude were part of her personality. Old family memories of Terri came to mind. She would whine and cry over minor details just to get attention. And now Ret couldn't help but figure that her attitude must have influenced her experience.

"What happened to the rest of your team? Can you still contact them?"

"No!" replied Terri. "After Pana threw me out, no one wanted to speak to me. All I could do was come here and try to find you."

"What am I supposed to do? I have nowhere to put you. Hibernation is imminent. Imminent! I can't fit you in my chamber with me; the closest tree line is far away. Forget about this Cliff snug. You need to do something about your situation. What are you going to do? Didn't you think about this before you came here?"

Ret began to panic. He was dumbfounded as he glared at his mindless sister standing before him.

"Are you serious? Do you think I need your help? Well, I don't!" she screamed proudly. "You think you know all the answers because you have a special hibernation chamber and these nice big living quarters. Well, I hope you enjoy your comfortable hibernation, Ret. Thanks a lot, brother!"

Before he could even respond to Terri's outburst, she bolted towards the front door.

"Where are you going?"

"Like you care."

Ret closed his eyes, tilted his head towards the ceiling, placed his hand on his brow and ran after Terri.

Ret stepped through the doorway but stopped suddenly for a moment, looking down at the curving ends of the hall. He listened to his instincts and then dashed into the lift area, hoping she was still waiting. She wasn't.

Once he reached the ground floor, he scurried over to the raised section of the lift area and frantically looked around in all directions. He glanced over at the main entrance far in the distance and squinted his red eyes. He spotted Terri. She was running out the front entrance.

Ret raced underneath the world clock without glancing up as it passed its caution marker. His attempt to save his sister clouded his rational thinking; he bolted outside without care.

The change in visibility hit him the hardest. A blanket of white fog made it difficult for him to find his bearings. He walked slowly with his arms awkwardly extended, trying to peer through the thick cloud cover. He spotted Terri's silhouette and followed in its direction.

Ret was in a dangerous spot. He wanted to find Terri, but the heat had intensified, and he could barely see his hands before him. Trying to make his way back to his building, the booming sounds of cracking thunder roared above. Knowing his limited supply of frost was melting he picked up his pace.

Ret was lost in the thick white nitrogen cloud and began to panic. Worst of all, Ret could hear that the red society building's large mechanical doorway was starting to close. He ran blindly in its direction. The sounds of gears clamouring and clanking became his only navigation.

A moment later, his hand smacked into a solid stone surface. Sliding his fingers along the wall, using it as a guide, he sprinted back toward the main entrance.

He reached the edge of the entrance, but he could feel with his hand that this doorway portion had been sealed. Terrified, he rushed over to the centre of the door, but his legs were starting to slow; there was only one reason for this. He swung his hand around to feel his frost bump. It was dry.

At last, he reached the middle of the doorway and tried to push his weakened body through the closing space, but he could only get one last glimpse inside his building before it sealed him outside. And what Ret saw then stole his last morsel of hope.

The sight he saw was more than just discouraging; it was crushing. It wasn't the truth about his outcast family, his tainted reputation, or even everyone doubting the idea that did him in. What ruined Ret was the sight of Terri running back across the grand foyer floor and over toward the lift area. Ret fell to the ground and placed his hands over his face after realizing he was the intended victim of Terri's clever scheme...

Revenge

"Okay, you two," asked a determined Hella. "Here's an easy one. Let's see if I can motivate you. Who was the first snug to develop the sound accelerator, and to which generation of Pagan did he or she belong? And remember, the first to answer gets a bottle of Jax."

Terri's face brightened as she shot her hand high above her head. Peering back to Ret on the other side of the bench, she exhibited her desire to win.

Ret raised his brow in mockery as he gawked back. Of course, he also knew the answer to this simple question. However, Ret enjoyed seeing his sister exert herself in order to beat him to the answer. Cracking a faint smile, he rested his head on his bent arm and curled up fist, watching Terri's mind hard at work.

"I know, I know! I know the answer, Mom!"

"What is it, Terri?"

"Don, from the one hundred and third generation," answered Terri, standing proud.

Shouting out hooray, Terri pushed out her chest before looking at Ret with a big grin. She held her head high and turned back towards her mother, who, at the moment, looked over to Sert sitting behind his matching green desk with his head in a book, totally preoccupied.

"Way to go, Terri. That was a really fast answer. We are very proud of you. Here is your bottle of Jax. Wasn't that a great answer, Sert?" asked Hella.

Ret rolled his eyes as he listened to his mother coddle his sister. He always felt that his parents' teaching methods were all wrong regarding Terri. Interrupting his sister's moment, Ret spoke out and addressed his concerns.

"Good work, Terri! Now answer this: what colour is the sky?" he asked sarcastically before facing the front of the classroom. "Come on, Mom. Pagan is looking for smart snugs. And she won't get smart if you keep giving her easy questions like this and congratulating her. We should push her harder."

"Shut your mouth, Ret! I am smart!" screamed Terri, raising her fists.

"Terri, calm down. And Ret, say that again? Please. Explain to us exactly what you mean. And think before you answer," suggested Sert in a firm tone, peering at Ret from behind his desk.

"We can all see that Terri is far behind me. I always answer your questions correctly, and I'm quick too. Terri needs to get smarter and faster." exclaimed Ret. "She won't be good or successful inside Pagan without having quick wits. You make her believe she's smart and reward her with a prize when she doesn't deserve it. I could have beaten Terri to the answer and stolen that bottle from her."

Hella felt shocked and offended. She raised her brow and turned to face Sert, who shared the same expression. Hella couldn't help but answer.

"You know what it's going to take to be successful, Ret?"

"Yes, I do. It takes…"

"Let me tell you something, Ret," said Hella, cutting in. "Take it from the two snugs in this room that have lived inside Pagan. One of the worst character traits is arrogance!"

"I know that, Mom. There are so many children who…"

"Ret! Listen up!" shouted Sert.

Taking control of the conversation, Hella walked towards Terri's side of the bench with the bottle of Jax in her hand. Courteously placing Terri's earned prize in front of her, Hella kneeled to her level and addressed her.

"Let me ask you, Terri. Do you respect Ret? When you get to Pagan, would you ever want to work with Ret on an idea? Would you ever let him be a part of your group?"

Terri smiled before answering her question. They both turned their head towards Ret, ruthlessly delivering a spiteful glower.

"No! There is no way I would ever let someone like you into my group. You are right, Mom. There are probably a lot of snugs out there that are smart, but if there is no respect, then they are not worth it."

"Take it from someone who has been to Pagan. I wouldn't form a group with you. Everyone dislikes those arrogant, self-righteous snugs that believe they are above everyone else. Everybody has their own natural skills and talents. Pagan is all about connecting all different types of snugs with different talents. And trust me. The judgmental and snobbish type snugs are always left out."

Ret pushed their remarks aside, shook his head, and pursed his thin blue lips. He looked to his father for support; Sert didn't give him a thing.

Terri glared back at Ret with a satisfied smile as she mustered up a few comeback lines in her mind. She pointed to her slouched over brother and opened her mouth. However, a loud knock on the front door interrupted her retaliation.

"Who can that be?" asked Hella.

Sert hopped up from his green chair and went to the window. He bent forward, rested his hands on the long window's edge, and looked down at their front walkway.

"There are two children at the front door. Siblings, I think. And it looks like they're holding a green pamphlet," said Sert. "Let's go see what they want."

Ret was free to behave as he pleased with the two responsible adults out of the room. He placed his hands on the back of his head and stared at Terri. Ret consistently underestimated his sister and believed he could control the situation with intellect. Still, where Terri lacked brainpower, she made up for it with her forceful temperament.

This time, though, Terri looked away. Trying to ignore her brother, she stood up from her side of the bench and walked over to the open window to see who was at the door.

She leaned over the edge of the frame and pushed her little body outside as far as she could. Balancing herself, Terri stretched out just far enough until she caught a glimpse of two young snugs holding out a green pamphlet. She could only decipher a few words as she pushed further from the window's edge. Trying her hardest to lean down, Terri tilted her head and finally heard the conversation. However, it didn't last long. Ret's deviant plan brought her attention right back into the classroom.

The distinct sound of a cracked open bottle sent Terri into a state of fury. Before turning around, she knew exactly what was happening behind her.

Without any hesitation at all, Terri pulled herself back in and turned to her brother, downing her well-earned prize.

"See, Terri. You should only get an award if you deserve it. After all, I could have answered that question way before you did. Consider this a lesson learned."

Ret slammed the empty bottle of Jax down on Terri's side of the desk, but to his surprise, he only had a moment to savour his victory. He should have known; Terri's response came swift and hard, smacking him on the right side of his head.

"You are such a puss bag, Ret!"

Fuming with rage, she screamed as she whaled on her brother.

"Terri, settle down!" screamed Ret. "Don't hit me! It's for your own good!"

She followed her strike with another loaded punch to the opposite side of his head. Soaked in a furious rage, she couldn't hear Ret shouting for mercy from within his curled up body. She overpowered her cowering brother and violently attacked him—punching, kicking and manhandling her brother in a crazed stupor.

"You might be a puss bag with your words, Ret. But me? I'm a puss bag with my fists."

"Alright, Terri! I'm sorry!" pleaded Ret from behind his hands as they covered his face. "Mom! Dad!"

Ret's cries for help went unnoticed and had little effect on her. The sound of her helpless brother seemed to fuel her intensity even more. Standing over Ret's humiliated body with her clenched fists and sinister smile, Terri's mind fixed on inflicting significant pain. Each powerful strike empowered her as adrenaline coursed through her body. Her mind turned vacuous; nothing could stop her.

Sert and Hella returned to the classroom, both dropping the green pamphlet in their hands.

"What is going on here?" screamed Hella. "Terri, what has gotten into you? Get off your brother!"

Terri stopped and looked at her mother with passionate red eyes, her hand tightly bound in a fist. Lifting her foot away from the side of her brother's face, pressed helplessly against the floor, she turned towards her mother to try and explain her actions.

"He drank my entire bottle of Jax when I turned my back! The entire bottle!

I didn't even have a chance to stop him."

Sert walked over to his desk, where he sat down and put his arms back behind his head, making himself comfortable as he listened to his daughter. He unsympathetically peered over to a frightened Ret and watched him collect himself. Sert felt proud of his daughter and understood why she reacted as she did. With a glance, he conveyed to his son that justice had been served. And, in turn, Ret looked back at his father with an unmistakable look of resentment.

"It doesn't matter, Terri! You never attack anyone! Never! Have some self-respect!" shouted Hella. "There is never any reason to hit someone!"

"That's not fair at all! Why does he get away with stealing my Jax and speaking to me however he wants to? How can you be mad at me?"

"I don't care, Terri. You don't hit others. That's a rule! Tell us if you're angry with someone, and we will take care of it! Understand?"

Terri nodded and sat in her seat, acting out the part while her mother continued her lecture. She looked up to her supportive father and couldn't help herself from cracking a smile as her mother blathered on. She pretended to listen, but inside she felt totally warranted by her behaviour. Terri realized that abiding by her mother's rules was an illusion to keep everyone in order. Terri got a small taste of injustice that day and felt vindicated, knowing she had defended her honour. Her belief system changed. No matter how much Hella tried to influence her, Terri realized that equality comes only if you fight for it...

Heartbroken

"**P**lease stop running, Terri. You don't have to listen to them."

Terri darted through corridors deep within the blue society. She paced herself to keep enough distance away from the snug trying to catch up with her. She ran as fast as she could, but his footsteps were getting louder.

"Stop following me! I don't want to be a part of your group anymore!"

"Just slow down a bit so I can explain. Please. You are what matters most to me. The rest of them will just have to accept that. And they'll have to get used to you being a half-breed. If you leave, then I will too. That's a promise."

Terri slowed and stopped, resting her body against the rough stone wall. She tilted her head and gazed through the gap separating the two buildings towards the orange sky.

"We have all been planning this for a long time, and you know how I want you to be our spokesperson," said the blue society member walking up behind Terri. "I want *you* to be the one to help promote and publicize our idea. You would be perfect for the part."

He extended his arm, placed it softly on top of her shoulder, and did his best to comfort her.

"How do you know that? I can barely even drip my frost around those snugs without having to explain myself. And Pana. She hates that I'm with you," explained Terri, trying to calm her nerves.

"If you just come back inside, we will straighten this out. I promise. I'll protect you, and I will be there for you. No matter what. They won't threaten you anymore. I'll make sure of that. You have to stay, Terri," he pleaded while calmly rubbing her shoulder with his hand. "Besides, there's only so much time left before hibernation. And as I said, you can use the spare chamber in my quarters. I'm the only one in my building with an extra one."

Terri loosened her shoulders. She spun around and stared deep into his green eyes, exchanging a comforting smile. She pulled his hand off her shoulder and grasped it tight.

"Let's go back up to my quarters and talk with everyone. If I have to, I'll make them understand exactly what I see in you, Terri."

"Thanks, Cliff," Terri whispered. "I just want things to be fair and to be treated as an equal. That's all I really want."

Cliff looked at the sky and raised his brows when he realized their time crunch. He scurried forward and tugged on Terri's small blue hand, hurrying her steps. They exited the corridor and scooted along a stone walkway leading to the front of Cliff's resident building.

The architectural design of the building was nothing short of a masterpiece. Its roof, extending in four directions converged seamlessly at a magnificent top point that glimmered against the orange hued sky. The dark blue brick walls displayed brilliance as subtle hints of light glimmered on all sides. The light snaked down the entire edifice and highlighted every window frame, protruding edge and contour on the face of the building. At the base, multiple floodlights were recessed into the sidewalk and shined directly upward, adding to the elegant facade.

Every level was built offset from the previous one, forming a corkscrew style design that flowed throughout the structure. These giant spiralling landmarks acted as a fitting monument inside the blue society, openly viewed from each corner of Pagan. Many ceremonial services were held in this location.

With little time to spare, the two snugs raced inside. Terri held onto Cliff's hand as they entered the foyer. The vast room featured many gleaming marble statues of former building engineers and designers. And the ceiling, a massive mural of intricately crafted etchings spanned from one side to the other. Detailing their society's historical timeline, the mural transitioned from early prehistoric works to fully detailed paintings of the most recent Terin accomplishments. The scene was jaw-dropping to those first laying eyes on it. However, for Terri and Cliff, it was the last thing on their minds.

Terri stayed optimistic and kept her spirits positive as they ran to the lift area.

She looked at Cliff as they stepped onto the lift, admiring his valour. If only their group could feel the same way about her.

*

"She's a half-breed. Who here really knows what her strengths are and what her history is all about? I said before: We can't afford to have a team member we can't trust," shouted Pana. "I will not stand by and let her infest our group!"

With a quick motion, a member of the red society raised her hands towards the ceiling and voiced her agreement, adding to Pana's disdain towards Terri. "I agree. There is no reason we need this incapable snug getting in the way of our goals. As a member of the red society, I can't see any similarities between her and me. She is not a true red," she exclaimed, pulling her hands down her smooth blue chest to caress her cherished identity piece.

"So, it's decided? I'm glad we all feel the same way about Terri. As soon as Cliff returns, we will all be adamant with our decision and give him our ultimatum."

Cliff and Terri approached his quarters and could hear through the open doorway the loud roaring sounds of encouragement from their idea group. They stood silently with their eyes wide open as they peered into the room. Terri harnessed her wits and prepared for battle.

"You want to say something to me, Pana?" shouted Terri as she entered Cliff's quarters. "I think it's about time I stood up for myself in front of you all."

Everyone inside the room stepped out of the way, leaving an inviting stage for this fierce quarrel. Terri and Pana stood facing each other, each taking a moment to size up their opponent before the dispute began.

"Trust me, half-breed; I won't be the only one you'll need to stand up to. This is something that will follow you for the rest of your life. That's one of the reasons why I want you out of our group. Everyone will turn on us if we keep you. How will anyone take us seriously knowing that a half-breed is part of our group? You have nothing to offer, only embarrassment."

"I have done nothing to you, Pana. You have this grudge against me, turning the entire group hostile. Why? Why is it such a burden to work with me? Why don't you believe in my abilities and how much I can contribute to this team? This is *not* fair!" screamed Terri.

"You don't have a history, and we can't trust you. Plain and simple. You think you deserve to be a part of this group; well you don't. What I know about you, half-breed, is that your father is from Tarni, the worst civilization in the world. And you didn't even place in the red competition." shouted Pana, addressing the room. "You are useless to us."

"You have no idea what I can do, Pana."

"Maybe not you. But I know what your brother can do."

Terri clenched her eyes as tight as her fists and tilted her head. When she opened her eyes again, they were solid red and glaring back at Pana.

"At least he came second place to Kin. I hear your brother has a group formulated and is working on getting it approved. See, at least he doesn't just sit back and whine and whimper about how we should feel sorry about him. *He's* doing something with his time here in Pagan. And that is much more than I can say about you. I would take him over you if it were a choice between you and your brother, you don't stand a chance."

Terri held her anger; it wasn't easy for her to resist. Instead of fighting back, she turned to Cliff standing in the doorway, looking for his support. Despite the promised patronage from her partner, when it was time for him to deliver, he stood in silence. He turned his head away, leaving Terri alone.

Her eyes instantly changed to black, and her clenched fists loosened. Terri dropped her shoulders, turned back to the group and faced Pana.

"You're not going to spoil our group's reputation, half-breed. You're not welcome here anymore. And you, Cliff, you better hear us out and listen for once because while you were outside running after this snug," Pana said, pointing a finger at Terri with disgust, "we were all in here discussing the next steps. We have all agreed that if you don't commit to us and banish her, you're gone too."

The sight of Cliff's nodding head sent a gut-wrenching blow into Terri's soul. Her one and only saviour turned on her; no one was there to help her anymore.

She looked around at the rest of her former group members and saw them all glaring back at her. She slowly shook her head and turned back to Cliff.

He disgracefully stood by with his head down, ignoring her silent cry for help. Terri stared at him in despair, yearning for one last glimpse of hope. Every moment that passed without receiving a sign from Cliff drove her feelings of care and adoration into revulsion and hate. A new belief set into her state of mind.

Terri's true colours were coming out.

Her instincts kicked in after realizing that her situation was hopeless. She reacted the only way she knew how. She clenched her fists, turned to confront Pana's smiling face, and lunged.

She tackled her to the floor and landed a couple of hard punches. Her rage was pouring from her soul. Noticing the crowd moving in, she dodged out of the way of two snugs trying to stop her attack, and delivered two more punches to Pana's shrieking face. Before she could deliver a final blow, other members barged forward and grabbed control of Terri's arms, pulling her away from the weeping yellow.

Terri was pinned. Glancing over at Pana, who lay in the corner of the room, she was taken aback by the overwhelming sympathy the rest of the group seemed to have for her. She couldn't understand how everyone believed Pana to be the victim in this situation.

Terri struggled to get up; three bigger snugs were pressing down on her shoulders and waist. She watched as Pana painfully leaned in and whispered into Cliff's ear. Cliff nodded, then turned and approached Terri.

"Terri, you have to leave."

"What?"

"You can't stay here anymore."

"No, you can't do this to me! Where am I going to go, Cliff? Have you looked outside? I won't be able to make the tree line. I could…"

"Good! I hope you don't find anything or anyone to take you in. You don't deserve to live in Pagan with us." shouted Pana.

"You can't do this to me, Cliff. I won't make it if I don't stay here!"

"I'm sorry, but you have to leave. I have to think of my future."

"You're future?' screamed Terri. "You puss bag! You are worse than any of these other snugs here! You were pretty convincing outside, but as soon as things get real and you have to pick a side…"

"I'm sorry, Terri. But I wasn't the one who attacked Pana. That's a serious matter, you know. Honestly, who hits other snugs?"

"Shut your mouth! She deserved what she got! And I felt great after hitting her! And now I want to hit you just as hard!"

Terri flailed her arms and managed to get free. She quickly got up and lunged forward, trying to punch Cliff's face, but to her disappointment, her arm was caught mid strike by one of the two snugs standing behind her. They pinned her arms behind her body and roughly clamped their hands over her mouth.

Everyone turned towards Pana and awaited her directions. She pointed to Cliff's doorway, stressing her demands.

"Get this half-breed out of here now!"

Ushered to the front door, Terri tried to shout, but the two snugs still held their hands tightly over her mouth.

"Wait," called Pana.

Pana marched to the doorway, placed her hand on the latch and swung open the door.

"You will never be one of us, half-breed. You are not, and never will be, worthy enough to call yourself a Terin citizen. Honestly, you and your brother don't deserve to be in Pagan with the rest of us. But I'll tell you one thing, Terri. I don't hate Ret. I only hate you. He at least has a small bit of our respect. As for you? I loathe you. Now leave and *never* come back!"

Without wasting a moment, the two snugs heaved her into the hall and slammed the door behind her.

Terri panicked. She sat in the dim hallway reviewing her choices, and Ret seemed to be the only option to save her life. The ongoing feud for equality between her and her brother, mixed with these fresh feelings of rejection, made her decision easy. She had always felt inferior to Ret and now transitioned her grudge against him.

Getting up from the ground, Terri glared one last time at the closed door, then took off and began her plot to exploit her brother and save herself. For most, a heavy conscience and a sense of guilt would sway one's decision to betray a family member, but not for Terri. She didn't second-guess her decision.

For her, this was final, and she felt justified.

Born Again

Three snugs from different coloured societies worked in unison inside a modernized control room. Their busy work area encompassed two substantial electrical panels on either side of a large rectangular reinforced glass window that displayed nothing but a thick white swirling cloud. After referencing large switchboards filled with circular dials and indicator lights, the group communicated the information.

The team sat fully alert in their black chairs, evenly spaced behind the oversized window, updating information in notebooks and verbally relaying the changing environment outside. Double-checking all the figures and managing each adjustment was crucial for this special idea group. Everything needed to be accurate.

"Alright, the atmospheric pressure is rising fast. For your sake, Rox, I hope you were right," said a yellow citizen sitting in the chair on the left side of the window.

"It's going to happen. I know it will. It's a matter of science," said Rox. "Trust me. Wait just a little bit longer. The cloud cover will rise high in the sky, and we'll be able to see everything on the surface. My thirtieth-generation elder discovered this when heated, surface nitrogen evaporates into gas. And because it's atomically light in weight, it will be stored…"

"We know. High up in the atmosphere." answered the arrogant yellow with a sarcastic look.

"Once all the ocean has evaporated, it will be clear. I promise you," answered Rox.

"Well, we didn't all hibernate early for nothing," answered the yellow citizen with a mocking tone. "Besides, if this thick cloud doesn't go away, we've got a bunch of thermal suits back there if we have to go out and do some testing. I really hope they can withstand the heat out there."

The third and final group member, a green society snug, swung around in his chair and responded.

"Oh ya, I tested them. They are rated for extreme temperatures, you could step outside in the middle of hibernation when the planet is superheated, and you wouldn't feel a thing."

"Yeah, I'm not going to be the first one to try that." said the yellow.

The yellow citizen chuckled and looked back at the temperature gauge on his side of the large panel board.

"It's getting hot out there, Rox. The thermal energy response indicator is very high. Wow, the temperature outside has really risen. Should be anytime now."

Feeling hopeful, Rox peered out the window, eagerly expecting the cloud cover to thin. If successful, this team would be the first snugs to witness the planet during hibernation. Living unharmed was only the first step in their dangerous task; the team was responsible for much more.

Rox and her team had proposed an idea that fit perfectly in Sal's vision of technical progression and his goals for the future expansion of his Pagan. They proposed a plan for harnessing thermal energy during the hot hibernation season. And after detailing many different methods, Rox argued the possibility of transforming it into raw energy. In fact, during their pitch, they justified to the board that risking their safety would be well worth discovering this natural resource. After long, drawn-out arguments with the board, Sal couldn't help but approve their idea; they had everything covered.

As she relished in her predictions and was on the verge of making history, Rox leaned forward in the chair, rubbing her knees with her hands, itching for her moment to come true.

"Hey! I can see the cloud cover thinning out. It's getting clearer!" shouted the yellow snug. "Look at that. You were right!"

Rox pumped her fists and hopped up from her seat, pushing her face next to the glass. Filled with enthusiasm, she pressed her hands on the window and smiled. The yellow turned around in his seat, faced his green society teammate, and pumped his fists.

Amid celebrations, Rox peered and pointed to something she could never have expected. She shook her head in disbelief and looked again. This time, she was sure; Ret's lifeless body lay in the middle of an evaporated ice road.

"What the… Is that a snug?" she ventured.

Rox snapped into action and rushed to an airlock protecting a thick iron doorway leading outside. She reached for the latch on the airlock door and opened it up.

"We have to help him! I think he's still alive!" she shouted. "One of you has to go out there and get him. We can't just leave him there!"

Rox stood at the open doorway leading into the small confined space encased with reinforced glass. The green was the first to jump from his seat, dashing away from the control panel and across the white stone floor into a small dressing area inside the lab. He reached for one of the three white thermal suits hanging close by.

The slim green unhooked the suit from the suspended cable and tossed it to the ground before dressing. "We did test these suits, right? I'm not going out there to have the glass face implode on me?" he asked nervously before putting the helmet over his head.

"What do you mean? You just finished telling us they were tested," said the yellow snug, sporting a grin. "We tested them, don't worry. Go get 'em, green. I got my eye on you."

The green made his way into the airlock chamber, and Rox followed right up to the edge of the glass doorway, closing him inside and latching it shut. The suited snug approached the exit and cautiously touched the outside door handle. After counting to three, he opened it.

Strong pressing winds grabbed hold of the door and swung it open. Swirling winds engulfed the green and forced him to step back. Fearing his suit would give way and rip open, he checked over his body, collected his thoughts and regained his footing. He rushed out the open door and entered a world no snug had ever ventured into, well, no conscious snug.

As the heavy wind pushed against him, the green drove his shoulder forward, and he shuffled his feet struggling to maintain his balance. Alarmed by the thunder and roars of cracking from the sky, the snug kept marching forward stoically. His eyes were jet black, and the frost from his bump started to pool at his feet inside the suit. To his surprise, the extra weight from the liquid helped stabilize his body. He firmly planted every step he took over the rocky surface, slowly gaining ground.

When the green was within reach, like a cat pouncing on its prey, he plunged toward Ret's unconscious body. In one quick motion, he scooped Ret up and slung his near lifeless body over his left shoulder. Rising, he spun around, picked up his pace and trudged back to the observation station.

The green rushed through the open entranceway into the airlock and placed Ret's flaccid body carefully on the floor. He spun around and thrust against the iron door. He bent his knee and drove his shoulder into the face of the door, fighting to keep it closed. With Rox cheering him on, the green reached for the latch and fumbled it after a gust of wind pushed on his body. The door swung back open, and the wind raged inside.

He swirled around, his arms flailing. Rox was screaming. The green found his balance and planted his legs again. He squared his body, pressed his hand firmly on the iron door and shuffled his feet. He slammed the door, grabbed the lock and secured the latch before dropping to the floor exhausted.

The yellow citizen raced toward the dressing area and prepped the floor with the remaining soft white thermal suits. Rox opened the airlock and dragged Ret's limp body into the station. They placed Ret face down on top of the plush pile of suits, and immediately both Rox and the yellow snug began scraping away frost from their backs, slapping it all over Ret's dried-out bump.

Ret's skin was transitioning from a solid, healthy blue to a transparent white, a sure sign he was overheating and in a critical state. Rox was panicking. She was so eager to help that she unknowingly used too much of her frost supply at the cost of saving Ret. Alarmed by her depleted frost bump, the yellow pulled on Rox's arm, trying to get her to stop.

"Rox, you won't have enough frost for yourself. You have to stop."

"You don't understand. I know this red! His name is Ret!"

○

Two Sides to Every Coin

Hella stumbled her way up the rocky trail on Mount Nite. She was pushing herself up the uneven terrain and trying to keep up with her energetic son. She fought through the pain in her aching feet, taking slower steps to conserve her energy.

Ret was far in front of her, gawking back at her with a sympathetic smile. He waved his hands enthusiastically and cheered her on, but unfortunately for Hella she was not in good shape and now crawled on all fours.

She collapsed onto a small pile of rocks that lodged into her abdomen, a sharp sting arced through her body, but her immediate concern was replenishing her low frost levels.

"I didn't know it would take this long," said Ret jokingly.

"Neither did I," whispered Hella.

Hella took his comments as scant encouragement and resumed her climb. She carefully rose to a kneeling stance and brushed off the embedded stones with a frustrated swipe.

"You just wait until you're my age. For some reason, things don't work well when you get older. And for the record, I *would* trade my wisdom for a younger body any day."

"We're almost there. Just a little bit higher. I can't wait to show you."

Harnessing the last of her energy, she secured her footing and finished climbing up the cliff. Finally making it to the summit, Hella lay face down with her back pointed to the sky.

"Yes. You did it. I knew you could," said Ret. "Now turn around and look at this. It's amazing."

Too exhausted to do anything else, she ignored her son and waited for enough frost to recuperate on her back. Closing her eyes, she lay perfectly still and soaked in the moment before Ret's youthful spirit demanded her attention.

"Come on, Mom. I know you're still tired, but at least turn your head around. It's really something."

"Alright, Ret, let me see what you want to show me."

A panoramic view of the calm yellow ocean encompassed their entire field of vision. Perched near the summit of Mount Nite, Hella and Ret were in awe, sitting on a wide-open cliff ledge jetting out from the mountain. The flat calm ocean appeared as a sheet of glass reflecting a pristine image of the yellow sky. The planetary ring between the two suns, dividing the sky, mirrored a perfect ring on the ocean surface.

Hella was amazed and inched closer toward the rocky edge to take in the view. She wanted this moment to stay undisturbed, but as soon as she reached the cliffside, she spotted her son sitting a little too close to the edge, and her maternal instinct kicked in. She extended one of her legs and positioned it right behind Ret's back, supporting his small body so there was no chance he could fall off. She could sense his irritation and addressed him with a kind grin, knowing full well that an argument was brewing.

"Take your foot off my back, Mom. I'm not going to fall. Why are you always like this? I'll be fine."

"Ret, I'm just making sure."

"Why? I'm safe, alright?"

"You're my child, and I wouldn't let anything bad happen to you."

Ret turned back around, frustrated and embarrassed. He continued his act by shaking his head and shrugging his shoulders.

"I have to admit it, Ret, this is a gorgeous spot you found. And I'm glad you showed it to me. I don't know if it was worth the hike up here, but I'm glad you brought me nevertheless," said Hella, chuckling.

Ret dramatically turned to Hella.

"Why are you so overprotective? You know you can't always be there for me, Mom. I'm not always going to be around. There will be a day when Terri and I move into Pagan, and I will have to fend for myself. I'll manage just fine without you watching my every move."

Hella sat back, and half ignored her son. She'd become accustomed to these tense scenes over the years and learned how to subtly sift through Ret's outlandish statements and pinpoint the real issues.

"I know Pagan isn't for a few years, but it will come sooner than you think. And I also know that you will miss us dearly when you leave," said Hella, watching Ret roll his eyes. "Just know that we want the best for you and Terri as you step into the next part of your lives. Pagan is *so* important…"

"I know it's important," said Ret. "You have to believe in me, Mom. I'm going to make something of myself. I know I will. You spend all this time worrying about how I could fail inside Pagan but never believe in what I could accomplish."

"I do believe in you, Ret. I think you have so much potential to be great. I can see it in your spirit. You have everything going for you."

"So why are you so overbearing? It's too much to handle"

"Because I'm your mother. And I know what Pagan is really like."

Hella watched as Ret cocked his brow at her statement, disregarding her wisdom and experience, but that didn't stop her from continuing.

"I wish I could be there to hug you every day inside Pagan, but I can't."

Ret rolled his eyes again, shrugged his shoulders in embarrassment, and turned away.

"Ret, you don't know anything. Pagan will stomp all over you and your attitude if you keep it up. I know that you are excited to get into Pagan but trust me, there is a lot more to it than just becoming brilliant and well-known, which is actually a rarity for most. Do you know what Pagan is full of, Ret? It's full of deadlines, obligations, clashing opinions, stress, and regret. Believe me! Nothing will work for you inside that wall without understanding how to manage your emotions. Not to mention knowing how to deal with other snugs. It's not as easy as you think. Everything in life isn't always as beautiful as this moment here. And you need to know that."

Ret stood with his back to his mother and pushed out his little blue chest, mustering up some courage to retaliate.

"You and Dad must be wasting your time then if all you've been doing for the past five years is educating us' seeing how I don't know anything. I'm pretty sure that I have been getting perfect on every test and assignment you have given me. Maybe it's Terri you should be having this conversation with. Didn't you just tell me I had everything going for myself?"

"Yes, I did say that. But Ret, intelligence does not determine success, and dedication doesn't always lead to accomplishment. However unfair you might think that is, it's absolutely true. Pagan is tough. Very tough. And you have to be, too."

"Pagan isn't going to be that hard for a smart snug like me, Mom."

"You'll see, Ret. You'll see…"

*

Ret played this memory repeatedly in his mind, drifting in and out of consciousness. He wished he could speak to his mother one last time. He finally understood what she was trying to tell him that day on the cliff; she was right.

Ret felt some strength in his body again as he became more aware of the room around him. He slowly opened his eyes and focused.

He was confused and in dreadful pain. Slowly, he began to move his limbs, and eventually he turned his body over and made out the silhouette of a slender figure walking toward him. Ret could feel Rox grasp his hand and begin rubbing his arm. She gazed into his eyes; his pain melted away.

"I knew you would survive. Try to stay still. Your frost bump is half full, and your muscles need rest. What were you doing? Why didn't you find cover before lockdown?"

Ret calmly replied to her questions trying to conserve his energy.

"Thank you for saving me, Rox. I remember you. From the red society community floor. On my first day."

Ret slowly pulled himself up to a seated position and gently stretched his torso out in all directions. He noticed a long, twisting hose running along the hard stone floor. It led into a small room filled with liquid nitrogen containers and one emergency hibernation chamber.

He lunged at the hose and started to suck back the liquid, desperate to replenish his depleted supply. Rox parked herself on the hard stone beside Ret and sat until he finished.

"You really shouldn't be alive right now. What you went through, any other snug would have, well, I'm just so glad you came through."

"Yeah, I'm just glad you remember me, too."

They gazed into each other's eyes, communicating their mutual interests with flirtatious repartee and sensual body language. Happily lost in this intimate moment, Ret relished her company even more as she continued explaining his rescue mission.

"It was a miracle we even found you. You were in our line of sight from our stone hut here. Peri, the green over there, got all suited up and battled the winds. He was the one who actually saved you."

Peri and a yellow team member turned around in their chairs and waved charmingly.

"You're alright?" asked Peri.

"I think so."

"Good. I guess it was worth it, then," interrupted the yellow.

"Oh, shut your mouth Len," said Rox.

Ret laughed at his response and instantly felt relaxed about the situation.

"You all saved my life? Wow, I don't know what to say. Thank you. By the way, Len, I don't suppose you are looking for another idea group after this, are you?" asked Ret with a chuckle to himself.

"Who, me? You would have to promise me the cover of my ancestry book. Can you do that?"

"Sure. That's an easy request. No problem," answered Ret, causing some laughter around the room.

"And what is it you're doing, Ret? Do you have an idea?" asked Rox.

Ret summed up the story in his mind before answering. But the moment he opened his mouth, something unexpected and alarming interrupted him. The immense sound of a powerful light bolt rattled the stone structure, shocking everyone inside. The phenomenon crackled and sparked through the sky as severe wind gusts blew across a vast stretch of superheated ground. Another large strike followed it. The team jumped up to set up their observations and record their findings.

"We need you over here, Rox. We got light bolts, and I'm hoping it will be a shower," shouted Len, turning around in his chair.

"What are light bolts?"

"Huge shocks of electricity. I'll explain later."

Ret sat by, astonished by the idea of light bolts, and watched as Rox and the rest of her team got to work. He observed the team. Impressed by their seamless communication and ability to multitask, he was amazed at how well they worked together. Slowly, he approached the group wanting to have a closer listen and see these light bolts firsthand. He gazed out the thick reinforced glass window, utterly captivated.

The stone observation station was set very close to the red society buildings and had a perfect view of the Pagan coastline, which was now a barren landscape. Across the evaporated land, small pebbles and moderately sized rocks were notable as the extreme rise in temperature heated them to a glowing bright orange. But high above the land, not even the bright light from the stars could penetrate the thick cloud. A mass of red nitrogen clouds swirled around the entire upper atmosphere forming a thick barrier high in the sky. Ret was soaking in everything he could see.

Ret waited for the next bolt to strike, anticipating a powerful demonstration of light. Ironically, it benefited him more than Rox and her group when it struck. While staring high into the atmosphere, Ret fixed on a small visible portion of the planetary ring peaking through the thick cloud cover.

"Here comes another strike. I can feel it," said an excited Peri. "Everyone, keep your eyes open."

An epiphany hit Ret after witnessing the bolt strike the planetary ring. Wanting to confirm his theory, he watched for another strike to ensure he saw it correctly.

As he watched the light bolt contact the copper rocks on the ring, he saw the concentration of electricity light up one band of the massive ring. Immediately he referenced the physics of his idea.

Broadcasting a sound wave using voltage as a platform was now very plausible.

The medium to transmit over long distances was none other than the planetary ring. He was astonished.

He recalled one study in particular that he and his group performed in his quarters a while back. It was to identify the physical properties of certain metals; copper being one of them.

Once a piece of copper is electrified, depending on the amount of current running through it, it will naturally emit an electromagnetic field. And, if a copper conductor is electrified, the flow of electrons will transfer the voltage from one end to the other. The flow will travel long distances using electricity as the medium.

"The ring can broadcast a signal around the world," whispered Ret.

Ret's mind was racing, so many ideas were exploding, and he needed to find anything he could to write all this down. He raced towards a small desk near the front of the room, and in mid-stride, stared back up to the perilous red sky and chuckled after hearing Peri's comments, knowing full well this discovery was about to change the world.

"Isn't it amazing how the light bolts travel around the ring when they hit it? Wow. That's incredible. The electricity goes all the way around the globe and back again."

Eureka!

○

Back Home

In the North Eastern Desert a vast stretch of sand dunes extended in all directions towards the horizon. Thousands of these sharp unusual features rose from the ground and extended into the calm yellow sky. These dunes were unlike what one would expect in a typical desert setting, constructed in the shape of a cone with a distinctly rounded summit. Each dune was crowned with a hardened layer of deep red sand, while the rest was composed of hard packed orange sand that blended with the ground's colour.

Stable and calm, the atmosphere was back to normal, coming off the heels of hibernation, and both stars delivered a wealth of light that radiated onto the desert below. The suns were positioned on opposite sides of the sky, resulting in a shadowless day.

Sert and Hella puttered down a long road, pushing their suffering glider to its limits. Worn down and struggling to perform even the most basic tasks, this gliding antique finally succumbed to its fate. It was still moving but had lost power and slowed to a crawl.

Sounds of electrical surges and agonizing sixty-cycle revs poured from the polarity switch underneath the chassis. The faded blue vintage glider had powered through the last of its efforts just before the vehicle halted to a final stop.

Sert jumped out of the glider and took off running. He entered the hills and looked around, inspecting each dune's face. He kept Hella in the back of his mind as he sized up the dunes around him, trying to choose one that would be easy for Hella to climb.

He made his choice, committed it to memory and walked back towards the broken-down glider, where he approached Hella lying back in her seat.

"Come over here. I want to show you something."

"Alright."

"Are you a good climber? What I want to show you is on top of that dune. Do you think you can handle it?"

Hella grinned as an old memory popped into her head. Sizing up the challenge, she summed up her strength and darted right for the sandy dune in one fearless motion.

She pushed her body over the rugged surface and raced up the incline. She swung her arms with every stride, dodging protruding rocks in her path and jumping over obstacles until she reached a steeper section just before the summit.

She felt all around the red sand that crowned the top to ensure it was sturdy and could support her weight. She took a firm grip of the upper edge of the peak and pulled her way up.

Hella managed to crawl toward the middle of the summit, got up from her kneeling position, and jumped in celebration with the last of her energy. Exhilarated by the climb, she extended her arms high in the sky, soaking in the moment.

She peered out from her elevated position and noticed the long span of dune formations spread across the land. She perused the land until she saw something that caught her attention. Not even the sounds of Sert struggling through his climb behind her could tear her eyes away from this spectacle.

After Sert reached the top, he took a moment to regenerate his energy and then introduced Hella to his homeland.

"This is Tarni."

"Wow."

Sert watched her from the corner of his eye. He saw that she was struggling with the reality of the situation, something Sert regrettably anticipated. Shaking her head in disbelief, she finally turned back towards him and listened as he explained the image in front of them.

"Don't be afraid, Hella. I wanted you to come up here and see it from a distance first."

Off in the distance, stretching high up, stood a stone wall, cruelly marked by an enormous crack splitting the face wide open. From their position, she could even distinguish the immense stone perimeter that, at one point, could have easily enclosed tens of thousands of snugs. Now, the visibly demolished structure portrayed a remorseful image to anyone looking at Tarni for the first time.

"What happened here?" asked Hella.

"There was a time when Tarni was prosperous. It might not look like much now, but we led the world in innovation and progression. For decades, we used that Pagan right there to its fullest potential. Our Pagan flourished with great ideas. We held the record for the quickest development rate among all the Pagans. I can still remember when our ruler Fig addressed the nation with that accomplishment."

Sert stood remorseful as he stared at his shattered homeland, witnessing what a pitiful sight it was. He readdressed Hella, who was paying full attention to his story.

"Our society was truly something. When I was young, my mom told me that all the other civilizations were trying to be as successful as us. *We* were the world's role models back then. We thought we were invincible. Now look at it. You know, Hella, I've grown to believe that the more you become accustomed to success, the more you think you can control it. A long time ago, during our prosperous years, a large group of elder snugs started to yearn for their children that recently entered into Pagan. If there's one thing a self-entitled elder can't cope with, it's the feeling of losing their son and daughter."

Hella's blue eyes started to turn black.

"Reg. We will forever remember that name around here. He was the first of all parents that stood up against the system. I still remember it like it was yesterday. He came from a highly successful background, and while inside Pagan he perfected the economy to a science. He constantly came up with new ideas and always invested in his creations, sitting in at least the top five productivity charts. Reg was smart."

"Productivity charts?" asked Hella.

"Our Pagan worked a bit different than yours. We didn't have coloured societies that distinguish your abilities as Terin does. And children weren't ranked before entering Pagan, either. Every snug inside our Pagan could do whatever they wished. But, snugs weren't allowed to leave Pagan until they participated in a number of ideas or services."

All these changes and alternate realities were a lot to take in for Hella. She tried to keep up with all the information as Sert explained his former Pagan social order.

"Anyways, back to Reg. He orchestrated a massive movement, and in no time, he rallied every elder and middle-aged snug he could and pressed his views onto them. And they all listened. Everyone, and I mean everyone, marched to our beautiful Pagan wall and began protesting. It wasn't long before my parents followed suit. I remember sitting on top of one of these dunes with my sister, watching our parents run towards us. They were shouting with pride, saying that we didn't have to go into Pagan anymore and that everything was going to change."

Sert turned his saddened expression downward and wrapped his arms around his squatted legs. He shamefully shook his head, regretting his youthful actions.

"I was so happy at that moment. I didn't want to leave my family, nor did my sister. We ran down the dune and jumped into our parents' arms. I remember my dad screaming for joy when he told us we would live together forever. At the time, it was the best day of my life. But little did we know, it turned out to be one of the worst things we could have done. I mean, we were just so excited. How was I supposed to know what would happen to Tarni? I'll tell you, Hella, if there's one thing I would take back in my life, it's that decision. Ahh, it wouldn't have mattered. The movement had already begun, and I couldn't do anything to stop it."

"How old were you when all this was happening?"

"Young, Hella. Very young."

Sert lifted his head, pushed away his troubled feelings of regret, and continued to explain.

"Then, our parents took both of us straight to the Pagan entrance, in the middle of the angry protest, and announced our loyalty to their cause and that we wanted to stay out of Pagan, too. We were forced to stand amongst a huge group of brainwashed and confused children, being told we were not to go into Pagan and to stay with our parents. I was holding tight onto my sister's hand. She was so frightened. Thousands of parents and elder snugs flocked to the front of the Pagan, all railing against our civilization. I almost couldn't believe what I was seeing. Everyone came, all bearing long iron picks and large masonry tools. I can still hear the crowd chanting away as hundreds of snugs threw long climbing lines to the top of the stone wall; day after day, they chipped away. I remember just before they breached one side of the wall, Fig, our ruler, came out from inside Pagan and addressed everyone."

Hella looked at the shattered Pagan city landscape, trying to imagine the horrific event.

"Fig didn't stand a chance. Once all the teens inside Pagan witnessed what was happening to the wall, it changed their beliefs. Everyone from inside Pagan began helping their parents destroy the wall. Fig tried to stop us. He preached in support of the Tarni traditions and laws, but it didn't take long before everyone turned on him and cast him out. We exiled him. Then, the day finally came. The large stone wall was felled. *We* caused that huge crack. And from that day forward, we all lived together—everyone. From parents to elders and children to teens, they all lived amongst each other. It's chaos. Our lives completely changed after that day. And, by the looks of things, it won't change back anytime soon."

Hella extended her arms and gave him a comforting hug. Remaining proud and strong, Sert turned around and started to walk down the dune.

"Come on, Hella. We have a long walk ahead of us. Well, until we find a haze."

"Wait. Was Tras being serious? You used to ride hazes to get around?"

"Yes, I did. And you are going to have to learn, too."

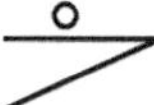

The Truth Always Comes Out

A small pack of Tarni snugs, all riding atop galloping hazes, cut across the desert floor. The gang raced between the Tarni dunes stirring up a thick trailing plume of orange dust behind them. Shouts of "hoorah" and high-pitched yips echoed over the land as the pack picked up speed.

Still standing atop his dune, Sert caught the sound behind him and spun around. He spotted the group of Tarni's heading in his direction and took off from the summit. He held his hands out and took short choppy steps down the incline, eyes peeled open, examining the terrain and avoiding rocky obstacles as he descended. He stomped on the desert floor and flailed his arms, desperate to hail the group. The thunderous roar of the stampede made his shouting inaudible. Caught in a panic, he was convinced there was only one way to stop them. Acting before thinking, he darted right into their path, raised his arms above his head and braced himself.

The lead guide posted off the haze, pulled back on the animal's shoulder blades and brought her to a swift halt. The others followed suit when they saw the lead haze drive her large muscular legs deep into the orange sand.

Just in time, the stampede came to a halt, leaving Sert surrounded by a thick orange cloud that blinded him and a mouth full of sand grains. He waved away the dust and peered through his squinted eyes to see an aggravated Tarni snug staring down from his haze.

"Are you insane? Who in their right mind jumps out in front of a large pack like that?" screamed the furious snug as he leapt off the backside of his animal. "Who do you think you are?"

Before the dust cloud had completely settled, the lead Tarni recognized Sert and addressed him.

"I don't believe this. Sert? Is that you? How long has it been?"

"Hey, Lip. Surprised to see me?" Sert responded while wiping dirt off his shoulders.

"Are you serious? If I had known it was you, I would never have stopped." chuckled Lip. "Hey, everyone. Look, it's Sert. He finally came back."

Sert clapped his blue hands together to clean off the last of the dirt from his palms and gave a pitiful wave of acknowledgement.

"Well, seeing some things just don't change is nice."

"Ok. Settle down there," Lip said lightheartedly. " Sertcy! It's been a while. Don't you want to catch up?"

"Catch up? Nothing has changed by the looks of it. You're still riding hazes. Why doesn't Tarni have ice roads yet? You realize that the rest of the world is years ahead of your civilization?"

"*My* civilization?" shouted Lip, extending his arms and pushing out his chest. "Don't believe for one moment that *you* belong to another civilization? Do you think you can just forget your past? Besides, what makes you think we even want you back?"

Sert glared away from Lip and over to Hella, who was making her way toward them. "Help us out, will you? Give us a ride into the city," suggested Sert, feeling his throat clear and his full voice return.

"Us? Who's us? We didn't trample over someone else, did we?" asked Lip, turning to look underneath his haze.

"See that gorgeous Terinian coming this way? Yeah, she's mine." Sert said proudly. "Maybe you should have left Tarni at some point and had a new beginning. You're just too old now, aren't you, Lip? It's too late for you to start over."

"Huh? I wonder how much she knows about you, Sert. Things will get better around here. It's going to take time, as we all know. But the last thing *I'd* do is desert my civilization and abandon the snugs that need me the most—all to start another phony life with someone who doesn't know *why* you left Tarni in the first place. I'm not trying to change *my* identity."

"Neither am I, Lip. I know where I came from. That's why I'm so surprised that this place hasn't changed since I left it."

"Well, it was *you* who was supposed to bring us back some good ideas, Sert! I'm not sure if you remember?" answered Lip in a mocking tone of voice. "We were all counting on you to gather information from other civilizations and bring it back to us."

"I know what I was supposed to do," snapped Sert. "Now quiet, please! Don't say anything else in front of my other."

Hella felt uncomfortable walking toward the pack. Each member shot her an admiring look while sitting astride their hazes. Suppressing her unease, Hella smirked and put on a brave face as she stood beside Sert, tightly gripping his blue arm.

"Hello all. My name is Hella. Nice to meet you. Did Sert scare the frost off your backs when he jumped out in front of you? Cause he sure made me cringe. What were you thinking?"

She ran her hand over Sert's upper back and cupped her extended arm, grasping a tight hold of his shoulder. Sert was proud to have her affection and held his head high, glaring at his antagonistic old friend.

Lip couldn't help feeling a sense of pity when he looked at Hella, though he did his best to hide his remorse. Inside, he knew she was oblivious to the real truth about Sert and imagined her reaction when she found out. He turned to face the group and leapt back up on his haze.

"Find someone to ride with, you two. We're headed towards the city. You need to speak with Dredge," instructed Lip. "Hold on tight, Hella. I'm sure this is your first time riding on a haze, and trust me; it ain't easy."

Responding to Lip's high-pitched whistle, two Tarni snugs pulled up beside Sert and Hella and extended their hands to grab on. Sert helped push Hella's awkward body up the side of the large beast, and he could feel her discomfort. She stumbled a few times climbing up, not to mention having to gracelessly swing one of her legs over to straddle the animal's back.

Sert frowned as he watched Hella struggle with her mount. He cracked a sympathetic smile and waited to get the okay from her before approaching his haze. He batted away the rider's extended hand and hopped up as if it were natural. He made a few adjustments, sat down comfortably and nodded to Lip.

Lip's haze stood on its hind legs, released a proud shriek, and took off leading the large group toward Tarni.

*

The jagged opening on the Pagan city wall was much larger than Hella expected. As they neared the huge crack that exposed the inside of the Tarni Pagan, she couldn't help but dwell on the devastation of it all. She could only imagine the lasting negative effects this devastated civilization had on its citizens; she was now starting to understand Sert's reasons for leaving.

Hella wondered how an entire civilization could destroy their own Pagan. The reality of the situation was hard to take in; she was trying to cope as best she could, but she found herself caught in quite an awkward situation. Concentrating on her feelings with the constant bouncing from the galloping haze was awkward. Fortunately, the ride was almost over as the pack went through the broken stone wall and into the Pagan city.

With the haze slowing its stride, Hella began to ease her grip after the group stopped in front of an aged temple-like structure in the middle of a large public square.

A sharp spear capped the top of a rounded structure surrounded by a vast array of overgrown and untrimmed red shrubs. Built out of large granite bricks, each layer of the fitted blocks was visibly eroded with signs of weather damage. Every brick on the outer layers of this building turned inward and resembled a half spherical shape as it ascended to the pinnacle above. The only welcoming aspect of this Pagan city's focal point was a stone staircase that angled upward from the ground and led to a rounded doorway. Hella's eyes were stuck on the open entranceway as she sat on the resting haze. Something suddenly came over her; she just didn't feel comfortable.

"You don't have to come in, Hella. You can just stay here," Sert proposed, standing on the ground next to her.

"Nonsense, Hella. You should come. It would be great if you came inside and met with our leader. Sert, don't be so rude. Don't you want to show her your roots?" interrupted Lip as he passed by. "You will learn a lot. I guarantee it."

Hella carefully dismounted the haze and hit the hard orange ground with both feet. She shook out a few kinks in her body and followed the group of Tarnis up the staircase to the entrance.

Hella peered inside the shadowy room, taking in the eeriness and distasteful setting. Circled around the dimly lit area stood a series of unfinished stone statues of former Tarni leaders. Ten solid black quartz carvings were only half completed, with signs of misshaped features and rough edges. They faced a wretchedly constructed white granite throne in the center of the darkened area. A thin beam of light shining down through the only skylight was all that illuminated the Tarni leader sitting slouched in his seat.

Carelessly lifting his half attentive head up from his relaxed position, Dredge's posture alone displayed one of the reasons behind this poorly managed civilization. Dredge appeared so uncaring and unmotivated even to address his new visitors that he could only raise his brow to welcome the group into his sanctuary.

"Hello, Dredge."

"What is it now, Lip? Will I have to get up?" answered Dredge, shrugging his shoulders. "We have company, I see. And who are these snugs? Especially the tall one? She's not from around here."

"Hella is her name, and you're right. She is a Terinian. They have both come a long way. How about you get up from your seat and address them hospitably?"

He darted his eyes away from Hella and glared at Lip.

"What did you say? Did you forget that *I* am *your* leader? I am not here to take advice from a subordinate. I believe that my actions are to be admired, not criticized. Do you understand me?" shouted Dredge, still unmoved from his position.

"Yes, I understand."

"Good. The last thing I want to hear from you is your opinion. You're lucky we're in the presence of company because otherwise, I'd be dealing with this backtalk a lot more harshly. And lucky for you, I'm in a good mood," shouted Dredge.

Turning his head away from Lip, the overzealous leader took his time sizing up Hella. He was fascinated with her and her origins. He smiled a courteous grin and asked her quite an intrusive question.

"What are you doing here, Terinian? I'd love to know about your civilization. Everything about it. What can you tell me?"

Hella immediately felt uncomfortable and turned her eyes towards Sert, hoping he'd take the attention off of her.

"And you. Who are you? What is your name?" asked Dredge, looking towards Sert.

"My name is Sert."

Dredge shot up from his seat and glared at Sert. "Sert? Really? Is that you? Ahh, nice to finally meet you. I always knew you were going to come back. No one else did, but I always had faith. And you even met a real Terinian. I'm surprised she's here," Dredge said playfully while approaching the pair and smiling with appreciation. "You are quite the couple!"

Sert's frost bump was dripping like a hose, and he tried to stay quiet for as long as possible. In an instant, his eye colour turned to black; he rubbed the top of his head before answering the Tarni leader.

"What do you want to know, Dredge?" he asked calmly.

"Anything and everything, Sert! Everything that *she* won't tell us. How about that?"

"As you probably know, Terin's Pagan is being run by Sal. And all of their citizens are focussing on the science of technological progression."

"Ok, that's a good start. I knew about Sal. But be more specific. What ideas are they working on? Any breakthroughs or anything we can steal and create ourselves? Tell me… tell me!"

"I didn't have that much time to research, to be honest. I was too busy raising my family. You see, I fell in love while I was there," said Sert, trying to cover his story.

"Half-breeds? Wow. How did they turn out?" asked Dredge with a chuckle. "But if I'm not mistaken, you did choose to be the one to leave Tarni and gather useful information from Terin. Isn't that right? We all expected you to return and give us at least something we could use. So let's hear it. You did do your job, didn't you?"

Hella's mouth lay wide open. Her spirit was crushed as the purity of her family history was once again tarnished. Even looking at Sert felt like torture. All his innocence and humility was a sham. Her only reaction was a quick shake of her head while her eyes reddened fiercely. She didn't say a word. Turning around and storming out of the building was enough to send a clear message to Sert.

All Sert could do was to lower his head in shame. He couldn't defend himself or his actions. He felt devastated, knowing he again deceived the only snug in his life who truly cared for him. And now Hella's trust, and most of all her love, the only value he had left in this world, was gone. He stood there, broken. There was nothing else he could do to harm his life partner. He took his punishment and looked back toward Dredge, who was wearing a sinister smile.

"Wow, Sert. I hope you were a better spy than you were a companion. Now, come on. What else do you have for us?"

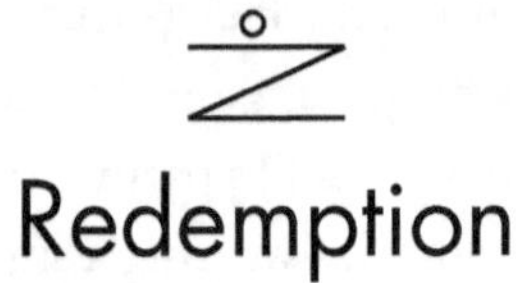

Redemption

From inside the Pagan tower, Sal sat on his pedestal and devoted his attention to a group of green society snugs, all standing in a circle and one yellow society snug in the middle. They all gazed up at the chief director, stuck in suspense, waiting for him to decide.

The idea approval process was always a nerve-wracking experience for snugs. Speaking before the board and delivering a formal request was a task no one enjoyed prepping for. The yellows prided themselves on being the finest presenters in Pagan and were always considered the best snugs for the job. However, this group in particular, was at a disadvantage. They were trying to submit a building design to the board, and their yellow was very young and underqualified.

Submitting a building proof was always a tough sell. All Paganers recognized the need for more free space in their overdeveloped city and knew it was difficult to gain authorization to build. Their planned structure would have been something to consider if the reason for its construction was justifiable.

Swaying his head from side to side, Sal weighed their idea. After tilting his head up to the ceiling, he waved his hand to his fellow leaders and asked for their advice; the panel was eager to share.

All the directors spoke up and out of turn. Their voices were deafening as they rose out of their seats, flailing their arms, sparking a heated debate.

Ret and his group watched from the back of the room, hoping this dispute wouldn't sour the crowd and hinder their chances of getting approval; they were up next.

"Everyone, calm down!" shouted Sal, smacking his hand against the top of his podium.

All the arguing stopped. The directors sat back in their seats and respectfully waited for Sal to mediate the discussion.

"There's too many talking at once. We'll get nowhere if everybody keeps this up. Blues? Seeing this group wants to build on your land, we'll start with you."

"Thank you, Sal," said the female blue society director. "First, please note that I have a very tough time believing and understanding your idea. It's far-fetched. To be clear, your idea is to observe the stars throughout our night season, which is only a couple of months out of our yearly calendar, and you, yellow, want to use this structure to study outer space. And our suns? Is that correct?"

She stared down at the yellow society snug, his bump dripping. Regrettably, the blue director was only the first of eight directors the yellow needed to convince.

"We all believe that there is something to learn from the outer reaches of our sky. Have you ever wondered if something or someone else was out there…"

"Out where? Out in the black nothingness?" the blue director rudely interrupted.

"Yeah. We want to try and discover if other beings are living on another planet. I mean, there must be something else out there."

The director displayed dissatisfaction as she listened further, closing her eyes and shaking her head.

"First off, get your thoughts together here, yellow. And second, every other civilization has studied the constellations for hundreds of years. We know all we need to know. I can't justify researching a subject totally irrelevant to our future vision."

"Alright, but…"

"There has been a lot of research on astronomy over the last few generations, young yellow. What makes this so different? It seems to me that we would be wasting time and resources on this project. Tell me what it is about the night sky that fascinates you?"

"Hear me out, everyone. Those stars are other suns. But they are very far away. Think of each one of those stars providing life for other beings just like us. Have you ever wondered about other beings living out there somewhere on another planet?"

Hit with a sudden epiphany, the female red society director stepped up from her podium and took over the conversation.

"Yes. I can see that being entirely plausible. It makes sense. The stars could be other suns way out in the distance. And you're saying that other beings could exist out there?"

"That is exactly what I'm saying," said the yellow excitedly. "This is a huge opportunity to expand our vision and understanding as a civilization. You have no idea how big this news could be if discovered. Does everyone get it now?"

"No, I still don't get it," replied the blue director.

"Ok, let me try and clarify," said the yellow. "If we find other life, this alone would be a breakthrough. Not just for Terin but for the entire world. We're going to take Kin's invention and expand on it. We plan on building a massive magnifier to see far into the dark sky. Not only are we going to build a tower, but we are also going to build a massive magnifying apparatus and install it at the top. This idea can lead to the biggest discovery we've ever witnessed," passionately explained the yellow while turning around and proposing his idea to everyone in the room.

"Alright, my turn." said the female yellow society director. "There's one aspect to this idea that we still haven't discussed. How do you propose we gather the materials needed to build such a tower? We have excavated almost all we can from Mount Nite. The resources for this project would take up a huge part of what's left up there. That is *my* biggest concern."

The room went quiet. Sitting back in his seat, a sceptical yellow director examined his young citizen as he stood baffled and scratching his head.

"Would this counsel not approve using only some of the remaining granite for a great idea?"

"For a great idea, we would," answered the yellow director. "However, this doesn't seem worth it in my eyes. We must be considerate and use what little we have left for practical projects. I think you did great with your presentation here, and I'm looking forward to seeing you back here, but I can't approve of it."

The young yellow held in his frustration. He wanted to burst out loud and try to sway their views one last time, but he didn't. The dispirited yellow snug smiled up to the yellow director, waved his hand to thank him, and turned towards Sal.

"Thank you, directors. I have heard enough and have made my final decision over this matter," announced Sal.

The group of greens gathered into a tight circle, and all linked arms around the yellow, standing in the middle of the floor. Giving the chief director their utmost respect, everyone stood proud, even though they knew what to expect.

"I hereby deny the request to build your observation tower," stated Sal.

Each member of the idea group bowed their head.

"The logistics and resources weighed heavily on this decision, my good team. I'm afraid the yellow directors are correct. We have very few resources left. Considering the size of your project and how it does not suit our ideals and future development, I cannot grant you this request. All rebuttals and appeals can be made at a later date and time. Do you understand?"

"No, I don't understand. This isn't fair! Our idea is cutting edge and will forever be…"

"Have this team escorted out immediately," instructed Sal, emotionless in his seat, cutting the awkward scene short. "Let's quickly move on to the next team in line."

Ret jumped into action. As he walked into the centre of the floor, his small team made up of a single snug from each of the coloured societies, followed close behind. The team stood in a disorderly cluster and waited for the chief to address them.

"Well, we have quite the disorganized team here, don't we? This should be interesting. I've never had a professional group begin their presentation without standing in a unified manner."

Looking at each group member, Sal was appalled when he spotted Ret standing before the panel.

"Ahh, that makes sense. I should have known the Tarni snug was a part of *this* group. Not a great first impression, Ret!"

The group's yellow society member stepped forward, ready to take over as presenter, but was stopped in her tracks by Ret's extended arm.

"Are you sure you want to present, Ret?" whispered the yellow.

"Yes, Trix. I have to do this."

This wasn't about what was best for the team. Ret knew having Trix deliver the presentation would give them much better odds for approval. This was about regaining his dignity and respect from the chief and everyone who had discouraged and abused him.

"Hello again, Sal. It has been a while, hasn't it?"

"Are you sure *you* want to be the one to present your group's idea, Ret? I wouldn't want you to spoil your entire team's chances because you're too stubborn to know your role in this."

Ret glanced around and ensured that everyone's attention was on him.

"Our idea that I'm proposing to you all today is something that is, first off, technologically groundbreaking…"

"Ret, I'm hoping for your team's sake that this is not about your global communication idea! Please don't do this to yourself again."

"Sal, Have you ever seen the environment outside during hibernation?"

"What?"

"The environment. Have you seen what it looks like during hibernation?"

"No, I haven't," answered Sal curiously, sitting back in his chair.

"Then I know something you don't, Sal."

The chief slapped his hands on the top of his white podium, and the sound echoed off every window and the high peaked roof.

"You think I'm going to take a comment like that from you, Ret? I don't know why I should let you and your team continue with this proposal. I've never been so insulted, and I won't tolerate it, especially from a half-breed like you."

"The ring," Ret spoke confidently.

"The what?"

"The planetary ring."

"What about it?" said Sal, still offended.

"I witnessed a breakthrough during our last hibernation season. Rox and her team saved my life…"

"I wonder why they would do such a thing."

"We're going to use the ring to send a broadcast across the planet. We already have the design to build a modulator to transmit the signal to the ring," Red proudly explained while pointing to the sky through one of the bay windows. "All that's left to do is set up a transmission station."

"And how big will this transmission station be?" asked Sal, intrigued by his theory.

"I'm guessing as big as or maybe bigger than the observation tower the last group was trying to get approved," said Ret mockingly. "About that big."

Sal put his head down in frustration then looked back up at Ret. This time, he was being sincere.

"Why are you wasting my time? Really, Ret. Have you not learned your lesson? Wasn't I absolutely clear? You know we have no spare resources, and you want us to give you a plot in our courtyard to build your idea?"

"No," Ret answered calmly.

"What do you mean 'no'?"

"It's already built."

"What? Where?"

Ret pointed out through the windows and towards the yellow society. Every snug in the room followed his finger and focused their sights on the copper tower on Mount Nite's peak. The large copper spear stretched from the mountain's summit, and, fortunately, it was aimed directly at the planetary ring.

"Alright, exactly what are you pointing at, and how is this part of your idea?" said Sal.

"Electrical currents," responded Ret. "Electrical currents can transmit sound decibels," responded Ret.

"What does that even mean?" asked Sal.

"Stop interrupting me, and let me finish," countered Ret.

Sal cut into the conversation, making quite the scene as he threw up his arms and shouted to Ret.

"Last chance, Ret! You better explain exactly how this idea works, or I will have your entire team escorted out."

Ret looked up at Sal, sitting frenzied on his podium. Taking a moment to collect his thoughts, he briefly closed his eyes and delivered what he wanted to hear.

"We plan on using the yellow society's tower to transmit a signal into the planetary ring, which will, in turn, broadcast it around the entire globe. Our idea will revolutionize the world and make you one of the most decorated chiefs in history."

Sal sat back down in his seat, a little calmer this time, and allowing Ret a real opportunity to prove himself.

"Since the last hibernation season, my group has worked hard on blueprints to build a signal transmitter. This device will be able to shoot a signal through the sky. If we hit the ring with our transmission, it should have enough energy to circle the world. We have found that generating enough voltage will provide all the energy to power a worldwide broadcast using the ring."

"Where did you learn this? And how do I know this is even feasible?" asked Sal.

"It's funny just how you learn certain things in life."

"Continue Ret." Sal insisted.

"I learned this by accident. Well, I hope leaving me outside during hibernation was an accident," said Ret, his words trailing off. "You can ask Rox and her group. They can all attest to the science behind this theory. I witnessed first-hand the bursts of static electricity known as light bolts. When they strike the planetary ring, the electricity runs worldwide along the ring's bands."

"You saw this with your own eyes?" asked the male red society director, standing up from his podium.

"Yes, I did," replied Ret after facing the director. "Now, copper is a terrific conductor of electricity, and thankfully, the planetary ring is all made up of small copper rocks. And we hope that when we electrify even one band on the ring, the electromagnetic energy will power the transmission around the globe."

"Hope?" questioned Sal.

"Trust me, Sal. It will work."

"Trust you... hmm. Well, I'm not convinced yet."

"The next objective is to build receivers that tune to the transmitted broadcast frequency. *These* are the devices that everyone will need in their possession to hear our communication. We have already developed a receiver. Simply put, it's a frequency tuner attached to a sound accelerator. It doesn't work to its fullest potential yet, but we know it will work. When we turn it on, we can only hear a static like sound. Noise, really. That tells us that it is working, ranging through the frequencies in the sky. We just have to transmit something for the receiver to pick up. So, once the connection is made between the transmitter and the receiver, you will be able to hear the voice of whoever is speaking into the transmitter. See, the signal will always be transmitting above us on the planetary ring, but the receiver is what fixes onto the signal."

"This seems like a…" Sal started to say.

"Great opportunity for both of us," interjected Ret.

Instead of saying anything rude or hurtful to the little Tarni snug, Sal forced out a light sarcastic chuckle and smiled after hearing Ret's idea. He now saw something in Ret that, at one time, he was certain he would ever see. It was hard for him to believe that after all the abuse this half-breed had taken since he entered into Pagan, he had persevered through it all and made quite the impression. Sal saw him in a new light and started showing Ret more respect.

"How long will it take your team to build the transmitter?"

"One year to a year-and-a-half, at most.."

"What types of materials will you need?"

"Just off the top of my head, we're going to need iron mouldings to build the casing of our transmitter, so I'll have to place an order with the green society metal workers with our design specifications. We'll need copper strands, solar panelling, and tools. I have a master list, and I can give it to the courtyard personnel as soon as you approve us," answered Ret, grinning.

Sal looked up to the ceiling again as he pondered his decision. Taking a long, drawn-out moment, he put his hand to his face and tapped his big blue finger over his mouth. He looked back down towards Ret's group, who were now walking into the middle of the floor in a straight uniformed line and staring up at him with conviction. Sal couldn't help but notice Ret was radiating with confidence.

"I haven't approved your idea yet," Sal insisted, holding back his acquiescing expression.

"Yes, you have, Sal. You just haven't said it yet," said Ret.

"Do you all concur?" asked Sal, looking around at his counsel.

Each member of Ret's group turned to face the directors, looking for anyone with a differing opinion. After a long silence, the group's excitement grew as the head nodding from the circle of directors confirmed their hopes. Sal also took their silence as a unanimous 'yes' and announced his final decision.

"I approve your group's request. You have been granted a courtyard plot and can commence your construction immediately. Well done!"

Don't Spoil the Moment

Ret ignored the melted frost dripping from his hunched over back as he worked inside the confined metal enclosure. He reached into his black tool pouch strapped around his hip, shuffled through the colourful assortment of handles, and fingered his options. He drew out a red fastening driver with one hand while holding up a shiny power inserter against the ceiling with the other. He fastened the equipment to the underside of the ceiling, twisting the driver and working his shoulder muscles to exhaustion. He grunted through the install with only one last pin to secure until the device was affixed.

He leaned against the wall in relief, wiped the back of his frost bump and shook the excess moisture off his hand. Staring out of his confined space, he prepared himself for the next and most demanding task. Everyone in his idea group stood in front of the metal cabinet, all waiting to activate this large piece of equipment.

"Remember, Ret, the electrical capacitors will be ruined if you spark it with a surge!"

Rony's unnecessary advice broke Ret's concentration, and he received an annoyed glare in response. After raising his arms in frustration, his restricted surroundings caused his hands to smack into the thick iron casing just above his head.

"Ow!" screamed Ret, adding to his irritation. "I know, Rony, I know! Remember, we were the ones that discovered the theory behind voltage controlled capacitors. But it was *me* that designed it. I think I know what I'm doing here."

Ret's entire team looked at him, unmoved by his response. His irrational tendencies were just something they had grown accustomed to.

"Just a friendly reminder, that's all! You don't have to be so bossy," answered Rony in an apprehensive tone.

"I know. I'm sorry," said Ret. "I'm just tired and anxious. I need this to work. Alright, let's get this thing started up. I'm hoping the power is charged."

Inside the iron enclosure were two open leads, suspended on a hook, fabricated from solid copper. The cables ran along the ceiling, clipped in place and connected to the positive and negative terminals on an electrical generating station built on the outer wall of the enclosure.

"Did anyone take a second look at the solar energy absorbers? Are the connections outside all dressed and in good working order?" asked Ret.

One of his green society group members climbed up to the side to double-check the connections. He wiped off the glass panelling secured to the roof using a soft cloth. He inspected the equipment to make certain that the connections were fastened down and in functioning order. After polishing all the bonded points, he gave Ret the go-ahead.

"Everything is in good shape, Ret. But keep in mind the electrical capacitors will be ruined if you spark it with a surge." chuckled the green.

"You're going to make him explode, Tre," said a blue group member, roaring with laughter. "We came all this way, we did all this work, and now you're going to make Ret keel over."

"Yeah, remember when the courtyard commissioners came over and asked about our progress, and Tre said to him, 'Yeah... well, just be glad we're getting some work done today,' " shouted Trix from the left side of the bunch. "I thought Ret was going to lose it."

"I know. The commissioner was so serious, too. No sense of humour at all." added Rony. "He even threatened to shut us down because he thought we weren't taking this seriously."

Everyone except Ret was swapping funny comments and amusing anecdotes, trying to keep the morale within the group light and airy.

"Yeah, and then Rony, you mocked him, saying how much you respected his opinion and how we couldn't do any of this without his guidance," laughed Tre, "all with a quirky smile on your face."

"What can I say? I'm the reason we're still here." answered Rony.

Waves of laughter overcame the group. Everyone was in great spirits, enjoying the moment.

"I don't know what it is, Rony, but you sure don't make it dull around here." smiled Ret as he approached the amused group.

"Well, Ret, just ensure you don't spark those capacitors with a surge!" Rony quipped in a playful tone.

"I won't."

Enjoying the cheerful ridicule, Ret and his group took a moment to relax before they put their efforts to the test. There was a lot to celebrate. This group was on the verge of building the first signal transmitter and taking their first steps toward making history. A little amusement to ease the tension was just what this group needed.

For a brief moment, Ret forgot about his stress, his obligations, and all the pressure he put on himself and his crew. He looked up into the sky when he felt the team was ready and shouted out loud.

"Alright, let's do this! Let's make the connection!"

The team moved into position, and Ret walked back inside the transmitter, turned around while inside the compartment, pulled down the two opposing leads from their hanging location, and secured his feet.

"Here goes nothing!" shouted Ret.

Attaching the positive bonds to the power inserter device was an easy connection. However, Ret and his group were worried about installing negative poles because these involve electrons. Any shift in the current or a sudden amplitude burst would destroy the internals of their prototype. Ret braced himself after polishing the end of the lead with a cloth. His hand hovered over the negative input. Ret wanted to connect the device, but uncertainty began to race through his body.

He held tight to the copper lead, anxious to make the connection. There was so much on the line for him, and after going over all his mental checks he began doubting himself. Transfixed, he reviewed the design procedures in his head and ensured that his group had followed all the right steps. But really, this was merely a cover to what he was thinking deep down inside.

The project details were, of course, a concern, but fear was holding him back. He was terrified. The risk of failure was stopping him from going forward. After putting in so much effort and gaining his peers' respect, he dreaded nothing more than being seen as a failure.

He was reminded of the events of his past and knew firsthand how devastating failure could be to his image and, more importantly, his spirit. And as he stood there, muffling out the sounds of his group members shouting over him, Ret couldn't help but think about how he would handle the outcome. The obligation to his team and the reputation he built were all at stake here. He just couldn't do it himself. It was just too much to handle. Luckily, a hard and comforting slap on his shoulder from Rony was all he needed to regain his focus.

"Alright, Ret. Let's do this. We're all here with you."

Ret's inner hesitancy started to melt away; he saw this moment as an opportunity, not a gamble. Ret looked back at his friend and steeled himself. He turned back to his task, closed his eyes, pushed his hand forward, and finally made the connection.

A loud resonating hum sent a wave of relief through his body, and a huge grin appeared. In a state of euphoria, he turned to face the rest of his idea group, who were all happily staring back at him. He ducked his head, hopped out of the grey steel compartment and joined his team.

Everyone showered their praise on Ret as they all celebrated their new invention. A sense of compassion fell over the group, and in this blissful moment everyone made wisecracks and poked fun at their past challenges and misunderstandings. But they each showed their utmost respect toward the group's journey.

"It works… It works!" exclaimed Ret. "I want to thank each and every one of you for all your dedication thus far, not to mention for putting up with me this whole time. That must have been the hardest part." he joked. "It sure wasn't easy, was it? Don't get me wrong, it's still far from over, but we managed—as a team—to get to this point, and I know everything else from here on out can be accomplished if we stick together. Thank you all for putting in this effort. We all deserve it! Next, we need to climb this thing up Mount Nite, connect it to the tower and shoot our transmission right into the sky!"

Feeling wildly optimistic, everyone raised their arms and released a roaring cheer. Their eyes all followed Ret's pointing hand up beyond the thick glass of the courtyard enclosure and onto the yellow society's copper tower set atop one of the tallest peaks on Mount Nite. Enthusiastic for the next and final phase in completing their idea, everyone felt the same as Ret and were ecstatic to take on the next challenge.

The sight of the large copper tower was not the only thing the group focused on. Stealing everyone's good spirit was Terri leaning against the entrance doorway, wearing an arrogant little smile.

"Hey, everyone. How is your idea going so far? Look at all of you just grinding it out. Giving your all for this great and wonderful Pagan system. It's all going to pay off, isn't it? And you are all going to be so famous. I bet you all just can't wait." smarmed Terri loudly in a very sarcastic tone.

Ret was shocked. This was the first time he had even looked at her since the incident, and there she was, slouching over, uncaring, smug and unapologetic. Her presence alone stifled all his good feelings, replacing them with a wave of loathing anger. He wanted to scream and rip into his sister, but all that came out was a short, irritated, pointed comment.

"What are you doing here?"

Terri carelessly pushed herself up from her leaning position and faced her brother.

"I'm here to tell you something. And only because you're my brother, Ret. I'm starting a new society to stand up against Sal. Every snug inside this Pagan that feels persecuted, misunderstood, or unaccepted can be a part of *our* organization," announced Terri as she entered the courtyard. "And because you are my family, I'm giving you and your friends an opportunity to be a part of our black society before it's too late. If you wait and resist what *my* organization stands for, I won't be able to help you later."

"Family? Family, Terri? Did you forget what *you* did?" screamed Ret. "You are not welcome around here, Terri. And I can't believe you have the audacity to try and force your way onto this group. Get out of here!"

"I *had* to use your hibernation chamber. I realize it put you in a dangerous spot, but I had to survive for good reasons. I am here to help all of you. My team is fighting for equality. Pagan is not fair. And snugs every day get discouraged because they cannot pursue what they want to do. *I'm* going to stop Sal and his directors. They will no longer have the power to judge us and be the ones to disapprove of our creativity. Look at our reputation, Ret. Aren't you angry about what Sal has done to you?"

"You want to change the order of Pagan? Whatever Terri. I don't have time for this. Now leave!" screamed Ret.

"Ret. Our numbers are growing, and I'm finding a lot of snugs inside Pagan that feel the same way I do. Sal has too much power, Ret. Don't you find it unjust to let one snug decide what's best for all of us? We should decide what's best for Pagan. All of us should have a say in our destiny. It's too much power for one snug."

"Grow up, Terri! Some things are not fair! Get used to it! You are such a weak snug. *You* are what's wrong with this Pagan. Go away, you puss bag and stop trying to influence my team."

Scowling back at her brother with fierce red eyes, Terri raised her arms above her head and exploded in retaliation.

"I'm what's wrong with Pagan? No, Ret, it's Sal. He's the problem. Plus, you are my family. How can you not agree with me?"

"You wanna talk about family? You disgraced our family. You disgraced Mom and Dad, and you disgraced your own image and reputation. I hope you're happy with what you've done and what you're doing. For the last time, leave now and don't ever come back! I ought to call our courtyard commissioners and have them escort you out."

"I know you are angry about what I did to you, but I had no other choice, Ret. Why can't you understand that?"

"You left me outside and stole my hibernation chamber! And now you want to try and change everything Pagan stands for because you feel it's unfair, Terri?"

Ret calmed his anger. He stepped closer to his sister and using all his inner strength tried to reason with her.

"Stand for something good, Terri. You have the power to make a change in your life. I started inside Pagan in the exact same horrible state you did. But I decided *not* to leave this place the same way. *You* have to make that change and believe in yourself, regardless of our past, because trust me, it will destroy you if you don't."

Ret's speech fueled her anger. She wondered what it was that turned Ret into such a coward. She instantly rejected his cheap and awkward lecture after realizing her plan would not include her brother. She glared at him, and turned her back. Before Ret could say anything else, she ran out of the courtyard plot, continuing her search for others to follow her beliefs.

∞

Now I'm Angry

Hella frowned as she gazed upon the Tarni resident home, now shabby and worn. Once an imposing and robust structure, it blended in with the rest of the neighbourhood's dilapidated properties. The foundation was in disrepair, the siding was partially torn off the frame, and the once reliable and flat roof was now tattered and buckled.

Hella paced back and forth. She closed her eyes, recited the words in her head, and finally nodded in agreement; she was ready to tell Sert how she felt. Hella approached the home with a sense of eagerness. She raced up the broken walkway and opened the faded yellow front door.

Barging into the main room, she surprised Sert and watched him spin around in shock. Hella was so keen on being the first to speak that she didn't notice Sert place his hand over his mouth.

"Hello, Sert. I have a few things to say to you, so listen before you interrupt. Things have been tough between us for a while now. Between your lies and, well, finding out about your lies and how they destroyed our entire family, I think I deserve a real answer. You need to tell me right now if there are any more things I need to know about, or else I'm leaving."

Sert looked up at her, mystified. He tried to act sober for the ensuing conversation, but his psychedelically fuddled mind took over. Before he could think of a way to hide his face, the harmful truth spewed out his mouth in the form of white mist.

He tilted his head upward and turned it from side to side to blow every bit of water vapour away from his body. Sert's imagination was racing, pushing away his high and trying to be sober, knowing his interrogation was imminent. He looked down to the ground and tried to take back control.

Hella was appalled. She glared down at Sert sitting on the torn-up couch, furious with the pitiful scene before her.

"You're sitting here taking shots of water? Are you serious? You have ruined everything in my life! And now I'm stuck with *you* in *this* horrible place? And what do you have to show for yourself? You're taking water shots, doing nothing to help yourself or even apologize to me for what you've done!"

She was screaming as loud as she could, erupting on Sert, sitting hunched over on one side of the couch.

"Answer me!"

Sert fought the intoxication and mustered up a response. However, only a slurred mixture of half-pronounced words came out of his mouth. And as for his face, the "high" forced an uncontrollable smile as he looked back at her; Hella was infuriated.

"Who do you think you are, Sert? You puss bag! You are going to pay for what you've done to me."

Looking at him with bright red eyes, Hella waited for a response, but Sert could only focus on trying to keep his balance. Keeling over to one side, he fell on the hard, uneven floor and began laughing hysterically. Hella shook her head in utter disgust and headed back out of the open doorway.

After Sert came to, he shook his head and got up from his contorted position, brushing away the orange sand from his body. Realizing the situation, he regained some of his composure and glanced at the open front door.

He burst out of the house, raced down the rubble filled walkway, and stopped at the end of the sandy road, unsure which way he should go. Turning his head from side to side, he peered to the left side of the dusty roadway and recognized the small image of Hella running off in the distance. He shook his body one last time to force out all the effects of the water and raced off in her direction.

Hella soon found herself running short of frost and, regrettably, had to stop. She cupped the bottom of her frost bump with her hand to gather all the melted nitrogen as it dripped down her back, and poured it back over her bump.

She was standing directly in the middle of a dirt road intersection with four identical buildings planted at each corner of the junction. As she looked around, she observed a number of Tarni snugs nonchalantly walking around this communal area, all conversing with each other.

The buildings on each corner were built on top of a square foundation, and each was topped with a rounded roof that featured a long spear centred on the tip of these once magnificent properties.

Resembling the Tarni theme in more ways than one, these four buildings had also suffered from major wear and erosion. Hella's new resident city was becoming a living terror. Everywhere she looked, buildings were in shambles, and everyone she encountered seemed to be living a dispirited existence—something she was not accustomed to.

"Hella!"

Hella stood in the intersection with her back to Sert. She could hear his erratic footsteps gaining on her. She wanted to run, but there was nowhere to go. Just like everyone else around her, she was stuck in her own despair. She stood frozen to the spot and closed her eyes.

"I'm really sorry about that. But it wasn't all my fault. Come on? Are you really that angry? You can't blame me for doing some water occasionally," he pleaded. "I mean, you do it too, you know. It's unfair to get mad at me because you walked in at a bad moment."

Hella twisted her head to the side and slowly turned around, peering into Sert's dumbfounded expression.

"You have got to be kidding me, Sert! After everything our family has dealt with because of you, you can't even bring yourself to apologize."

"What would you have me do, Hella? You can see around you, can't you? I think it's pretty evident why I wanted to leave. I don't know if you noticed, but life on the other side of the world was just a little bit better than here."

Their dispute gathered the attention of some passing Tarni snugs who quickly encircled the arguing pair.

"You've got some nerve, Sert. Do you realize the sacrifices our family has made because of you? You are so selfish. Our children are tainted and going through problems I can only imagine. And me? Having to leave my home and be forced to spend my final years living in Tarni, of all places."

"You didn't have to leave Terin, Hella. It was your choice."

"You told me during our journey here that you wanted to leave Tarni. You told me in your words that you *had* to leave this place because it was too horrible to live here. But that was all a lie! Sert, you came to Terin to spy on us. Do you hear what I just said? You were chosen to spy on me and my civilization! Who are you, Sert?" She screamed. "And you're wondering why I'm upset that you're drinking water and doing nothing to help your own civilization? Not only that, but you're trying to get *me* to understand *your position*? Oh, trust me, Sert. I understand! You have no consideration for Ret and Terri, or for me. It's pretty clear that all you care about is yourself!"

Sert dropped his chin and his shoulders. He wanted to find anything to comfort Hella and help put her mind at ease, but it was too late. Standing before a large crowd of his fellow Tarnicians, he looked into Hella's fiery red eyes and listened carefully to her rant.

"Do you think I will stand by you after you lied to me? Well, I'm not! Not to mention—look at this place! This city is wretched! Look around, Sert. Why haven't any of you Tarnis done anything to help your cause?" shouted Hella, spinning around and raising her frustrated arms to all the spectators. "You can all see what I'm seeing. But you would rather live in these broken homes, downing water shots and feeling sorry for yourself."

"Now, wait a moment," interrupted Sert. "It's not my fault things are the way they are around here. You know what happened here. I don't think you understand what it was like for all of us when we had to watch our own Pagan getting destroyed. And watching our parents doing it! Do you think we can all just go back to normal? It takes time to mend the problems we all faced as a society all those years back. I left, yes. Even if it was for the wrong reasons. But I wanted a better life, Hella, and I did what I thought was right."

Hella shook her head in disappointment and took in all the ill-mannered and rude comments from the large circle of Tarni citizens around her.

"That wasn't the right thing to do, Sert! You think that running away is the answer? You think abandoning your problems will make them go away? You have no idea, do you? Even when times were good between us, you never tried fixing our problems. You just forgot about it and pretended that nothing had happened. Well, it's time for you to smarten up. Sert, I'm done with you and your selfish ways."

"What do you mean you're done with me? This is your last year. Are you never going to talk to me again? Really? And where are you going to go, Hella? You can't just run away now."

Hella's eyes were bright red, her brow crunched down, and her shoulders were tense. She stepped close to Sert, put her hands on both his shoulders, and pressed her face against his blue cheek. Firmly holding onto his body, she whispered her final words.

"I'd rather run away and live in the cold orange sandy desert than spend any more of my time here in this worthless place next to you. You have ruined my last years, Sert. You have ruined our children's lives back home. And you will pay for everything you've done. Now get away from me."

She shoved him hard. Sert took a few steps back and was about to respond, but it was too late. Hella turned around in her spot and marched through the hostile crowd of Tarnis, ignoring their comments. The last thing she cared to do was apologize to all these unsympathetic Tarni snugs. Hella ran away from the mob as fast as she could, down the sand filled roadway and away from everyone.

—∘•—

Compromise

Hella kept her eyes pointed down on the sandy ground. She was dragging her feet as she wandered around the inner perimeter of the Pagan wall. At times she pulled her head up and looked around, but the images of Tarni reinforced the feeling of despairing pain inside her. She stood tilting her head to one side, shoulders slumped, unimpressed with her forlorn surroundings.

Every standing structure was visibly damaged and neglected without any type of upkeep or maintenance. The outdated architecture added to the distasteful appearance throughout the area; the building styles were so old-fashioned they resembled structures built before her birth.

Adding to the aged appearance were many noticeable areas of stress and erosion. She focused on one building in particular set off in the distance. Every stone block was eroded from the foundation up, leaving four corroded pillars holding up the roof riddled with hundreds of small holes.

She shook her head and turned away. What was it, she thought, what could cause an entire civilization to end up like this? As she made her way further inside Pagan, she discovered the answer.

Built out from the base of the Pagan wall was a long chain of seating areas, each distinguished by a worn-out cloth overhang and personalized by a different colour and design. She strolled from partition to partition and kept her eyes focused on every apathetic Tarni snug lazing around and doing absolutely nothing. The one thing they had in common was their feckless attitude and thick white mist expelling from their opened mouths. She vigorously waved the excessive mist away from her disgusted face.

Reaching the end of the line, Hella stopped, turned around, and looked back. Puffs of white mist rose from underneath the shadowy edge of each overhang. She stood with her mouth wide open and shaking her head, stunned by these young dispirited snugs with their wasted lives.

"It's quite the problem around here, isn't it? Hey, you there. I'm talking to you."

Hella half turned her head and saw an elderly female with attentive blue eyes and a half-hearted grin.

"I guess you're not from around here, are you?" asked the elder Tarni.

"What makes you think that?" answered Hella as she turned her body fully around to face the seated snug.

"Well, you're standing there, appalled at seeing what's happening with our younger generation. Plus, you're taller than me—and any other female Tarni, for that matter."

Hella looked down at her body and chuckled before reconnecting with her new acquaintance.

"What's your name?" asked the intrigued snug.

"Hella."

"Well, Hella. Have a seat."

From behind the brown table, the elder Tarni extended her arm with an open hand directing her invitation to a small rickety looking chair across from her. Hella momentarily paused questioning her gesture, before stepping under the white and orange striped overhang and pulling out the offered seat.

"As I said, it's quite the problem," said the elder female.

"There seems to be a lot of this happening, problems."

Hella bent her knees and parked herself on the wobbly chair. She crossed her arms over her chest, stared into the face of the elder, and listened closely as she began to speak again.

"There's no motivation and drive with these young snugs anymore. Honestly, I don't know how we'll ever return to being a productive civilization with how things are going. Something big has to happen. Really big."

Right away, the elder caught Hella's attention. She reassuringly uncrossed her arms and placed them down on the table. Hella was about to ask her to go into more detail on the subject, but the elder began to explain.

"They all just sit around and do nothing but socialize and take shots of water. No motivation to do anything. No drive; just a bunch of wasted talent. If I knew this was how the future would turn out, I never would have helped my parents tear down our Pagan. It's ironic when you think something is for the best, but it actually turns out for the worst," she said.

"You can say that again."

"The more time that goes by, the harder it will be to return to being a productive society again. I really could go on talking about this all day, Hella. And I'm sure you aren't here in Tarni for a good reason. So tell me, why are you here? One upsetting story should always be compared to another. And it looks like you have quite a story."

"Oh, it's upsetting alright, and well, very complicated. I'm not sure I want to get into all of it. It's not going to leave a good impression."

"Please, Hella. Look around. Do you realize where you are?"

Hella nodded her understanding at the elder's signal as she pointed her open hand toward the malaise around them.

"Well, it's just that I'm finding out after all this time that I never really knew my other. He kept everything a secret from me. Everything. And now I realize I spent half my life with a stranger."

"Where are you from, Hella?"

"Terin."

"You're from Terin? What are you doing here? As much as I don't like saying this, you snugs are the best. Your civilization is the most productive of the entire world. I would give anything to be a Terinian."

"What's your name?"

"Gini."

"Well, Gini, not all of us Terinians are who you think we are. And don't let our nationality fool you. My other was banished, and I can never show my face there again, thanks to him."

Gini crossed her arms over her chest and sat back in her seat, letting Hella lead the conversation.

"We ruined our children's reputation just two months before they left for Pagan. And I can only imagine what they've had to go through," Hella said, shaking her head and looking down at the ground. "That's what makes me feel the most guilty. Our Paganers aren't going to be too kind to…"

"Half-breeds," interrupted Gini. "So you're Sert's other, aren't you?"

Hella pulled her head up to face Gini and slowly nodded her head.

"Wow. Now it's starting to make sense. I was wondering why he returned after all this time. We all thought he had moved on to a better life. How did they find out who he was?"

"We were part of the red society."

"Red society?" prompted Gini.

"Yes, the red society. Everyone in Terin has to, well, choose to be part of one particular society. There are four in total that divide our civilization."

Gini hung onto every word while Hella explained Terin's social structure. She was astonished to learn how organized and focused Hella's society was in comparison; her wide-open green coloured eyes communicated her amazement.

"Sert made a deal with the chancellor for our children's futures. That puss bag. Once the chancellor confronted Sert about his origins, he wanted to expel all of us immediately. So Sert felt he had no choice and gambled our future on Ret winning the competition. He came in second place. And he could have won."

Gini sat hunched over and reached out to Hella's hands resting motionless on top of the table and rubbed them, trying her best to comfort her.

"So? If Ret lost the competition, why isn't he here with you, too?"

"Because he's smart, and like any other Terinian, he deserves to be there. He saved himself and his sister by answering a tough question on the spot. Dek, one of the chancellors, saw Ret's true potential right then and let my children into Pagan. However, everyone inside Pagan knows them as half-breeds. And to be honest, I've worried about them every day since we left. I suspect they are living a tough life inside our Pagan, especially Terri. She was always a very emotional child. I hope for her sake that she grew up strong."

"Yeah,"

"The biggest problem now is that I don't know how to talk to Sert anymore. We have grown so far apart. Whenever I look at him, I'm constantly reminded of his lies. There is nothing good about him anymore. All the things I used to love about Sert are gone. I just don't know anymore."

Gini sat stunned for a moment as she stared back at Hella. There was a time when Hella would try to put on a happy face no matter the situation, but this time was different and she didn't care who saw it. She chuckled, but it was clear she was feeling distraught.

Gini was concerned. She wanted to say something that could possibly cheer her up. She scrambled to get a few thoughts together and faced Hella, ready to say her piece, but right before Gini could speak, she was interrupted by her children.

"Mom. We need some more water. Everyone else ran out," shouted a young teenage snug.

With an annoyed expression, Gini turned away from Hella and answered her son standing to the left side of the table.

"Kreg, can you think of anything better you can do with your time? I don't want to keep giving you and your sister water shots. All you do is just sit around and drink all day. And don't interrupt me like that again. Can you not see I'm speaking with somebody else right now?"

Her daughter curtly rolled her eyes and slammed her hands down on the opposite side of the table.

"Oh, sorry for interrupting Mom! I don't know why you need to make this so difficult. We need more water, and you have an entire bottle behind you. Plus, my friends are all out as well. And we owe them. So, come on, Mom. We have to pay them back."

"Alright, you two. If I give you two another few shots, you have to promise me that you will get working on an idea of your own."

"Fine," screamed her son standing impatiently on her left.

"I'm serious. You need to start taking control of your life."

"Yes, we know, Mom. Now just give us the water," shouted her daughter.

Gina pulled up a large insulated bottle from behind her chair and placed it on her lap. Without any courtesy, both children held out smaller bottles and opened the lid. Gini moved the bottle down to the middle of the table, stood up from her seat and unscrewed the circular opening.

As she began tilting the bottle as both children acted like infants, fighting over which one would be served first. Kreg overpowered his sister and pushed her behind him so he could be served first.

"Quick, now. Seal it up before it freezes."

"Yeah, we know, Mom. We're not new at this."

"Remember what I said about starting an idea."

Both children tightened the tops of their bottles and scurried off without any gratitude or appreciation. Gini shook her head in shame and placed the large insulated container back behind her seat. She tried to avoid her guilty feelings by shaking her head, but Hella saw right through her charade and glared back at Gini.

"Are you serious?"

"I know, Hella. And I hate myself for it every time I give in. But they are my children, and deep down, I want them to be happy."

"Well, they don't look very happy to me."

"They don't know what happiness is. They have no idea what life is all about, and as you can see, a whole generation of them are just wasting away."

"You're not helping their cause. And soon, we're both going to be gone. And then how will they cope? You said to yourself you want things to change around here."

Both of Gini's aged blue hands slammed firmly on the table. She got up out of her seat in a fit of fury. Offended by Hella's direct comments, she shook her head a few times before responding.

"I know, Hella! I know. We were the ones that believed our parents were doing the right thing when they destroyed the wall. We were the ones that believed in the change. And most of all, I realize now that we've all turned into a stubborn and selfish society that cares only about ourselves. I wish I could take it all back. I do. But I can't, Hella. What's done is done."

Hella slowly moved her head from side to side and stared at Gini.

"Just because something like this happened does not mean it can't be fixed or undone. You *all* need to have faith. Forget about the past. It's not about that anymore. You're right. What's done is done. But a new beginning always starts with one step, and it doesn't matter how old or hard you think it will be. If you believe in it, it's simply worth doing."

Gini closed her eyes and hesitated for just a moment before she opened them again. She stared deep into Hella's face and articulated something she needed to hear.

"Well, Hella. You're absolutely right. And if it's worth it for me to fix my situation, then wouldn't it be worth it for you to fix yours? Wasn't there more to Sert than just being a spy? Maybe he did want to change and start over, and it didn't matter to him how he got out of here, just as long as he did. We are both in our last year of living, Hella. You and Sert are both the same age. Do you want to spend your last year hating him or forgiving him? You can re-discover the good inside him again if you let yourself. The big thing for you is to try and understand the changes he made in his life."

Hella contemplated her advice and wondered if there was anything between her and Sert she could hold onto.

"I get it, Hella. We both have huge problems to fix. And I know that it's a lot easier said than done. So how about I make a deal with you? If you try and fix your problem, then I will too. Is that a deal?"

"I don't know, Gini. It's not that easy. Sert will have to show me that he can change, or else I won't be able to see the good inside of him. I'll only be reminded of all the bad."

"You're right. He needs to change. We *all* need to change. You know, Hella, I knew Sert years ago, and if he's anything like he was when he was younger, I can tell you that *he* can change for the better and lead others to change as well. If there is anyone that can be inspired to change things around here, it's Sert."

"I hope so, Gini, I hope so."

Congratulations

Thousands of Paganers were packed around a wide circular stage in the blue society's centre. The flawless construction was highlighted as white stone interlocking bricks bordered the outer perimeter and glimmered in the sunlight. Elevated just above the heads of the surrounding audience, the stage provided a perfect vantage point over the crowd, who at the moment were cheering on eight group members standing atop the smooth polished platform.

Ret, with his team, looked out to the enormous group of snugs, bowing and waving to their supporters. Rolls of colourful streamers were being launched upward into the sky from a number of individuals in the audience, and handfuls of glitter were being hurled up, forming small puffs of sparkling dust that shimmered in the sun. Taking in the festivities, Ret spotted one streamer with his eye and watched as the spool uncoiled and snaked its way down toward the crowd, only to be thrown back up.

A massive ceremonial geyser hole provided a serene backdrop behind the stage. The perimeter of the cavern, dwarfing the stage in front, was constructed with thick white granite blocks encircling the hole. At the moment the geyser sat dormant; however, sounds of sonorous hollow whistles hummed from inside the chasm, a sure sign an eruption was imminent.

Adding to the aesthetic, four distinct and beautifully designed buildings stood tall behind the geyser. Erected perfectly offset on either side of the geyser, these structures were built in the blue society's renowned corkscrew design. Each one was topped with a high peaked roof and illuminated in their distinctive blue colour, affirming this location as the perfect venue for commemorative festivities inside Pagan.

Sal marched onto the stage, waved his hands down, approached the microphone at the centre, and tapped on the capsule.

"Ret, we are all standing here today because of you and your team."

The crowd erupted, and Sal again waited for the audience to settle.

"What an accomplishment," shouted Sal. "I'll never forget the day you and your team connected the transmitter to the ring. I was watching you from my podium using my magnifying eye-rod. I was so nervous watching you. I thought you were going to plummet," said Sal as he turned towards Ret, harbouring a crafty smile. "You didn't fall in the slightest, though. You rose right to the top."

Ret smiled as he listened to Sal, still in shock. He looked out to the crowd, cheering on his team, and he soaked in all their recognition. Accepting their praise, Ret took advantage of the adulation, raised his arms and lifted his hands, charging up the crowd and watching them deliver a unified cheer.

Savouring the moment, Ret closed his eyes and drifted back to the day his team made history. It was like he was back there.

"Hold on tight, Ret. Whatever you do, don't let go of that cable," shouted Rony.

Strapped near the tip of the copper tower, built on the summit of Mount Nite, above the Pagan city, Ret grasped his hands onto a thick copper cable and planted his legs firmly on the edge of the smooth tower surface. Seated in a horizontal position, he faced the sky and squinted his eyes, trying to block out the glaring sun as he carefully made his way down, spiralling the cable around the tower as he descended.

"Wrap it tight, Ret. We need a good connection. And remember to keep it evenly spaced," shouted Rony from the tower's base.

"Yeah, I know, Rony. Just let me do this," screamed Ret.

Another enormous cheer pulsed from the audience, dragging Ret out of his daze. He peered over to Sal, having fun with his crowd, pumping them up at every chance.

As for Ret, he chuckled over the memory, glanced over towards Rony and shot him a beaming smile. Rony gave him one in return.

"I was worried about you, Ret, climbing to the top of that tower. All of my directors were cringing, " said Sal. "I was so relieved when you made it back down."

Ret nodded his head and smiled. And as Sal continued his speech, Ret couldn't help but fade back into his memory again.

"Wow, Ret. You actually made it down. Good thing. Our idea would've been ruined if you fell. Plus, we'd miss you, too." chuckled Rony. "Now, connect the power cable to the transmitter, turn it on, and get off this mountainside. I hate heights."

"Yeah, let's get this thing hooked up," answered Ret. "Alright, all the connections are on the back. Wish me luck."

"Good luck to you, Ret. I'll keep an eye on you."

Due to the limited space on the summit of Mount Nite, the cabinet was installed on the edge of the tower's small stone foundation. It was fastened with study lag bolts and secured to the base of the tower with a tightly wrapped chain; there was no risk of it coming loose. However, Ret needed to get to the power ports on the other side of the cabinet, and there was only one way around.

The team had no choice but to fix the cabinet to only one-half of the foundation, leaving one side of the cabinet hanging over the cliff's edge. Unfortunately, Ret was given the risky task of swinging around the cabinet to reach the other side,

He stood in panic on the cliff's edge, visualizing his plan. He noted his hand placements, footing and body positioning, acting out every movement in his mind; his bump was drenched. Ret did one last mental check, reached for some courage deep within, wiped his back and began his traverse.

With one shaky hand, he took a tight hold on the top edge of the transmitter casing and, with the other, clenched the end of the thick copper cable as his feet dangled thousands of feet over the yellow society.

"You got this, Ret!"

With his body suspended, he inched his way across; he was in control and confident until he felt his grip loosen. Despite mentally preparing himself, he realized that he had forgotten to dry his hands after wiping his back, causing his fingertips to slip.

"No," he screamed.

Ret dug his fingers into a vent hole on the roof as tight as he could. He frantically rushed along the face of the cabinet, using his knees to help guide him.

He had no other choice; it was either hurry or die. His frost bump was sweating profusely, dripping down his back, off his body and down to the yellow society below his feet. He swayed his torso back and forth in one last effort, grasping the copper cable with a death grip. He built up just enough momentum, and as he swung forward, he pinpointed his landing spot and released his hold.

Ret hit the ground and dropped to his knees. Taking a moment, he spread his body, face down and gratefully patted the surface beneath him. He opened his eyes and stood up; his legs trembled as he returned to his feet.

"Tre? I'm back here. When I give you the signal, turn on the power supply and hope for the best.

Ret gathered his melted frost with his cupped hand and splashed it in his face. He shook his head and focused on the main output in the centre of the machine. He quickly dressed the end of the cable and clamped it to the port. By now, he was physically and mentally exhausted and didn't even take a moment to admire his work before shouting over to Tre, waiting in position.

"Alright, Tre. Hit it!"

Another eruption of roaring applause pulled Ret back from his reminiscence. He began to cheer with the crowd and raised his arms to the sky, motivating them to roar even louder. As Ret looked at the audience, he pinpointed Rox standing near the front of the crowd cheering with the rest. She glanced up with an inviting gaze and smiled. Ret stared back down with glossy green eyes, raised his brow and conveyed an alluring grin.

Stress, anxiety, and the pressure to succeed were now a thing of the past. Not only was Ret celebrating this accomplishment with Terin and the world, he realized that he had redeemed himself and his spirit. It was his resiliency he was proud of, his tenacity, and most of all, the drive he maintained to never give up on his dreams. However, the one thing he cherished the most, was now, after all his time in Pagan that hardened shell he wore to protect against all the spiteful, vengeful and hateful snugs was beginning to wane. He was ready to start putting his trust in others again.

"I remember the moment you turned on the power to your transmitter, Ret," announced Sal. "We were all huddling around the recie…. What do you call it again?"

"Receiver box."

"Receiver box! Yeah, that's it. I knew it would work because as soon as you turned on the power, the sound went from a rustling static sound to silence. And not a moment later, we heard your first groundbreaking words: 'We just made history.'"

Ret revelled in the moment by mouthing the four words at Sal.

"What a fine day that was, Ret," said Sal, smiling graciously. "And even now, as we speak, every civilization worldwide follows Ret's team's design, constructing transmitters and receivers. Well, almost every civilization."

Sal shot a sympathetic glance towards Ret, and right away Ret understood the hidden message. He wondered about his parents and how they would've reacted to this news. Unfortunately, this wish could never come true for Terin snugs. Ret stood and reflected on the speech Hella gave him on the mountainside when he was younger. He cracked a cheeky smile and looked up to the sky, grateful to have had someone like her in his childhood.

"In fact, let's have Ret come up here and say a few words on behalf of his group," shouted Sal, gesturing to Ret to step toward centre stage.

Ret marched to take his position. Sal exchanged positions and gave a thankful nod as Ret walked into the centre. He took a moment to gather his thoughts and looked out of the crowd, and then he spoke.

"No more messenger snugs. Can you believe that?" shouted Ret. "My time here in Pagan has been something—an experience on all levels. There's a lot to handle inside these walls, but we made it here, on this stage, today. I'm still stunned at the outcome. We're all so fortunate to be a part of this place. It's funny; as cruel and unfair as things may seem, you just have to keep fighting and persevering through all the obstacles Pagan throws at you. After all, knowing that we would be standing here one day kept me going. A few hibernations ago, there was a time when I thought this place couldn't take anything else away from me."

Taking a moment to savour his statement, he looked down before readdressing the crowd.

"It's ironic, though, because that was just the beginning. This place can be amazing in every way. Good and bad, hideous and beautiful. And I wouldn't trade any experience I've had in Pagan. It has made me the snug I am today."

He paused to look out to all of his fellow snugs. "Never give up on what you believe in. Trust me, keep going, keep fighting, even against all odds. This world will not do the work for you. I strongly believe that the more you want something, the more the world tries to hold you back. The strong-willed learn from their failures and work through."

Ret turned to face his group and extended his pointing hand out to every snug in the line.

"Just ask my team here. How many problems and conflicts did we face and have to work through? And I think *I* was probably the biggest problem of all," said Ret, smiling at his group. "Working as a team and creating an idea from scratch took hard work, patience and understanding. It was tough, and it took every fibre of my being to work through it all. However, it was the struggle that made us better, made us smarter. We all had to endure it. But our struggles are not over. We're about to enter into parenthood next year. And if I have children that are anything like my sister and me, then I think I'm going to experience my hardest challenge yet."

The audience burst into laughter, and he gave them a moment to regroup. "You all have a choice in this world. You can choose to be strong. You can choose to be weak. You can choose to be caring, and you can choose to be cruel. Your choices will determine your outcome. When you make a choice, whatever it is, understand that you will be remembered as such, and your life will reflect your choices. So make them wisely and make them count. You never know where you're going to end up. Just believe in yourself and fight to pursue it."

Ret wrapped up his speech with a beaming smile and a lengthy courteous wave before announcing one last motivating message to the audience.

"And be proud to be a Terinian."

Clapping along with the crowd, Sal approached Ret and turned his back to him, setting up his posture for a generous backside bump. Reacting in kind, they both showed their respect and waved to the audience.

"Let's thank Ret for that wonderful speech. We have only a few moments before the blue geyser erupts, so I must say this quickly. Ret, I know that most of your team is your age, and I wish you all a fun and relaxing retirement year on Pagan Island. I'll be around on my monthly visits to see how you are all doing. I can't wait to play a round of fetch; just don't expect to win." boasted Sal. "You have made great names for yourselves, and you have built a reputation not only inside Terin but across the world. And with that being said, I had the honour of speaking with all of your society directors."

Pausing for a moment, Sal purposely built the audience's suspense before delivering a piece of wonderful news to Ret's group.

"Every one of them granted you all the cover of your ancestry book."

As the crowd cheered, one director from each society walked out onto the stage holding a stack of ancestry books. They started at each end of the stage and worked inward, addressing their individual group members and handing over their ancestry books. Every team member was thrilled to receive them back with the cover picture printed on. Unfortunately for Ret, no one approached him.

Ret was dumbfounded. What did he have to do to be recognized as a citizen? He was crestfallen. Why wouldn't they now consider him to be one of them? Ret's temper rose. He was on the verge of bursting into a scene when Sal approached, wearing a genuine smile.

"I think you deserve this, Ret. It's my honour to present the first entry in *your* ancestry. Now all you need is a book to put it in. It's personal, so I didn't want to pick one out for you."

Sal handed him a loose leaf. Ret grasped the page with both hands and examined the illustration to ensure it was real; the cover image jumped right up at him. On the face was a picture of their bright yellow planet centred in the middle of the page. A black backdrop surrounded the planet to represent space, with small white dots depicting faraway stars. The most noticeable feature was the planetary ring; it radiated a deep orange colour that signified its new energetic properties. Clearly this was the focal point of the artwork.

Ret's shoulders dropped, his head tilted to the side, and his glossy eyes gazed into the cover. He soaked in the moment as a warm, comforting sense of belonging coursed through him, an experience he hadn't felt in a long time. And to lighten his spirit even more, he chuckled when he saw his trainer's name etched in the bottom left corner.

"You're welcome, Juke," whispered Ret.

"Alright, everyone. Get ready. The geyser is about to go off," shouted Sal to the assembly.

Right on cue, rumbling sounds emanated from below the surface, prompting the audience to quieten and listen for further signs of seismic activity. As anticipation grew, the ground beneath their feet began to shake, and all eyes were fixed on the geyser behind the stage, waiting for it to surge. Just in time, Ret diverted his gaze from his cover and caught the first glimpse of the erupting geyser.

The geyser exploded like a flare. Large quantities of built-up gases raced from the planet's core and lit up the blue society. Shades of red, orange, and green spewed out fiercely from the deep cavern. The expansive and colourful display shot up high into the sky, adding to the celebrations and turning the event into a grand spectacle.

Ret gazed into the geyser, and vivid memories of his father rushed into his mind. Knowing this wish to see his parents was impossible, he recalled the last time he witnessed such an event; Sert would have been so proud.

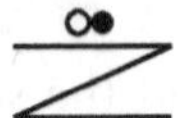

Actions Speak Louder Than Words

Sert was exhausted. He strengthened his grip around the handle of a block hammer and squinted his eyes at the last nail. He swung his arm all the way through his range of motion and struck the peg. After wiping away the melted nitrogen from his bump, he sprawled out and lay on his back, staring at the sky.

Sert was aware of his unhealthy position. He was suffocating his frost bump on purpose. His guilt was wreaking havoc on his conscience, and to inflict his self-punishment, he refused to flip over. He lay there, gasping for energy, questioning if he deserved to live.

As he battled this inner fight of good versus evil, honour versus dereliction, it was clear that his only saving grace was that now, he was willing to do something to fix the past. Not only was he trying to reconstruct his own tarnished image, he was also trying to rebuild his and Hella's rundown Tarni residence, one proverbial step at a time.

With one morsel of hope, Sert shook his head, slowly spun his body around, and pushed his back toward the sky. His frost bump immediately began to recuperate as it filled with a thick layer of yellow frost. Glancing over the rooftop, a genuine smile came over his tired face. This newly repaired surface was a mirror to his self-reconstruction. It was a small step, but it was his first.

He heard choppy footsteps racing towards the front of the house and exhaustedly turned his head to the approaching snug.

"What are you doing up there?" shouted a little Tarni from the edge of the eroded stone walkway. "Are you doing what I think you're doing? You can't do that, Sert!" The little Tarni placed three fingers above his squinting eyes to act as a visor and scowled up at Sert.

"Why would you go to all that trouble, Sert? You know it's pointless to try. Where did you get the material? Did you run it by Dredge? He's going to be angry."

"I have to do this," whispered Sert.

"And why would you start with the roof? My father used to construct buildings and always said, 'start from the bottom.' You're never supposed to start reconstruction from the top. Everyone knows that! You shouldn't have done this, Sert. We all have to decide on big things as a group, and Dredge has the last say in our actions. I know you have been away for a while…"

"At least I'm trying to do something to fix this broken place. Who else is?" shouted Sert, shrugging his shoulders. "I'm tired. I'm so tired of living in fear and guilt. I can't do it anymore. You hear me?"

"What are you talk…"

"It has cost me *everything*! I've betrayed everyone I love."

"Sert you can't…"

"And now, after all this, what do I have to show, huh? Well, it ends now. Even if this is my last living year, I can't go out feeling the way I do. It's about time we started doing something about it and stopped living in the past."

"Things are not where we want them to be, Sert. I'll give you that. But what do you want me to do?"

"You? It's not about you. It's about us. How can we keep living under the command of an uncaring leader who does absolutely nothing? Can't you see that we're all living in misery? And no one here has any drive to want change."

"It wasn't us, Sert. It was our parents that…"

"We always put the blame on our parents. They are all gone. The problem is now with us, the ones that sit back, cry about how bad things are and do nothing about it," screamed Sert. "You want Dredge to know what's going on, then go tell him! And bring him back here. I'd love to see his reaction."

The little Tarni snug was shocked. He slowly stepped backwards, spun around and raced down the roadway, shouting out to every passing snug. A malicious grin was printed on Sert's face as he watched the Tarni run away, fulfilling his request.

*

Hella traipsed along the sandy road with her head down, staring at the tops of her feet. With a glum look on her face, she bobbed her head from side to side, reflecting on her relationship, struggling to find a way to forgive her other. She tried to convince herself to stay but realized that no matter how much she wanted to pardon Sert, there was no trust or respect. She stopped in her tracks, nodded, turned around, and began marching down the road, determined to confront Sert with her decision.

She now walked with more confidence in her stride, upright and determined. This was her final year of living, and there was no way she would live her last chapter feeling betrayed. She believed that moving on and out of Tarni and completing her life by venturing into the unknown was a real option. Any place was better than Tarni, she thought. Picking up her pace, she marched with her head high.

Faint sounds of roaring cheers caught Hella's attention. She tilted her head to the side, honing in on the sound, trying to pinpoint the direction of what sounded like hundreds of Tarnis gathered together in celebration.

As she gazed out into the barren surroundings, she spotted a stampede of hazes off in the distance galloping in her direction. She stepped off to the shoulder of the road clearing the path as the horde passed by. She swivelled her head from side to side, politely acknowledging every passing Tarni with a wave. Most were unrecognizable to her. However, one snug, in particular, stood out from the rest.

Dredge posted up, grasping his animal's jagged shoulder blades, sneering at Hella as he passed.

Hella pulled her arm down and shot back a look; a perfect mix of confusion and irritation was impressed on her face, feeling as if it was a burden for Dredge to even lay his eyes on her. She shook her head after the group passed and then corked her head to the side as she stared down the road and into the large dust cloud kicked up by the stampede. Feeling intrigued she took off in their direction.

*

"We can make this a better place for your children to live. We can start right now and rebuild this civilization. We can be on the cutting edge of progression again. We have power in numbers. We just need motivation in all of us to do it. We can, Tarni. And we will," Sert shouted from the roof of his half restored resident building.

"Everyone! Before I came back, I was part of a great civilization. I lived there for years and knew what it was like to belong to a rich society and have a good life. Terin is very successful, and we can be, too," shouted Sert as he paced back and forth on his model rooftop, livening up his audience. "I learned a lot over there and know what changes to make. I can lead every one of you to a life of value. But it all starts with one step. Look at my home," he exclaimed as he turned around with his arm outstretched to display his handy work. "I *just* built this rooftop. And I'm standing on it. It feels great. I *know* what it's going to take to fix this place up. And I'm up to the challenge. I look around Tarni, and I can see—just like you all —other projects just like this one that we can all take part in repairing. It will take a lot of time, yes. However, if we all work together, we can make this happen. Are you with me?"

A loud, roaring cheer echoed throughout the land. Everyone flocked their way in from the outskirts of Tarni, drawn to the crowd, hoping to get a closer look at Sert. He was alive. The more he spoke, the more the crowd grew in size, and as each Tarni newcomer approached, Sert's motivated spirit unified them, all cheering together. He pumped his arms in the sky and encouraged a loud uproar, commanding the crowd as he stood firm on his roof.

Unfortunately for Sert his moment didn't last, his hands dropped and his smile straightened at the sight of Tarni's counsel barging in from the back of the crowd.

Dredge posted up on his haze, stealing everyone's attention and glared around the audience. He hopped down from his haze and shot a scornful snarl up at Sert.

"You will not continue on with this! Who do you think you are? You left us years ago, and now you want to persuade my citizens? You had your chance to help us. We instructed you to bring back knowledge about other civilizations, but you didn't. The only reason you came back was because you were found out and banished from Terin," screamed Dredge. "You never wanted to come back here, Sert. You never wanted to help us. Since you returned, you've told me practically nothing about Terin. And now you have the nerve to try and persuade my snugs? Well, I hereby banish you! And your other, Hella."

As he moved through the audience, each citizen backed up and formed a path for Dredge, eventually creating a lane that led right to Sert's rickety yellow front door. He marched confidently down the pathway and sneered at his nation in disgust.

"How could you all be so weak? After everything I have done for you. This is how you repay me? I have *protected* all of you. I have *helped* all of you, and this is how you show appreciation. This will not go on."

Dredge pointed into the crowd and singled out an individual.

"Lou," he said in a condescending tone. "Remember when you couldn't find your children after they ran into the dunes? Who was there for you and lent you a haze to find them? Me!"

The snug responded with a feeble cry. Dredge scoffed at him, turned away and identified another individual in his debt.

"And you, Rae. Who gave you somewhere to stay after the last hibernation washed away your old home? Again, it was *me*. I could go on for a long time listing off everything I have done for you as a leader. And you think you are going to throw all that away? For what?"

"For a better life. And a real leader," shouted Sert, still standing on his rooftop.

Dredge shot up a lethal glare. Sert did his best to anticipate Dredge's reaction, but at the moment, he was intimidated. He felt the brunt of Dredge's stare and struggled to drum up the courage to retaliate.

"You will *never* be allowed inside Tarni again. And my citizens will *not* listen to you! You don't have the right or the power to justify your actions," screamed Dredge as he looked up from the base of Sert's house. "But before you leave, you will watch all of us tear this house to pieces."

Feeling a loss of respect from the crowd, Sert looked over his audience, and for an instant, he let Dredge's disheartening speech discourage him. He dropped his shoulders and tilted his head down.

It was easy for him to lose faith. Hunched over, Sert looked over the agitated crowd and wondered if he had made a mistake. His plan required willpower and fortitude. It required a group effort and a strong belief to execute. And most of all, it required everyone to stand up for a true leader, someone they could trust without fear. Was he that snug?

His confidence had diminished. It would've vanished altogether; however, glancing around the audience, Sert spotted Hella standing in the background, encouraging him to take back his power with her glossy green eyes and yearning look of hope. He gathered his thoughts, and with an unwavering determination, he urged himself to show her what he was made of; after all, Hella deserved it.

"Stop, Dredge. We won't listen to you," screamed Sert before turning to his audience. "You all don't have to feel guilty and ashamed anymore. I know what it's like to feel discouraged and depressed. I've been there. I'm still there, and I've had enough! I want to change for the better, and I know all of you do, too. No more sitting around, feeling bad for ourselves, and doing nothing about it. We can *all* change if we just believe in ourselves."

"You don't tell them…"

"Enough! We are *not* going to listen to you anymore, Dredge. It hasn't solved anything."

"You think you know what it takes to solve our problems, Sert? Have you forgotten that this is your last living year?" argued Dredge. "Do you all want a leader like him? He is not supportive of you. The only thing Sert knows how to do is run away."

"That's not true," screamed Hella from behind the crowd.

Sert's confidence flourished as he watched Hella march toward him defending his cause.

"I understand, Sert! I understand why you felt you had no future here. And I understand why you want to fix this place," declared Hella as she walked through the crowd. "If you all don't already know, I have been with Sert for a long time. I know him better than any of you, and I can tell you that he is courageous. He is determined. And he is a great leader. Just ask my two children. The ones that we both raised. I know both of them are leaders, just like Sert."

"You will *not* listen to this Terin snug," shrieked Dredge, beginning to lose his command over the crowd.

"That's right. I am a Terin citizen. And you know what, Dredge? So is Sert. We know what it takes to be successful, " argued Hella as she passed Dredge and entered through the rickety doorway.

"Stop! I command you to stop right now. There will be no more of this. I want you all to return to your homes."

"What homes?" shouted a snug from the crowd as he edged his way closer to Dredge. "You mean the houses and buildings around here that you refuse to repair? The homes you have neglected for years? Those homes, Dredge?"

Dredge responded with a spiteful glare and an annoyed grunt. Before he could muster up any words, another Tarni approached him.

"How would you even know what's really going on with us, Dredge? You spend all your time sitting on your throne, ignoring us all. We need someone like Sert. Someone who wants to change. Someone that sees the problems around Tarni and wants to fix them. I'm with him."

The female Tarni finished her rant and pointed to Sert, standing proud on his roof.

"Let's start *right* now," shouted Sert. "We can all do our part to make a difference in Tarni. But we need all of you. The time to put our pasts behind us and build ourselves up as a productive and capable society is *now*. Are you with me?"

A surge of energy poured over the audience as every citizen cheered in unison. Dredge screamed his frustrations, but they held no weight. He looked up at Sert with black eyes before walking to his haze. He kicked his leg over the animal, secured himself, and glared at the chanting crowd. He sat dumbfounded, slowly glancing from side to side as thousands of his former supporters barked for his removal. He scowled one last time at Sert, smacked his hand on the back of his haze and took off, taking with him all the repression rooted within this civilization.

Sert eyes turned bright green as he watched his other climb up on the roof. His legs were shaky. As Hella approached, she raised her arms and delivered a gracious smile. With roaring cheers behind him, he grabbed a tight hold of his love, pulled her in, and hugged her.

Hella pulled her head back and looked into Sert's eyes. Fulfilled and more than ready to forgive, she caressed his cheeks.

"So, I guess you *were* worth it after all."

Act
2

Vacation

"How about this one, Ret? It's two levels, quaint and close to the blue auditorium. We can have it if we want. Wait! How about this one? It's three levels. No, hold on, this one, Ret, this is the one; what do you think of this one?"

Ret stared out onto the calm nitrogen sea from his ocean view terrace. He crossed his arms, placed them behind his head, and leaned back on his couch. Half attentive, he casually turned his head towards Rox and shrugged his shoulders.

"No more worrying, Rox. No more having to do anything. Let's just sit here and enjoy ourselves. Now take your eyes off that brochure and come over here."

Ret circled his hand on the seat next to him, gazing towards Rox with an inviting grin. She played right into his flirtatious act and sat on the red cushion beside him. Ret extended his arm behind Rox and confidently pulled her in close.

She draped her submissive body over Ret, allowing him to take control. Returning the favour, Ret pulled her shapely blue chest against his, securing her with a powerful hold. Interlocked in a passionate embrace, they edged closer, lying cheek to cheek. However, right before their lips touched, Rony's voice cut into their intimate session.

"Hey, Ret, Rox? Where are you?" shouted Rony from inside their retirement residence. "I know I'm early, but I want to practise before the fetch tournament. Hello? Where are you two?"

"I'm going to finish you off later," Rox whispered flirtatiously.

Ret slammed his hand down onto the empty padded seat next to him. He turned to glare at his friend, standing alone inside Ret and Rox's open concept living room.

Rony stood stunned as he stared through massive floor to ceiling windows, gazing out at the yellow sea.

"I wish I had this view."

He strolled outside and walked over a smooth interlocking brick patio; his head turned towards the ocean. As he moseyed his way over, he clumsily fell over the back of the plush red couch and landed beside Ret.

"You *had* to come over right now, didn't you?" Ret asked.

"Why? Were you two doing something? Did I interrupt?"

"No, not at all, Rony. We were just looking over a few blue society houses for us to live in after Pagan. Ret wants to be in the blue society to raise a family," answered Rox.

Ret glanced back to Rox and cracked a knowing smile, and Rox responded back with a grin of certainty. She had the blue society's retirement brochure open, and before she looked back down, she forcefully flipped the page with her fingertip and winked at Ret.

Ret, of course, wanted to reside as a red. However, Rox felt that the blue society would be the only place to raise children, no matter how much Ret contested the idea. He looked back at her coquettish face, submitting to his role in the relationship.

"Alright, Rony, let's talk fetch. What do you think Sal's first move will be?" asked Ret.

"Remember last time when I approached Sal at the start of the match and called him out as a cheater? Ya, I don't think I'll do that again."

"Really?" answered Ret sarcastically. "Besides, he wasn't even cheating. And then he embarrassed us when his team beat us three nothing."

"Three nothing," said Rony, reaffirming his answer. "Well, we'll show him this time, Ret. We can't let him go first, though; it's such an advantage to go first."

"It's only a game, Rony—no big deal. It's not like we're still working on an idea in the city. No need to get all riled up."

Ret exaggerated a long stretch as he readjusted his body. He laid back, peering out over the yellow sea.

"We have to leave soon, Ret. We should formulate a plan of attack if we want to beat Sal. Are you with me?"

"Rony, we'll beat him, or we won't. Let's just have fun and not put so much into always having to win."

"Who are you right now, Ret? We haven't been on this Pagan island that long, and already it's starting to take away that arrogant nature I grew to admire about you. Snap out of it, will you?"

"If anyone deserves a full year of peace, it's me. Let me be and forget about trying to make me care. I deserve this time."

Rony glanced toward Rox and watched her pull her head up from the brochure. She slumped back in her chair, released her tense brow and looked out onto the calm ocean surface.

"Alright, Ret, you're not ready to prepare for today's tournament."

"Rony, sit down. The tournament isn't important. So stop stressing over it and just enjoy this."

Rony let out a big sigh of relief and dropped his tense shoulders. He laid back on the red couch and placed his arms behind his head, trying to match Ret's body position and gazed into the open scenery savouring the peaceful moment.

*

"Ahh… Alright, you two. Let's get a move on. We have to get to the main beach," announced Ret.

He walked over to Rox and wrapped his arms around her body, motioning to her for a kiss.

"Later on, Ret. I promise," whispered Rox. "We have to get going. Plus, Rony is standing right behind you, trying not to look."

He smiled back at his partner, gently released his grip and grasped her hand.

"Can we go already?" asked Rony.

"Let's go, Rony, lead the way," answered Rox.

Rony tried to hurry his teammates along to the sandy beach, but his directions went unnoticed. Ret and Rox were too busy in their own world, exchanging coy smiles and casual hugs. They stopped momentarily to search for flat stones and took turns skipping them over the ocean surface; Ret's highest count was thirty-five skips.

Rony was beyond irritated; the more he tried to push, the more Ret and Rox resisted.

"Can you two hurry up?"

"We'll get there when we get there," said Ret.

As they arrived at the main beach, both stars illuminated a massive stadium sprawled along the oceanfront. From their vantage point, the dark stone encasement rose up to the sky and reached heights that blocked out one of the Sirra stars positioned midway up the skyline. Roars from the audience inside erupted out of the open top stadia, as waves of cheering sent a warm welcome to the three approaching.

Inside was a square playing field, well lit from the sky above with tall stone walls bordering the sandy surface. Spectators were provided grandstand seating that extended high up on all sides, reaching the top edge of the stone encasement.

Row upon row of excited retirees filled the arena. The stadium was divided into two distinct groups of supporters, black and white. On one side, the fiery audience waved black flags from the stands, and in response, the opposing side raised crisp white flags.

"I can hear them calling for us, Ret. We have to hurry," shouted Rony. "Come on, you two. Everyone is waiting for us."

"We're right behind you, Rony; go in and greet everyone and we'll be right there," shouted Rox.

Rony entered the stadium to a thunderous cheer from the audience. And as he performed a few laps around the sandy arena court, he stopped and raised his arms to the audience. Every white supporter rose in a surging uproar.

In response, the black side leaped off their seats, cheering for Sal as he entered the field with his two other teammates. He made his way to the middle of the court, held out his arms and waved them down to simmer the crowd.

"Welcome, everyone and thank you all for attending the match today," announced Sal. "You're all in for quite a show. Those blacks have no idea what they're up against. Hey, wait, Rony, where's the rest of your team?"

Annoyed, Rony glanced at the entrance to see Ret and Rox stroll inside.

"We're here, everyone. Don't worry," shouted Ret, as the white supporters whistled and applauded.

"Yeah, we're really sorry about being late," said Rox coyly.

Bursting into a chuckle, Sal watched the two snugs mosey across the playing surface.

"Enjoying yourself, Ret?" asked Sal, sporting a playful expression. "Ok, Rony. I'll let you decide. Do you want to go first, or should we?"

"You go first, Sal. Alright, everyone. Let's play!"

"Wait, I thought you didn't want them to go first," asked Ret.

"Well, I do now!" Rony answered decisively.

"Alright."

Sal raised his arms in the sky, which prompted another roaring cheer from the audience; the players took their positions.

In two opposing corners, three moving red targets were unveiled. Like a pendulum, they swung from side to side, attached to a thin cord anchored to a bulkhead above. Each target was manned by a snug dressed in a yellow smock who kept the targets moving constantly. These snugs, known as officials, were trained never to change the swing speed of these targets and to keep score. The object was simple; each team must hit the opposing targets with frostballs, and the first team to strike all three wins the match.

Sal took a moment and placed his teammates strategically on his side of the playing field. He positioned one snug midway up the field, close to the left edge, and then took his second player and placed her front and center, directly behind a thick red line that ran across the field connecting two corners. The field was purposely divided into two large triangle-shaped zones; either team would be penalized if they stepped across.

Both players on Sal's team stood up straight, faced forward, and pushed out their frost bumps, signifying they were ready. Sal subtly bobbed his head up and down as he walked backwards to his corner, satisfied with his strategy.

Countering Sal's defence, Rony began to place his team in the same setup as his opponent. Quickly, he led Rox midway up the right side of their zone, and

Ret was placed in front of the opposing team's player, directly behind the red line at the front of the field. Rony walked backwards to his starting position, double-checked his game plan and nodded to the field official.

The official slowly raised his arm and turned his head to both team leaders. The crowd roared when the snug chopped his arm down. Rony and Sal took off from their corners.

Rony ran behind Rox and scraped enough frost off her backside to make three medium-sized frostballs.

"Watch out, Rony. Sal is throwing now," shouted Rox

Rony tucked and rolled, ducking the onslaught of incoming frostballs. He peered behind Rox and saw Sal waiting for his teammate's bump to restore. He took the opportunity and ran out from behind Rox, launching three frost balls at Sal before racing to Ret. He leaped off his feet, diving behind Ret and landing hard on the sandy floor.

"Sal's throwing another one," screamed Ret, standing firm in position.

Sal read the situation perfectly and saw Rony was landing just a bit outside of cover; he cocked his arm and released the ball with all his power. It flew in a perfect line and struck the centre of Rony's chest. Sal raised his arms and rejoiced with his supporter after they burst into a blaring roar.

Rony looked up to his side of the stadium and felt encouraged by his fans, cheering for him to get back on his feet. He picked himself up, dusted off the sand from his midsection, and returned to his corner.

"One free throw is awarded to the blacks," announced the field official as he pointed to Sal, offering him his free throw.

The black supporters clapped in unison as Sal approached the centre of the red line, tossing a trusty frostball up and down in his right hand. Ret stood in front of Sal, sporting a cheeky grin and tried to wreck Sal's concentration by shouting out before he released the ball. It didn't have the effect Ret wanted. Sal locked in his target, pulled his arm back and hurled the ball. The black supporters hailed Sal after the ball smacked one of the three swinging red targets dead centre.

"Two left for the blacks, and whites are still at three. Everybody back to your corners, and let's start the next round."

The match went on, and both teams were grinding it out. Sal was a skilled thrower, and Rony was a great defender; the match-up couldn't have been better. Midway, the score ticked over with two targets left for Rony and only one for Sal.

Rony was going for a hail mary attempt to win back points. He stood at the very back of his field, near the corner and launched a few low percentage shots from deep in his zone. He had three attempts, and on the last try he struck one of the swinging targets in Sal's corner. His supporters rained down their praise as Rony pointed to Sal with a gritty look on his face. He was back in the game, but he was disadvantaged.

Rox was forced to kneel and regain her energy after he scraped the last bit of frost off her bump. Rony rushed around the open court with one of his teammates out of the competition, dodging each of Sal's throws. The crowd was wincing in suspense.

Caught in open territory, as Sal chucked several frostballs, Rony was blindly throwing a few in return, zigzagging around the court and managing to avoid every shot except one. Regrettably, he finally got hit on the left thigh.

Rony pounded his fist on the ground and sneered over at his opponent. He expected Sal to celebrate and the black supporters to explode in cheer, but they didn't. As Sal glared back at Rony he wiped off a frostball mark from his knee.

"Yes, Rony. You got him too!" screamed Rox.

"Free throw for both teams," announced the official.

Both opponents walked to the center of the field and faced off. The commotion within the crowd was deafening around the stadium. Each side taunted and shouted at their opponents as Rony and Sal scowled at one another.

The official approached both snugs, the audience was hushed in anticipation. Looking at Sal and Rony the official hemmed and hawed for what seemed like an eternity as he decided which of the two snugs would be the first to throw. The crowd booed and hissed at the official until he finally made his decision.

"The black team was the first to score. Therefore, I grant him the first throw. Sal, take your place."

Heckling from the white side contrasted with hearty applause from the black supporters.

Without hesitation, Sal stepped up to the line, planted both his feet and studied the timing of the swinging target. In one smooth motion, he pulled his arm back behind his head and launched his frostball.

The closer the ball got to the swaying target, the audience were stuck with anticipation. Rony watched on with wide-open eyes. However, his hopes quickly dashed after the ball struck the moving target square in the center. Sal's arms rose above his head, and the crowd roared.

It was now up to Rony. With one last opportunity to send the game into overtime, he threw his hands up toward his supporters behind him, initiating a massive cheer. All fired up, he turned around and focused on the final swinging target.

He took a long moment, firming up his stance and readdressing his aim, trying to find his composure. After making a few final adjustments, he felt confident and stepped into his pitch. Rony squared his body, secured his feet and hurled the ball.

Everyone cowered as they watched the ball flying through the sky. Rony raised his hands and gave a cagey grin as the ball reached the target, yearning for the hit. But when he saw the ball fly past the edge of the swaying target, he bowed his head in shame and stomped his foot on the sandy floor.

All the white supporters sunk back down on their benches, deflated and dispirited, as they watched Rony lashing out in frustration.

As for Sal, he ran back into his zone, hugged his teammates and turned around to face his crowd. Every black flag in his section flew as the supporters shouted for joy. Thick black streamers rained down on top of the snugs as they celebrated relishing in their victory.

"Don't worry about it, Rony. You did great," said Rox, patting him on the shoulder.

"Yeah, Rony, you shouldn't feel bad at all. Sal is a really good player. He rarely loses," answered Ret.

"Why can't I ever beat him?"

"Don't get so angry. There is always next time," said Rox.

"Sorry, Rony, about the match. Listen, we'll see you later, ok? And do us both a favour. Don't come over for a while." said Ret.

Before Rony could respond, Rox turned her head and shot an suggestive glance toward Ret; he instantly read her mind. The two impetuous snugs ended theconversation, quickly grabbed each other's hand, and gave Rony a hurried goodbye.

Rony chuckled as he watched his friends run for the exit. He turned to the playing field and was startled by Sal standing behind him.

"Good game, Rony. Maybe next time?"

"Yeah, next time. It isn't over, Sal! I will get you before my year ends. There are a few matches left, and I will beat you at least *once!*"

"Well, I hope you do, Rony, but to be honest, I think you need a better team. Ret and Rox weren't focused at all."

"You noticed that as well?"

"Yeah, and they sure left in a hurry."

"They're obsessed with each other," said Rony, rolling his eyes.

Before answering, Sal placed his arm over Rony's shoulder and patted him on the back.

"Yep. They're in love."

‰

Seeding

Ret and Rox hurried across the white sand beach, very much in love. Stuck in their passion they grasped each other's bodies and dropped to the ground. After rolling around in the soft white sand they descended to the shoreline, splashing their legs in the nitrogen. Then lying cheek to cheek, Rox took the lead and mounted Ret, forcing him to lie on his back. He looked up into her eyes and smiled at her salaciously.

"Take my hand," whispered Rox.

Ret interlaced his fingers and drew his eyes from Rox's blue society ring over the soft skin on her arm, up to her toned shoulder line, and onto her smooth neck. He unlatched his fingers, reached around her body, placed one hand behind her neck, and pulled her in close.

He stared captivated, looking adoringly into Rox's eyes. Rox looked back. However, he felt she was anxious; he could see the apprehension on her face. He tried to keep the spark alive but felt pressure against his hands as she pulled away ever so slightly.

Showing physical affection by touching and caressing was always innocent fun, but for Rox this next step was the most important decision of her life. She caressed both sides of Ret's face with her fingertips and veered her eyes toward his thin blue lips. She was still a little uncertain about making the connection.

She wanted to give in to the moment, but the first kiss was an important life decision. Rox needed assurance that she would not regret it. After all, once they kissed, her future would be sealed and would forever be a mother to their children.

Ret took on his role dutifully. His strength and hard-headed persistence gave her the security she was looking for. With a subtle tug from his hand and one final comforting stare, he gracefully pulled her head down and planted his pursed lips right onto hers. His gesture was exactly what she needed to make up her mind, and she subsumed herself to her partner with her mind, her body, and her spirit.

They wrapped their hands around each other's bodies, and grasping onto their bumps began scraping off small pieces of frost, a sign of fondness and devotion between two loving snugs. With their legs intertwined below the shallow ocean and their chests held firmly together, the couple focused all their attention on their kiss.

Ret was surging with adrenaline. He picked Rox straight up and into a seated position, cupped her bottom with his hand, spun her around and placed her back down on the smooth white sand. Rox guided her long blue legs around his waist and slid her arms around his midsection, latching on to his scraped frost bump.

Rocking back and forth, both snugs thirsted for each other. Their love making was so passionate and trusting it naturally brought about one of the most profound moments in any snug's life—seeding.

Slowly, Rox opened her eyes and was astounded by what she saw in her partner. Radiant white light was bursting out from Ret's eyes. He pulled his left leg up and planted his foot firmly into the sand, leaving one knee anchored in the ground. He slid his arms underneath Rox, and with all the power coursing through his body, he raised her up from the white sand and pressed their chests together.

Rox squeezed onto Ret as she hovered over the sand. She gazed into his glowing eyes, completely awestruck. Held in suspense, she tried to keep their lips connected and dug her fingers into his shoulders; then suddenly, a loud high pitched howl emitted from inside Ret's body, and with it every muscle contracted. Soaked in a craze of ecstasy, Ret harnessed his power and pressed his lips hard onto hers as the loud shrieking cry deepened.

Rox was struggling to keep their lips sealed. Overwhelmed, she touched his chest and tried to push him away. However, right before pulling back, she felt a hard acorn shaped seed drop into her mouth.

Every limb on Rox's body shot out in all directions, and her eyes opened wide, radiating the same bright white light she saw in her other. A surge of euphoria coursed through her body. Her head flung right back, her arms and legs continued extending out in all directions, and her mouth was left wide open, moaning.

Ret clenched his arms around her waist as her body jolted with waves of elation, crying out as she climaxed. He peered into her glowing eyes, watching them burst with light every time she was hit with a shock of exhilaration. As the waves started to diminish, Rox slowly placed her hand back on Ret's shoulder, still quivering, and stared at him with a serious and submissive look; she was ecstatic.

Both snugs urged their feelings onto one another as they gazed deeply into each other's bright white lit eyes. The two lovers were emitting the same howling shriek as throbs of pleasure engulfed their bodies, fulfilling their every desire.

Still keeping eye contact and now casually kissing, Ret lowered Rox to the sand. The light was dimming in her eyes. He unlatched his pressed lips from Rox's and rolled over, lying face up beside her, smiling and sated. They held hands and stared up into the bright sky as they took a break to restore their exhausted bodies.

Turning his head out to the calm nitrogen ocean, Ret glanced at the Pagan city skyline right over Rox's feet and followed his vision up her smooth legs, her silky torso, and finally into her deep green eyes.

Using only a few words, Rox reassured him that they were now a complete and mature couple. Thrilled to announce the news, she turned on her side and spoke with a delighted smile.

"I'm pregnant!"

Things Are Going to Change Around Here

Sal was being guided down a long corridor by four snugs curtly enforcing a brisk pace. As he marched on, playing along with their charade, he glanced at each snug and noticed not one was wearing an identity piece. He slowed his stride and rolled his eyes; he thought these snugs were taking their protest a little too seriously.

"Keep walking, Sal. Let's go!"

"Keep walking? Please. It's *me* who leads *you*! Don't ever forget that!"

Everyone stopped abruptly, and the snug in front, leading the way, turned around, tilted his head and glared at a smiling Sal.

This resistance was widely anticipated within Pagan, hence the reaction. But for Sal, he wanted to see how serious they were. He tested the young snug's patience and realized that the group's emotional stability was questionable. Negotiations were out of the question for these befuddled young minds.

"You really have no idea how much damage you've done to us, Sal? I can't wait to see your face when everything falls apart inside Pagan. You hurt all of us, and now we get to hurt you! A snug like you and the rest of your kind out there will break into pieces after you witness what we will do to Terin."

Sal kept his emotions under control. He looked back with glaring concern. He had no interest in listening to their terms; to Sal, these protesters were a fringe minority of snugs with no direction and no respect for the existing Pagan rule. All he was focussing on was figuring a way to stop this rebellious group before it got out of hand.

"We are not incompetent, Sal. This movement is what saved us. We will have a say in our future without you judging us."

"Calm down, Wita. *We* don't need to talk to him. We didn't bring him here to talk to us. We brought him here so he could talk to Terri. She will be our voice now."

The tall snug shook his head and regained his composure. His eyes changed from a vibrant red to a tranquil green before he turned around and continued the march. A forceful shove from behind pushed Sal into action as they walked toward Terri's quarters.

Stern voices and loud shouting poured out into the hallway as Sal approached the open door guarded by two militant snugs. And, after noticing the chief director making his way down the hall, the guards shifted their slouched posture and stood to attention.

"I still have that effect on you all. You don't have the power you think you do," said Sal as the group reached Terri's quarters.

"She is waiting inside for you," said Wita.

In all the years commanding his nation, Sal, for the first time felt nervous. Beneath all the resentment towards Terri's new organization, he was conflicted; her ability to spark a movement of this magnitude impressed him. Terri's results to date were well beyond his expectations, and her influence on others seemed to have grown exponentially as word spread of her project.

Still, Sal's admiration did not outweigh his feelings of betrayal. As he stood by observing everyone's disloyalty, the memory of the first time he met Ret and Juke raced through his head.

Maybe he shouldn't have been so strict on the idea approval process, and maybe he shouldn't have been so hard on those half-breeds. With strength of purpose, Sal pushed away his thoughts and refocused on the situation. Projecting a noble and honourable persona, Sal reigned in his anger as he strode past the two lookout snugs and into the lair of his political nemesis.

He was instantly hit by Terri's presence. Right away, he felt her confidence radiating as she sat firmly on a padded green coloured chair in the middle of the large oval room lined with many serious looking snugs, all standing in abeyance. Accenting her power, she was the only snug sitting, centred in front of a bay window displaying the entire Pagan city from high above the green society. Cocking her head to the side, she ordered one of her snugs to provide Sal with a small stool. Sal rebuffed the offer with a dismissive wave, and stood steadfastly upright as befitting his office.

"Hello, Sal," announced Terri.

Sal couldn't help his anxiety rise as he tried to relax. He took some time to collect his thoughts and settle his emotions before answering.

"I let you know that I was coming here today, Terri, because I think we should get to know one another a little better, and try to understand both our points of view about our Pagan. I thought it would be good to show up here, but no one from your little group has shown me any respect."

"How does it feel?" Terri responded calmly.

"How does what feel?"

Terri gazed at him and cracked a sarcastic smile.

"The point at which you started to believe that this organization could impact your precious Pagan system. Now you must understand what it's like to be mistreated, misunderstood, and afraid of what the future might bring. And that now you don't have a say in any of it. Tell me, Sal. How does it feel?"

Sal waited to respond. He looked around and noticed the tension in the room rise palpably as she finished addressing him without a fragment of courtesy. Her confidence resonated with every snug in the room.

"Like I said when I walked in, Terri, you have a long way to go. This organization of yours doesn't even have one percent of the Pagan population on your side. Believe me, I'm impressed. That's the truth. But I came here today because I want to talk to you and find some common ground you and I can agree on."

"You are wasting your time, Sal. This is a group dedicated to changing the system of Pagan. It would be wrong for us to work something out together. *You* are the one we want to change. You and everything you stand for. Our numbers may be small now, but they're growing every day. All thanks to you."

"Terri, you have no clue what you are doing and where this project will take you. Do you really think this movement is best for our civilization? Have you considered the future if everyone lived in your new system? You believe everyone should be equal and free to do what they want, right?"

"That is what we are all striving for, Sal. I will not stop until…"

"Do you even know what happened to Tarni? It was a very prosperous civilization at one point. And just like you, Terri, some of them decided that things were unfair. Everyone decided to overthrow their governing system, and it destroyed their entire culture in less than a generation. And to this day, nothing has changed. That will be our future under you, Terri? Is that what you want?"

"Please, Sal. We all have better sense than that. Just because it happened to Tarni does not mean the same thing will happen to us. Especially if *we* are in power."

Slowly shaking his head, Sal looked down and crunched his brow before raising his hand to his forehead, trying to assuage the frustration.

"Terri, you don't have the slightest idea of how to manage a civilization. You have a radical view of how things work here and believe everyone is treated unfairly. How can you be the voice for everyone when everyone has a different view? I see them every day arguing back and forth between ideas. It's a hard position to take on, Terri. But someone has to mediate the situation and take the side that best serves Pagan."

"You said it perfectly, Sal. Why do you get to make that decision? Why do you have the power to tell anyone what they can or cannot do? If I want to build a tall tower to observe the night sky, why do I need permission? Remember Yun? He pitched that idea to you, and you denied him!"

Following Terri's pointing arm, Sal turned to the left side of the room and saw the angry former yellow staring back at him.

"You are missing your yellow bracelet, Yun," said Sal.

Like everyone else in the room, this snug had removed his identity piece, proving his dedication and allegiance to Terri.

"Snugs like him feel the same way I do about this system. We all want change, Sal. You will no longer be the one we need to impress anymore."

"So, they will be answering who, you Terri? Well, you only have so much time left here. What will you do when you have to leave Pagan and begin your family life? And, to bring up another point, is this what you will teach your children when you're outside Pagan?"

"I have been through a lot, Sal. You can't imagine what I went through in my younger years inside this precious Pagan of yours. No one can understand the hardship and suffering I had to endure. Looking back now, I respect the struggle I went through because now I can relate my experiences with everyone here in this room, and all of those out there who support this cause—who need this cause as much as I do. To answer your question, Sal, I will be a great mother because I know what it is to feel pain… *real* pain. And I know how to overcome it! That is something *every* child needs to realize about life. No one can teach that except *me*!"

"Ret can!"

Terri turned her head, slammed her fists on her armrests and rose to her feet, but Sal continued talking.

"I saw Ret not too long ago, Terri. He is spending his last year in retirement on Pagan Island, a place all of the snugs in this room could have been awarded in their last year if they had just focused on an idea and followed through with what was expected of them. Instead, *this* is what you have spent all your time inside Pagan focusing on—feeling mistreated and taking your frustrations out on everyone else. It's selfish, Terri. Your time in Pagan is almost up, and this is what you have to show for it. It was supposed to be your retirement year, too. You could have taken this time to yourself if you had just adhered to the Pagan rules. By the way, have you met Rox yet? She and Ret are having a great time on Retirement Island. I think they are in love!"

"This is not about Ret!"

"You know, Terri. I do feel bad about how I treated him when he was younger. If anyone has had a tough life inside Pagan, it's him. However, he came out strong and, most importantly, respected!"

"Don't say another word about him!" screamed Terri.

"I look at both of you. You both started with the same disadvantage inside Pagan. I respect the struggle you have faced and the road that you felt you had to travel. I didn't expect either of you to end up where you did. But Ret acted the right way; instead of filling his mind with hatred, he developed something everyone could benefit from, unlike your idea."

"You don't think I'm doing this for everyone? I am doing this for every snug inside Pagan who wishes to pursue their ideas. This movement is for everybody you have denied. It's for everybody you pushed away," screamed Terri.

"No, it's not, Terri."

"Yes, it is," screamed Terri as she raised her arms above her head.

"You're all just self-serving snugs with your own agendas. What good changes can you create? How can you make the world a better place?" shouted Sal, standing tall and proud, fighting back against his opponent.

"The good changes start with you, Sal," said Terri, calming herself. "*You* came here today because you are afraid. You are afraid of real change. You are afraid of us winning. Because it will involve you stepping down. The fact that you even left the Pagan tower and showed up here tells us that you are scared of something. You would have never visited us if you didn't believe that we have the power to change things…"

"Terri, that's not why…"

"And for your information, Sal, I'm not trying to be like my brother. My entire life, I was always compared to my brother and shamed for not being like him. It's different now. Instead of trying to be like Ret, I'm finally being myself. And so is everyone in this room," said Terri, pointing to her supporters. "Each one of us has been a victim of the system Sal. We are not going anywhere; we have an idea of the future and we have the power to command it."

"You are not going to stop fighting me, are you, Terri?" asked Sal trying to find some closure to the conversation.

"Only if you stop fighting me. That's the only way. You cannot interfere with us, Sal."

"Oh, I can't? Are you saying I won't try to stop this?"

Terri turned in her spot, stepped back to her throne, and gracefully descended onto the padded seat. While keeping her posture straight and her deep green eyes on her new rival, she mustered a patronizing smile.

"You can't stop this, Sal, even I can't stop this now. No one can. It has begun. And now that it's out, I can't be put back. You asked who is going to take over after I leave Pagan. It doesn't matter. Someone will fill the position just like someone will fill your position after you go."

Sal shook his head, feeling pity for the assembly of snugs all standing around her. Figuring that there was no way to rationalize with her group, Sal summed up his last thought.

"Well, Terri, I just hope you don't have a guilty conscience when things end badly."

"It's only going to end for you, Sal."

Miracle

Ret was tense. From inside his family room, he sat in his blue reclining chair with both arms crossed over his chest. He glared through the window onto the Pagan wall reminding himself of all the accomplishments he had worked so hard to achieve; his discouraged spirit needed it.

This effort to lift his mood just didn't seem to work. None of his empowering and rewarding memories could combat the agonizing scene before him. As he sat inside his newly decorated nursery room within his blue society home, Ret was quite literally facing his worst fears. Rox's giant wall-to-wall frosted over shell that housed her and their two unborn children was ready to crack.

Since Rox's first day of pregnancy, something has changed inside Ret. The radical transformation from a successful Paganer to an everyday civilian had hit him hard. It didn't take long to feel depressed, having to live outside of Pagan, and on top of that, inside the blue society.

Ret's anxiety was getting tougher by the moment. As he had watched Rox's cocoon grow bigger over the months, not only was the reality of becoming a father placing a heavy burden on him, he also wasn't used to the drab lifestyle and slow pace of living outside of Pagan. It was mind-numbing.

Ret closed his eyes, slid back into his chair and replayed in his memory the first day Rox fell into her long pregnant sleep.

*

"Alright. Ret, you have your list, right?"

"Yes. Well, I did. Where did I put it?"

Rox glowered toward Ret as he frantically searched for her list of tasks. And, as she watched him run around the nursery room trying to find it, her uneasiness intensified.

"Ret! Did you lose it? You have to know what's on that list," shouted Rox from her lying position. "I'm obviously going to be doing my part for our family over the next while. You have to as well. We need to be able to count on you too, Ret! Can your family count on you?"

With his back turned, Ret rolled his eyes. He knew she was scared and had a lot of emotions running through her body. He also knew his role and tried to comfort Rox as best he could, but inside a part of him was looking forward to her time inside her shell.

"Well, Rox, you counted on me inside Pagan, and look where it got you. Into this large wonderful house. And we *are* here in the blue society."

"I know, Ret. I'm sorry for being a pain. I'm just scared, and I can use some support before I sleep."

"I will always be there for you, Rox. I'm not going anywhere. You are the most important thing in my life. Yes! Here it is," Ret shouted as he waved the list over his head.

"Hurry, Ret. I want to go over it with you before I fall asleep. I can feel it coming."

Ret ran across the room, sat on the floor next to Rox's lying body, and while holding out the shortlist with both his hands, he glanced over and noticed her eyes clouding. He placed his hand on her shoulder and gave her a shake.

"I don't have much time. I can really feel my body taking over," Rox whispered.

"I'll go over it. Just lie back and listen," Ret softly answered as he caressed her head. "Alright, first things first. We need two little support cradles. I will build them right here in this room, so they will all be ready when you break free from your shell."

"Perfect."

"Then, after you enter the first stages of your cocoon, I will complete all the registration forms for our children and submit them to the blue society counsel. I have everything I need for that. All of your Pagan information and your ancestry book history outline is drawn up. And mine. Well, my ancestry is pretty easy to summarize," chuckled Ret. "You know, thinking back, I have to say that my father was pretty creative in making up a fake summary of his history. I wonder what it said?"

Before continuing, he looked down into Rox's fully clouded-over eyes.

"Rest well, Rox. I am so proud of you, and I'm so excited! The next time I see you, we will be parents to a wonderful family. And you will see how great of a father I will be."

*

Ret shook his head and pulled himself back to reality. He glared at the frosted over shell that took up one side of the room, turned and scurried over to the other side of the nursery, resting his trembling hands on the window's edge. He gazed out to the ocean, unable to find solace. Ret grimaced, pushed himself away from the window and marched over to his newly built infant cradles, staring at them with a conflicted glare.

Fabricated out of granite, both small stone pedestals sat on the opposite side of the room. He stared at the saddle shaped cradles and anxiously tapped one of his fingers over his lips. His mind was racing.

At the beginning of Rox's pregnancy, everything was moving quickly for him. With the support of Rox, he didn't have an opportunity to contemplate what life would be like as a father. He didn't have time to think. Everything was changing at such a rapid rate. Between the transition from Pagan, settling into a new home, and adjusting to the blue society, Ret was overwhelmed with change, and his outlook for their future was a novelty at best.

Everything was about status up to this point in his life. Always striving to be a success; it took a lot of work to change his mindset. Over the last few months of solitude, he tried to combat the psychological changes he was experiencing. Life was becoming less about competition and more about long-term planning and obligations. A new attitude started to take shape, and he didn't particularly like it.

He tried to fit into his new surroundings. He made trips to the blue society auditorium for monthly gatherings, learned about the history of the blue society, and went as far as working with the blue counsel, trying to be open to their passion for artistic expression. Still, it just wasn't who he was.

Ret ran to the other end of the room. Now hysterical, he was desperate to devise a plan to re-enter Pagan. The idea of living his life this way until his death was birthing a senseless frenzy within him. Only the crazed psyche of a despairing snug would ever believe that he could immerse himself inside Pagan while abandoning his family.

He lunged towards a frostboard at the front of the room, picked up the black pen and shook it with his fist. He started scribbling a loose diagram and shouted a few verbal hallelujahs. He threw the pen to the ground and snickered after glancing over his work. He was ready and willing to put his plan into action. With his back facing Rox's cocoon, he finalized his decision and took his first step toward the doorway. Thankfully, the faint yet powerful sound of a small crack stopped him.

He couldn't ignore it. He stopped mid-stride and slowly turned toward the source of the sound. He closed his eyes. Another sharp crack reverberated through the room and sent Ret rushing over, placing his hand on the surface of the cocoon.

"Rox," he whispered.

He traced his fingers across every fracture of the surface as sounds of splitting were getting louder and more frequent. His limbs were quivering with anticipation.

Ret stepped backwards after a loud crack struck the inside of the shell. The first fragment of organic material fell and landed next to his feet. He looked up and saw that more and more pieces of thick frost were flipping away from the wall.

"Ret!"

He rushed to her side. Refusing to wait, he ripped away large portions with all the energy he could muster. He could see the top of the nest inside, and as he chiselled his way down, he could hear Rox's exhausted voice encouraging him to keep going.

He hollowed out a large opening and stuck his head inside the barrier; his body instantly calmed, and his eyes turned pale yellow. Frozen in awe, he got his first glimpse of his beloved other and their two new little family members.

Rox's gleaming face stared at Ret, holding their newborn son and daughter in each of her arms. Overflowed with joy, Ret gazed at their small light blue bodies as their innocent expressions enriched his spirit. He watched his daughter turn her head, locking her large glossy green eyes onto his and reaching out her tiny arm. His soul melted. As Ret stared back, he was hit with more than a sense of belonging. Her gaze conveyed what Ret needed to understand.

Nothing else mattered anymore. Shaking his head, Ret rejected the foolish plan he was trying to devise, barely a few moments ago. His past insecurities vanished, and with a deep sense of acceptance, Ret realized that his life didn't belong to him anymore, and he was just fine with that.

Clash of Opinion

Rox ran up the stairwell inside her blue society home. She hurdled two steps at a time, swinging her arms with every stride. She reached the landing at the top of the stairs and hurried beside a shelf displaying both ancestry books. A thick beam of light shone down from a skylight in the arched ceiling, highlighting the two artifacts standing proudly atop the shelf's glossy brown finish.

She raced down the hallway and abruptly stopped at the classroom, gripping the door trim with one hand and waving a black pamphlet to catch Ret's attention with the other.

Ret glanced up from the front of the room, stopped his lesson and stared at her with a raised brow. "What do you have there?" Ret asked sarcastically.

His smug tone irked Rox as she approached him. Ret looked over to their two young children sitting behind their desks, looking back in awkward silence.

"These snugs were originally from the red society, right?" asked Rox, showing him the pamphlet. "That means that *you* know who they are."

"Yeah. It's Bri and his…"

"Do you know who they just teamed up with?"

"How about we talk about this after my lesson? And away from the children."

"These snugs are destroying Terin! Have you read this pamphlet?" shouted Rox, "It's all about being part of Terri's black society. And how her band of snugs are all building a *black* society out in the flat rock. Do you know how this looks on us?"

"Rox, you need to settle down. Can we talk about this after?"

"Why?"

"I can't do anything to stop this from happening; to be perfectly honest, no one can. It's something that will just have to…"

"No, I disagree. We all need to do something about what's going on. I thought this was just some stupid project that Terri was trying to organize inside Pagan because she was miserable with her life. I didn't expect it to become what it is today. We have to stop this before it's too late."

There was a time when Ret opposed overthrowing the Terin government. Remodelling Terin's long-standing and successful social structure was a cause for concern. However, his outlook was now different. And throughout his years within Terin, he realized that in life, things change.

He found that putting himself in the position of others and trying to see from their point of view was a much more productive way to cope with change. Observing life from another perspective made him more understanding, and instead of trying to force his opinions onto others, he listened first. This was one character trait he wanted to teach his children, and Rox.

"I know how you feel about this, Rox, and don't get me wrong, I don't support this group at all…"

"Why am I sensing that you'll say something I won't agree with?"

"Rox. It's different now. I would much rather focus on them," answered Ret, pointing to his children. "It's our obligation to discuss this with Rus and Carin and give them all the information about what's going on, so they can decide for themselves what is best for their future."

"Future? They are going into Pagan as a blue. I will not stand by and watch our children be influenced by anyone that wants to change that. That's my life, and everyone in my family has led. And that will be the life that Rus and Carin will lead. Isn't that right, kids?"

Looking to the front of the room, Rus nodded and puffed out his chest.

"I will be the best blue citizen Pagan has ever seen. And these other snugs? I want no part of it. The next time I see one of them, I'll throw frostballs at them," shouted Rus before climbing onto his desk.

After hearing her son's response, a big, luscious smile spread over Rox's face; she looked back to Ret, shaking his head.

"Ret? Don't judge me! This is a major issue. We have to fight this."

"Yeah, Dad. Why aren't you on our side? You should be angry. Do you even like Terin?" said Rus, still standing on his desk, contorting his face.

Ret rolled his eyes.

"Rus, you're not even old enough to know how to feel. You haven't gone through anything yet. You are standing up for something you know nothing about."

"What's that supposed to mean, Dad? I know a lot."

"Ret, I need to know that we are all in this together," demanded Rox. "We need to be strong as a family. I need to hear you denounce your sister. I need to know that we are all on the same side. Cause if you're not…"

"If I'm not on your side, then what, Rox? I don't respond to threats. What's happening with Terri's group is happening, and we can't stop it. And even if you could, would it be for the better? What is better? Do you even know? Cause I don't."

"Our way is better, Ret. The Terin way is better. It's always been the best civilization. And that is the way it's going to stay," screamed Rox. "Who are you right now, Ret? I feel like I don't even know you anymore. How can you side with those good-for-nothing snugs that only want to destroy our way of life? Our perfect life."

"If it were so perfect, Rox, this wouldn't happen. If Terri were wrong, no one would follow her, and her black society wouldn't grow. A huge number of snugs feel the same way she does."

Rox tilted her head to the side and cunningly posed her leading question.

"And what about you, Ret? Do you feel the same way they do?"

"I told you, Rox, I don't agree with it. So let me put it another way. Our generation was one of the most unproductive generations to date. And it was due to snugs feeling that they had no freedom and having to conform to what the directors wanted. Did you know that seventy-five percent of the ideas proposed to Sal were denied because they did not match his future vision."

"And where did you read this? I have a hard time believing it, Ret," answered Rox.

"You asked me to answer the question, so I did," Ret responded before turning to his children. "See, your mom and I were lucky. My dream had everything to do with Sal's vision, and so did your mother's. She was one of the first snugs ever to propose harnessing the heat during hibernation and converting it into energy—something a group is trying to perfect right now inside Pagan. We had ideas that were accepted within Pagan and had everything to do with technological progression."

"Ya, we listened to our leaders and did what they told us. I don't see anything wrong with that," said Rox.

"How about all the others that had great ideas and were shot down by the board? Why does one snug have the power to make decisions for all of Pagan?"

"That's how we do it here, Ret, you know this," shouted Rox.

"Rox, if you constantly get denied approval, you will end up working on a project that just doesn't interest you, and even worse, you get the feeling your ideas don't matter."

" I will always be smart and tough enough to be a leader inside Pagan!" shouted Rus.

"Rus settle down," shouted Ret. "How about you, Carin? What do you think about Pagan?"

Carin dropped her hands from her face, opened her glossy green eyes, and slowly opened her mouth.

"I guess I'll do whatever I need to do. Pagan kind of scares me, and I will miss you too much. I really don't want to go."

Ret pushed an awkward grin to the side of his mouth; he needed to help her become more confident. He stepped over to his daughter and sat on the corner of her desk. He placed his fingers under her chin and lifted her head.

"You have what it takes, Carin, to be a proud Paganer. You have to find your passion and push to pursue it. That day is going to come. You are both going to be sent off into Pagan. I admit it will be hard, but you must be strong."

"I just don't want to become like Terri and the other snugs mom talked about. I don't want to be someone everyone hates. I just don't want to fail like them."

"She is by no means a failure, Carin. If I can be honest, Terri is tougher and more of a success than I've ever been."

"What?" answered Rox with a sharp tone.

"If anyone in our civilization can be considered a leader, it's Terri. Carin, I respect what she has put into this project. Really, I'm astonished at how she's developed such a following. And, even though many other Terinians believe she is destroying our culture, she has become a great example of what it is to be strong. She single-handedly addressed the social issues that have been oppressing snugs for years within our Pagan. Some say it's hate or resistance to the Pagan rule. But me, Carin, I think it's a powerful message of standing up for what you believe in. Please don't ever feel like you can't make a difference. Anyone can make a change in this world, and that, Carin, is what Terri is showing all of us right now."

A glimmer of green in the centre of her eyes swelled out until it filled the entire eye cavity. She slid up in her seat, straightened her posture and gave an encouraging look toward her father. Ret smiled back.

"Ret, can I see you outside in the hallway? We need to talk. Right now!" said Rox.

Ret knew what was coming. He smiled down at Carin, slid off her desk and sauntered towards the doorway. He glanced over to his son sternly and snapped his fingers; one pointed at his chair. Rus shrugged his shoulders, climbed off his desk, sat back in his seat and hunched his head down on his desk as Ret stepped outside the classroom.

"What are you doing?"

Ret flinched at the anger in her voice and was startled by her pointing finger shoved in his face.

"You look up to Terri? Do you have any idea what kind of impression that's going to leave on Carin?"

Ret took a moment and planted his stance before he pushed Rox's pointing finger away. Crunching his brow, Ret stared at her with red eyes.

"Do you realize what kind of impression your words will have on them? I am their father, and I have a say in how they are raised just as much as you do. I know that you and a million other snugs in this civilization have an issue with what's going on with Terri's group, but…"

"No, Ret. I know what you are going to say, and it is not the right answer. You have no right telling them that what Terri is doing is to be modelled over. It's not even up for discussion."

"You can't tell me how to raise my children, Rox…"

"Do you realize how tough it is being your other? Especially now when everyone is talking about your sister and what she is doing to all of us."

"How have I changed because of that…"

"You have no idea what it's like, Ret. Everyone knows you're a half-breed. And I have to sit there and defend you to everyone who remarks about *you* being a half-breed. How do you think I feel when I hear that? If you're a half-breed, I'm a half-breed, and our kids are half-breeds."

"If there is anyone who knows what you are feeling, it's me. I went through that— a million times worse. But you must choose not to listen to that and tune out all the negativity. I can't change what has happened. I can only try to work with it. I have been doing this my whole life," shouted Ret, trying to force his point onto his partner.

"So you want me to believe that you are *not* siding with Terri, and then you tell our daughter that she is a leader and one of the strongest snugs in Pagan? Why are you telling Carin to be like Terri?"

"Rox, Terri is my sister, and I know her very well. She has bad qualities and good qualities, just like everybody else. Our daughter needs to work on her confidence. Without it, she doesn't have a chance at becoming something inside Pagan. And I will do everything I can as a parent to provide her with the insight to stimulate the power inside of her. She needs us now, Rox."

"She might be on the timid side, yes, but I will not have her influenced by anything that tarnishes the image of Terin. And that's that, Ret."

"Did you see the reaction on her face after I told her about Terri?"

"It doesn't matter."

"It's not about you. It's about them now. And Rox, I will coach them using any life experience I lived through or any form of wisdom to help them develop into a better, stronger snug, even if that means not taking your side. I'm sorry, but it's the truth. I love you, Rox. I always have and always will, but we are not the priority."

Rox walked down the hallway to the main level without a final thought or reaction. She grasped the knob on the front door and swung it open. Before going out, she turned around and shouted up from the foyer.

"If you don't change your ways, Ret, I won't stand by your side anymore. You are outside of your mind. And I won't be there to help you when everyone turns on you—again."

Tension

"We must take this situation into our own hands *now*," said the blue society leader, addressing everyone within the blue amphitheatre. "No more putting up with this black society. Anyone involved with this uprising will be held accountable for their actions. We have all seen them sneaking into our communities and handing out pamphlets. If anyone sees one of these snugs wearing black fabric wrapped around their arm, you have every right to tell them to leave and never return. We will not stand for these acts of treason anymore. We must put an end to this once and for all."

Ret sat annoyed as he watched Rox and thousands of other blues rejoice. Sitting thirty rows back, he tried to focus on the speaker standing firm on the stage below. But the two snugs in front, blocking his view, crossed their arms on each other's shoulders and extended their free hands up to the sky. Ret tilted his head from side to side, trying to find a gap between them; failing to find even a sliver between the pair, he rolled his eyes and looked around at the rest of the audience.

Ret focused on a few snugs on the lower levels facing the audience and encouraging everyone to partake in a unified bow. Acting out the charade, they stretched their arms up and repeatedly bowed to the speaker, trying to motivate the audience to follow suit. Ret sat unmoving.

The leader of the blue society's counsel embraced the support of his spectators, and with his hands thrown high above his head, he inspired the audience around him with every pump of his fists. The crowd began to hush after he approached a microphone fixed to a straight iron rod in the middle of the stage. He paused momentarily, polished the blue gems on his identity ring with his hand, and then readdressed the audience.

"Terin will prevail. And with the help of other societies, we will force this problem away with all of our combined power. We will strike hard and fast. We will be merciless. We will make an example of this disgraceful black society and show the world what happens to all who choose to defy us."

Ret shook his head as he listened to Rox cheering on every word. She looked back to Ret, and knowing his opinions wouldn't budge, she delivered a condescending eye roll. Nothing was a compromise. Even mundane and day-to-day conversations were peppered with smug answers and judgmental responses. It didn't take much for a simple misunderstanding to set off a full-blown argument.

Ret raised his brow and turned his head towards his two children watching with roaring acceptance. He knew it would take much more than his words to influence his children. Sitting back in his seat, he pulled his eyes away from them and focused back on the stage.

"We will organize ourselves between all four societies—blue, red, yellow and green united. Our counsel has maintained contact with the yellow's union, the green administration, and the red's chancellors. Every Terin snug inside each society will be a part of this. We will all become one massive unit of force and coordinate our actions together. This is the only way to stop those destroying our system. Are you with us?"

Waves of roaring cheers fueled the speaker. Calming his crowd, he lowered his open hands to the stage floor before he addressed them again.

"In just over a month, every adult snug will begin marching to the east side of Terin, where Terri and her small group of outcasts are operating. We will force every black society snug to leave Terin and never return. Sorry children, only adults can join in the barrage."

Thousands of children moaned across the crowd. Ret cracked a little smile.

"My young ones. We cannot risk having you be a part of this. We need all of you to focus on yourselves and your future inside Pagan. You have my word that no one from Terri's society will be allowed inside our great wall. Who wants to grow inside Pagan with snugs that want to destroy our way of life? I will not stand by and let that happen."

Another supportive cheer erupted from the audience, and adding to the commotion, Ret turned his head to Rox as she screamed her support. "I will *never* let my children be exposed to that future. I am with you, Luc! My children and I are with you to the end! Terri must be stopped."

She raised her hands and cheered along with the crowd. Her two children followed suit.

Ret tilted his head up and looked at the ring. He recalled his childhood and the last family glider ride they took to the red competition. He imagined his family sitting happily in their glider, all laughing together. The trip was pure delight from what he remembered, even if it was embellished, and a long-lost sense of joy filled his soul. If only it could have lasted forever.

"Ret, Ret! It's time to go. The congregation is over."

Rox gave him a forceful shove pulling him out of his daydream. He shook his head and noticed the stage was clear, and most of the audience was leaving. He blinked his green eyes a few times, stood up, and followed his family, walking up the aisle in single file.

*

They approached their glider sitting in its parking spot. The vehicle's body glimmered in the sunlight as each contour sparkled in its notable deep blue. Ironically, Ret and Rox were the recipients of this stylish glider as a reward for being one of the most successful couples inside Pagan. However, if there were a reward for being the most successful parents, Ret and Rox wouldn't even be in the running.

Ret sat in the driver's seat and waited for his family to fasten their seat straps. He pressed the ignition button and zipped out of the parking space. Ret hoped the ride back home was going to be pleasant. "You know what needs to be done, Ret."

It wasn't.

He focused on the long stretch of road ahead. The open shoreline expanded the horizon on his left, mirroring the deep yellow sky. On his right, small dunes set off in the distance were carpeted with a rough sandy texture as they rolled up to the valley of Mount Nite. He tried to soak in the scenery and avoid answering Rox, but she didn't stop.

"You don't care about our children at all, do you? I mean, you just sat there and said nothing. This is big news, and if you are part of Terin, then we all need to know that you are with us. And if you're not, then you are just as bad as Terri."

"Rox, I am absolutely impartial to all of this. To be honest, I don't even know what's right and wrong anymore."

"What do you mean? That's not what you said when *you* told both of our children that you admire Terri and think she is a leader."

"Rox, I don't want to fight in front of the children. I'm tired of fighting. I don't wanna do this anymore."

Ret had lost the fiery nature he once had as a younger snug. Maybe it was that his older mind was now more analytical, or was it due to his bias? Whatever it was, he was just too tired of having to take a side and defend it. He wished the situation could just vanish and things could return to normal. Whatever normal was?

"Look at you, Ret. You can't even take a side and be there for your society, let alone your family. What kind of father are you? You have no feelings about anything anymore. And right now, your children need you the most," shouted Rox before turning in her seat. "Are you two upset with your father? It's ok. You can say it. You should tell him how you feel. Everyone should. Your father doesn't seem to care about you like *I* do. He grew up in a family that abandoned him, so I'm not surprised that it's happening again to you. But I won't let anything happen to you. You two can trust *me* over your father."

"Who do you think you are, Rox?"

He had it.

"Don't you *ever* tell them not to put their trust in me? I will *always* be there for them. And if you think I'm anything like my father, you're wrong. That congregation back there was an act of fear. I have *no* idea what will happen with Terri, our children, or even us, Rox, but I will *not* support a group fueled by hate. I saw too much of it when I was in Pagan. And now, with this, it has exploded into something that I never thought Terin would become. "

"Can you stop fighting, please," said Carin piping up from the backseat.

"*We* are being hateful?" screamed Rox. "What about your sister? How can you sit there and not see that this is a reaction to the evil she is spreading? Look at everything Terin has given you, Ret. Our house, this glider, and a great legacy. You would have nothing if it weren't for Terin."

"Terin didn't give this to me, Rox. *I*… well… *we* earned it."

"You think *you* were the one to earn everything between us?"

"That's not what I meant."

"You think *you* have the power in this relationship, don't you? Well, you don't, Ret. Did you forget that *I* was the one who saved you? You wouldn't even be here if it wasn't for me. Maybe I should have…"

Rox ended her rant and faced in the other direction.

"Maybe you should have what? Left me?"

"All you do is fight," screamed Carin.

"It's getting really old," shouted Rus. "Will you both just stop."

Ret slammed his hands on the steering wheel, and a long, awkward silence ensued. The animosity between him and Rox cut so deep that he didn't know how to resolve their issues. In his experience with friendships, he knew the only thing that made a partnership strong was respect, and it was clear between them there was none. While blinking his fiery red eyes, Ret came to terms with the hard truth about his relationship. Love, it seemed, didn't always last forever.

⊶

Family First

Once a year, this lone yellow planet moves to the outer edge of its orbit and traverses past the Sirra star. Slowly, the face of the planet turns outward, exposing the world's only landmass to the blackness of space, leaving every inhabitant in total darkness for three long months.

Stuck in a perpetuating state of trepidation, snugs have learned, over time, to combat the isolation of night by gathering together, strengthening their community. For centuries, pioneer snugs assembled into large gatherings to promote past accomplishments and recognize opportunities for the new year. The idea was to celebrate all achievements by praising everyone in one big commemorative festival.

Today, modern practices are much larger in scale—mass congregations from across the globe. For Terin, the red society banquet hall was always the communal location. For the blue society, assemblies were held inside the blue amphitheatre. Terin was so organized that each year every member was provided living space and required to partake in their colour's celebrations. Everyone had a home, and everyone felt a sense of belonging. Well, everyone except the black society.

East of Terin, a large gathering of black society snugs assembled inside their makeshift garrison. Their buildings, modest in nature, were constructed of raw granite and scrap metal from discarded Pagan projects.

Their newly formed perimeter encircled all the members of the society, which stood a thousand strong. Located in the middle of her fortress, standing confidently atop a stone pedestal and surrounded by all her group members, Terri raised her head and grinned before she addressed her small nation.

"Our first night season, I can't say how proud I am of every one of you. Look how far we've come; we only have you to thank. In the beginning, I felt alone before we even started this movement. Like most of you, I felt Pagan was a place where we couldn't be ourselves. We've all heard the lies, experienced the manipulation and felt the lack of self-expression inside that wall. None of us had the freedom to be who we wanted and follow our beliefs. We were all just cogs in the system, the system that hated us and wanted us to conform. But we know now. Never again will others dictate how we should live our lives. If *we* have our *own* ideas, we should have every right to pursue them."

Terri paused her speech and raised her clenched fist to the sky, cheering on her supporters.

"All of you here have made a big difference, and together we can make a change in Pagan. Everyone is scared of us because, deep down, they know we are right. They just don't want to face it, but the time is now to show everyone we will stand up for what's right. No one can take away our voice now."

Terri's blue skin was gleaming from all the burnlights shining on her as she stood strong, arms held out, palms facing the sky.

"It wasn't long ago when we first settled here on the flat rock and began constructing our home."

"It wasn't easy," someone shouted from the darkened crowd.

Chuckling along with the rest of the group, Terri grinned and nodded her head.

"Yeah, my muscles are still hurting. Yours must be, too, Bri! I don't think anyone worked as hard as you, chiselling out all that rock," answered Terri.

"I almost fell into two geyser holes! So trust me when I tell you I'm committed to being a part of this society," Bri shouted.

"I'm still amazed how we managed to build this society using the brittle granite from around old geyser holes," exclaimed Terri. "But that just shows everyone just how determined we are. And we are here to stay."

A great hearted laugh poured over the crowd in the darkness.

Terri continued. "It will never be easy. Was it easy inside Pagan when we stood up to Sal?"

"No!" the audience shouted back.

"Was it easy to build this society?

"No!"

"The hardest obstacles are yet to come. Whether it be dealing face-to-face with the four societies or spreading our influence with them inside Pagan, I want… I *need* you all to understand that this group has more power, ambition, and will, than any of Sal's followers. I see a strong future, and as each day goes by, more and more snugs are walking across that flat rock and coming over to join us. *You* have made this a reality. Now let's take our goals to the next level and influence Pagan as a whole."

Black society devotees shouted in kind, roaring their acceptance to an empowered Terri standing firm on her podium. Beams from burnlights shone out into the darkened sky from all the snugs raised arms, pinpointing their position on the flat rock.

The bleak landscape around her society was desolate, even more so now throughout the night season. This made for an ideal setting for the black society to inhabit an area far enough away from Terin that would provide stability and little resistance from Terin snugs.

The only snugs who made the trek across the flat rock knew the risks of their venture. On a one-way journey, the blacks always accepted these recently turned snugs. It was a journey that more and more Terin snugs were taking daily.

However, this night one lonely snug ventured across the dark landscape. Not to become a black society member and not to defend Terin's traditions. He marched across the flat rock to try and save his sister from Terin's extermination plan.

Ret trudged his way through the pitch black. Exhausted and out of frost, he paused momentarily, dropped to one knee, and waited for his bump to recover. He stared out onto the flat rock and spotted white beams of light shooting high into the sky, giving him clear directions to Terri's society. Ret pushed his body back upright, released a long exaggerated groan, stretched out his arms and continued.

As he marched across this bleak panorama, he began to see the dark silhouette of the makeshift structure and plodded towards it. He tried to ignore the pain in his legs and the bottoms of his feet, but his body wasn't only struggling; his mind was taking the brunt of this torture.

Thoughts of his sister raced through his mind, and at times, Ret questioned what he was doing. Terri never showed Ret any respect; she was irrational with her feelings, and of course, he could never forget what she did to him during that one hibernation in Pagan.

Even though he harboured resentful feelings towards Terri, he believed in her capabilities and, most of all, her cause. He was not trying to betray his society or the Terin civilization. All he was trying to do was warn Terri of Terin's plans. The way he saw it, she was family, and even after all of their history, he still believed that family came first.

Finally, he reached the short rock wall that bordered black society and immediately fell to his knees. He dropped straight down onto the hard rocky ground, barely able to push up onto his backside. He grimaced in pain as he spread his appendages out and shouted.

His howling shriek of exhaustion caught the attention of a few meandering snugs he swiftly found himself surrounded. Too tired to even look up, Ret lay there gasping for energy and did nothing but thank the blacks as they swooped in and grabbed his lifeless body.

"We got you now, spy," one of them screamed. "Look! He's wearing a blue society ring. Grab his legs. You are not going anywhere."

"I'm not a spy!"

"Well, we're going to find out. Now get up. You're coming with us."

Forced to his feet by a powerful thrust, both black members took Ret's arms and shuffled him inside. Flashes of white light illuminated the ground as angry snugs yelled insults from all around. He tried to look up to see what was happening, but his captors pressed his head down again, walking him like a hostage.

"We just found a Terin spy. Look, he's wearing blue rings on his hand. He was sent here to gather information and use it against us."

"No, I'm not a spy. Where is Terri? She is my sister," shouted Ret.

Their grip eased off Ret's neck, and a confused hush took over the immediate crowd. He blinked his eyes in relief and pulled his body upright, facing the group. He shook his head, looked around, and noticed all the beams of light were funnelling together, illuminating Terri standing directly in front of him.

"So you had to become a spy just to say hello to me?" Terri asked with a smirk on her face.

She gestured to his captors to let go and stepped away. Before releasing their grip, one of the snugs patted him on the shoulder.

"If you were any other Terin snug, we would have made an example out of you."

"Nonsense. We won't stand for cruelty. However, we will reciprocate any action done to us," exclaimed Terri. "Is that? Really? Someone, point a light onto my brother's hand."

Turning his wrist, Ret tried hiding his blue identity piece.

"A blue? Really? I can see you being a yellow or green before, but a blue? You would look better with a black tag tied around your arm. Listen, Ret. Are you sure you want to join our group and be part of black society? We aren't conventional with how we do things in these parts. I'm not sure a snug like…"

"They're coming."

"What?"

"All of the societies are forming a union and coming after you and every-one here."

Terri laughed at the threat and kept her followers calm.

"Good. We need more supporters."

The groups chuckled along with her.

"That's why you came here, to tell me this. What do they think they are going to do?"

"They are coming to destroy this society and banish you. They are going to force all of you out. None of your children will be allowed into Pagan, and from here on out, you will be considered outcasts and can never return to Terin."

Terri reacted as a true leader and tried reaffirming confidence within herself and her snugs. She wasn't about to let this public spectacle ruin the integrity of her project. She encouraged her followers to keep their faith.

"Remember what I said. We knew this was never going to be easy. To be honest, right now, I feel privileged to have made such an impact on Terin. This tells me that we are making a statement. Our word has spread, and our hard work is being rewarded. We have induced fear into all those who have oppressed us, abandoned us, and taken advantage of our good ideas within that wall.

This retaliation against our simple freedom will be met with an equal reaction. They will not push us around. We'll confront anyone that tries to smother our freedom. We will stand and fight them head-on."

Terri looked around and finished her speech with a decisive nod. Her followers responded generously and raised their arms, displaying their black arm straps.

Approaching her brother with a broad and loving smile, Terri opened her arms and hugged him.

Ret felt uneasy. He irked out a little grin, stepped in and patted above her frost bump with one of his hands. Playing the part of a loving brother, he shook off his awkward feelings, pulled his head back, and faced her with a smile. "I would have brought a bottle of Jax, but I probably would have drank it before I arrived!"

"Yeah, you would have!" chuckled Terri. "Ret, allow me to take you around our society. There is a lot I want to show you. Here take this burnlight."

They walked to the far end of the improvised society, approaching a series of rough and ready structures fabricated from uneven stone cuts. He examined one makeshift building as they approached a wide, asymmetrically shaped doorway inside the darkened grey exterior.

With his light source held in his hand, he took note of the weak foundations of the two-story building. He noticed several black flags erected on the roof, and directly below a series of irregularly shaped windows were cut out from the second story.

Terri poked her head out the main door and waved to Ret, directing him inside. Ret cautiously stepped in.

"Why are you here, Ret?"

Straight to the point, Terri confronted her brother.

"The last time we spoke was not the most comfortable conversation. From how things were left off, I can't imagine you ever wanting to talk to me again. So forgive me, Ret, 'cause I'm wondering why *you* are really here."

"Come on, Terri. Do you think leaving me outside in the heat of hibernation was something to hold a grudge over? Really?" Ret replied sarcastically.

"You really *are* a spy, aren't you, Ret? How clueless do you think I am? I'll tell you exactly what *I* would think if I were you. Knowing that your life almost ended because of me, I would have lost all hope in rekindling any relationship. I wouldn't even consider you to be part of my family anymore. I would never forgive you and I would eventually find a way to get even. I would devise a plan to take revenge on something you have put your life into. And then, after I crush your dreams and accomplishments, I would look you in the eye and tell you how I was the reason your empire crumbled. *That's* what I would do, Ret. So let me ask you again. Why are you here?"

"Yeah, Terri, you would do that."

"Yes. I definitely would," she answered with a serious expression.

"Aren't you tired of being angry?"

Terri's harsh expression instantly diminished; she let her brother continue.

"You realize that you have formed a society that goes against centuries of tradition. You are trying to destroy everything Terin stands for because you resent how it treated you? Did you think this would go on forever unchallenged, that no one in Terin was going to try and stop you?"

Shaking her head, Terri burst out into a spat of frustration.

"You got lucky, Ret! You developed your communication technology, and then bang, everyone in Pagan respected you. No one remembered or even cared about Dad after you built your idea. You got a fresh start and then lived a great life in Pagan. A life that I and everyone else out there never got to experience. We were all cheated. It wasn't fair."

"Spare me your struggles, Terri, because so many of us have been through it and don't want to hear what you have to say. It's a weakness, Terri, plain and simple. You are all weak. That's the truth."

"So easy for you to say, Ret. You have a great other and a great legacy. Your children will grow up with everything they need inside Pagan. You can't imagine what it's like for us inside Pagan."

"You deserve it, Terri. You deserve it!" screamed Ret. "And I'm not what you think I am. I have so many problems with my family because of you. Rox hates me because I defend you. I look into her eyes, and there's nothing anymore. And my children are conditioned to believe only one thing. To hate and destroy you and this black society. You have stirred up all of Terin. You've pushed your views and this idea on them so far that now, just like you, snugs either hate Terin or they hate you. You should feel very proud of what you accomplished."

"We have both suffered. We have both risen above the challenges we faced, Ret. And we both have been in positions of power," Terri said, calming her voice. "You know I can't change this or take back what I've started. If they want to try and push us away, we'll just have to push back. And that's that."

"Terri, as much as you might not believe this, I'm proud of what you've accomplished. Really, I am. That's why Rox hates me so much," said Ret as he cracked a faint smile. "But in all seriousness, how will you defend yourself from the entire population?"

Terri caught sight of a light beam dancing on the wall beside her. She spun around to see two small snugs standing behind her.

"I thought I told you two to stay inside our quarters."

"We heard a lot of shouting out here, and we wanted to see what was going on. Is everything alright, Mom?"

"Everything is fine, you two. Come over here. There is someone I want you to meet."

Ret was shocked. He pointed his light toward the two children and smiled at the curious little snugs before him.

"Rey and Tam, I want you to meet Ret, my brother."

"Really, *You're* Ret? I've heard so much about you," said Rey, shining his light onto Ret's face.

"So, are you the one that developed the communication system?" asked Tam as she tried reaching for the light in her brother's hand. "Give me the light, Rey. You aren't shining it right."

"Go away, Tam. I'm doing it just fine."

"They are sure like us when we were their age, aren't they?" said Terri, snickering.

Ret was so caught up in the moment that his only response was a cackle and a dramatic head nod.

"Mom always talks about you and how smart you are. She always says how she wishes she could be as strong as you. She says you were the one she wanted to be like growing up, always winning competitions. Mom always tells us that she wants us to be like you."

Ret looked into Terri's eyes with compassion, as she stood behind her children and harboured a gracious smile.

"Well, your Mom is very kind. But trust me, you two, I want you to be yourselves. Most of the time, I don't want to be me."

"That can't be true. You're the best. When I get into Pagan, I also want to change the world. Do you think I can, Ret?"

The feeling of sorrow hit Ret hard. He knew these two innocent children might never have an opportunity to be a part of Terin, let alone Pagan. But he held in his emotions, kneeled in front of both little ones, and returned the flattery.

"Of course you can, Tam. And so can you, Rey. You can do whatever you want."

Before standing up, Ret followed his encouraging words with a big smile, reaching his arms out and rubbing the tops of their heads.

"Alright, you two. Go back to our quarters. I'll be there soon," said Terri.

"Bye, Ret. It was very nice to meet you," said Rey.

"Bye, Ret," said Tam.

"Wow! They're great, Terri."

"Yeah, they are. They are the ones I'm fighting for. They are the reason I'm so adamant about making Terin fair. There is no way I want them going into Pagan and through the same torture we faced, Ret."

"We became the strong snugs we are today because of our challenges, Terri. You have to see that. I couldn't have done anything if it wasn't for what I faced inside Pagan. You know, you were the reason I found the idea for my group. And you were the reason I found Rox. If it weren't for you, Terri, I wouldn't be the snug I am today."

Ret and Terri shared a righteous moment for the first time in a long time, or maybe ever. The hard nail driven between them loosened just a bit. He knew he couldn't change who she was, nor did he want to. All Ret wanted to do was protect her from what was to come, and, at that moment, he felt good about himself and so did Terri. For the two long-lost siblings, all they needed was to show each other an act of kindness, as one good deed usually follows another.

Without feeling pressured, Terri faced Ret and repaid her act of kindness. For years she had buried her feelings beneath her pride, but today she was ready to give Ret something he'd yearned for. And even though she couldn't change what had happened, it was time for her to apologize. In one small sentence, she reciprocated the good deed and rekindled a new start to their relationship.

"You know, Ret. About that day I left you… I… I'm sorry."

War

A sliver of sunlight peeked out over the horizon, emitting rich and radiant energy across the land, and a single black society member sat slouching at his lookout post, gazing into the rising star at the front of the black garrison. His glazed over eyes shot wide open before jumping to his feet. It took a moment for his mind to process and needed more than three or four glances and a few blinks to confirm what he was witnessing. With a firm shake of his head, he saw an army of snugs marching in their direction. "Terri! They're coming! Everyone position yourselves. Get out in front of our society wall now."

A heavy siren shook the black society into order. Everyone jumped into action and scurried to their posts, ready to fight.

Terri ran to the base of the stone podium high above the society's walls and shouted up to the snug, staring out to the horizon with his black eyes peeled.

"How many, Ric? How many of them are there?"

The snug tried to answer Terri but words deserted him.

"Ric! How many?" screamed Terri. "I need you now!"

"Tens of thousands. Do you hear me, Terri? Tens of thousands!"

Terri snarled. His weakness aggravated her. Terri's beliefs were simple: face your fears and never give in to your emotions, especially when it involves a challenge from your enemy. Darting from the podium's base, she dodged and weaved through the frenzied crowd of snugs, giving orders to a few waivering individuals as she raced to the front entrance.

Standing directly behind two granite stone gates, she gathered the attention of her snugs before she gave the order to open the doorway. "We knew this was coming, everyone. Ret was right. We all need to take control of ourselves and face this challenge head-on," she shouted, turning to address every snug in the crowd. "This is the reaction we were all hoping for. We did it, everyone. And we will meet every challenge that faces us. Let's show them the strength of the black society!"

Two lines of snugs were positioned on either side of the gates, gripping long ropes attached to a pulley rig. At the sight of Terri's arm chopping down each line of snugs bent their knees and began tugging on the rope. Two thick stone slabs slid over ice tracks, bottoming each granite slate. Once the doors opened, every black citizen took a conscious step back after witnessing the oncoming horde of snugs marching toward them.

Terri grimaced as she squinted her eyes. She readdressed her citizens, trying to keep them focused. "We will not back down. They want a fight? They want a war? We're going to give them exactly what they came here for," screamed Terri as she glared outside the doorway. "I will lead all of you through this. Stand behind me and fight for our society—and most importantly, for yourselves."

Terri turned around and looked out into the horizon. She raised her left hand high into the sky and took the first steps outside the gates. Her devoted patrons delivered on their promises and stayed close behind.

Out in the open flat rock, Terri's group was heavily outnumbered. The Terin army marched in unison, sending vibrations through the ground. And as the small group of blacks made their way over the flat rock, the ground shook harder as they approached. "We have the strength. They are afraid of us. That's why they are here. We are free. They are not."

Terri's anxiety was building as her loyal followers moved farther away from their secure position and onto the exposed land. She was close enough now to see the colour of the enemy's eyes. Angry shades of red stared back at her as they trooped forward. Responding in kind, Terri and her group scowled back with eyes just as red. "Throw the rocks now."

Well within firing position, the blacks hurled hand sized rocks onto the Terin army, staggering their throws to keep a constant rate of fire. Terri cheered as the stones rained down, smacking several Terin citizens square on the head. As they drew closer, she commanded her followers to keep advancing and not to give in or be weakened.

After several more steps, Terri felt they were close enough and signalled her clan to halt in their place; the Terinians, however, did not stop their march.

They gathered around the black society members and encircled the entire group, barricading them. Realizing their superior tactic, Terri snarled as she looked behind her and saw a smaller group of Terinians running towards her society building, equipped with heavy tools and bulky mallets. Hooting and shouting, the group raced to the edge of her black society and began ripping the walls apart.

"Who do you think you are? You will not get away with any of this. I will dest…"

"You deserve this."

Interrupting her rant was the stentorian voice of the red society chancellor. The noble snug was recognizable by the red jewelled sash wrapped around his shoulder and midsection.

"I'm Razo, Terri. I took over from Dek after they sent him off to die."

"Call them off. Call your slave snugs back from destroying our home."

"I won't do that," answered Razo, shaking his head. "I know you grew up as a red, so we all figured I was the most suitable snug for you to speak with…"

Terri stepped closer toward Razo, her enraged red eyes piercing as she pointed her finger at his face.

"You think you can come here and take our lives away from us without a fight? Did you think we were just going to back down? You can't do this."

Turning in her place, Terri addressed her army.

"I hope all of you can live a life of conformity and compliance. You all know that you are here because of them. These pathetic leaders of Terin. This civilization is only for the powerful snugs who don't care about your dreams or creativity. I am the only one that can promise you absolute freedom from everyone and everything. It's up to you to take a chance and give that to yourself. Don't listen to the society leaders…"

Razo forced Terri to halt her speech with a solid shoulder strike right to her chest. The Terin army howled.

"Don't say another word, Terri," Razo commanded.

She didn't listen.

"Question everything. Don't listen to him or the directors. We're all here for…"

Fueled by the support of his army, Razo grabbed Terri's shoulder, spun her around, and faced her fiery red eyes and devilishly smirking mouth. Without hesitation, he swung his right hand with all his power, connecting it devastatingly on her cheek.

Terri crashed to the ground. Nursing her pain, she opened her left eye and looked up at Razo, who had both arms held high into the sky. An ear shattering roar erupted around him.

She put her hand to her face and kept her aching eye closed. She looked back at her supporters and smiled after seeing her brother come to her defence.

"Enough," screamed Ret as he walked towards Razo. "Nobody hits my sister!"

"Well, this isn't a surprise at all. We should have known you were going to join up with her, Ret. I wouldn't have expected anything less."

Pulling his right arm up to Razo's face, Ret clenched his fist and showed the chancellor exactly where his allegiance lay.

"Blue rings. Can you see them? I'm blue for my family," Ret said in an aggravated tone. "I would do anything for my family."

"Your family," said the chancellor sarcastically. "Your family put Terri here. Ret, I would have banished you and Terri years ago."

"Your society wouldn't have been as renowned if it wasn't for me, so don't go thinking that we did nothing for you," replied Ret in a defensive tone.

"You are not a red anymore, Ret. And right now, you are not blue, either. A snug like you would hate the blue society. Don't stand here and tell me you're a blue. You're black at heart. Tell me, how is everything back home in the blue society? Does Rox still love you? I know she must be on our side. She obviously knows about your past and Terri's. And your children? I wonder what their lives will be like inside Pagan."

"Terri's society is becoming more and more appealing the more you speak," answered Ret.

"You know, we came here to get rid of Terri, but both of you are the problem. I'm going to follow through with what Dek should have done. You are hereby banished from Terin. You, Terri, and every single black society member here will leave our land and never return."

Ret sneered into Razo's red eyes without breaking his focus. A hush fell over the tens of thousands, standing anxious and uncertain.

Terri was the only one to break the silence after rising spiritedly to her feet.

"Not without a fight, you're not," she threatened.

She raced towards Ret, placed her hand on Ret's shoulder, and then lept out from behind him, delivering a hard strike directly into Razo's left eye. Razo dropped to the ground in front of all his supporters. The Terinians answered back.

Instantly the army charged the centre of the circle with their arms raised. Each side began throwing punches and knocking the other to the ground, savagely releasing all their pent-up anger.

Terri shouted and raised her black identity piece high in the sky before taking a running start towards the first Terin snug she set her sights on. She sprinted towards the frontline, cocked her arm back, and released a brutal punch on the first Terin snug to approach her. Invigorated by the pandemonium, her followers relished her actions as fuel and followed her lead.

Sounds of screaming and heavy cracking of bone-on-bone contact heightened the bloodthirsty spirits of both sides. Black society members were swinging their limbs in every direction, trying desperately to land a few strikes against a sea of enraged Terinians countering their attacks with pummelling blows. Those who fell to the ground were kicked and stomped on by waves of snugs screaming their fury. The only defence fallen snugs could use was curling their knees to their chest and stretching their arms to cover their head. No quarter given, no quarter taken.

Peering through a swarming barrage of bodies, Ret pushed off a few attackers with quick elbow shots to their backs and punches to their faces. His head was swivelling all the time. He glanced to his left and saw one black society member pummelled by several Terin supporters stomping on his helpless body. He pressed his way through the crowd.

With a running start, he leaped onto the back of one of the attackers and clenched his arm around their neck. Contending against the sounds of everyone's battle screams, Ret shouted in fury as his grip tightened. Round and round he went as the Terin snug spun his body, trying to throw him off. Ret clasped on until his frost was depleted, and he fell to the ground. Smirking with satisfaction, Ret peered out of the corner of his eye and saw the snug he was helping rise back to his feet and immerse himself back once more into the fight.

As for Ret, they attacked him on the ground; punches, kicks, and stomps reigned down on Ret's face and body until finally a few black members rescued him.

The situation was growing grave. Terri fought off several unworthy attackers while keeping a close eye on Razo, who at the moment was fighting off another black society member. Anticipating the chance for a one-on-one battle with him gave her the strength to combat every aggressor she faced. She gained confidence each time she injured a worthless challenger by swiftly knocking their bodies to the ground with a quick swipe of her leg and a finishing kick to their chest. She held nothing back. She swung her head and saw Razo standing before her, squaring off and staring her down. She was ready for the ultimate challenge.

All around them were snugs furiously battling one another, providing the perfect backdrop for Terri and Razo. Both leaders circled each other. Terri answered Razo's loathing demeanour by mirroring the same sneer eyed and vile facial expression onto him. Suddenly, Terri charged him; Razo charged back.

Flying fists, hard-hitting knee strikes, and an exchange of screaming fueled the fight. Terri got the edge over her opponent by grabbing his red sash, pulling his body in close, and delivering a walloping head butt to the centre of his face. Staggering back in pain, Razo placed his hand on his face. Terri holding onto his sash ripped it from his shoulder. Smiling, she threw the sash to the ground, grinding the stones into the rocky surface with her foot.

The battle around them stilled as the crowd reacted to Terri's discourteous insolence against the chancellor and his office. Everyone stopped fighting and gathered around the two leaders to watch the duel of their leaders.

Razo shook off the pain of Terri's strike and cast his fiery red eyes around. The roaring sounds of the crowd stoked his anger. He clenched his fists and sneered at Terri, arrogantly standing with her back to him.

Terri had her arms raised proudly with a mocking smile on her face. She pulled her head back and lifted her face to the sky. She savoured the moment a little too long; Razo was almost upon her, soaked with vengeance.

Not even the warning sounds of the other snugs gave Terri enough time to react against Razo. At the last possible moment, her internal alarm alerted her to the voices of her supporters shouting from the perimeter.

"Terri, watch out."

Razo lunged. Using his shoulder, he speared her lower back with the full weight of his body. Terri's arms and legs flailed backward as her midsection folded forward, smacking the ground hard. Her body lay still and unconscious. The vicious strike had done irreparable damage, but Razo ignored it. With his anger intensified, he turned over Terri's lifeless body and jumped on top of her, straddling her midsection. Without wasting a moment, he began lambasting her motionless face. His glossy red eyes were wide open. The crowd's intensity shifted to a disturbed silence as they all watched Razo destroy her face. For everyone present, this traumatizing act was well beyond what any of them could have imagined. No one had thought that it would have resulted in this. Every snug watched terrified as Terri's body was annihilated..

"Stop! Stop it, Razo!"

Trying to push his way through the perimeter of snugs, Ret was the only one not entranced by the scene. He was the only voice to stand out; everyone else was in shock, staring blankly at Razo, still delivering punch after punch.

Ret barged his way into the circle and jumped onto Razo's back, pulling his body away from his sister and flinging him to the ground.

Ret kneeled over his beaten sister and tried to shake her body awake. He consoled her face with the palm of his hand and looked at her with poignant blue eyes before turning his head to the sky and wailing a heartrending bellow. With no snug ever having seen an act of violence so terrible in their life, no one present had any idea what would happen next. "Look at her eyes. Is she?"

Astounded at what he saw, Ret stood up while keeping his eyes locked on her face. It was unthinkable to explain what her body was going through.

Throughout history, death has been a mystery for the snug species. To their knowledge, every Terin snug that lived out their twenty-five years spent their last remaining time out in the darkness of nightfall only to vanish from the planet. Dying of natural causes was the only way every snug in their world had ever understood the progression of dying; until now, as they all witnessed Terri's unnatural demise.

Lying still, her unmoving eyes filled with abundant bright white light. The brilliance of the light grew and strengthened until it was too intense to watch. Ret turned away from the beaming glow now shining out of Terri's entire body. Not even Ret's palms covering his face could block it out. Everyone was kneeling, emitting shrieks of panic. Screaming in fear, Ret was about to take off running. However, as he rose to his feet the light disappeared.

Blinking his eyes open, Ret waited for clarity to return to his vision, as he rubbed his tender face with his hand. He looked around and saw the legion of snugs all staring in shock, their black eyes focussed on the spot where Terri once lay. Ret shook his head, wiped the dust off his front and looked for his sister.

"Where did she go?" whispered Ret.

I'm Sorry

"I can't wait for our snugs to return home from their fight! We should all be so proud. We have finally taken action and banished Terri and her followers from our civilization. The Terin way of life is the only way of life. And no one will ever try and change that now."

Hundreds of Terinians gathered at the border of the flat rock, cheering on a female snug standing before them. She bowed to her audience and projected a brimming smile. Standing firm within the audience, Rox wrapped her arms around her two children standing at her side, shouting her acceptance to the female speaker.

"Soon, our snugs will return from the black society, and we will celebrate our victory. We will praise all the snugs that chose to fight for this cause and help destroy black society. We have once and for all eliminated them from Terin forever. No more worry about our children's future being tainted. Everything is back to how it is supposed to be," the female said, pumping her clenched fists above her head. "Now, there is someone here I want to commend. She is someone who has been through a lot and should be praised for her efforts. Where is she?"

She searched through the pack and settled her gaze on Rox, singling her out with an extended finger.

"Rox. *You* are an inspiration to all of us. I am so proud of you. I know that you have been dealing with difficulties at home. Her other, as everyone knows, is Ret, Terri's brother—and a half-breed himself. Rox, I want to tell you that I'm delighted that you stuck to your beliefs through all of this. It really means a lot to us. *You* were the one that raised your children, and I know they have the same beliefs as all of us. Because of that, I can look past their partial Tarni roots and see them as our equals."

A loud, supportive cheer rumbled across the crowd as everyone showed their admiration for Rox and her children. She turned and faced everyone with green eyes, waving to the audience around her. She stood proud, nodding her head, soaking in the praise from her supporters; however, on the inside, she was coming to a serious realization about Ret, and wondering just how he could go against an entire civilization. She pushed her thoughts aside and spoke out.

"Thank you all. This means so much to us. It has been hard. And yes, our home life has been a challenge. But I knew this whole time that I was right. You are all showing me that today. I battled Ret for years. It wasn't easy. He's a very stubborn little snug, and it's hard to sway his opinion. I don't understand why he doesn't see the evil in his sister. The things that I see. The things that we *all* see."

"We're all here for you, Rox," a voice shouted from the crowd.

"You don't need him anymore. You have us," another voice followed.

"Thank you. And I'm so glad to have all of you. I'm no longer going to put up with Ret. And if that means I have to go ahead and live my life without him, then that's what I'm going to do. He has done nothing but defend Terri. He even went as far as calling her a leader."

The crowd let out a unified gasp. She nodded her head as she turned to show acknowledgement of the group's reaction.

"*Yes*! I couldn't believe it myself. He supports her and her society. In fact, I wish I could tell him how I feel right now. But I don't know where he is. At some point in the night season, he left the house and hasn't returned. For all I know, he could have turned on us, become a black society member, and reunited with his sister. So, I guess he did all the hard work for me. No need to push him away anymore."

Rox's eyes were solid green, with a wide grin spread across her face. She paused to take in the moment before letting out a loud cheer and returned her attention to the lead female snug smiling back.

"Let's all thank Rox for her courage. You are doing what is right for *your* children. After our snugs return from destroying the black society, you will realize that you made the best decision for your family. Ret is the one who is missing out. Now, let's all stand proud and wait for our snugs to come in from the flat rock."

Everyone turned towards the horizon, waiting for the first sight of Terin's army to return. A few snugs were scuffing their feet, kicking up small dust clouds on the stone surface, eager for their heroes to come home.

Far in the distance, a small silhouette of the first snug peaked over the horizon. A roaring cheer erupted, but to their surprise, he did not react in kind. As he made his way over the hard granite, he slowly swayed from side to side, dragging his feet and staring at the ground as he led his massive Terin legion in from the flat rock. Dodging the geysers in the ground appeared to be the only sense of awareness this snug seemed to have.

"Look, here they come. Let's all greet them with a big hooray," the lead female snug announced.

Rox looked out to the horizon; she couldn't believe what she saw.

She squinted her eyes, trying to block out the bright sunlight and noticed their wretched body movements as they slowly walked in.

A silent confusion encapsulated the crowd. Rox shook her head and raised her brow, questioning the look of horror printed across each one of their faces. She felt utterly mystified as each snug sauntered past, all looking melancholy.

"What's wrong with them, Mom? And why aren't they stopping? Do they even see us?" asked Carin.

"Yeah, it's like they all saw something that frightened them," said Rus.

"I don't know," answered Rox. "But I'm going to find out. Hey. What happened out there? Can someone tell me?"

Rox shouted out to a few passing snugs, but everyone ignored her. Yelling even louder and with more force, she demanded a response. However, her voice was useless. No one stopped or even looked up. Rox was not impressed. Losing her control, she grabbed hold of one passing snug and pulled him in, forcing her red eyes onto his.

"What happened to Terri?" she screamed.

The snug slowly looked at Rox with black eyes. Rox gripped his shoulders and shook him a few times, trying to force out an answer. He was trembling in front of her. Closing his eyes and shaking his head, the snug bawled in dread. He finally opened his eyes and told Rox in two words the reason for all of their suffering.

"She's dead."

"She's what?" answered Rox.

"She's dead. We—beat—her—to—death?" answered the snug as he pulled his hands to his face.

"What? What do you mean, dead?" answered Rox.

"She is dead, Rox. We made her die early. She disappeared. No one knows what happened to her body after she died. She just vanished."

"We took her life away?"

"Yes, Rox. We all stole her life."

"I still don't understand."

"Razo, he beat her face so much that her life ended early. There was a huge glow of white light around her body after he beat her, and then she disappeared."

"So, he ended her life?"

"Yes. Now, I'm going home. Don't bother me anymore."

He pulled Rox's arms off his shoulders and forced her out of the way. Struck with shock, Rox began to believe his story when she studied the facial expression of the others walking in from the battlefield. She shouted out to another passerby; he delivered the same message to her.

"Did we really just end Terri's life?"

"Yes."

"No…"

Rox slouched her shoulders and tilted her head down. Her body was trembling. With her eyes half open, she dropped to her knees as her children approached her, trying to understand the situation.

For years after the birth of her children, Rox took on a much more dominant role within her family. A protective, nurturing approach with her children had, over time, distilled into a controlling abrasive attitude. Her maternal nature was always being tested, and as her children grew up and began to challenge her, she created a more demanding and stricter set of rules that she enforced to keep the household under control. Being a mother changed her, and it seemed that her role as a parent was what had hardened the free spirit she once had. But her parental duties weren't the only reason she had transformed into the snug she was today.

It didn't help that Terri was part of her extended family. In social settings, she always felt the need to be overly cruel and callous towards Terri when the topic was brought up; and it always was. It was easy for her children who she loved unconditionally, to be painted with a brush of persecution. She tried to battle everyone's biased judgement by taking a harsh position that reinforced her disdain towards the black society. Reiterating everyone's hateful views of Terri helped her keep her friendships healthy and protect her children—or so she thought.

As the years passed, Rox's position on Terri grew into a boiling hatred that infected her rational thinking. Her once kind, understanding and considerate attitude was replaced with a narrow-minded, argumentative and judgmental outlook. Animosity buried its clutches deep into her soul, and as the years evolved she gradually changed for the worse. Hatred it seemed was the catalyst.

"Look, Mom! There's Dad!" shouted Carin.

Returning to the present moment, Rox rose and tried to spot Ret walking in from the horizon.

"Where?" she shouted frantically.

Rox followed Carin's pointing hand to the middle of the group and spotted Ret limping towards them.

"Dad. We're over here," shouted Rus.

Devastation splashed over Ret's face, his black eyes glaring at Rox as he walked closer. He stopped before her, squared his body to hers and waited for her to share her thoughts. Any comment that would convey Terin's triumph over Terri or even the smallest remark that would applaud their result, would cause Ret to cut off all relations with her, and she knew it.

Rox was quivering as she slowly pulled her eyes up to meet his. She struggled to even look at him; her shame sat heavy in the pit of her gut, weighing her down. Ret deserved a sign of good faith. Harnessing her courage, Rox grabbed his hand, closed her eyes and cried out the only words that resonated with her other.

"Ret, I'm so sorry."

Peace

R et reclined on his comfortable blue couch, savouring the silence. He stretched his hands behind his head and interlaced his fingers. He looked at the lofty ceiling in his blue society home and let his mind drift. Trying to soak in the tranquil moment, he closed his eyes and relaxed his matured body that was now very quick to tire due to his age—a realization he so wanted to deny. Just as he settled into the soft cushions, the sound of Rox's voice roused him as she came dashing through the front door.

"It came, Ret. The newsletter came. Along with this big package," she shouted as she entered the living space. "I read over the front index, and the four societies have finally released what they promised."

"And it only took three years," answered Ret sarcastically.

Holding up the blue society's newsletter above her head, she showered her excitement onto Ret, and was annoyed by the snarky comment. She slapped the envelope on his chest and shook the package listening to the rattle of the contents.

"Aren't you excited? We—well, you—have been waiting for this since Terri — you know. It's about time they informed us and honoured her for her sacrifices. Here, Ret. I want you to read it out loud."

Rox placed the wrapped package on the edge of the black table before Ret and urged him to open it up, but his sluggish hand moved too slowly for her liking. Finding it hard to resist, she swiped the document from his hand and began prying it open.

"Well, if you're not going to take an interest in reading it, then I will. If I could just open this stupid thing."

Rox put the newsletter in between her knees and heaved on it. Ret smirked in his recliner and watched Rox grimace as she struggled. She turned to the table, and in a fit of frustrated excitement, began slamming the envelope against the table's edge. Ret held out his arms and offered help.

"Here, let me try."

"No, I got it. It's almost open. Yes. It's open."

She grasped the newsletter with her extended arms and stared at the cover. A vibrant picture of their society's identity piece was displayed in the centre. Filling in the background was a picture of Pagan's blue society cityscape, enhanced with a glossy finish. The newsletter cover was always identical; however, this issue was slightly different. Rox pulled the cover closer to her face.

"Why is the middle stone on the ring black? Have you ever seen that before, Ret? Do me a favour and grab an old copy of the newsletter."

Ret reluctantly got up from his seat, stepped towards the far edge of the long black table, and rummaged through a drawer beneath the polished surface. Grabbing the most recent copy of the blue society newsletter, he returned to Rox and placed them side-by-side.

"Yeah, you're right, Rox. In this picture, all three jewels are blue. Hmmm, I guess they made a mistake."

They quickly disregarded the misprint and opened the first page.

"Wow, the index page is full of information. We should sit down for this, Ret. It looks like there's a lot to go over here."

Ret shuffled back over to his side of the couch, sitting at the far end and stretching his elderly body.

"Alright. So let's get started with news from inside Pagan. I hope Rus and Carin are part of a productive team. I want them to have the best opportunities while they are there."

Learning about Paganers was important for Ret, especially now since his own children were in their third year of Pagan. The newsletter provided great information and always gave blue society parents an idea of what their children were focused on. It also gave Ret the assurance that no other snug, as of yet, has made a significant accomplishment that surpassed his achievements. So far, to his knowledge, no idea group in Terin has created a global change as consequential as his. With his ego uncontested and his integrity upheld, he listened on.

"No breakthrough ideas yet," said Rox. "It says here that this two-hundredth generation in Pagan has changed the future. And that they have revolutionized the traditional Pagan system. 'This generation has become a self-serving society that promotes ideas based on the majority of others.' Hmm, I wonder what that means?"

"I know. I don't understand, either. The majority of others?"

"Ok, well, let's come back to that. There's a lot more here about other civilizations worldwide and groundbreaking developments."

Ret was kept in suspense as he watched his other mouth the words on the page. He pulled himself off the couch and shrugged his arms towards Rox, who was still reading over the report.

"I never thought this could have ever been possible. There is no way this can be true," said Rox

"What? What is it? Tell me."

Ignoring his insistence, she shook her head in disbelief, and looking up from the newsletter she paused before delivering the announcement.

"Rox. What is it?"

"We can fly," she whispered before turning her head over towards Ret.

"What? Are you serious? That can't be. Read that entry out to me."

"'It took ten generations and more than one hundred attempts, but the northern green skinned snugs have finally discovered a method of self-propulsion flying. This multigenerational invention was founded on the principle and physical properties of flight. Apparently, these properties demonstrate that flying is possible if given the appropriate velocity and design."

"Wait, You can't really be serious?"

Ret became more annoyed than impressed. After all, this announcement could detract from his reputation. Crossing his arms in front of his chest, he slid back in his seat and nurtured his bruised spirit.

"Yeah, believe it, Ret. Look at this."

She flipped the newsletter around and presented a picture of a prototype sketched alongside the article. Ret studied the picture and examined the design, remarking on the odd shape of the vehicle.

"That won't last at all. Maybe it works, but who in their right mind will risk their body by test-driving one of those? Besides, it looks ridiculous. What are those two large flaps hanging off both sides? My invention is way better."

Rox rolled her eyes and read on. "'The skyglider, in short, dives off the highest summit found on the north rimmed mountains, and after it gets up to the necessary speed, a solar generated motor powers on at the front of the vessel, keeping the skyglider at a constant altitude. Once the speed is reached, the skyglider can sustain flight. It can even maneuver through the sky and climb to higher altitudes. This is really amazing, Ret. We are entering a new age of technology that none of us had ever thought we would see."

With a subtle glare, he urged Rox to finish her commentary. She moved quickly to the next piece of news.

"Ok, Tarni, here we go. It says here that their civilization is showing signs of great improvement. Hold on," she said as her eyes skimmed ahead on the page. "Let me read into this a little."

Warm feelings washed over Ret. Before Rox finished reading over the article, his imagination ran with the idea that maybe—just maybe—both Sert and Hella were the reason Tarni was improving. He smiled and nodded, believing his premonition. Without a doubt, he knew, deep down, that they were Tarni's inspiration.

"Well, it looks like Tarni has made some serious changes. They have ice roads all throughout their society now. They are soon to complete the restoration to their Pagan. What else? Let's see." said Rox as she flipped through a few more pages. "They have also formed a new style of government and social structure that includes using different colours to identify different social groupings and skill sets. Wait, That's just like us."

Ret released a loud howling cackle as he threw his arms above his head. Tarni having an identical social order as Terin was the only evidence he needed to support his theory about his parents. He felt a fond warmth inside him that he hadn't experienced in a long time. He couldn't stop his mouth from forming a wide childlike grin.

"Why are you so excited?" asked Rox as she read on through the article. "This is strange. Tarni is now using the same social model we use. Where do you think they learned that?"

Ret stayed silent in honour of his parents and held onto his response. He gave only a casual shrug of his shoulders. This was one secret he was keen on keeping to himself.

Rox skimmed through the section that gave a few bulletins on educational aids, parental obligations, and study subjects to teach the blue society's youth. Still coping with the loss of her children entering into Pagan, she always found it difficult to read over any news that reminded her of them. Rox closed her eyes tightly, pushed away her feelings and skipped to the last part of the newsletter.

"Here we go, Ret. Finally!"

Pulling his body back upright, Ret sat at attention. He even tried studying Rox's ever-changing facial expressions as she read over the article. After a few moments, his patience vanished.

"Rox! Rox," shouted Ret. "Read it out loud. I have to know what it says."

"Alright, hold on. I'm reading it."

"Rox!" "Wow, Ret. You are going to be so proud of Terri."

"Really? What does it say?"

Taking a long moment to answer his questions, she held up her index finger as she read. Playing on Ret's nerves, Rox smiled as she soaked in the entire article before sharing the information. Ret was frozen in place, absolutely quiet, allowing her all the satisfaction she needed.

"Come on, Rox! Tell me," Ret pleaded.

"This is pretty amazing, Ret. Let me read to you what it says. 'Declared to all Terinian citizens, and in respect to all members of the former black society, these governing bodies proclaim this Freedoms Act as an acknowledgment and respect to those that fought, risked or lost their lives defending their own beliefs and ideals. This developing act of freedom of expression will ensure that all present and future generations of snugs who choose to follow a path of prosperity will be given every opportunity and encouragement without being faced with inequality, subordination, indifference, or discrimination. The existing equal rights, opinions, and beliefs will now be honoured and defended by the Terin governing body, provided it proves to be a viable resource to the community. Every idea, proposal, vision, and inspiration of social status or construct will be voted on by the public through fair poling.'"

Looking up from the document, Rox glanced over at Ret. He stared at the floor, smiling. She looked back down at the newsletter and finished reading.

"'The Terin government's new responsibility will be to provide support and mediate the general public it serves. Addressing public viewpoints and communicating the majority rule will be the only duty of the political officials appointed by Terin citizens through annual voting. They will select a single pair of head directors for each society from a majority tally of free voters acting solely in the interest of that given society. Due to the nature of this new democratic government, the position of Chief Director will forever be abolished.'"

"Wow!"

Ret got up and paced around the room, letting the news soak in. The wrapped blue package sitting on the glossy black table caught Ret's attention. He lunged over and grabbed the parcel.

"What do you think is inside, Rox?"

"I have no idea. I'm sure it's something good, though."

Without wasting time, Ret tore through the wrapping, and after throwing the paper to the floor, he ripped open the top and pulled out one of two small boxes. He gripped the flap with his thumbs and pushed up its edge. At a loss for words, Ret and Rox stared down at their new identity piece radiating in the sunlight that streamed in from the skylight above.

The structure and design of the ring hadn't changed. The size and shape of the three jewels also kept with the traditional look; however, nestled between the two deep blue jewels was a shimmering black gem mounted as the centre stone.

"Is this just for the blue society? Did they only change our identity pieces?" asked Rox.

Gazing down at the polished black stone, Ret couldn't find the words to answer. He couldn't take his eyes away. In honour of Terri and all the black society members, he closed his eyes, praising his sister with a moment of silence.

"Look at this."

Rox flipped to the final page, and illustrated on all four corners was a glossy print displaying the changes made to all the identity pieces within Terin. The modified red medallion on the top left-hand corner exhibited a distinguished black outline around the prominent red centre. Ret nodded, accepting the change to his former society's identity piece.

Right next to the red medallion was the yellow society's bracelet. A thick stripe of black encircled the bracelet around the forearm, and another band of black around the wrist portion. Imagining the long bracelet over his arm, he looked at his aging blue wrist and clenched his muscles. Returning to the newsletter, Ret searched for the final identity piece.

The thick green belt incorporated a square black clasp in the buckle's centre. The belt was to be worn by every green society member with the clasp in front.

They both went silent as Rox placed the open newsletter in the middle of the table. Ret took a moment, standing proud and looking up to the skylight, paying tribute to his sister's efforts. He of course, regretted all the years of resentment and all the time they spent begrudging one another, but more so now, he felt grateful that before the end of her life, both he and Terri found peace. Feeling a sense of triumph on Terri's behalf, he valued this moment and thanked her for pursuing her hard lived ideals. Sharing the moment, Rox looked at Ret with her eyes bright green.

"She did it, Ret."

"Yeah. She really did!"

Family Reunion

“To all of our send-off snugs, we want to thank you for living such a wonderful life and for contributing everything you have to Terin and the blue society.”

The counsellor's voice radiated over the audience through large sound accelerators high up in the blue society's amphitheatre.

Ret turned his head and scanned the jubilant crowd. He couldn't discern many faces as the audience was shrouded in darkness, and the spotlights aimed at the stage washed out the crowd in a fog of white. He swung his head around and faced the blue society counsellor standing centre stage beside a line of elderly snugs, Ret being one of them.

The counsellor placed his hand on the shoulder of the first snug in line.

“Your children are doing very well in Pagan; you should be very proud. I know your children are in the same idea group, working on a plan to redesign the burnlight to make it more efficient, longer-lasting, and brighter. This idea is almost in the final stages of approval. They have been voted on twice by their peers in the blue society. However, they still have yet to get a majority vote to give them a courtyard plot,” stated the counsellor before turning his head toward the audience. “Let's all wish them well.”

Ret smiled as the supportive audience cheered and clapped. The send-off snug mustered up a little grin as he waved to the audience and then back to the blue counsellor.

“You are free.”

A powerful force rushed through his body. His arms shot down towards the floor, and his head tilted toward the sky. Suddenly, a shimmering white glow radiated through his wide-open eyes. He was surging with energy and ready to fulfil his destiny. He turned his head towards the counsellor, standing beside a large doorway outside the amphitheatre. With a burst of youthful energy, the blue snug dashed outside through the two heavy iron doors and vanished into the darkness, never to be seen again.

Ret was next in line. He stood up straight, in complete suspense, feeling the aged muscles inside his knees begin to tremble.

"Ret, who here doesn't know about Ret?" the counsellor asked rhetorically. "I could list all of your accomplishments, my dear blue society member. However, I think everyone here knows what you have done for Terin."

Grasping Ret's tense shoulder, the counsellor spun around, gazed at the silent crowd and grinned.

"Not one snug in the entire history of our world has lived a life like yours, Ret. I can only imagine the struggle, confusion, and injustice that you have faced throughout your life. The red society has informed me that you and your sister did not have an easy childhood or Pagan life. I need to ask you one question. How did you get through it?"

Ret was caught off guard. Trying to find an answer to the question, he found himself at a loss for words. He blinked his eyes a few times before pulling his thoughts together. He cleared his throat and spoke out.

"The last thing my father told me when I was younger was to embrace life's struggles and never give up on what you believe in. I never really understood what he meant when he said that to me. And throughout my life, I never thought about it," said Ret as he spoke to the audience around him. "I guess you have to go through struggles in your life to see what you're really made of. Everything troubling that I have witnessed has actually been the root of real change. It has been a wild ride, everyone. And I wouldn't change a thing. I know now what my father was trying to teach me that night. I wish I could tell him where my life led me."

Taking the mic away from Ret's mouth, the counsellor smiled, pulled his arm off his shoulder and looked at the crowd.

"I'm sure they would be proud of you, Ret. I know Rox was proud of you at the end of her life. The night of her send-off, she said you were the best snug she had ever met."

The crowd applauded before the counsellor moved on to the next portion of his ceremony. Ret knew what was coming. Eager to hear about his children's Pagan life, he couldn't help but recall a bittersweet memory as he stood and waited, closing his eyes.

*

"I can't wait for Pagan," shouted Rus before throwing his arms above his head and sitting on the edge of his seat in the classroom. "I'm going to be an amazing blue. One of the best they have ever seen."

The heartbreaking comment struck Ret and Rox as they sat behind their desk, watching their young rejoice. Selfishly cheering for their new beginnings as Paganers, Rus and Carin sat ready to take on their new world, completely unfazed by their parents, sitting melancholically at the front of the room.

Ret was overwhelmed with feelings of grief. He struggled to find an upside to the moment but still managed to smile as he looked at his daughter, standing up from her seat.

"Everyone will be on my side, Rus. You just wait and see," she said, pumping her clenched fists above her head. "We can do anything we want to, Rus. I'll start as soon as I wake up inside my quarters, spreading the word of my idea and making friends with other snugs who share my vision. And I won't waste any of my time on no good, useless small-minded snugs. This is my idea and my goals, and once it's approved, I won't stop until it's complete."

Ret was astounded listening to Carin's speech. He was pleased to see his daughter utilize her newfound confidence. Forgetting about his emotions for a moment, he praised himself on his parenting, knowing that his daughter's confidence reflected his teachings. He nodded and looked over to Rox, who was staring back at him, sporting a touching smile. She extended her arm behind Ret's left shoulder and rubbed his back. Savouring the soft touch, Ret looked into her eyes, smiled, and placed his hand on her knee.

*

"I love you, Rox," Ret whispered before turning to the counsellor.

"Well, we do have some news about your children in Pagan. We'll start first with Rus. He has been in many idea groups so far. However, he is still trying to find a group with an idea suitable for approval. There is one area of concern that I have to tell you about. Rus, along with a few other snugs within Pagan, are protesting the new social system of annual voting and communal idea group approvals. They are fighting against Terri's system. We all knew some pushback was bound to happen within Pagan after the chief director role was abolished. This comes as no surprise. He is a strong snug, Ret. And I do see him having the same fighting spirit as Terri did. And just like her, he's not giving up."

"He does get that from her. And, if he's anything like me, I can see him annoying everyone in his group, too."

Following Ret's answer, a widespread chuckle entertained the audience. The counsellor waited for a calm pause from the crowd before informing Ret of his daughter's progress.

"When you were present during Rox's send-off ceremony, I announced that Carin has been with an idea group for the last two years. And Ret, you will be happy to find out that the yellow society has approved her idea group. Her team was voted in by the yellow majority a few months ago to receive a courtyard plot. They have already begun construction to create a synthetic stonelike material that can be used to offset the shortage of granite. She is quite the leader, and you should be proud."

He didn't even have the opportunity to soak in the news of his daughter's success before the counsellor said his final send-off words.

"And now, Ret, it is your time to move on. You are free."

Charged with a surge of energy, Ret felt an exhilarating sense of youth course through his body. He clenched his fists as tight as he could, trying to control the power radiating inside. Ret felt an overwhelming liveliness as an intense white glow burst from his open eyes. He turned his head towards the doorway held open by the counsellor and instantly took off running through the iron doors.

This vibrant force completely controlled Ret's mind, body, and soul. He was running along the cold landscape at a quick pace, heading towards the Terin border.

He was a slave to his body. Without hesitation and feeling no pain, he ran as fast as he could manage and crossed over the blue society boundary into the unclaimed lands of the northwest—a mountainous region full of steep slopes and slick rocks.

He was gaining ground towards Mount Nite. His eyes, still wide open and glowing white, led his body up the mountain. He charged up a well-travelled pathway that led to a midpoint summit up the side of the mountain. Familiar with the trail, he quickly scaled up the rocky incline.

He was not showing any signs of fatigue. Alarmed, he pulled one of his swaying arms behind his body to feel his frost bump. He was certain it was drying out. Surprisingly, he found that he was powerless over his appendages and could not even command his muscles to do as he wished, no matter how much he tried.

When he reached the midpoint summit, he turned his head around to all sides of the rocky terrain. He recognized the area from when he was a young snug. He had brought Hella hiking here once. But this time, before he could admire the view, his head moved, and his eyes locked onto a steep overhang far up the mountain slope and his body took off towards it.

He climbed hand over hand up the rocky incline, his glowing eyes focused on its target as his body crawled closer to his destination. He paused at a familiar lookout, a spot that he had always hiked to when he was younger, but his body wouldn't stop. Before he knew it, he reached the small pinnacle, facing out towards the vast yellow sea below him.

From this vantage point, he overlooked the black star speckled nitrogen ocean. He gazed down into the darkened sea and waited, wondering exactly where for the next phase of his death. His mind and soul were growing restless until his fate revealed itself.

The bright reflections of every star that mirrored the cosmos began taking shape across the vast ocean's surface. Ret watched in wonder as a visual illusion played out before him, toying with his mind.

Growing in size and changing colours, thousands of stars intertwined and built an abstract design on the ocean surface. The whirling array of colours grew in vibrancy and eventually covered most of this calm nitrogen canvas that expanded over the ocean's surface. Ret stared down in shock.

Finally, the intense colourful event below started to take shape, and as Ret peered down with his eyes, he was humbled when he recognized the image below. Waiting a few more moments, he looked down onto the ocean until every detail of his parents' faces was clear. To his astonishment, Sert and Hella were smiling up at him.

"It's been a long time, Ret," announced the lively image of Sert. "We missed you."

Trembling on the spot, Ret looked on. He wanted to speak, to say something—anything—but he just couldn't.

"We are so proud of you. We have been waiting for this day for so long, Ret. It is so nice to see you again," said Hella, giving Ret a warm, comforting smile.

Finally finding the courage to speak, Ret addressed his parents.

"… I …I have… I have so much I want to tell you… I missed you so much…"

His voice was shaky. His legs were quivering, and his thoughts were racing. He dropped to his knees and placed his hands on the cliff's edge, yearning to reconnect with his parents.

"We missed you too, Ret. Everyone is here. Everyone is waiting for you."

"Is Terri there?"

"Yes, Terri is here."

"Is Rox there?"

"Yes, Rox is here. Be with us again. Come, Ret…"

Ret kept his glowing eyes focused on his parents and didn't realize that he was edging farther off the small rocky ledge. He slowly raised back to his feet, stood straight up on the cliff, and hovered one foot over the edge.

Without hesitation, he pushed his body towards the tender words of his family, as he stepped off the rocky overhang, falling straight down into Sert's and Hella's smiling faces.

He closed his eyes and plunged gracefully through the sky, letting go of everything—every memory, every event, every feeling he once had, good or bad. It didn't matter anymore. And as he reached the ocean's surface, a blissful sense of true peace engulfed his soul after receiving the one thing he longed for.

Ret reunited with his family.

About the Author
Dan Miwa

Daniel Cameron Miwa is a man of diverse heritage with Japanese and French Canadian roots. He is also a devoted father to a young son, who has become his co-author in a series of children's books entitled "The Adventures of Pickleville."

While he has a successful career as a Senior Project Manager for a major Canadian telecom operator, Daniel is also an accomplished polymath with a passion for organized sports, cooking, travel, and music. He even hosts his own cooking show and can often be found strumming his guitar in his spare time.

Despite his many interests, Daniel's true love is science fiction. He has recently published his first novel in the genre, Ret, showcasing his boundless imagination and original ideas. With his talent for storytelling and his dedication to his craft, there's no doubt that Daniel Cameron Miwa is a rising star in the science fiction universe.

Acknowledgements

I would like to thank my supporters throughout my writing and publication journey.

To my family, Barry, Shauna, Matt, Aunt Vicki, Aunt Chris and Grandpa Harold, I wouldn't be here without your ongoing support.

To my friends Kim Collins, Beverley Neilson and Geoffrey Cotton, you were all pivotal in providing constructive feedback that ultimately made this novel what it is today. I am truly grateful.

And to my editor, Richard Tardif, thank you for all your guidance and expertise throughout our journey. You have impacted me in such a positive way with your knowledge of the written word and your ability to navigate this project through the publishing world. I see you not only as an editor but also as a mentor and friend. Thank you for all your help.

www.ingramcontent.com/pod-product-compliance
Lightning Source LLC
Chambersburg PA
CBHW071554030726
47593CB00001BA/159

9781990093838